"We both know this marriage is one of convenience, a business arrangement."

Exactly what Elizabeth wanted to hear, wasn't it? Then why did Ted's words sting? Well, business arrangement or not, how could she wed a stranger? "I...I can't marry you."

Ted turned to her, searching her face. His expression softened. He took her hand in his. His gentle touch gave her a measure of comfort...and far too much awareness of the man.

"This isn't easy for either of us," he said, his eyes filling with tenderness. "But I want you to know, I'll be kind to you. Work hard to provide for you. I don't have much, but all I have is yours."

Elizabeth didn't want to marry, but what choice did she have? She didn't have a penny to her name. Didn't have a single idea what to do.

A proposal would solve all her problems.

Except this proposal was offered to another woman. What would Ted say once he knew her true identity?

Janet Dean
and
Carla Capshaw

The Substitute Bride
&
The Gladiator

HARLEQUIN® LOVE INSPIRED®CLASSICS

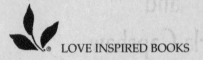

LOVE INSPIRED BOOKS

Recycling programs
for this product may
not exist in your area.

ISBN-13: 978-1-335-47362-2

The Substitute Bride & The Gladiator

Copyright © 2019 by Harlequin Books S.A.

The publisher acknowledges the copyright holders
of the individual works as follows:

The Substitute Bride
Copyright © 2010 by Janet Dean

The Gladiator
Copyright © 2009 by Carla Hughes

www.Harlequin.com

Printed in U.S.A.

CONTENTS

Janet Dean grew up in a family with a strong creative streak. Her father and grandfather recounted fascinating stories, instilling in Janet an appreciation of history and the desire to write. Today she enjoys traveling into our nation's past as she spins stories for Love Inspired Historical. Janet and her husband are proud parents and grandparents who love to spend time with their family.

Books by Janet Dean

Love Inspired Historical

Courting Miss Adelaide
Courting the Doctor's Daughter
The Substitute Bride
Wanted: A Family
An Inconvenient Match
The Bride Wore Spurs
The Bounty Hunter's Redemption

Visit the Author Profile page
at Harlequin.com for more titles.

THE SUBSTITUTE BRIDE

Janet Dean

And we know that all things work together for good to them that love God, to them who are the called according to his purpose.
—*Romans 8:28*

To my wonderful Steeple Hill editors
Melissa Endlich, Emily Rodmell and Tina James.
Thank you for your encouragement and wisdom.
To my beloved grandchildren Tyler, Drew,
Lauren and Carter. God bless you for giving me
fresh eyes, endless joy and hope for the future.
To the Daves, our sons by marriage,
and my husband, Dale—your steadfast faith
is a role model for our family.

Chapter One

Chicago, spring of 1899

Elizabeth Manning had examined every option open to her. But in the end she had only one. Her heart lurched.

She had to run.

If she stayed in Chicago, tomorrow morning she'd be walking down the aisle of the church on Papa's arm. Then, walking back up it attached to Reginald Parks for the remainder of his life, which could be awfully long, considering Reginald's father was eighty-two and still going strong.

Papa said she had no choice, now that their circumstances had gone south like robins in winter. He'd reminded her that as Reginald's wife, she'd be kept in fine style. Probably what the keepers said about the tigers at the zoo.

She scooped her brush and toiletries into a satchel, then dropped it beside a valise crammed with clothes. No, she couldn't rely on mortality to get her out of the marriage.

And as for God…

Martha had promised God would help her. Well, Elizabeth had prayed long and hard and nothing had changed.

Her breath caught. Perhaps God had washed His hands of her. If so, she could hardly blame Him.

The time had come to take matters into her own hands. Once she got a job and made some money, she'd return—for the most important person of all.

She dashed to her four-poster bed, threw back the coverlet and yanked off the linens, then knotted the sheet around the post, jerked it tight and doubled it again for good measure. That ought to hold her weight.

A light tap. She whirled to the sound.

"Lizzie?"

Elizabeth flung open the door. Skinny arms and legs burrowed into her skirts. "I don't want you to go," her brother said, his voice muffled by tears.

"I don't want to, either. But I've explained why I must."

Robby's arms encircled her waist, hanging on tight. Her breath caught. Could she do this? Could she leave her brother behind? "I'll be back, as soon as I find a job. I *promise*."

With few skills, what job could she do? Could she find a way to support them? All those uncertainties sank like a stone to her stomach. Refusing to give in to her fear, she took a deep breath and straightened her shoulders. She would not fail her brother.

"What if you can't?" Robby's big blue eyes swam with tears. "What if—" he twisted a corner of her skirt into his fist "—you don't come back?"

Looking into her brother's wide eyes filled with alarm and hurt, Elizabeth's throat tightened. Was he afraid she'd die like Mama had?

"I'll be back." She knelt in front of him and brushed

an unruly lock of blond hair out of his eyes. "We're a matched set, remember?"

Robby swiped at his runny nose, then nodded.

"We go together like salt and pepper. Like toast and jam. Like—"

"Mashed potatoes and gravy," Robby said, voice quavering.

"Exactly." The smile on Elizabeth's face trembled but held. "In the meantime Martha and Papa will take good care of you."

"But—but when we move, how will you find us?"

One month until the bank tossed them out on the street. One month to forge a new life. One month to save her family. Her stomach dropped the way it had at nine when she'd slipped on the stairs and scrambled to keep her footing. She hadn't fallen then and she wouldn't fail now. "I'll be back before the move."

Tears spilled down his cheeks. "I want to come with you."

If only he could. But she had no idea where she'd go. What conditions she'd face. "Eight-year-old boys belong in school." Elizabeth forced the words past the lump in her throat.

Tugging him to her, she inhaled the scent of soap, thanks to Martha's unshakable supervision. A sense of calm filled her. She could count on Martha, who'd raised her brother since Mama died, doting on him as if he belonged to her.

Robby's eyes brightened. "Can you get a job on a farm, Lizzie? So I can have a dog?"

His request pressed against her lungs. What kind of a father gave his son a fluffy black-and-white puppy for Christmas, then turned around and sold it in January?

Reversals at the track, he'd said. As always with Papa, luck rising then falling, taking their family and their hearts with it.

A chill snaked down her spine. What if Robby caught Papa's fever for gambling? If she didn't get him away from here, her brother might spend his life like Papa, chasing fantasies.

"I can feed the pigs and chickens," Robby pleaded, his expression earnest.

"I don't have the skills to work on a farm, sweet boy, but once we're settled, you'll have the biggest dog I can find." She kissed his forehead. "I promise."

Yet another promise Elizabeth didn't know how she'd keep.

A smile as wide as the Chicago River stretched across Robby's face. "You mean it?"

"Have I ever failed to keep a promise?" She ruffled Robby's hair. "Now promise me you'll be brave while I'm gone."

His head bobbed three times. "I will."

She wrapped her brother in one last lingering hug. "I love you." She blinked back tears. "Now, tiptoe to your room and crawl under the covers." She tapped his nose with her fingertip. "Sweet dreams."

His lips turned up in a smile. "I'm gonna dream about a black-and-white fluffy dog."

She forced up the corners of her mouth as Robby took one last look back at her then slipped out the door.

No longer able to hold back her tears, Elizabeth leaned against the wall, fingering the cameo hanging from the delicate chain around her neck, the last tie to her mother. She would miss her room, her home, the place she'd lived all her life. Her watery gaze traveled the tiered moldings, crystal chandelier and wood-planked floor. Once this bedroom had held a mahogany writing desk, hand-carved armoire and handsome Oriental rug.

Here one day, gone another.

Like her life.

"Elizabeth, we miss your company."

Papa's booming voice was followed by the muffled mumblings of her want-to-be groom.

She swiped the tears from her cheeks, then hustled to the half-open door and caught snatches of Reginald's conversation. "Tomorrow...at my side...ceremony."

"I assure you, Reginald, she'll be there," Papa said, his voice carrying up the stairs, putting more knots in her stomach than she'd tied in her linens.

He'd promised her to Reginald Parks much as he had the armoire he'd sold to Mrs. Grant last week and the cherry breakfront he'd shipped to the auctioneer the week before. He expected her to bail him out as Mama's fortune had, until he'd squandered every dime and worried poor Mama into an early grave.

How could Papa believe Reginald was the answer? She couldn't abide the man. He had no patience with Robby, even hinted at sending her brother to boarding school, as if losing his mother hadn't been enough upheaval in his young life.

Surely God had another answer.

She sighed. If only she and Robby could have a real home where a family shared their meals and the day's events at a dining table that stayed put, where a man considered his family first, where love didn't destroy.

"Elizabeth Ann!" Papa called. "Reginald is waiting."

She heard the familiar creak of the first step—Papa was on his way up. With her heart thudding in her chest, she eased the door shut and turned the key until the lock clicked. Then she jammed her hands into her kid gloves, grabbed her handbag and the small satchel stuffed with necessities and tore to the open window.

She looked down. *Way* down to the lawn and shrubbery along the back of the house. She gulped at the prospect of following her possessions out that window. Now was not the time to lose her nerve. She dropped the satchel. It bounced but stayed shut. When the valise hit, the latch sprung, scattering clothing across the lawn. Praying she'd hold up better when she alighted, Elizabeth flung the rope of sheets over the sill.

A rap on the door. "Be a good girl and come downstairs."

She grabbed the footstool and set it below the window.

"Reginald promised you a lovely matched team and gilt carriage as a wedding present," Papa said, his tone cajoling.

Elizabeth hiked her skirts and took a step up.

He pounded on the door. "Elizabeth Ann Manning, I'm doing this for your own good!"

Papa might believe that, but in reality, her father had one goal—prosperity. Through the door, she heard him sigh. "Sweetheart, please. Don't embarrass me this way. I love you."

Her fingers fluttered to her mouth as tears filled her eyes. "I love you, Papa," she whispered.

How could she abandon him? She stiffened her spine. *He'd* made the choice to gamble away their money, not her. Years of watching him take them on this downward spiral had closed off her heart. In her mind, he had only himself to blame.

Well, she and Robby wouldn't go down with him. Together they'd start a new life. She'd find a job somewhere, then return for her brother. After they got settled, she'd find a way to help Papa. She'd find a way to save them all, a way that didn't involve marriage to Reginald Parks. *To anyone.*

Papa slammed his body into the door. Elizabeth gasped. The hinges quivered but held, thanks to Mama's well-built family home, a home far enough west to have survived the great fire. A home they'd soon lose.

With one leg in and one leg out the window, she clung to the sheet and somehow managed to get a knee up on the ledge. Soon both legs dangled from the second-story window. Gathering her courage, she lay on her belly, ignoring the metal stays of her corset pinching her ribs.

The pounding stopped. She heard a creak on the stairs. Papa must've gone in search of Martha and her ring of keys. He'd soon be back.

Holding her breath, Elizabeth relaxed her fingers, and down she went, faster than a sleigh with waxed runners—until her palms met a knot and broke her grip. She landed on the boxwood with a thud, and then tumbled backward onto the lawn.

For a moment, she lay sprawled there, dazed, then gathered her wits and scrambled to her feet. No time to gather her clothing. She snatched up her satchel and purse and darted for the cover of the carriage house. Slipping inside, she tore through it and out the back, easy to do since Papa had been forced to sell their carriage.

Out of sight of the house, she sprinted down the alley past the neighbors', no small feat in silk slippers. By the time she reached Clinton Street, her breath came in hitches.

Once Papa found a key and got her door open, he and Reginald would be out searching for her. Two doors down, a hack rounded the corner and dropped off a passenger. She slid two fingers into her mouth and let out one of the peace-shattering whistles that had sent Mama to her bed with a cold compress draped across her brow.

The hack pulled up beside her. "Where to?"

Robby's words marched through her mind. *Can you get a job on a farm? So I can have a dog?*

Her brother yearned to live in the country, a good place for a boy. Not that she knew the first thing about the life, but a farm would be far from Reginald.

Perhaps a farmer's wife would want help with…whatever a farmer's wife did. Elizabeth was strong. And she could learn.

She gave the driver her destination. Then she settled into the corner of the coach and wiggled her hand into the slit she'd made in the lining of her purse. And came up empty.

A moan pushed past her lips. Papa had taken the small stash of money she'd hidden for just such an emergency. How low would her father stoop to feed his compulsion? She dug to the bottom of her bag and found enough coins to pay the driver. She wilted against the cushions.

How would she buy a ticket out of town?

Well, she'd face that later. Knowing she had no money, Papa wouldn't look for her at the depot, at least at first.

She wasn't going to walk down an aisle tomorrow morning, so how bad could her situation be?

Right before dawn, Elizabeth woke. She'd tossed and turned most of the night, as much as the bench would allow, listening in the dark to every sound. But Papa and Reginald hadn't come. In fact, no one had paid the least bit of attention to her.

She twisted her back to get out the kinks, sending three sections of the *Chicago Tribune* sliding to the floor. Thankfully the news that she'd bedded down at the depot wouldn't make the Society Page. Not that anything she did these days merited a mention.

Carrying her possessions, she tossed the newspapers into the trash and strolled to the lavatory. Through the window, the rising sun lit the sky with the promise of a new day. What would this day bring?

In front of the mirror in the large, tiled room, she pulled a brush through her hair, twisted it into a chignon, and then pinned her hat in place.

The distant shriek of a whistle shot a shiver along Elizabeth's spine. She grabbed her belongings and hustled to the platform. Porters hauled trunks and hatboxes to baggage carts while soon-to-depart travelers chatted or stood apart, sleepy-eyed. Her heart thumped wildly in her chest. A ticket. She needed a ticket. But tickets cost money. What could she do?

Smokestack belching and wheels squealing, the incoming train overshot the platform. Amid clangs and squeaks, the locomotive backed into position. Soon passengers flowed from the doors to retrieve luggage and hail hacks.

Elizabeth had to find a way to board that train. Her stomach piped up. Oh, and a spot of breakfast.

Near one of the station's exits a robust, plainly dressed young woman huddled in the corner weeping. Passersby gave her a brief glance then moved on. The stranger met Elizabeth's gaze. Her flawless skin glowed with health, but from the stricken look in her eyes, she was surely sick at heart.

Some inner nudge pushed Elizabeth toward her. "Can I help?"

"I... I can't go through with it. I can't marry him."

Another woman running from matrimony. "Who?"

"The man who sent me this." Out from the woman's hand stuck a ticket, a train ticket. "Eligible bachelors are few and far between, but..." Tears slid down her ruddy cheeks. "I'm homesick for my family already and I've only come as far as Chicago."

Pangs of longing for Martha and Robby, even Papa, tore through Elizabeth. She'd left a note, but that wouldn't stop them from worrying. Worse, Papa and Reginald might appear at any moment.

"That's my train." The stranger pointed to the rail cars across the way. "I feel terrible for spending his money on a trunk full of clothes, then leaving him in the lurch. He's a fine Christian man and doesn't deserve such treatment."

Elizabeth's stomach tangled. A twinge of conscience, no doubt for neglecting church since Mama died. For not heeding the Scriptures that Martha read each morning while Papa hid behind the headlines and she and Robby shoveled down eggs. No doubt the reason God hadn't heard her prayers.

Her gaze latched onto her means of escape. "I need to leave town. What are you going to do with your ticket?"

Brushing at her tears, the young woman's sorrowful eyes brightened then turned thoughtful. "The ticket is yours—if you want it."

"You're *giving* your ticket to me with no strings?"

"Well, not exactly no strings." The woman gave a wan smile. "More like a tied knot."

"What do you mean?"

"My groom's expecting Sally Rutgers…me. If you're up to starting a new life, take my place."

Elizabeth took a step back. "I couldn't."

"If you don't like his looks, use this round-trip ticket to take the next train. That was my plan."

As Elizabeth scanned the throng milling on the platform, her mind scampered like hungry pigeons after a crust of bread. *Marry a stranger?* There had to be another way to take care of Robby without marrying *anyone*.

Her heart skipped a beat. Not fifty yards away, Papa, looking handsome, vital and by all outward appearance, prosperous, stood talking with Reginald. From under Reginald's bowler, white tufts of hair fluttered in the breeze.

Twisting around, Elizabeth grabbed Sally's arm. "Tell me about this man."

"He lives on a farm." Sally sighed. "Oh, I doubt that appeals to a fine lady like you."

A farm. Robby's dream. Was this God's solution? "How will I know him?"

Sally removed a stem of lily of the valley from the collar of her traveling suit and pinned it to the bodice of Elizabeth's dress. "Wear this, and he'll find you." She checked the nearby clock. "Better hurry. Your train leaves in ten minutes."

Elizabeth glanced over her shoulder. Papa and Reginald had stopped a porter, probably giving her description. She had nowhere to go except back to Reginald. She'd rather ride a barrel over Niagara Falls.

That left her one alternative. Wear the lily of the valley and take a gander at the groom.

"Where to?" she asked.

"New Harmony, Iowa."

Where was that in Iowa? Did it matter? In Iowa was a farm, the answer she sought.

Clutching the ticket in her hand, Elizabeth thanked Sally, then dashed for the train. She boarded and found her seat, careful to avert her face. Within minutes, the engine worked up steam and lumbered out of the station. Once she'd presented her ticket to the conductor, she lost the hitch in her breathing.

The seat proved far more comfortable than the depot bench and she nodded off. Her last thought centered on the man who had sent for a bride.

What would she find in New Harmony, Iowa?

New Harmony, Iowa

Pickings were slim in New Harmony.

One last time, Ted Logan started down the list of the single women in town. There was the schoolmarm who'd bossed him like one of her errant pupils before they even made it out the door. He wouldn't let himself be pulled around by the ear. Or subject his children to a mother who wore a perpetual frown.

And then there was Ellen, Elder Jim's daughter, a sweet, docile creature who quoted the Good Book at every turn. With the church and all its activities at the center of her life, he doubted she possessed the gumption to live on a farm.

Strong as an ox, the blacksmith's daughter could work alongside any man. But Ted couldn't imagine looking at that face for the rest of his life. Well, he might've gotten used to her face, if she'd shown the least bit of interest in his children. From what he'd seen, she preferred the company of horses.

Then there was Agnes, the owner of the café, who came after him with the zeal of a pig after slop and appealed to him even less. Something about Agnes set his teeth on edge. Maybe because she forever told him he was right and perfect. Was it wrong to hope for a woman with a bit of vinegar? One who wasn't afraid to set him straight when he went off on some tangent? And how would she handle his home, family *and* the café?

All godly women, but most weren't suitable mothers for Anna and Henry. And nothing about any of them drew him.

That left his bride-by-post.

God's solution. A woman of faith who loved children and life on the farm.

Ted tugged the brim of his hat lower on his forehead and scanned the passengers leaving the train. A young woman stepped to the platform, wearing the sprig of lily of the valley pinned to her clothing. His pulse kicked up a notch. Sally, his bride.

Gussied up in a fancy purple dress, not the garb of a farmer's wife. Even gripping a satchel, she carried herself like a princess, all long neck and straight spine and, when she moved, as she did now, her full skirts swayed gracefully. He could hear the petticoats rustle from here.

She turned her head to sniff the flower, putting her face in profile. The plumed hat she wore tilted forward at a jaunty angle, revealing a heavy chignon at her nape.

He swallowed hard. Sally was a beautiful woman. He hadn't expected that. She didn't have a recent likeness. And he couldn't have sent the only picture in his possession—of him and Rose on their wedding day. In the three letters he and Sally had exchanged, he had described himself as best he could, even tried to be objective, though he hadn't told her everything.

It appeared she'd taken liberties with her description, too. Light brown hair, she'd said. Well, he'd call it more blond than brown, almost as blond as his.

Blue eyes, she'd written, though from this distance, he couldn't confirm it.

Tall and robust, she'd promised. Tall, all right, but slender, even fragile.

He noticed a nice curve to her lips.

And a jaw that said she liked having her way.

Sally didn't look strong enough to handle even part of the chores of a farmer's wife. Well, he'd prayed without ceasing for a suitable wife and God had given him this one. He couldn't send her back like he'd ordered the wrong size stovepipe from the Sears, Roebuck Catalog.

His stomach knotted. When a man prayed for wisdom, he shouldn't question the Lord's answer. Still, the prospect of marrying what amounted to a stranger was unsettling.

But Anna and Henry needed a mother to look after them. This morning, and countless others like it, left no doubt in his mind. He didn't have what it took to manage the farm, the livestock and his children. Never mind the house and cooking.

Even if Sally couldn't handle heavier chores, she'd said she could cook, clean and tend a garden, as well as Anna and Henry. That'd do. With all his qualms forming a lump in his throat, he moved out of the shadows. Might as well get on with it. The preacher was waiting.

He strode across the platform, nodding at people he knew. New Harmony was a nice town, though folks tended toward nosy. The news Ted Logan was seen greeting a woman down at the depot would spread faster than giggles in a schoolhouse.

When he reached his bride, he stuck out a hand. "I'm Ted."

Not a spark of recognition lit her eyes. Had he scared her? He was a large man. Still, he hadn't expected the blank stare.

"The flower…in the letters, we agreed—" He clamped his jaw to stop the prattle pouring out of his mouth. "You're Sally, aren't you?"

Her eyes lit. He gulped. They were blue, all right. Like forget-me-nots in full bloom.

"Oh, of course." She offered her hand. "Hello."

He swallowed it up with a firm shake. She winced. He quickly released his hold then held up callused palms. "Sorry, chopping wood, milking cows and strangling chickens have strengthened my grip."

Her rosy skin turned ashen, as if she might be sick. How would he manage if he married another woman in failing health?

Chapter Two

Elizabeth swallowed hard. She'd never considered how
fried chicken or cold milk arrived at the Manning table.
Drat, she'd have to scrub her glove. Not that Sally's intended looked as if he didn't wash. He smelled clean,
like soap, leather and sunshine.

Mercy, the man was brawny, wide at the shoulders
with a massive neck, chest and powerful forearms. Not
someone she'd care to cross. White creases edged his
eyes in his tanned face, evidence of long periods spent
in the sun. Those intense blue-gray eyes of his appeared
to see right through her.

She hoped she was wrong about that.

But all the rest…well, she couldn't find anything to
complain about. She'd expected another Reginald Parks
and another reason to run. But something about Ted
Logan kept her rooted to the spot, unable to look away.

Decency demanded she tell him she wasn't his bride.
But if she did, would he insist she take the next train
back? She needed time to think. To take a look at the
town and see if she could find employment here.

She couldn't forget the importance of that farm, the

fulfillment of her brother's dream. If only that didn't mean she had to marry the man, and all that entailed. She shivered. Well, she wasn't foolish enough to give her heart to this man.

Through narrowed eyes, he looked her over. "I expected you to have brown hair."

She gulped. "You don't like my hair?"

"The color of your hair doesn't matter a whit."

"Glad to hear it." She leaned toward him. "And so you know, I happen to like the color of yours. It's lighter than I expected, but it's tolerable."

His lips twisted up at one corner, as if they tried to smile without his approval. "I can't decide if I like a woman talking to me like that. Especially one I'm about to marry."

Elizabeth's stomach flipped at the mention of matrimony, a subject she intended to avoid. Her gaze traveled to a field of cows grazing not far from the tracks. "It's better than talking to the cows, isn't it?"

With a large hand, he gently tilted her face to his. "Yep. And a far sight better view."

A woozy feeling slid over her. Without thinking, she grabbed hold of his arm for support. And found rock-hard muscle. Beneath her feet, the ground shifted. She hadn't eaten in what seemed like forever. That had to be the reason for her vertigo.

He gave her a smirk and pulled away. "I'll get the rest of your things."

"Things? Oh, my luggage." Once he discovered she had no trunk, he'd send her back. Without money for food or housing, how would she take care of Robby? Moisture beaded her upper lip. "I, ah, left the trunk unattended in Chicago, only for a minute." With guilt at her lie niggling at her, she added, "When I returned, it was gone."

"Everything you bought with the money I sent—is gone?"

She nodded. Twice. "I'm sorry."

"Didn't you think to check it?"

"Didn't you ever make a mistake?" she fired back.

"Sure have," he said, arms folded across his chest, "but I've never lost all my clothes."

She grabbed a fistful of skirt. "Well, neither have I."

He sighed. "We'll have to stop at the mercantile."

If only she'd had time to gather her clothes scattered across the lawn. "I'll make do."

Waving a hand at her dress, he arched a brow. "With only that frippery to wear day and night?"

"That frippery is silk shantung, I'll have you know." She poked the rumpled lapel of his suit. "Do you think you're qualified to judge *my* fashion sense?"

He grinned, a most appealing smile. Or would be if he wasn't the most exasperating man she'd ever met.

"It's not your *fashion* sense I'm questioning."

Determined to stare him down, she held his gaze. Neither of them gave ground as travelers swept past them, tossing an occasional curious glance their way. "I'm smarter than you think."

"Smart enough to sew a new dress?"

"I can sew." She ducked her head. *Did embroidering pillow slips count?*

"We'll purchase fabric, whatever you need later."

Perhaps the store could use a clerk. The possibility eased the tension in her limbs. Instead of arguing with him, she'd better keep her head if she hoped to escape this mess. But without food she could barely keep on her feet.

Ted plopped his straw hat in place then took the satchel from her. "Better get moving. The preacher's waiting."

His words cut off her air supply as effectively as if he'd wrapped those large hands of his around her windpipe and squeezed. "So soon?"

"Did you expect to be courted first?"

She'd expected to remain single but wouldn't say that. "Well…no."

Behind them, the locomotive emitted a whistle, the call of "All aboard!" Wheels turned, picking up speed as the train chugged out of the station, taking with it her means of escape.

Elizabeth's eyes roamed what appeared to be the town's main street. Maybe she could find work here, though not a solitary establishment looked prosperous. She gnawed her lip and faced the truth. Unless a shop needed a clerk who could recite the multiplication tables while pouring tea, she had slim chance of finding employment.

Hysteria bubbled up inside her. She clamped her mouth shut, fighting the compulsion to laugh. Breathe in. Breathe out. Breathe in. Thankfully, the giddy sensation passed, replaced with the heavy weight of responsibility. Robby was depending on her, not a laughing matter.

Ted took hold of her elbow and ushered her along the platform. "We both know this marriage is one of convenience, a business arrangement."

Exactly what she wanted to hear, wasn't it? Then why did his words sting like a slap? Well, business arrangement or not, how could she wed a stranger? Elizabeth dug in her heels and yanked out of his grasp. "I... I can't. I can't marry you."

Ted turned to her, searching her face. His expression softened. He took her hand in his and ran his thumb along the top. Her stomach dipped. His gentle touch gave her a measure of comfort...and far too much awareness of the man.

"This isn't easy for either of us," he said, his eyes filling with tenderness. "But I want you to know, I'll be kind to you. Work hard to provide for you. I don't have much, but all I have is yours."

Elizabeth didn't want to marry, but what choice did she have? She didn't know a soul in this town. Didn't have a penny to her name. Didn't have a single idea what to do. That made her—a desperate woman.

A desperate woman with a proposal on the table.

A proposal that would solve all her problems.

Except this proposal was permanent—*and* offered to another woman. What would Ted say once he knew her true identity?

"My farm isn't much," he continued, his voice steady, calm. "But with God providing the sunshine and rain, the earth gives back what I put into it."

Such a simple yet profound statement. This man gave instead of took. He relied on hard labor, not luck. Ted Logan had planted his feet, appeared as solid as the earth he worked, the exact opposite of her father.

"I have cows, pigs, chickens, horses." He paused, then chuckled. "A dog."

Elizabeth's heart skittered. "What does your dog look like?" She held her breath, every muscle tense as she waited for his answer.

"Black and white. Shaggy." Ted shrugged. "Lovable."

Goose bumps rose on her arms. The exact description of the puppy Papa had given Robby, then taken away.

Martha always said there was no such thing as coincidence, not for a praying believer. Could Ted Logan be God's answer for Robby? Without a doubt her brother would adore this hulk of a man. Yes, Robby's dream stood before her with the promise of a wedding band.

Ted held out an arm. "Are you ready?"

A business arrangement he'd said. Maybe if she dealt with the marriage that way, she could go through with the wedding.

For Robby's sake she would.

She slipped her hand into the crook of his waiting arm. They strolled along the street. The occasional passerby gave them a speculative look, but by now most people had left the station.

Ted stopped at a weathered wagon with nary a speck of gild, nor springs or leather on the wooden seat to soften bumps in the road. Two enormous dark brown horses wearing blinders swung their heads to get a better look at her, their harnesses jingling a greeting. Her carriage waited. The matched pair were built for hard work not pretension, like Ted.

"That's King and his missus, Queen. They're Percherons," Ted said, a hint of pride in his voice.

Elizabeth didn't know much about breeds to work the farm, but Ted obviously cared for his animals, another point in his favor. She ran her hand along a velvety nose. "They're beautiful."

"And mighty curious about you."

Clearly she'd traded a fancy carriage for a rickety wagon, but a far more suitable groom. Her fingers toyed with the lily of the valley pinned to her dress. Could she go through with it? Could she marry a stranger?

Before she knew what happened, Ted handed her up onto the seat with ease, as if she weighed no more than dandelion fluff, then swung up beside her. Elizabeth shifted her skirts to give him room, while the memory of those large hands, warm and solid through the fabric of her dress, spun through her, landing in her stomach with a disturbing flutter.

She glanced at Ted's square profile, at this strong, no-nonsense man. The eyes he turned on her spoke of kindness. Even excluding Reginald Parks, she could do far worse. No doubt Ted Logan was a good man. He'd be kind to Robby. To her. That is if he didn't retract his offer of marriage once she revealed her true identity.

He clicked to the horses. "I left my children at the neighbor's. I'll pick them up tomorrow after breakfast."

Elizabeth swayed on the seat. "Children?"

"Don't tell me you've forgotten Anna and Henry?"

Sally hadn't mentioned children. "I'm just…tired."

How old were they? Since Mama died, Robby's care had been left to Martha. Sure, Elizabeth had read to her brother, taught him to tie his laces, but she had no experience caring for children.

What did she know about husbands for that matter?

And the tomorrow-morning part—did he intend a wedding night?

Well, if he had that expectation, she'd call on her touchy stomach. No bridegroom would want a nauseous bride.

Though if she didn't get something to eat—and soon—there wouldn't be a wedding. For surely the bride would be fainting on the groom.

Chapter Three

On the drive through town, Ted's bride glanced from
side to side, worrying her lower lip with her teeth. From
the dismay plain on her face, the town disappointed her.
Ordinarily he wasn't the edgy type, but this woman had
him feeling tighter than a rain-soaked peg.

Not that Ted thought the town paradise on earth, but
he hoped she didn't look down her aristocratic nose on
the good people of New Harmony.

Silence fell between them while she plucked at her
skirts. "I'm... I'm sorry about my clothes."

"No use crying over spilt milk."

Though money was always a problem. Because of her
carelessness he'd have to spend more. Would he rue the
day he'd advertised for a wife?

No, if Sally was kind to Anna and Henry, he could
forgive her most anything. From what she'd said in her
letters, she liked children and would be good to his.

If not, he'd send her packing.

His stomach knotted. He hoped it didn't come to that.
Since Rose's death, his well-planned life had spun out of
control. Every day he got further behind with the work.

Every day his children got less of his attention. Every day he tried to do it all and failed.

To add to his turmoil, he'd felt the call to another life.

A life he didn't seek. Yet, the unnerving summons to preach was as real, as vivid, as if God Himself had tapped him on the shoulder.

Him.

He couldn't think of a man less qualified. Yet the command seared his mind with the clarity of God speaking to Moses through the burning bush.

As if that wasn't enough to leave a man quaking in his boots, his bride, the answer to his prayers, now harbored second thoughts.

Lord, if this is Your plan for our lives, show us the way.

Up ahead, Lucille Sorenson swept the entrance of the Sorenson Mercantile. The broom in her hand stilled as she craned her neck to get a look at the woman sitting at his side. He tipped his hat as they rolled past, biting back a grin at the bewildered expression on her face.

They passed the saloon. Mostly deserted at this hour.

"Does that tavern foster gambling?"

Ted's breath caught. "Reckon so. Never been in the place."

"I'm glad." Sally smiled. "I'm sure I'll like...the town."

"I've lived a few places and the people here are good."

"Good in what way?"

"Folks pitched in after Rose died. Insisted on caring for the children and doing my chores. They've kept us supplied with enough food to feed an army of thrashers. I owe them plenty."

"People like that really exist?"

He raised a brow. "Aren't farm folk the same in Illinois?"

A flash of confusion crossed her face, but she merely shrugged. A prickle of suspicion stabbed at Ted. Something about Sally didn't ring true. Before he could sort it out, they reached the parsonage.

Ted pulled on the reins, harder than he'd intended. No reason to take his disquiet out on his team. "Here we are."

"Already?"

"Doesn't take long to get anywhere in New Harmony."

He set the brake, climbed down and walked to her side, reaching up a hand to help her from the seat. She took it and stood, wobbly on her feet. Was she sick? He looked for signs she'd be depositing her lunch in his hat brim. But all he saw was clear skin, apple cheeks and dazzling blue eyes.

He'd never seen bluer eyes, bluer than the sky on a cloudless day. His attention went back to her skin— smooth, fair with a soft glow about it. He'd have no trouble looking across the table at that face.

Or across the pillow.

Why had he thought she wouldn't suit?

He wrapped his hands around her waist, so tiny the tips of his fingers all but touched, and lowered her with ease. With her feet mere inches from the ground, their eyes met and held. Ted's heart stuttered in his chest. His gaze lowered to her mouth, lips slightly parted...

"Are you going to put me down?" she said, color flooding her cheeks.

"Sorry." He quickly set her on her feet.

She sneezed. Twice. Three times. Then motioned to the road. "This dust is terrible."

Ted looked around him, took in the thick coat of dust on the shrubs around the parsonage, further evidence of the drought that held the town in its grip. Unusual for New Harmony.

"Is it always dusty like this?"

"'Cept when it rains, then the streets turn to mud."

She wrinkled her nose. "Can't something be done?"

"Like what?"

She waved a hand at the road. "Like paving it with bricks."

"No brickyards in these parts."

"Hmm. If the dust turns to mud, why can't that mud be made into brick?"

An interesting point, one he hadn't considered.

"Well, I shall have to think about the problem," she said, tapping her lips with her index finger.

Thunderation. She sounded like the governor. Did she mean to send him out with a pickax and set to work making a road before sundown? "What are you, a reformer?"

She raised a delicate brow. "Would that bother you?"

"Hardly think you'll have time to reform much more than my kitchen." His gaze swept Main Street, mostly deserted at this time of day. Folks were working either at home, in the fields or the town's businesses. All except for Oscar and Cecil Moore lazing on a bench in front of Pete's Barbershop, whittling. "Even if you did, you'll find nothing much gets done in New Harmony."

"Why? Are people here lazy?"

"For a farmer's daughter, you don't know much about farming. Farmers don't have time to fret about roads and such. We work and sleep. That's about it."

"What do you do for fun?"

"Fun?" He opened the gate of the picket fence and

offered his arm. They strolled along the path to the parsonage door.

"Don't you have socials? Parties?"

"Some, but this isn't the city. We're a little...dry here."

The breeze kicked up another cloud of dust and she sneezed again. "*That* I believe."

He chuckled and rapped on the wooden door, which was all but begging for another coat of paint. Jacob kept his nose tucked in the Bible or one of the vast number of books he owned. And let chores slide. Maybe Ted could find time to handle the job on his next trip to town.

Lydia Sumner opened the door, neat as a pin and just as plain, wearing a simple brown dress with a lace-trimmed collar, nut-brown hair pulled into a sensible bun. She had a heart of gold and, like now, a ready smile that she turned on Sally.

"Lydia, this is Sally Rutgers. My mail— Ah, fiancée."

"Hello, Miss Rutgers. Please come in." She stepped back to let them enter the small vestibule, then motioned to the closed door of Jacob's study. "My husband's working on Sunday's sermon. He'll only be a moment."

Ted doffed his hat and they followed Lydia into the parlor, where dollies and doodads covered every tabletop. "Glad we didn't hold him up."

"Can I offer you a spot of tea?"

Ted shook his head. "No thank—"

"Oh, I'd love a cup," Sally chimed in. "Do you have some cookies, perhaps? I'm famished."

"Why, Ted Logan, you didn't think to feed her?"

At half-past three? "Uh..."

Lydia patted Sally's arm. "The ladies at church vie over appeasing my husband's sweet tooth. I'll just be a minute."

Bald head shining like a beacon in the wilderness, Jacob passed his wife leaving the room. Tall, long limbed with the beginning of a paunch, most likely the result of that sweet tooth, his pastor beamed. "Sorry to keep you folks waiting."

Once again Ted made introductions and he and Sally took seats on the sofa, leaving a chasm between them wide enough for a riverboat to navigate.

Jacob clapped Ted on the shoulder. "Shall we get started?"

"Yes," Ted said.

"No," Sally said.

Ted's jaw dropped to his collar. "No?"

She gave a sweet smile. "I hoped to have that tea first."

Used to cramming every waking moment with activity, Ted reined in his desire to hurry her along. Unsure this feisty woman would comply if he did.

Once Sally devoured two cups of tea and three cookies, she dabbed her lips with the snowy napkin. "Thank you, Mrs. Sumner."

Ted lowered his half-filled cup to the saucer. "Now are you ready to get married?"

She shot him a saucy smile. "I thought you'd never ask."

A chuckle rumbled in his chest.

Jacob slipped his glasses out of his coat pocket. "Do you have the license, Ted?"

"It's ready to go, filled out with the information Sally sent me in her last letter." He withdrew the neatly folded paper from the inside pocket of his suit and handed it over.

Jacob scanned the document. "Everything appears in order."

Sally lifted a hand, then let it flutter to her lap. "Pastor Sumner, you…ah, might want to change one teeny thing."

He readied his pen. "Be glad to. What would that be?"

"The name."

All eyes swiveled to Sally. Ted frowned. What in tarnation?

The ticking of the mantel clock echoed in the sudden silence, hammering at Ted's already shaky composure.

"I'm, ah, not Sally Rutgers. My name is Elizabeth Ann Manning."

Had Ted heard correctly? The woman at his side wasn't Sally? He frowned. That would explain her odd behavior on the way over. Clearly his children had come as a surprise to her. No wonder she hadn't remembered anything from those letters he'd exchanged with Sally.

He'd been duped.

Pulse hammering in his temples, Ted rose to his feet, towering over her. "Why did you lie about your name all this time?"

"I haven't lied *all* this time." She lifted her chin. "I've lied for less than an hour."

Jacob stared at the bride as if she'd grown two heads, one for each name. Lydia wilted into a chair, her smile drooping.

"What are you talking about?" Ted shoved out through his clenched jaw, his tone gravelly.

"Have you ever been down on your luck, Ted Logan?"

The question caught him like a sharp blow to the stomach. He shifted on his feet. "Well, yes, of course."

She ran a hand over her fancy dress. "Despite what you see, I'm destitute. So when the real Sally changed her—"

"What?" he bellowed.

"You're making me nervous, glowering at me like that. It's not my fault Sally got cold feet."

His pastor laid a hand on Ted's shoulder. "Let's stay calm. We'll get to the bottom of this."

Ted staggered back. "Who are you?"

"I told you. Elizabeth Ann Manning, your bride. That is—" she hesitated then forged ahead "—*if* you can ignore a small thing like an identity switch."

"A small thing?" He pointed toward the door. "Use the other half of that ticket. Go back to where you came from."

Wherever that might be.

Tears glistening in her eyes, she slumped against the sofa, her face pale and drawn. "I can't."

Lydia hurried to the impostor's side and patted her hand. She shot Ted a look that said she blamed him for this mess.

Him!

"I should've told the truth right off, but I was afraid you'd send me back," she said, her voice cracking, tearing at his conscience. "I'll get a job and repay you for the ticket."

Unable to resist a woman's tears, Ted bit back his anger. Something terrible must've happened to compel this lovely, well-bred woman to marry a stranger. Still, she'd deceived him.

Not that he hadn't made plenty of mistakes of his own. God probably didn't approve of his judging someone, especially someone with no place to live, no money and, in this town, whether she knew it or not, little prospects of either.

Still, something about her claim didn't ring true. If she was destitute, then it must've been a recent development.

"Our marriage is one of convenience," she whispered. "Weren't those your words?"

"Well, yes," he ground out.

She gave a weak smile. "Sally's not here. I am. How much more convenient can I be?"

Lydia released a nervous giggle. Looking perplexed, Jacob's brow furrowed. Obviously nothing in those books of his had prepared him for this situation.

Scrambling for rational footing, something Ted took great pains to do, he struggled to examine his options. He'd spent most of his cash bringing his mail-order bride to Iowa. He couldn't afford the time or money to begin another search.

Still, could she be hiding something else? "Are you running from the law?"

She lurched to her feet and planted fisted hands on her hips. "Most certainly not," she said, her tone offended.

Unless she was a mighty good actress, he had nothing to fear there. Trying to gather his thoughts, he ran a hand across the back of his neck. "Will you be good to my children?"

"Yes."

"Do you believe in God?"

She hesitated. Her hands fell to her sides. A wounded expression stole across her face. "Yes, but God's forgotten me."

God forgot no one. Elizabeth's forlorn face told him she didn't know that yet.

Had God ordained this exchange of brides? Ted had prayed without ceasing for God to bring the wife and mother He wanted for him and his children. Had this woman been God's answer all along?

Lord, is this Your will?

A potent sense of peace settled over him, odd considering the circumstances. "Well then, let's get on with it."

His pastor turned to Elizabeth. "You do realize the vows you are about to exchange are your promise before Almighty God."

Elizabeth paled but whispered, "Yes."

Though Jacob didn't look entirely convinced, he changed the bride's name on the document.

Lydia unpinned the flower on Elizabeth's dress and handed it to his bride, her bridal bouquet, then reeled to the organ in the back corner of the room. Her voice rose above the strains of "Love's Old Sweet Song" while Jacob motioned them to a makeshift altar. The song ended and Lydia slipped in beside Elizabeth.

"Dearly beloved, we're gathered here today to…"

Ted considered bolting out the door. But he couldn't plant the crops with Anna trailing after him and Henry riding on his back like a papoose. He had priorities that demanded a wife, even if he hadn't picked this one. He trusted with every particle of his being that God had.

"Ted, did you hear me?"

"I'm sorry, what?"

"Join hands with your bride," Jacob said in a gentle tone.

Ted took Elizabeth's ungloved hand, soft, small boned, cold, like his. Under that forceful exterior lived a woman as uncertain and unsettled as him.

"Elizabeth Ann Manning, do you take Theodore Francis Logan to be your wedded husband, to live together in holy marriage?"

She swallowed. Hard. "I do."

Ted gave her credit for not getting weepy on him. He couldn't handle a woman's tears.

"Do you promise to love him, honor and obey him for better or worse, for richer or poorer, in sickness and health, and forsaking all others, be faithful only to him so long as you both shall live?"

Elizabeth glanced at Ted, at the preacher, then back to him. "I'm… I'm not sure I can do the…obey part."

A strangled sound came from Lydia. Jacob frowned into the book he held, as if searching for a clue on how to respond. Ted opened his mouth but nothing came out.

"But I promise to try," Elizabeth added with a feeble smile.

Jacob yanked out a handkerchief and mopped his brow, then the top of his head. "Is that acceptable to you, Ted?"

He nodded, slowly. This woman had nerve, he'd give her that. She wasn't one bit like Rose. Good thing they weren't standing up in front of the congregation. If they were, after this, every man he passed would be guffawing.

Looking eager to get the knot tied, Jacob righted his glasses. "All right, Miss Manning, do you agree, then, to what I just said, except for adding the word *try* to the obey part?"

Elizabeth beamed. "I do." Then she repeated the vows after the preacher, cementing her to him.

"Will you repeat after me, Ted?"

This marriage would be legal, binding like a business arrangement, but far more than that. As his pastor said, Ted would make his promises to this woman before Holy God, the foundation of his faith and his home.

Ted gave his "I do" promise, then Pastor Sumner recited the words, words Ted echoed in a voice hoarse with strain.

"I, Theodore Francis Logan, take thee, Elizabeth Ann Manning, to be my wife." *What was he letting himself in for?* "To have and to hold—" *Would she allow that?* "—in sickness and in health, for richer and for poorer—" *She could count on the poorer part.* "—and promise my love to you until death do us part." *He'd try to love her about as much as she tried to obey him.*

He turned his gaze from the preacher to his bride. She licked her lips, no doubt a nervous response, sending his stomach into a crazy dive.

Next thing he knew, Jacob had Ted digging in his pocket for the ring, a slender gold band he'd ordered from the catalog. It had cost him over a dollar, but he'd ordered fourteen-karat so the metal wouldn't discolor her skin.

"Slip it on her finger. And repeat after me."

Ted did as he was told, repeating the words, "With this ring, I thee wed."

He released her hand. Elizabeth looked at the ring as if a ball and chain hung from her finger.

"Inasmuch as you have pledged to the other your lifetime commitment, by the power vested in me by the State of Iowa, I now pronounce you man and wife in the name of the Father, the Son and the Holy Ghost." Looking around as though he addressed a church full of witnesses, he warned, "Those whom God has joined together, let no man put asunder." Smiling, Jacob rocked back on his heels. "You may kiss the bride."

Ted had forgotten that part. He lowered his head as she turned her face. Their noses collided.

"No need..." she said softly.

Well, he had no intention of letting her believe he couldn't manage a simple kiss. He cupped her jaw, tilted up her face. Her eyelids fluttered closed, revealing long, dark lashes. He leaned forward and brushed her lips with his. She tasted of tea and sugar, all sweetness with a bit of bite.

Her eyes opened. Startled, bright blue, a man could get lost in those eyes. He had an impulse to pull her to him and kiss her more thoroughly. But kissing her like that would most likely stand Lydia's hair on end. And scare his bride. After all, she hadn't married for love. And neither had he.

Like a racehorse crossing the finish line, Jacob blew out a gust of air. "I've got to admit, this has been the most unusual wedding I've ever performed."

"And for the handsomest couple," Lydia said, beaming. "We hope you'll be very happy."

The wary look in Elizabeth's gaze no doubt mirrored his, but they murmured their thanks.

Jacob ushered them to a desk, dipped the pen into the inkwell and handed it to Ted. "Now all you have to do to make this legal is sign the license," Jacob said, examining their faces as if expecting one of them to refuse.

Ted signed and passed the pen to Elizabeth.

She wrote her name with a wobbly hand, then glanced at Lydia. "Could I bother you for a couple more cookies?"

"Why, of course." Lydia giggled. "You have quite the appetite."

A few minutes later, Ted ushered his new wife, clutching a fistful of cookies, into the sunshine. A cardinal chirped a greeting from the top branch of the ancient maple sheltering the lawn. His horses twitched their tails, chasing away flies. The sun still hung in the heavens.

Around him, nothing had changed. Yet in less than an hour, everything had.

A troubling truth struck Ted. He knew more about his

livestock than about the woman he'd just married. But then she must feel the same disquiet about him.

One thing was obvious. Unlike Sally Rutgers, Elizabeth Manning had courage. Courage based on desperation, not on the desire for a family. What had driven his wife to switch places with his mail-order bride?

What was she hiding?

What other lies had she told?

Chapter Four

Outside the parsonage, her new husband turned to Elizabeth, the chill in his steely gray-blue eyes raising goose bumps on her arms. "I've got to ask. Where are the clothes I bought?"

Elizabeth looked away. "With Sally."

His mouth thinned. "When you said someone stole your trunk, you lied."

She swallowed. "I didn't know how to tell you the truth."

Suspicion clouded his eyes. "If you're lying about anything else, I want to know it. Now."

Elizabeth dropped her gaze. She did have one more lie, a three-and-a-half-foot, blue-eyed whopper.

But if she told Ted about Robby, about the real reason she'd run from Chicago and into this marriage of convenience, he'd march her into the preacher's and demand an annulment. What would become of her brother then?

"I'm sorry I lied. But Sally's clothes wouldn't fit me."

His gaze traveled over her, bringing a flush to her cheeks, and a rosy hue beneath his tan. "Reckon not."

He helped her onto the wagon seat, then scrambled

up beside her, released the brake and pulled back on the reins. "We'll stop at the mercantile to pick up what you need."

As they rode down the street, Elizabeth's focus settled on the rumps of the horses. How long before she could bring Robby here?

How long before Ted lost patience with her inability to handle a household? Or care for his children? Her stomach lurched. What would happen then?

Well, she wouldn't fail. Couldn't fail. Too much depended on it.

She scrambled for a change of subject, a way to smooth the rough waters between them. "Pastor Sumner performed a lovely service."

Ted gave a curt nod.

Wonderful. A husband of no words. Well, she knew how to fill the gap. "He didn't seem like one of those hellfire-and-brimstone preachers."

"Jacob can rise to the occasion if it's warranted."

Elizabeth cringed. Would she be the topic of his next sermon on deceit? She tamped down the thought. Perhaps she had a way to get him to open up. "Were you born here?"

"No."

Talking to Ted was like pulling teeth with a fraying thread. "Then where?"

"St. Louis."

"What made you leave?"

"No reason. Just looking for something, I guess."

Elizabeth couldn't imagine what he'd been looking for that had stopped him here.

One street comprised New Harmony's downtown. A blacksmith stood at a forge in front of his shop, hammer-

ing a red-hot horseshoe while a young woman prepared
the steed's hoof. A few doors down, a man wearing bib
overalls entered the bank. Two women stood talking
outside Sorenson Mercantile, the younger bouncing a
baby on her hip. Signs tacked to the fading exterior advertised a post office and seed store in the back. Make
one stop and you'd be done for the day.

The door to a café stood open to catch the afternoon
breeze. A barber's red-and-white-striped pole caught her
eye among the other nondescript buildings. Not much
of a town compared to Chicago, compared to most anywhere.

Still, New Harmony provided more chance to social-
ize than being tethered to a farm. That might be Robby's
dream and she'd done all this to give it to him, but she
dreaded life in the country. How would she survive for
the next ten, twenty, goodness, forty years? Still, her
situation could be worse. She could be wearing Reginald Parks's ring.

Once she handled Ted's household reasonably well,
she'd have the courage to tell him about Robby. At the
prospect of reuniting with her brother, her mood lifted,
putting a smile on her face. Robby was the warmest,
sweetest little boy. He never judged. Never manipulated.
Never let her down.

In the meantime, maybe a neighbor would befriend
her. Or were these people as shallow and unfeeling as
her so-called friends in Chicago, once word got out about
the Manning reversals?

Ted said he'd be kind to her, take care of her and give
her all he possessed. But if she didn't fulfill her end of
the bargain to his satisfaction, would he forget all his fine
words? Were Ted's promises as meaningless as Papa's?

She fingered the gold band encircling her finger. Like most young girls, she'd dreamed of her wedding day, marrying a man she adored, a man who cherished her in return. But her parents' marriage had taught her that real life didn't measure up to fantasy.

The wheels caught in a rut in the street, jostling the wagon. Clinging to the seat, Elizabeth glanced at her husband, the flesh-and-blood man sitting next to her. Firm jaw, solid neck, wide shoulders. Ted had called their union a business arrangement, a binding contract. No matter what she told herself, Ted Logan didn't look like a line on anyone's ledger.

At Sorenson's Mercantile, he pulled back on the reins, set the brake, then jumped down and tied up at the hitching post. His long strides brought him to her side. He lifted her to the street, his hands strong yet gentle. If only she could trust Robby's future to this man.

Up ahead a plumpish woman made a beeline toward them, the ribbons on her bonnet flapping in the breeze. "Hello, Ted. Who's this?"

"Afternoon, Mrs. Van Wyld. This is Elizabeth, my wife."

Her blue eyes twinkled. "Well, imagine that? I hadn't heard about your marriage." She turned to Elizabeth. "Call me Johanna."

Obviously this woman kept up with the news. Still, her warm greeting brought a smile to Elizabeth's face. "We just came from the ceremony."

"You did? Well, congratulations!" She beamed. "Why, I must be one of the first to know." She said goodbye then rushed off, calling to a woman down the way.

Ted harrumphed. "No need to put an announcement in the paper now that Johanna knows."

Elizabeth's optimism tumbled at the expression on his face. They'd have no friends. No family. No party to celebrate. "Were you hoping to keep our marriage a secret?" *In case it didn't work out.* But she didn't finish the thought.

"No." He opened the mercantile door. "It would've been nice to get used to it ourselves before the whole county knows."

Inside, Elizabeth gaped at the wide array of goods filling every table and ledge. The scent of kerosene, vinegar and coffee greeted her. Behind the long counter, shelves stocked with kerosene lamps, china teapots, enameled coffeepots, dishes and crocks rose from floor to ceiling.

Barrels of every size and shape lined the front of the counter, leaving enough space for two customers at the brass cash register. Overhead, lanterns, pots and skillets hung from the ceiling. Picture frames, mirrors and tools of every size and description lined the walls.

Ted pointed to a table in the center of the room piled with bolts of fabric. "Get yourself some dresses."

"I...don't see any dresses."

He gave her a curious look. "Uh...that's because they aren't made yet."

"Oh. Right." She marched toward the bolts. "I'll take the fabric to the dressmaker's—"

He laid a hand on her arm and then jerked it back, as if afraid to touch her. "Dressmaker's?"

"Well, yes, won't she—" The look on his face cut off Elizabeth's protest. "Oh." Her fingers found her mouth. "I'm the dressmaker?"

"You said you could sew."

She avoided his eyes. "I may have...exaggerated." She'd figure out how when the time came.

He chuffed but let it go. "Don't take too long making your selection. It's getting late."

Elizabeth glanced at the afternoon sun streaming in through the front windowpanes. "Late?"

"I'd like to get us home before dark."

A jolt of awareness traveled through her, squeezing against her lungs. She gulped for air then forced her attention to the material, trying to ignore the implications.

Lovely bolts of restful blue gingham, cheerful yellow dimity, sweet sprigs in pink twill. She ran a hand over a length of lavender checked cotton, cool to the touch. Not exactly the silks and velvets of her gowns back home, but nice.

"The blue would look pretty with your eyes," he said, his gaze warm and intense.

His inspection set her hands trembling, a silly reaction. Clearly she needed a meal, far more than a few cookies. "Then I'll take this one," she said, indicating the blue.

"Get enough for two, one to wear and one to wash."

Laundry, another to add to the long list of chores she'd never done.

Thinking of the closet full of dresses in Chicago, she bit back a sigh. Then she remembered Ted's concern about money. Offering two was generous. She motioned to her dress. "I can wear this."

"To church maybe, but you'd make a pretty scarecrow wearing that in the garden." He hesitated. "Get enough to make three."

Had he just called her pretty? And offered three dresses?

Yes, and called her a scarecrow, too. Her new husband could use lessons in chivalry.

Heavenly days, she didn't know how to make *one* dress. Still, she couldn't refuse his gift. Under his rough exterior, Ted Logan possessed a soft heart.

A woman wearing her salt-and-pepper hair in a tight bun and a crisp white apron over a simple blouse and skirt lumbered over, her smile as wide as her hips. "Why, Ted Logan, who do we have here?"

Ted made introductions. The shop owner jiggled all over at the news.

"Well, I'll be! *Huuubert!*" she cried, the way Martha had when, as a child, Elizabeth had ignored her calls to come inside. "Come here and meet Ted's new wife!"

"I ain't deaf, missus." A ruddy-faced splinter of a man, his suspenders crossing his humped shoulders, moseyed in from the back, carrying a bag of seed. He laid it on the counter then ambled to where they stood. Smiling at Elizabeth, he shook Ted's hand. "Well, Ted, you married yourself a looker."

"Oh, she certainly is," Mrs. Sorenson said. "Resembles one of those ladies in the Godey's book, all fancied up and pretty."

Heat climbed Elizabeth's neck. "Thank you."

"How long have you two been married?"

Ted shifted on his feet. "We just came from the preacher."

"Why, I saw you ride past. You must've been on your way to the parsonage then." Mrs. Sorenson elbowed her husband in the ribs. "Tell them congratulations, Hubert."

"I'm about to. Much happiness." He turned to Ted and clapped him on the shoulder. "You're a lucky man. Can't say I recall seeing your missus before. If I had, I'd have remembered." He smiled at Elizabeth. "Are you from around these parts, Mrs. Logan?"

Elizabeth's new name socked her in the belly. She was a missus now. Her belly flipped faster than Martha's Saturday pancakes. "No, I—"

"We're here to buy a few things," Ted interrupted.

He must not want people to know she was a mail-order bride, and not the original bride at that. Did he believe they'd think she popped up under a rosebush?

Mr. Sorenson waved a hand. "What can I get you folks?"

Ted motioned to the stack of bolts Elizabeth had selected. "She needs enough fabric to make a dress from each of these."

Mrs. Sorenson stepped forward, her gaze running up and down Elizabeth's frame, muttering gibberish about yardage and seam allowances. She grabbed up the three bolts Elizabeth indicated and lugged them to the long counter.

Elizabeth and Ted followed, watching as Mrs. Sorenson unrolled the blue gingham, sending the bolt thumping across the counter. Soon she'd cut and stacked all the fabrics in a neat pile. "Will you need thread, needles?"

Elizabeth glanced at Ted.

"Plenty of thread at home, needles, too." He glanced away. "But Elizabeth does need…a…few other things."

Mrs. Sorenson nodded. "Like what?"

Ted tugged at his collar, squirming like a liar on a witness stand. He may have been married, but as a gentleman, he couldn't speak of a woman's unmentionables. "Get her two of whatever she requires."

"Of course." Mrs. Sorenson grinned. "Right this way, Mrs. Logan."

As Elizabeth followed the older woman to a table at

the back of the store, she wondered if she'd ever get used to hearing herself referred to as Mrs. Logan.

Ted stayed behind, talking grain with Mr. Sorenson. Grateful not to have to select undergarments with her new husband looking on, Elizabeth unfolded a pretty white nightgown, a sheer, lacy thing.

"Oh, your husband will love that," Mrs. Sorenson whispered, her voice warm with approval.

Glancing back at Ted, she found him watching her. She dropped the gown like a hot biscuit and grabbed a long-sleeved, plain, high-necked nightgown. Not exactly body armor, but close.

"It's hot around here in the summer," Mrs. Sorenson put in.

Heeding the hint, Elizabeth selected a sleeveless square-necked gown with no trim. Ugly and plain. *Perfect.*

"That's serviceable, but this is beautiful." Mrs. Sorenson pointed to the sheer, lacy gown.

"It's too…too…" Elizabeth grabbed up the tag. "Pricey. You know new husbands."

"Yes, I do," the older woman said with a wink, "which is why I suggested this one."

Elizabeth quickly gathered up two pairs of drawers, an underskirt and two chemise tops in cotton, all simple and unadorned, whether Mrs. Sorenson approved or not.

At the counter, the shop owner totaled the purchases. When Elizabeth heard the number, she gasped. A sudden image of her father harassed by creditors popped into her mind. Had she and Mama spent too much money on clothes? Jewelry? Had mounting bills forced Papa to gamble? If so, why hadn't he gotten a job like most men?

"Add that to my account," Ted said, his voice thick and gruff as if saying the words hurt.

Was she to witness yet another man's financial ruin? She vowed to watch her pennies. Well, when she had pennies to watch.

Mr. Sorenson opened a book, the pages smudged and crammed with names and numbers; cross outs and additions. Elizabeth couldn't imagine how he kept track of who owed him what in such a messy ledger.

Mrs. Sorenson wrapped the purchases, then handed two bundles to Elizabeth. "I look forward to seeing you again, Mrs. Logan."

Elizabeth blinked.

Mrs. Sorenson chuckled. "Why, Hubert, she forgot her name."

"Oh. Yes." She gave a weak laugh. "Thanks for your help, Mrs. Sorenson."

"Anytime! Enjoy the sewing."

Ted took her elbow. If she could find an excuse to linger, Elizabeth could ask Mrs. Sorenson's advice about dressmaking.

The store's proprietor turned to Ted. "Are the children at the Harpers'?"

Ted grabbed up the seed. "Yes, Anna loves their new baby."

"Hubert, get that precious child some candy."

"I am, missus, if you'd stop issuing orders long enough to notice."

Elizabeth bit back a groan. Another model of wedded bliss. Why had she taken such a drastic step?

Mr. Sorenson removed the lid from a large jar of peppermints on the counter, dipped out a brass scoopful and dumped them into a small sack, then handed it to Elizabeth. "These are for Anna."

Ted raised a palm as if to refuse, then nodded. "That's thoughtful. Thank you."

"Give a kiss to Henry," Mrs. Sorenson added.

These shopkeepers were warm and generous, different from those Elizabeth had known in Chicago.

"We'd better be on our way," Ted said. "I promised dinner at the café."

"Could I speak to you, Ted?" Mr. Sorenson asked.

"Sure." He turned to Elizabeth. "Will you be all right for a minute?"

"Of course," Mrs. Sorenson said for her. "That'll give us a chance to talk. Maybe your wife will share a favorite recipe."

Elizabeth gulped. Unless calling the maid for tea constituted a favorite recipe in these parts, she was in deep trouble. Surely only the beginning of her woes.

Chapter Five

Ted stowed the seed in the wagon, then took the packages from Elizabeth and wedged them in tight. For a man in a hurry, he had a patient way about him. She'd never been patient about anything in her life. A trait like Ted's could either drive her to distraction or make life easier.

Right now, he dallied when her stomach demanded speed. "I'm starved."

"Getting married must give you an appetite," he said, giving her a smile.

Mercy, the man set her off-kilter with that lopsided grin of his.

They walked up the street to Agnes's café. Inside the spotless, simple dining room, he led the way to a table in the corner. He murmured greetings to the diners they passed, but didn't stop to introduce her. The way people put their heads together, the room suddenly abuzz, Ted must have lost his wish for privacy.

He sat across from her, studying his menu while she studied him.

Ted looked up. Met her gaze. A baffled expression crossed his face. "What?"

Her face heated and she grabbed the menu. "I'm thinking about my order."

"Good evening, Ted." Carrying glasses of water, a round-faced, dark-eyed woman with black curly bangs smiled at Ted. When she looked at Elizabeth her warm smile faltered. "This must be your wife," she said, stumbling over the word *wife*.

"News travels fast. Elizabeth, this is Agnes Baker, proprietor of this establishment and the best cook in town."

Agnes and Elizabeth nodded a greeting while Ted scanned the single sheet as though he'd never laid eyes on a menu before. "What's the special today?"

"Your favorite. Chicken and dumplings."

"I'll take a plate of that." He turned to Elizabeth. "Know what you want?"

Elizabeth's stomach rumbled. The cookies and tea had kept her on her feet, but her stomach had met her backbone a long time ago. "I'll have the same." She smiled at Agnes. "I'm glad to meet one of Ted's friends."

A sheen of sudden tears appeared in Agnes's eyes. "It'll only be a minute," she said, then sped toward the kitchen.

Elizabeth glanced at Ted, who fidgeted with his silverware. Did he realize this woman adored him?

If so, why had he sought a bride by mail?

The gazes of their fellow diners burned into Elizabeth's back. Apparently everyone knew everybody else in a town this size. Well, she'd rather be here, the topic of speculation, than on the way to the farm with Ted. And the night ahead.

Her heart lost its rhythm.

A tall man loped over to their table. "Reckon this is

your missus, Ted. Johanna came in earlier, making her rounds." He cackled. "Thought I'd say howdy to your bride, seeing I'm the mayor of sorts." He looked at Elizabeth. "Not that I'm elected, but mayor's what folks call me." He stuck out a hand. "Name's Cecil Moore."

"Nice to meet you, Mr. Moore."

Agnes arrived, two steaming plates in her hands.

"I'll let you lovebirds eat in peace," Cecil said, moseying on to the next table where the occupants looked their way, smiling.

Agnes set Ted's plate in front of him. "Hot and piled high, the way you like it."

"Thanks, Agnes." Ted blushed, actually blushed, no doubt aware of Agnes's devotion.

Then the proprietor plopped Elizabeth's dish down on the table without a glance and returned to the kitchen.

Elizabeth's gaze dropped to her food. Her portion didn't measure up to Ted's but, far too hungry to fuss about it, she attacked her food. Mmm, delicious.

She glanced at Ted's untouched plate and lowered her fork.

"I'll say grace," he said, then bowed his head.

Cheeks aflame, Elizabeth bowed hers.

"Lord, thank You for this food. Walk with Elizabeth and me in our new life as man and wife. Amen."

Elizabeth's gaze collided with Ted's. She quickly looked away. Not that Elizabeth had neglected praying about her problems, but God had withheld His answer.

Well, she'd found her own. And he sat across from her now.

Ted picked up his fork. "How long since you've eaten?"

His words reminded her to take dainty bites, not pig-at-the-trough gulps. "I had tea and cookies at the parsonage."

His brow furrowed. "You didn't eat on the train, did you?" he asked softly.

She stared at her plate. "No."

"Look at me, Elizabeth."

She raised her chin and looked into his eyes, which were now clouded. Was it with dismay?

"I may not have much in the way of money, but my cellar's stocked. You won't go hungry. At least if you're a good cook," he added with a chuckle.

She fiddled with her napkin. "I'm sure I can."

"You've never tried?" he said, his tone laden with amazement.

Elizabeth took a swig of water. "I grew up in a home with maids, a cook, laundress, tutor, butler, even a nanny."

Ted frowned. "You said you were destitute."

"I am. Of late."

"What happened?"

"What happened isn't a topic for good digestion."

She wanted to ask how long it had been since Rose had died, but it didn't seem like the right time, either. Instead she returned to her food.

Ted took a bite, obviously enjoyed the tasty dish and ate every morsel, and didn't end the meal with a belch.

Uninvited, a memory invaded her mind. Of the three red-faced, ho-humming, toe-tapping times she'd sat in the parlor with Reginald after dinner, swishing her fan until her arm ached, trying to dissipate the silent belches rocking his spindly body and the unpleasant odors chasing after them. She'd tried to be kind, to turn the other nostril, ah, cheek, but he'd been…distasteful.

Papa had said Reginald Parks was short on manners but long on cash so he had to be forgiven. Instead of forgiving Reginald, she'd defied her father. A heavy weight squeezed against her lungs. Would Papa find it in his heart to forgive her?

Would Ted forgive her once he knew about Robby?

She looked up to find Ted studying her in that quiet way of his. He wiped his lips on the napkin. Nice lips. Full. At the memory of Ted's kiss at the end of the ceremony, Elizabeth's pulse leaped. His lips had been soft. Gentle. Enticing.

The one time Reginald had lowered his whiskered face to hers, he'd triggered spasms in her throat that threatened to make her retch.

Another point in Ted's favor.

Though, at the moment, her stomach tumbled. Too many uncertainties churned inside her.

The door burst open and in marched Mrs. Van Wyld, followed by a knot of ladies, beaming like sunshine. Johanna led the procession to their table.

"The folks of New Harmony, leastwise those I could round up, are here to give you newlyweds a party." She gestured to Cecil Moore. "If I know the mayor, he's got his harmonica. His brother will be along with his fiddle."

Grinning, Cecil flipped the instrument out of his pocket and played a few merry notes. Ted looked as if he wished the floor would open up and swallow him, but Elizabeth's toe tapped under her skirts.

People came over, shook Ted and Elizabeth's hands, offering their congratulations.

"Would you like a piece of Agnes's pie?" Johanna said, once the crowd cleared.

Ted took a step toward the door. "We really need to be going."

"My treat," Johanna persisted. "Sorry it's not cake, but it's mighty good."

In case she needed to escape tonight, Elizabeth couldn't risk putting the sheets to the test. She turned to Ted. "Is your house one story or two?"

"One."

"Oh, I'll have a slice of pie, then. A big one." She smiled at Ted, resting her chin on her palm. "Pie is my weakness."

Johanna waved to Agnes. "They'll have pie. I'm paying."

Agnes appeared at their elbows. "I've got sugar cream and cherry today."

"The sugar cream, please," Elizabeth said.

Ted frowned as if he didn't approve of the turn of events. "None for me."

"Don't be silly," Johanna said. "This is your wedding day. Your bride shouldn't eat pie alone."

Ted sighed. "All right—"

"Cherry and coffee black," Agnes said, obviously familiar with Ted's tastes.

With Johanna issuing orders, diners moved the tables, opening space in the middle of the room. The mayor let loose on his harmonica. A heavyset, squat fellow strode in carrying the fiddle and joined in. Cecil's brother Oscar, Johanna informed Elizabeth.

Four couples formed a square, moving up and back, square dancing or so Johanna explained.

Agnes arrived with coffee and pie. Flaky golden crusts piled high with luscious filling. Elizabeth thanked her, and then dug in. Mmm, cinnamon. Sugar. Cream.

She licked her lips, capturing a speck from the corner of her mouth. "This is delicious." She glanced at her husband.

Ted sat motionless, his fork hovering over his plate. Did the man pray before each course? No, he was staring at her lips. Had she missed a crumb? She dabbed at her mouth with the napkin.

His face turned a deep shade of red. Blue eyes collided, hastily looked away and then back again. He dropped his gaze to his plate, slicing his fork into his pie and then lifting a forkful of cherries and crust to his mouth. Her stomach dipped. When had pie ever looked better going into someone else's mouth besides her own?

In all of Elizabeth's years she had never been unable to finish a piece of pie. But tonight, her wedding night, she pushed the plate away. "I'm stuffed."

Ted smiled. "Glad I finally got you filled up." He glanced out the window. "Time to head for home."

"We can't leave." She waved a hand. "Your friends have done all this for us. To celebrate our marriage."

"Johanna's turned our wedding dinner into a spectacle."

"My dreams for my wedding day hardly match our ceremony."

Ted had the decency to look contrite. He rose and offered his hand. "May I have this dance, Mrs. Logan?"

"If you'll teach me the steps, Mr. Logan."

"It'll be my pleasure."

Her pulse raced at the warm, steady pressure of his hand on her back. At the warmth radiating from his very masculine body. At the breadth of those powerful shoulders.

No doubt Ted could protect her from any danger. Yet she'd never felt more threatened. More out of control.

Surprisingly light on his feet for a hulk of a man, Ted led her through the dance. But even with the unnerving awareness that others watched every move they made, smiling and nodding approval at her attempt to join in, she wanted to stay. Leaving would mean being alone with her husband.

Right now, if she could, she'd stamp Cancel on their mail-order nuptials. But that meant she couldn't give Robby a home.

So like a self-assured bride, she smiled up at her groom, but under her skirts, her knees were knocking.

What had she gotten herself in for?

Neither Elizabeth nor Ted said much on the trip to the farm. As dusk crept in and a full moon rose overhead, lights appeared in the houses they passed. Elizabeth kept her gaze off the man beside her, who took up more space than a mere man should, and focused on the fields. The turned-over earth exposed parched soil as cracked as old china. An owl hooted overhead, an eerie, lonely sound that crawled along her skin, raising the hair on her nape.

"You mentioned a weakness for pie. Any other flaws I should know about?" Ted said at last, his voice laden with humor.

No doubt an attempt to ease the tension crackling between them. Well, she'd do her part. "I'm emotional. A talker."

He turned toward her, his pupils reflecting the moonlight. "What do you mean, emotional?"

She squirmed under his stare.

"Are you a weeper?"

"Just the opposite. I have a temper." She pinched her fingers together then opened them a tad. "A teeny temper."

"Ah, I see." He chuckled. "Thanks for the warning."

"Do you?" Elizabeth asked.

"Do I what?"

"Have a temper?"

"Nothing makes me mad, except deceit. How can you trust a man if he can't be taken at his word?"

Fortunately for her, he didn't say *woman*.

Elizabeth fidgeted with her ring. "Couldn't there be a good reason a person would lie?"

"The truth sets people free."

She'd be set free, all right. If Ted learned about Robby, he'd rip this simple gold band off her finger and get an annulment faster than Johanna Van Wyld could spread the news.

Ted shifted on the seat. "Seems odd to be married and know so little about you."

"I feel the same."

"It'll take some getting used to, especially for my children."

Elizabeth gulped. She'd forgotten about Ted's children. From what she could remember about Robby, babies cried a lot and forever needed a change of clothes. "How old are they?"

"Anna's seven and scared, I think. She understands a lot."

Robby had been six when Mama died. Even though Martha had taken care of her brother when Mama took sick, Robby had cried for his mother. Rose's death had to be even more traumatic for Ted's daughter.

"Henry's fourteen months. All he cares about are his

meals and a soft lap." He lifted a brow. "That is, if you're one to cuddle a baby."

She'd cuddled Robby. No problem there. Besides, a lap meant sitting and from all Ted's talk about work, sitting sounded good. "I'll have a lap anytime he needs one—at least when you're not available."

"As long as you're gentle with my children, you have no need to worry about overstepping. I'll expect you to mother them whether I'm in the fields or in the house."

Elizabeth suspected little ones cared not a whit about who you were, how much you owned or where you came from. Long as they had that lap and a ready meal.

But cooking, well, she hoped Ted and his children had low expectations, bottom-of-a-burned-pan low.

Approaching a house near the road, a dog barked a greeting, leaping along the bank as they passed. Inside, people gathered around the table. Good people who lived by the toil of their hands. Not trying to make money without working for it like Papa had, and losing most every time.

Still, as furious as Papa's gambling made her, she still loved him. He was an affectionate, jovial, handsome man who had a gift with words. In that careless manner of his, he loved her, too, and was probably worried about her now.

Tears pricked at her eyes. She'd propped a note on her dresser, assuring him of her love. But love might not heal the breach she'd crossed when she'd defied him.

Her attention drifted to Ted, which didn't do much for her peace of mind. She shifted, trying to ease the tightness between her shoulder blades. How could she relax, knowing once they reached the farm, she and her new husband would be totally alone?

Ted had made no move to touch her, other than to help her from the wagon and a polite offer of his arm. Still, they'd signed a marriage license. And surely he'd noticed that baffling attraction between them at the café.

She wrung her hands in her lap while the pie and noodles waged war in her stomach. He'd better keep his distance. They'd only scarcely met.

Desperate to end the silence between them, she said, "I don't mean to criticize, but Mr. Sorenson's ledger could use some organizing."

"Sorenson has a heart of gold, not a head for bookkeeping. He asks me for advice, but can't seem to implement it. Sometimes I think the store is too much for him."

Elizabeth's heart skipped a beat. Could this be the solution for earning the money to bring Robby to New Harmony?

"We're not far from my place." In the gloom, Ted's deep voice made her jump. "Sorry, did I scare you?"

"I don't frighten that easily."

"Me, either," he promised.

She stiffened. "You should be scared, at least of me."

"Oh, I thought you only had a teeny temper. I'm not afraid of that." He chuckled. "Appears my wife's the timid one."

"Me?"

"Yes, you." He tipped a finger under her chin for a brief, heart-stopping moment and then went back to the reins. "I don't see any other wives around, do you?"

"Well, maybe I am, a little."

He laughed. "Thank goodness, because I'm terrified of you."

Laughter burst out of her into the clear night air. For

the first time in ages she felt more in control of her situation.

She cocked her head at her new husband. "You're a handsome man, Ted Logan. And from what I've seen of New Harmony, probably the most eligible male in town."

Eligible for Chicago, too. Anywhere. But she wouldn't tell him that.

He looked mildly uncomfortable with her appraisal. "I'm a married man, remember?"

As if she could forget.

"Why would you advertise for a wife when I suspect you could've had Agnes, probably a number of other women, too, by simply saying the word?"

He cleared his throat. "I thought it better to marry for convenience rather than marry someone who'd expect love."

Obviously Ted held no illusions that this marriage would lead to love. Good. Love wasn't her goal, either. She only wanted a happy home for Robby.

"Would you be marrying anyone if you didn't have two children to care for?"

The reins hung limp in his hands. "No."

"That makes you as desperate as I am."

He flashed some teeth, pearly white in his tan face. "Reckon so. So why did you decide to take Sally's place?"

That quickly Ted gained the upper hand. Unaccustomed to feeling out of control with beaux, too young, too old or too self-absorbed to be taken seriously, Elizabeth's brow puckered.

"I came to Iowa to…" She took in a deep breath. "To get away from a marriage my father arranged…to a much older man, a man I couldn't stomach marrying."

"Why would your father insist you marry someone like that?"

"Money. The man's rich." She sighed. "So I ran."

"Into marriage with me. Guess I should be flattered you consider me the lesser of two evils."

"To be honest, I'd planned to find a job here, not a husband. But one look at the town destroyed that strategy."

He chuckled. "No danger of getting a swelled head with you around. Not sure I've ever met a female like you."

Ted's tone held a hint of awe. Did he understand the tedium of propriety, the yearning for something she couldn't name? "I'll take that as a compliment."

He reached across the space between them and brushed a tendril of hair off her neck. "You know, Mrs. Logan, this marriage might just be fun."

His wife scooted about as far from Ted as she could get without tumbling from the wagon. Not a typical bride. But then not a typical wedding, either.

He stood over six foot tall. Hard work had broadened his shoulders and strengthened the muscles in his arms, an ox of a man, some people said. Was she afraid of him?

Well, if so, she needn't worry. He was far more afraid of this slip of a woman from Chicago. If she smelled any sweeter, he'd need to sleep in the barn instead of the children's room, his plan for tonight.

The decision made, he felt an odd sense of relief. Elizabeth might be his wife, but she was a stranger. A charming stranger at that. She made him laugh, something he hadn't done in far too long. And as now, he could barely tear his gaze away from the curve of her neck, her tiny waist—

"What happened to your wife?"

Her question doused his interest like a glass of cold water in his face. "Rose died of nephritis." He tightened his hold on the reins. "Her kidneys began shutting down after Henry's birth."

"I'm sorry."

Nodding an acknowledgment, he turned the horses into the lane leading up to the house, relieved to reach his farm. And avoid the topic of his deceased wife.

As they bounced over the ruts, he remembered his citified wife's complaints about the condition of New Harmony's streets. He made a mental note to haul rocks from the creek to level the surface after he'd finished planting.

The road curved around to the back of his house. They passed the garden plot. In the barnyard, he stopped the horses and set the brake. Tippy bounced into view, barking. Ted climbed down and gave the dog a pat.

Night was falling, putting the farm in shadow, but Ted knew every building, fence and pasture. He'd earned all this off others' pain. A straight flush had paid for the house, a full house repaired his barn and a four of a kind had bought his livestock.

Yep, the best poker player on the Mississippi, that had been him. Not that he'd planned on being "Hold 'Em" Logan when he'd joined the crew of that riverboat.

He'd seen men die over a game of cards, women toss their hearts after gamblers who loved their whiskey and the hand they held more than any female. He'd watched men and women lose everything they owned. Not a decent life. A life he now detested.

He'd started over here. Put his mark on this land. Everywhere he looked he saw evidence of his hard work, his daily penance for his past.

Shaking off his dreary thoughts, Ted walked to Elizabeth's side. Even in the dim light she looked tired, worn to a frazzle, as his mother would've said. He encircled her waist with his hands and she laid a gentle hand on his shoulder for balance. Light in his arms, she surely needed fattening up if she hoped to handle the chores. Her hand fell away and he quickly released her. A strange sense of emptiness left him unsteady on his feet. Must be the strain of this eventful day.

Elizabeth bent and ran a hand along his dog's shaggy back. His white-tipped tail wagged a greeting.

"Tippy is gentle as a lamb," Ted said, "and the best sheepdog in these parts."

While Elizabeth got acquainted with Tippy, Ted retrieved their purchases from the back of the wagon. When he returned to her side, she gave the dog one final pat, like she'd met a good friend and didn't want to say goodbye.

"Go on in. The door's unlocked." Ted handed her the packages. "I'll be along as soon as I bed down the horses and feed the stock."

She turned to face him, hugging the bundles close. "I've got to ask…"

He waited for her to say whatever she had on her mind.

"Where will you be sleeping?"

Ted gave her credit for asking him straight out. "In the children's room. If that's agreeable with you."

"That's fine. Perfect." She released a great gust of air,

her relief palpable in the soft night air. "You're a good man, Ted Logan."

Would she still say that if she knew about his past?

Chapter Six

With the sleeping arrangements settled, Elizabeth walked toward the house with a light step, suddenly curious about her groom's home. At the back door, a whiff of lilac greeted her, transporting her to the ancient, mammoth bush behind the Manning carriage house. To the gigantic vases Mama filled to overflowing, giving off the heady fragrance of spring. *Home.*

Tears stung her eyes but she blinked them away. Refusing to dwell on what she could not change, she whistled Tippy inside. She'd found a friend and had no intention of leaving him behind.

The door led into the kitchen, a huge room that ran the entire depth of the house, from back to front, cozy, if not for the chill in the air. A stack of newspapers all but covered the faded blue cushion of a brown wicker rocker.

In front of the chair, Elizabeth spied dried mud in the shape of a man's boots. Didn't Ted shed the footgear he wore in the barn before entering his house? Well, if he expected her to clean, that would have to change.

A large table, legs sturdy enough to support an elephant, dominated one end of the kitchen. Its porcelain castors sat in a sea of crumbs. "Come here, Tippy." The dog made quick work of the tidbits. Elizabeth patted her personal broom.

A high chair was set off to one side of the table. A spoon was glued to the wooden tray with oatmeal and, from the smell of it, soured milk. On the back of a chair, a garment hung haphazardly.

"Oh, how cute." Elizabeth picked up a tiny blue shirt that stuck to her fingers. "Uh, maybe not."

She put the oatmeal-painted apparel back where she found it. Tippy sat on his haunches watching her every move, as if he wanted to oblige her by licking her hands clean.

At this preview of marriage to Ted, her knees wobbled and she slumped into a chair.

She should leave. Maybe Reginald Parks wasn't so bad after all. Well, no, *he* smelled like sour milk. Far worse.

She surveyed the smudgy oilcloth covering the table. Over the center Ted had tossed a blue-checked square, covering whatever lay underneath. Hide it and run—a cleaning plan she could relate to. She lifted the corner of the lumpy cloth, exposing a sugar bowl, a footed glass filled with spoons and one nearly empty jar of jam.

In the sink, a pile of oatmeal and egg-encrusted dishes filled a dry dishpan. As if waiting for her. *Welcome home, little wife.*

Obviously Ted needed help. Well, she might not know the first thing about housekeeping, but she could handle this clutter better than Ted. Couldn't she?

A mirror hung over to one side of the sink. An odd place for it. She unpinned her hat and then couldn't find an uncluttered spot to lay it.

Carrying her hat, she climbed the two steps leading to the living room. Nothing fancy here—two rockers around a potbelly stove, a kerosene lamp in the center of a round table stacked with *Prairie Farmer* magazines. On either side of the table a navy sofa, chair and ottoman looked comfy. A sloped-top desk stood under the window with a ladder-back chair tucked beneath. Not so much as a lace curtain to soften the glass.

Nothing like their parlor at home with its lavish velvet curtains, brocade sofa, wing chairs and prism-studded chandelier. Well, that room had been stuffy and suffocating.

Now it stood empty.

Shaking off the maudlin thought, she walked to the four-paned side door that opened onto a covered porch. The shadow of some kind of a vine blocked her view of the lawn and sheltered a wooden swing at the far end. A pleasant place to read. Though farmer's magazines hardly interested her.

Well, she'd see about changing that on her next trip into town. Surely New Harmony had a library.

She crossed the room and opened a door. A small rumpled bed clung to one wall. A crib hugged another. Anna and Henry's room—the place where Ted would sleep tonight. He'd surely be uncomfortable curling his massive frame onto that small space.

A bureau filled the niche between the beds. Tiny clothing dangled from three open drawers. Elizabeth stuffed the garments inside. As she pushed the drawers closed, her gaze rested on a framed photograph on top of the dresser.

She recognized Ted immediately. Wearing a suit, face sober, he looked vaguely uncomfortable, as though his collar pinched. In front of him sat his bride, her dark hair covered by a gauzy veil, gloved hands clasped in her lap. Rose. Elizabeth studied the mother of Ted's children. She read nothing in her expression but quiet acceptance.

Along the opposite wall a rocker was positioned next to a washstand. A cloth floated in a bowl of scummy water and a still-damp towel hung from the rails of the spindled crib. Her new husband couldn't be accused of fastidiousness.

When her father no longer had the money to pay servants, Martha had gladly taken over all the duties in their house. She'd be in her glory here. Elizabeth cringed. Now *she'd* have to play Martha. Well, she'd spiff this place up in a matter of hours. Show Ted she could handle the job of wife.

Back in the kitchen, she shivered. How long did it take to bed down a pair of horses? She should start a fire. She bent toward the black behemoth. *Home Sunshine* in raised letters on the oven door hardly fit her mood. She took hold of a handle and opened a door. Ah, ashes. Must be where the fuel should go.

She grabbed a couple of small logs from a large, rough-hewn box, then squealed when a bug crawled out of one of them. She tossed the infested firewood into the stove.

Where were the matches? Her gaze settled on a metal holder hanging high above little hands. A flick of the match against the side and it flared to life. She tossed it on the wood and stepped back in case of sparks.

The match went black. She needed something smaller than that log, something more flammable. She crumbled a big wad of newsprint, lit another match and tossed the whole thing into the stove. The paper lit and blazed. Soon the log would ignite.

She glanced at the dog. "See, nothing to it."

Tippy whined.

Elizabeth shut the stove's door. "You're a worrywart."

Once the fire took off, she'd heat water and wash these dishes. That would show Ted his new wife could carry her weight, *and* his, by the looks of this place.

The acrid odor of smoke reached her nostrils. Tippy barked. Elizabeth dashed to the stove and flung open the door. Black smoke poured out of the gaping hole, enveloping her in a dark, dirty, stinky cloud. She coughed and choked, waving at the smoke hanging stubbornly around her, stinging her eyes.

The screen door banged open. Ted raced to the stove, tossing his suit coat on the rocker as he passed. He turned a knob in the pipe and slammed the door shut. "Didn't you know to open the damper before you lit the stove? You could've burned the house down!"

She sniffed and swiped at her burning eyes. "Are you going to yell at me on our wedding day?"

The sour expression he wore turned troubled. "No, I don't suppose I should." He met her gaze. "I'm sorry."

He yanked up the windows over the sink and opened both doors, then cleared the smoke with a towel. She watched the muscles dance across his broad back. When he turned around, he caught her staring.

"Ah, thanks for taking care of the smoke," she said weakly.

With a nod, he inspected the kitchen, as if trying to get his bearings. "As soon as the fire gets going, we can have a cup of coffee. Or tea, if you'd prefer."

"Tea would be lovely."

He swiped his hands across his pants, and then filled a shiny teakettle with water. "Sorry about this mess. I wanted the place to look nice."

"It's, ah…homey."

"I meant to get the dishes done before we left, but things kept happening." Ted set the teakettle on the stove. "Henry spilled his milk. Anna tried to wipe it up but slipped and bumped her head on the high chair. They both needed holding before it was over. Everything takes more time than I expect."

Elizabeth smiled at the look of dismay on Ted's face. This father cared about his children, loved them. Like Papa loved Robby and her. A nagging unease settled over her. Could Papa love her when he'd tried to use her to discharge his debts?

But of course he did. Hadn't he always told her so?

"What's the dog doing in here?"

Tippy hung his head, appeared to shrink into himself. "Doesn't he live here?"

"Not inside, he doesn't." He opened the back door. The dog gave one last pleading glance at Elizabeth. "Out you go, boy. You know better than to come inside."

"I don't see why he can't stay."

"He's a working dog, not a house pet. And the way he sheds and attracts mud, you'll be glad of it, too."

"Then that must be his mud in front of the rocker?"

He harrumphed.

She smothered a smile.

The teakettle whistled. Ted gathered two cups and a blue willow pot, then rummaged through a cabinet, mumbling. His broad shoulders filled every inch of space between the wall and table. Elizabeth squeezed past him as if she thought he would bite, then pulled a container marked *Tea* from behind a bag of cornmeal.

Her gaze lifted to his. She swallowed hard. "Here it is."

He reached for the tin, his fingertips brushing hers. "I...ah." He blinked. "Thanks. I spend half my time searching for things."

She smiled, remembering Papa's inability to find something right in front of his nose while she could spot a sale on gloves from three stores away. She picked up the kettle and filled the teapot with water, dividing the rest between the two round pans, then added dippers of cold. She chuffed. And Martha said she didn't have a domestic bone in her body.

Ted waved a hand at the mess. "They'll wait till morning."

"No time like the present." She sounded smug even to her own ears. But keeping busy meant avoiding her new husband.

The sink hung in a wooden counter supported with two legs at one end and a cabinet at the other, the space under the sink skirted. What an odd arrangement.

"What's the mirror for?" she asked.

"I shave there sometimes. And it helps me keep track of Henry." He smiled. "Like having eyes in the back of my head."

In no time, Elizabeth worked up some suds by swishing a bar of soap in the pan, then dipped a plate through the bubbles, but dried yellow food still clung to the plate. She scrubbed with the dishrag. Still there. Running her thumb over the hardened mess, she crinkled her nose as the nasty stuff filled the space beneath her nail. Well, she wouldn't let dried-on egg yolks defeat her. She rubbed harder. Her thumbnail gave way and tore. She dropped the plate into the pan. It hit bottom with an ominous clunk.

Ted stepped up behind her. "What was that?"

Elizabeth brought up the plate. It looked fine. Fishing beneath the water, she found a cup, a handle-less cup. "Oh, my."

Ted didn't say a word, merely turned away, but from the tight expression around his mouth, she imagined he blamed her for squandering his possessions.

"The cup isn't the only thing that's broken. My nail is practically down to the quick."

"Around here nails take a beating."

Obviously she'd get no sympathy from Ted. Well, she'd finish washing these dishes if it cost the nails on both hands.

Careful not to let them slip between her fingers, she attacked bowls of dried oatmeal. The fork and spoons ranked the nastiest. Finally she'd laid the last utensil to dry and dumped the water down the drain, smiling at her achievement.

Then she shrieked. Water gushed over her shoes—her only shoes, and formed a puddle of water and debris on the planks.

Pulling himself away from staring out the back door while she killed herself in his kitchen, Ted grabbed two towels off the hook alongside the sink and mopped up the mess.

"The drain leads to a bucket under the sink. Reckon it needed emptying."

"What kind of a drain does that?" she wailed, looking at her shoes.

His brow creased into a frown. "*My* drain," he said in a want-to-make-something-of-it tone.

He gathered the drenched towels and draped them over the lilac bush out back. She stepped aside so he could return to the kitchen where he heaved the large bucket out from beneath the skirted sink.

"The other bucket under here is a slop jar for the pigs. They eat most anything so you can dump table scraps and peelings into that one. Don't mix them up. Pigs aren't partial to soap."

He grabbed the full-to-the-brim drain bucket by the bail and carried it to the door. Beneath the weight, his biceps bulged. Her stomach did a strange little flop. As the door slapped shut after him, Elizabeth slumped into the wicker chair.

She removed her beautiful silk slippers, now water stained. Irritating tears stung her eyes. What had she gotten herself into? She buried her head in her hands. "I can't do this."

"Yes, you can," Ted said softly. Ted wadded up a few newspapers, stuffing them into the toes. "That'll help keep their shape. You can wear my mom's boots until I can get a pair of shoes made."

"You make shoes?" She hiccuped.

"They won't be Sunday-go-to-meeting shoes but you can work in them. And save these."

She sniffed back her tears. Ted Logan might not spoil her like Mama had, nor bribe or cajole her like Papa, but the man could be kind. She'd give him that.

He took her hand, his grip sending unwelcome heat through her veins. "Let's have that tea."

At the table, Elizabeth tucked her stocking toes over the rungs of the chair and added a teaspoon of sugar to her cup. Ted drank his plain, the way he drank his coffee. While she stirred her tea, she thought about Ted making those serviceable shoes.

What did he expect her to do besides work in the kitchen? "A farmer's wife must be busy cooking, doing dishes and…" She let the words trail off, hoping he'd supply her with a list. A short list.

"Besides caring for the children, Rose baked bread for the week, cleaned, mended, washed and ironed and weeded the garden. Oh, and collected the eggs. In the fall, she canned."

"With all that to do, how will I find time to sew dresses?"

"Oh, you'll find the time." He gestured at her frock. "That won't last long hoeing and gathering eggs."

Hoeing? Whatever that was, it sounded hard. The prospect of doing all those chores weighed her down. "What do you do all day?" she snapped.

"Milk the cow, feed and care for the livestock, work the land from planting through harvest." He ticked off each chore on his fingers. "Plow the garden so you can plant. I've got machinery to mend, the barn to muck, tack to clean and repair and firewood to chop. Now a pair of shoes to make." He'd used his last finger so he stopped. "Always plenty to do."

"Can't you get in some help?"

His expression turned troubled. "I know I don't have much to offer you, a woman who's accustomed to a staff waiting on her."

"Those days are gone."

"What happened?"

"Bad investments." She threw a hand over her mouth to stifle a sudden yawn and further questions.

"You'd best get to bed," Ted said. "The day starts early."

How early? she wanted to ask but didn't dare, certain she wouldn't like the answer. She gathered her purchases. "I'll say good-night, then."

He flicked out a section of the paper. "Good night." He gave her the briefest glance then returned to the farm news.

In the bedroom, she turned the lock, satisfied by the firm click that followed. Not that Ted had given her reason to fear him. But something about the man made her insides tremble.

She lit a kerosene lamp on the nightstand. An open Bible filled most of the space. Sally had called Ted a godly man and so he appeared. Compared to his untidy kitchen, Ted's bedroom was immaculate. A chamber pot, dry sink with white pitcher and bowl, even a fresh towel. Under the window sat a black contraption with a spool of white thread on top. A sewing machine—another reminder of all she had to do with no inkling of how to do it.

The bedroom had a chill in the air. Shivering, she didn't waste time getting into her nightgown, new and soft as down. Inside the chifferobe, she found Ted's clothes and a few items of women's clothing, obviously Rose's. Did Ted still love his wife so much he couldn't get rid of her things?

She pulled a robe from the hook and tried it on. Though it barely covered her shins, the robe would cover her nightgown in the morning. She didn't relish donning her soiled dress, especially if she got an opportunity for a bath. But with no bathroom in the house, where would she find privacy?

She sighed and slipped between the sheets. They smelled clean, sweet and fresh. Obviously Ted had managed to change the linens. She stretched out her body, thankful to sleep in a bed.

Long before this, Robby would be tucked in for the night, an extra pillow clutched in his spindly arms, while Martha heard his prayers. She hoped he wasn't missing her or, worse, crying. Her heart squeezed. To give her brother his dream, she must first find a way to manage Ted's home and children. Tonight proved she could handle the cleaning. Learning to cook should soften Ted up enough to tell him about Robby.

She had less than a month to become a passable farmer's helpmate, less than a month to earn the money for two return train tickets. If Mr. Sorenson needed help, she might be able to handle his books.

But how would she get to town?

Who'd take care of Ted's children so she could get away?

She had plenty of questions, but no answers. She sighed. Take it one step at a time. Tomorrow she'd learn to cook. Martha had tried to interest Elizabeth in the culinary arts, or so the nanny called meal preparation. Up till now, Elizabeth had only one interest in food. Eating it. She suspected that was about to change.

Chapter Seven

The clatter of pans brought Elizabeth straight up in bed. For a second she didn't know where she was. Then memory hit with the force of a gale wind, tossing her back against the pillows.

She'd awakened in Ted Logan's house. Married to the man. No doubt that was Ted, her dear, considerate husband, up and raising a ruckus in the kitchen.

Through the curtain, she could see the slightest glow from the rising sun. A rooster crowed, heralding the day. Gracious, why was everyone in such a hurry?

Yawning, she tossed back the covers, slid out of bed, shivering when her bare feet hit the floor. It might be spring but during the night the temperature had dropped. She slipped on the robe, cinched the belt tight and padded to the kitchen. Today she'd prove herself by handling the cooking.

Ted sat at the table, bent over at the waist, pulling on his boots. His thick blond hair showed the tracks of a comb. A sudden urge to run her fingers through the silkiness brought a hitch to her breathing.

Raising his head, Ted took in her attire with a silver-blue disapproving gaze. He opened his mouth as if to say something and then clamped it shut.

Elizabeth looked down at the robe. "I hope you don't mind if I wear this." A war of emotions waged on his face, telling her plenty. She turned to go. "I'll take it off."

"No, you need a robe and that's a perfectly good one."

"You're sure?"

"Yes, seeing you…just surprised me is all." He jammed his stocking foot into the second boot. "I'm heading out to the barn. Can you manage breakfast?"

"Of course." She'd handled the dishes, hadn't she?

"I started the stove and made coffee." He rose, towering over her, then grabbed a jacket from a hook near the back door and shrugged it on. "I should finish the morning chores in about an hour."

"Wonderful." She put on her best smile but the robe fit her far better. "Uh, what do you usually eat?"

"Fried eggs, bacon, biscuits. Nothing fancy." He tossed the words over his shoulder as he strode out the door.

She sank onto a chair. Eggs, bacon, biscuits? Couldn't he ask for something that matched her experience? Like cold cereal and milk. Well, she'd drink a cup of coffee to get her brain working, maybe two. Then find a cookbook. And start on the road that led to Robby's dream.

Martha was a nanny, not a cook, but she'd whipped up plenty of meals. How hard could cooking be?

Butterflies fluttered in her stomach. *Hard* was the arrival of Ted's children later today. If only she knew a recipe for motherhood.

Two cups of coffee and a roar from Elizabeth's stomach motivated her to unearth *The Farmer's Guide Cook Book*. Rose had apparently put the volume to good use, judging by the stains on the cover and looseness of the spine.

Under Breads—Quick, she read, "The ability to make good biscuits has saved the day for many a housewife."

Well, it better. On page eleven the list of ingredients for baking powder biscuits read like Greek. Flour, baking powder, salt, lard and...sweet milk. What on earth was sweet milk?

Inside the cabinet near the pantry door, she found the baking powder and lard. The flour had to be here somewhere. Pulling back a sliding panel, she discovered a metal contraption with a spout at the bottom and a wire sticking out from the side. She gave the wire a couple flips and a volcano of white poured onto the work surface, soaring into the air and onto the front of Rose's robe.

Elizabeth sneezed then sighed. She'd get to the mess later. Maybe when Ted came in the back, a big gust of wind would blow through and send the flour out the front door.

Yeah, that was about as likely as Papa giving up gambling.

Rummaging through the doors and drawers, she dug out a large brown crockery bowl, measuring cups and spoons, then washed her hands.

The ever-helpful cookbook read, "Sift together 2 cupfuls flour and 4 teaspoons baking powder with half teaspoonful salt." Sift? Did that mean mix? She shrugged and scooped flour off the work surface into the cup then dumped it into the bowl. Twice.

"Add 2 tablespoonfuls lard and work well with tips of fingers."

Ew. Whose fingertips?

She sighed. No one here but her.

The clock ticked away at an alarming speed. Best get it over with. With one hand, she attacked the lard, squeezing it through her fingers. It stuck, seeped under her nails until her hand looked like a dough ball. She tried to scrape it off with her other hand, but the mixture stuck to that hand, too. Her stomach somersaulted. Cooking was nasty.

The clock struck behind her. A half hour until Ted returned. She'd better get the rest in. Add seven-eighth's cup sweet milk. Well, cow's milk with lots of sugar would have to do. She grabbed the pitcher from the icebox, guessed how much less than a cup she needed then added sugar. She tried to stir it into the flour mixture with a spoon but resorted again to her fingers. The dough had become a gummy, thick mess.

She read, "Roll lightly to half inch in thickness and cut any size desired. Bake 15 minutes." Thankfully, they wouldn't take long to bake.

She grabbed up the blob and plopped it on the floury work surface, sending more flour into her face. Her nose itched. She ran the back of her hand across it.

The door opened. "I forgot to mention that you'll need to feed the fire so—" His eyes widened. "What happened to you?"

She followed Ted's gaze first to her robe, dusted with white, then to the planks in front of the cabinet where she could plainly see her tracks in the flour. She swiped her hands over her middle, then rubbed a hand over her cheek. "The flour bin exploded."

A grin curved across his face. His light blue eyes sparkled with humor. He let out a chuckle that became a howl. "Looks like you've been in a pillow fight and you lost," he said, once he got himself under control.

"You should've seen my opponent," she said with a toss of her head.

He chuckled again. "You missed some. Here." He stepped closer and brushed the tip of a finger along her jaw, sending tingles down her neck, dispelling every trace of mirth between them. "And here." He moved to a spot on her cheek.

Their gazes locked. Something significant passed between them, drawing her to Ted like filings to a magnet. Her spine turned to jelly while Ted lurched toward the wood box, grabbed a log, fed the fire and, without a backward glance, headed to the barn.

Disoriented, as if cobwebs filled her brain, she struggled for her composure. What had just happened? Whatever it was, she wouldn't let it occur again. If she hoped to bring Robby here and find a modicum of peace, she'd need to keep her wits. And hang on to her heart.

Returning to the task, she laid her hands in the flour then rolled the dough around until it took the form of a loaf of bread. Using a large knife with a razor-thin blade, Elizabeth whacked off slices, making some thick for Ted, others thin for Anna and Henry.

What to bake them on? She opened and closed cabinets until she found a metal pan. With her finger she drew a daisy on a few. Once she got the hang of it, cooking was kind of fun.

She washed the mess off her hands, not an easy task, then picked up the pan of biscuits, a feast for the eyes. She grabbed the knob on the oven door, almost dropping the pan. First rule to remember—stove handles are hot.

Once she'd safely tucked the biscuits inside, she

wrapped her hand in a wet dishrag and tied a knot in it with her teeth. She rummaged in the icebox, emerging with a crock of eggs and a slab of bacon.

By the time Ted hit the back door the second time, she had the bacon and eggs draining on a platter and the bottom-burned biscuits pried from the pan and piled on an oval glass plate that read "Bread is the staff of life."

Well, this batch had nearly killed her.

Ted washed up at the sink then wiped his hands, smiling at her. "Smells good in here." His expression turned wistful. "I'm starved."

Something suggested he meant more than his stomach. Elizabeth hurried to the table, putting as much distance between them as she could, and wilted into her chair. To sit at the table with Ted, just the two of them alone in the house, had her feeling tauter than an overwound clock.

She'd been up a little over an hour but felt she'd worked half the day. She took in the floury mess and smears of dough on the handles of the cabinets. Tippy wouldn't relish lapping up this.

Ted bowed his head and gave thanks for the food and this time Elizabeth remembered to wait for prayer before diving in.

He picked up the platter and scooped two eggs and four slabs of bacon onto his plate. After pulling off the undersides of two biscuits, he buttered the salvageable parts.

"Remember to put the bottoms in the slop jar. The pigs will be glad to get them."

Maybe Ted hadn't meant anything by it, but more than likely she should feel insulted. She would if she had the energy.

He raised a bite of egg to his lips and chewed, then caught her watching. Nodding, he turned up the corners of his mouth, lifting a weight from her shoulders.

With enthusiasm, she took a bite, only to find the egg much too salty. When she cut into the side meat, one end shattered into a hundred pieces while the other wiggled beneath her fork. Even minus the burned bottoms, the biscuits tasted terrible, bitter in spots and hard as stones.

Her shoulders sagged. Nothing resembled their cook's food in Chicago. Or Martha's, once she took over the household.

Ted took another bite, grimaced and swallowed. "Not bad," he said gallantly, and then cleaned his plate.

The man had a strong stomach. She'd give him that.

"Why not be honest?" Elizabeth said. "The breakfast is terrible."

Ted took her hand and gave it a gentle squeeze. "I won't criticize the answer to my prayers."

"How do you know I'm the answer to your prayers when I'm not the woman you planned to marry?"

He released her hand and studied her, probably wondering how to quickly retract his statement as he had his hand. "I'll admit the switch threw me at first. But God's given me a sense of peace about our marriage."

"What do you mean by a sense of peace?"

"God laid a gentle hand on my spinning thoughts, calming them like He did the Sea of Galilee. Like Peter, I felt called to take a step out of my boat and onto the water with Him."

Whatever was Ted talking about?

"I'll get the Bible and read that passage."

No doubt he'd seen on her face the confusion she felt. He disappeared, returning with the Bible. "I always start my day with Scripture. The story is found in Matthew."

The words Ted read of Jesus calming the Sea and Peter walking to Him on the water were spoken with a reverence that stabbed at her conscience and filled her with longing for more.

When he'd finished, Ted met her gaze. "The words Jesus spoke to Peter came to me at the parsonage, not audibly, but just as real. 'O Thou of little faith, wherefore didst thou doubt?' And I knew no matter how bad it looked, I wasn't to doubt that you were the one...the answer to my prayers."

Elizabeth had never connected stories in the Bible with her life. She could identify with Peter sinking beneath those waves. But how she could be the answer to anyone's prayers baffled her.

"Walking on the water isn't comfortable. May even feel like lunacy," Ted said.

Tears filled her eyes and she glanced away.

He cupped her chin with his palm and turned her face to his. "You and I are out of our boats, Elizabeth. Two very different boats, I might add." He smiled at her. "No matter how afraid we feel, God's help is only a 'Save me' prayer away. He'll stretch out His hand and never let us sink."

If only Elizabeth shared Ted's confidence. God might save him, but God didn't listen to her. If He did, surely He could have found an easier way to give Robby a home.

Ted laid the Bible aside and rose to get his boots. "I gathered the eggs for you this morning."

Relief swished through her. "Thank you."

"The egg money is yours. You can keep whatever Sorenson's paying."

"Really?"

"Tomorrow morning I'll introduce you to the chickens, give them a chance to get used to you."

"Get used to me?"

"They can peck your fingers if they're nervous. Or worse, stop laying." He grabbed his coat. "I appreciate the meal. A man has to eat to work."

But the words he didn't say, the words Elizabeth discerned—that her cooking didn't measure up to Rose's—hung between them. Most likely chafing against that peace he had about their marriage. How could Ted believe she was the answer to his prayers?

He buttoned his denim jacket. "I'll get more wood for the box," he said, then left the kitchen in a rush.

Elizabeth took another bite, choked it down then shoved her plate away, tears springing to her eyes.

She didn't blame him.

She'd leave, too…if she had somewhere to go.

Stomach rolling in protest at the meal grinding away inside, Ted gathered up an armload of firewood from the huge mound he'd stacked in even rows against the shed. From Elizabeth's expression earlier, Ted suspected she remained unconvinced that their marriage was God's plan.

He suspected she didn't know much about The Word and even less about listening for God's quiet voice. But she'd soaked up the Scriptures he'd read like a woman hungry for their comfort.

Probably desperate for reassurance that she hadn't made the biggest mistake of her life. If so, he couldn't blame her disquiet. She had far more adjustments to make than him.

Back in the kitchen, he found Elizabeth at the sink, doing dishes. She might be slower than sorghum, but he found her jaunty profile appealing. And when she wasn't scowling at him, her smile warmed a man better than a hot brick at the foot of a bed on a cold winter night.

He dumped the wood into the bin then stepped outside for another load. Elizabeth followed behind, broom at his heels, sending flour, straw and dirt onto the stoop. Hustling back inside, she returned with a dustpan. Using one hand to hold the pan and the other the broom, she swept the debris into the dustpan, looked around, then shrugged and tossed the contents into the lilac bushes alongside the stoop.

He chuckled. His wife had a way of making the simplest task an ordeal…and life a whole lot more interesting.

Next thing he knew she strode toward him, stopping mere inches away, and folded her arms across her chest, the dustpan aimed skyward. And thankfully not at him. She must have heard him laugh. Appeared he was in for it now.

"From here on," she said, "please take off your boots before you enter the house."

"Seems to me that mess in the kitchen was your doing."

"I couldn't help that the flour exploded, but you and those boots you wear *in the barn* need to part company before you take a step inside."

He smiled, enjoying her rosy-cheeked snit. An urge to pull her into his arms crashed through him. But in her mood, she'd likely crown him with that dustpan. "Is this that teeny temper you warned me about?"

"You haven't seen anything yet, if you don't cooperate." She wagged a finger at him.

"In that case, yes, ma'am. From now on I'll remove my boots." He doffed his hat and bit back a chuckle, then another bubbling inside him. If he laughed, she might get all teary on him as she had last night. The prospect squelched his mirth faster than a hailstorm could destroy a crop in the fields.

She nodded curtly. "Thank you."

Without a word, she turned toward the house. Unable to take his eyes off his bride, he watched her sniff the lilacs, putting her pert face in profile. Upturned nose, slender neck...

He shook his head. This dawdling wasn't getting the sheep moved to the north pasture. He whistled for Tippy. From the porch, the dog rose from his nap in the sun and trotted over, his tail wagging. Ted leaned down and scratched the canine's ears, rewarded by a lick on the hand.

On the way to the barn, Ted took one last glance toward the house. Elizabeth was nowhere in sight. A peculiar sense of disappointment plowed through him and pushed against his lungs.

"Come on, Tippy," he said, grouchier than he'd intended.

In the barn, he gave the ewe he'd bottle-fed as a lamb a pat on the nose. Tame as a dog, Suzie followed him everywhere, as she did now, out of the barn with the rest of the small flock falling in line behind like baby ducks trailing their mama. Tippy hung back, nipping at the heels of stragglers daring to stop and graze along the way.

At the north pasture, Ted lifted the wire loop then

swung open the gate. His neighbors poked fun at him for raising sheep. But he liked the reminder they provided of the Good Shepherd and His wandering lost sheep.

A robin swooped from a tree, hopping across the grass, and then stopped, cocking his head toward the ground, listening. Suzie and Tippy did their jobs and Ted returned to the barn, which, from the odor, was badly in need of mucking. He could use more hours in the day. With Elizabeth here, he hoped to get caught up with the chores.

His gaze lifted to the haymow overhead. Not exactly pleasant accommodations, but Anna and Henry would be back in their room tonight. He needed to talk to Elizabeth about the sleeping arrangements. He'd compared their marriage to a business deal, though he doubted God approved his assessment. Still, a wise man wouldn't push a woman into intimacy. Time would solve the issue. Or so he hoped.

As he strode into the yard, Elizabeth emerged from the back door, carrying a dress in her arms, her hair tied back with a length of twine. Water sluiced off the heavy fabric, dripping down the front of *his* shirt. The flannel plaid hung to her knees, making her look like a skinny sack, while *his* denims ended in rolled cuffs resembling feather-filled bolsters sagging at her ankles.

He stopped, dumbstruck at the sight. Rose might've worn pants under her dress on the coldest days, but this—

His pulse tripped in his chest at this woman standing before him.

Cocking her head, she met his gaze, all innocent-eyed while at her bare feet a puddle formed on the slab of concrete outside the kitchen door. One of her little toes was crooked. For some unknowable reason he found the slight imperfection endearing.

He chuffed at his silliness. He'd have to find those boots today.

"I washed my dress."

As if he needed an explanation with all that dripping going on. "So I see."

"I had to put on something. Knowing you weren't too happy about me wearing Rose's robe, I made do with these."

He opened his mouth to argue the point, but couldn't. Seeing Elizabeth in that robe had been a sucker punch to the gut. His resistance to Elizabeth using whatever she needed had not been fair.

How was she holding up his pants, anyway, with those slim hips and tiny waist? "Can't figure how my pants would fit you."

"Twine works for a belt." She raised her chin. "I can improvise."

"Which would explain your hair."

"You don't like how I look?" She parked a fist on her hip.

He liked how she looked, all right. "I didn't say that."

Lugging the dress, she headed for the clothesline, barefoot like a tot barely out of nappies. Didn't she know she could pick up a nail or a thistle or get bit by a spider?

She heaved the bodice of the dress over the line and it hung from the waist, the skirt almost touching the ground. She turned back to him, a self-satisfied smile on her face. Behind her, the weight of the wet skirts pulled her freshly washed dress over the cord and onto the grass.

His expression must've alerted her. She spun around. "Oh, no!"

"Clothespins might help."

He walked to the bag hanging on the line, pulled out a handful of wooden pins and sauntered to her. He took the dress from her clutches and pinned it in place by the hem as he'd seen Rose do countless times. Then he took the rod leaning against the post, raised and propped the line.

She grabbed a pin from the bag and stuck it in between two of his. "Five might work but six is better."

Her gaze locked with his and her wide blue eyes dared him to disagree, setting off something that coiled in his stomach. This turmoil didn't have a thing to do with breakfast and everything to do with the woman before him.

Well, he wouldn't let those eyes make him lose sight of what he wanted from Elizabeth—a mother for his children—and help getting a grip on his off-kilter world.

He'd better remember, if he let this woman get close, she'd unearth his secrets and the open wounds he'd sealed.

"My children are coming home today." He looked toward the barn. "I've rigged a bed in the loft."

Color dotted her cheeks. "I appreciate it."

Nodding, he glanced at the sun rising in the sky. "As soon as I haul my things to the barn and finish the morning chores, I'll pick Henry and Anna up at the Harpers'. We'll be back in time for dinner."

She smiled. "That gives me plenty of time."

"Dinner is at noon in these parts."

"In Chicago we call that lunch."

"Call it whatever you like but make it big—I'm plowing this afternoon. You'll find canned food in the root cellar outside the front door. Oh, and don't forget to ladle off the cream, then put the milk and cream in the icebox."

She shot him a glare. "You're good at barking orders, Mr. Logan. Have you forgotten I'm not so good at obeying?"

"How could I forget?" He ran a hand through his hair then plopped his hat in place. "Well, the children and I'll see you at noon."

A parade of emotions marched across her face. Apprehension. Uncertainty. Not that he could blame her for feeling nervous. He shared her qualms. The biggest—would his strong-willed daughter accept Elizabeth's presence in the house?

By the time Ted drove the wagon down the lane, he whistled a tune. His relationship with his wife might be fragile, but at least he'd given his son and daughter a mother, a huge step toward returning their lives to normal.

Elizabeth pulled open the slanted cellar door and ambled down the stone steps, thankful a stream of sunlight lit her way. Bushel baskets of potatoes, wrinkly apples, onions—some growing roots—lined the walls. Dried herbs hung from the ceiling, little upside-down bouquets. Elizabeth inhaled those fragrances mingled with the cellar's musty smell. Not perfume, but not unpleasant.

Crude wooden shelves lined one wall and contained row upon row of filled glass jars of green beans, applesauce, tomatoes, corn and grape juice. Many with homemade tags hanging from the necks, identifying the friend or neighbor who'd sent it, wishing Ted peace, giving Bible verses or even a recipe. Apparently, friends and neighbors continued to look after Ted's family. Elizabeth remembered how her family's friends in Chicago had looked away, whispering behind their hands. Her heart squeezed. No doubt that was the difference between squandering wealth and losing a loved one.

She plopped four potatoes and an onion in the wide pockets of her apron, grabbed a glass jar of tomatoes and a crock of canned beef, ingredients for the soup she intended to make for lunch, and carried them up the steps.

Inside the kitchen, she added more wood to the red embers and got the fire going again. Following directions, she chopped the ingredients, regretting the onion the minute the tears started. Other than one cut on her index finger, preparing the soup went smoothly and it soon bubbled away on the stove, releasing a mouthwatering aroma.

From what she'd seen Ted consume at breakfast, he had a voracious appetite. Yet he didn't have an ounce of fat on his solid, muscular frame. A man built for the work he did.

With the meal under way, she rushed outside to check her dress. The dog rose from the covered porch and ambled over for a scratch. A beautiful animal, he had a gentle disposition and eyes that settled on her with the warmth of an old friend.

Robby would love Tippy. How long before she could bring her brother here? Already she'd prepared two meals. Cleaned up the kitchen twice. Tomorrow she'd gather the eggs. Why, she'd practically completed her list of chores. A week of egg money would surely pay for their train tickets. Wouldn't it?

Soon she'd tell Ted about Robby. Her smile faded. How would a man short on cash react to the news that he'd have another mouth to feed?

At the line, Elizabeth found her dress still damp. Perhaps that would make it easier to iron. She carried it inside. The quiet of the house had her beckoning the dog to follow. Tippy hesitated, but only for a moment.

Elizabeth found the flatirons and the padded ironing board where Ted said they'd be. She placed both irons on the stove and wrestled the board upright. She didn't know the first thing about ironing. If only she'd paid attention to the running of the Manning household. But she'd only thought about parties, fancy dresses and the latest hairstyle. Of late, that life had seemed meaningless and her friendships shallow.

Life on the farm provided food, an existence forcing people to rely on the basics, to look out for one another. But it had taken less than a day to discover the work was pure drudgery. How could she survive the endless tedium?

By remembering Robby would love the farm.

But would Ted's children take to him? To her?

Elizabeth tightened her jaw until her teeth ached. What if she couldn't manage to care for Anna and Henry? What if they resented her? What if her inexperience brought them harm?

Perhaps if she prayed about it, God would give her some of that peace Ted had talked about.

Well, she wouldn't meet Ted's children wearing anything but a proper dress. She picked up an iron and laid it on the collar, which had bunched up on one side. As she smoothed the fabric, a little hissing sound startled her into moving the iron. When she did, a scorch remained in the exact shape of the tip. "Oh, no!"

Elizabeth propped the flatiron and raced to the sink for a cloth, but no amount of scrubbing erased the scorch.

Well, who needed a collar, anyway? A collarless dress would be unique.

This time she kept the iron moving. When one iron lost its heat, she exchanged it for the other. Pressing the yards and yards of fabric made her arms ache. Ted had called them sadirons. Good name for the heavy, ugly instruments of torture. Just when she thought she couldn't stand the discomfort another minute, she met up with the pressed side of her dress.

Except for the collar, she'd done a fine job. She laid the garment over a chair while she set the table for four. When she'd finished, she grabbed up the dress, took the shears from the pantry and hauled them to the bedroom.

The waist was still dampish, but her dress smelled like sunshine. With endless stitches holding the collar in place, she didn't have time to remove the seam. Using the shears, she trimmed away the lapel, slipped into her undergarments, and then donned the dress. From her reflection in the mirror she decided even with the missing collar, she looked presentable, except for her hair. She untied the twine, brushed and then twisted her tresses into a chignon. Now prepared to meet Ted's children. Or so she told herself.

In the kitchen, Elizabeth stirred the soup. Some of the vegetables had stuck to the bottom. Well, it couldn't be helped. How could she watch the soup and get ready? In an attempt to disguise the taste, she added pepper and salt. When she ladled up the soup, she'd avoid the bottom of the pan.

Suddenly exhausted, she flopped into the kitchen rocker. Tippy laid his head on her lap. She gave his nose a pat, and then leaned back against the chair, closing her eyes.

A sense of exhilaration slid through her, odd considering her fatigue. She'd never accomplished this much, never experienced this satisfaction.

In Chicago she'd lived like a sailboat without a rudder, without a compass, blown to and fro, getting nowhere.

Now as Ted's wife, she had a ready-made purpose. A job. Responsibilities.

The weight of those responsibilities sat heavy on her shoulders. Yet they also gave her a new view of her life. One where waking up in the morning meant hard work, yes, but also…

Fulfillment. That was the word.

Elizabeth giggled. All that insight from preparing a bowl of soup.

But then reality reared its disagreeable head and the joy drained out of her faster than a bottomless jug.

Could she really do this? She knew nothing about motherhood, about anything outside of teas and balls.

Like a dress off the rack, she suspected the role wouldn't quite fit. Well, when the job got too big, she'd pin a section here and there. Squeeze into the confining areas that chafed. Though the garb would surely feel more suitable for a costume ball than for her.

Regardless, she'd find a way. Do whatever she must to ensure her brother had a happy life.

But at what price?

Chapter Eight

"I don't like you." The pale blue eyes staring at Elizabeth were defiant, strong, so like her father's, and not about to be dissuaded by a scorched bowl of soup.

No matter how hard she tried to pretend otherwise, Ted's daughter's declaration squeezed against Elizabeth's heart. For a second she wanted to rush in with words, to find a way to soothe the waters between them. But really, what could she say that would change Anna's mind? Why wouldn't Anna dislike the woman she'd see as her mother's replacement?

As if Elizabeth held any such aspiration.

She wouldn't get attached to anyone in this house. Opening her heart might lead her down a risky road she dared not travel.

Elizabeth gave a bright, friendly, let's-work-together smile. "Well, Anna," she began, seeking a truce between them. "We both live in this house so what do you say we try to make the best of it?"

Anna shoved folded arms across her chest. "I don't want to."

"Let's try." Elizabeth bit back a smile at the all-too-familiar stance she'd used as a child. "We can start by—"

"You're not my mommy. I don't have to do anything you say." Anna's eyes narrowed to icy slits. "Why are you here?"

Good question.

No, Elizabeth had an important motive for marrying Ted. Her brother.

"Ahem." Ted stood in the doorway. From the wary look on his face he'd heard her exchange with Anna.

He shot her a smile, then another to Anna, trying to ease the standoff between them. How long could he sustain that resolute smile plastered on his face before it cracked?

Anna streaked to her father's side. Solid, well muscled with thick blond hair and a stubborn jaw, she was a replica of her father. "My, it's good to have you home, sweet pea," Ted said, giving his daughter a kiss, then hoisting Henry in his arms. "You, too, big boy."

The toddler planted his chubby hands on his father's cheeks as Ted nuzzled Henry's nose. His son let out a squeal then lunged closer, every ounce of his body bouncing with joy.

A pang rose in Elizabeth, a deep yearning for her family—for Papa, Robby and Martha. Not that the nanny was her mother, but she was a substitute of sorts. Perhaps, with thought, Elizabeth would see how Martha managed to walk that line. Then she could do the same with Anna.

Ted crossed to the stove. "Hmm, soup. Your favorite, Anna."

Leaning against her father's leg, Anna screwed up

her face at Elizabeth then brightened as she faced her father. "Sit, Daddy. I'll get it for you. Like I always do."

Ted tugged his daughter's braid. "Yes, pumpkin, you've been a big help, but Elizabeth should serve since she made the soup."

Anna's face flattened. The spark in her eyes faded to a vacant stare.

"You can put milk in the glasses." Ted slipped Henry into the high chair. He tucked a towel around his son's middle, securing the ends to the back, and then tied a bib around the boy's neck. "Try to keep your food on this, my boy."

His hand lingered on Henry's shoulder, a fatherly, most likely absentminded connection Ted didn't realize he made, Henry probably barely felt and Anna didn't see.

But Elizabeth noticed. She saw the love that simple contact embodied, and almost felt it.

How often had she wiggled free from her mother's touch because of some silly irritation with Mama? Now those opportunities were gone, along with her mother. Gone too soon. Gone before Elizabeth appreciated the simple gift of her mother's touch.

She shook off the loneliness that threatened to unravel her. The past couldn't be undone. She had a job to do here. She'd focus on that. And be extra patient with Anna, who'd lost her mother years before Elizabeth had hers.

She crossed to the counter to load a plate with cheese sandwiches, bringing her near Anna. The child carefully balanced the pitcher of milk as she poured it into four glasses. Though the container was heavy, she didn't spill a drop.

"Nice of you to help," Elizabeth said. Anna rewarded her with a frosty stare.

Well, apparently Elizabeth had a lot more trying to do if she wanted peace between her and Anna. The only trouble was she had no idea how to create harmony with a seven-year-old hurting child. For now she'd concentrate on ladling up the soup, something she could manage.

As she stood at the stove, Ted came up behind her, filling the narrow space with his overpowering presence. She caught the scent of his soap, clean and fresh, as crisp as a March breeze. Like a doomed moth drawn to a flame, she turned to him. The heat from his skin, from the intensity of that silver-blue gaze burned in her cheeks, muddling her thoughts.

Determined to sever the connection, she whipped back to the stove. But her hands shook and she slopped soup over the brim of the stoneware like an old lady with tremors.

"I know this has to be hard," he said near her ear, his breath drifting along her jaw. "I'll do what I can to make it easier, but…"

Unable to resist, she faced him, took in his expression now shadowed with worry, darkened by uncertainty. Evidence he held the same doubts as her. A comfort Elizabeth hadn't expected, but held close to her heart.

"But you're as new at this mail-order-bride thing as I am," she said, then grinned. "Sally's not the only one with cold feet."

He laughed—a deep, hearty sound, dissolving her concern faster than the cookstove melted butter. "Anna will put the fire to our toes, that's for sure," he whispered, then asked her to put only vegetables in Henry's bowl, the moment over.

Ted struck up a conversation with his children about nothing, really, but enough for Elizabeth to feel like an outsider peering in the window of a family home. She clutched her bowl. Well, she lived here, too, and soon—

Soon she would feel like she belonged.

A part of her whispered belonging meant joining. Belonging meant being part of a family in all ways, not just cooking for them. Belonging meant opening her heart.

Her stomach dipped. She knew how much it could hurt if…if things didn't work out. Time and time again, she'd learned by watching her parents that what a spouse gave could easily be withdrawn. Better to keep her distance than try to join an already complete circle.

While she served the soup, Ted scooted the high chair closer to the corner of the table then took the seat at the head with the children on either side of him. As she had at breakfast, Elizabeth sat to his right, close to the stove.

Anna pointed an accusing finger. "She's sitting in Mama's chair. She's not s'posed to."

Ted nodded slowly. "I know, pumpkin, but women sit where they can keep an eye on the food."

Mama's chair.

Elizabeth's mind rocketed back, far from this simple kitchen to the elaborate dining room, to the ornate, massive chair where her delicate mother had always sat. Now empty. Her eyes stung, remembering a hundred meals spent with her guilt-ridden, grieving father filling his place at the other end of the table while she and Robby avoided looking at that chair. Or tried to.

No other woman had claimed her mother's place. In that chair. Or in Elizabeth's heart.

A wave of sympathy crashed through Elizabeth. How would she have felt if someone had taken her mother's place at the table? Probably much like Anna. Anna wanted Rose, not a stranger. Not just in this chair, but here, in this house.

Elizabeth searched for the right thing to say. The words Robby must've craved at Anna's age. None came. But there was something she could do. She picked up her bowl. "Would you like to trade seats, Anna? You should sit in your mother's chair."

Tears welled in the little girl's eyes. She nodded and then, carrying her bowl, took Rose's seat at the table. Now Anna would fill it. No one would look at that empty chair. A good solution or so Elizabeth hoped as she took Anna's place.

If Elizabeth had expected gratitude she didn't get it. Well, one small step at a time might bring peace. Eventually.

Sending her a nod of thanks, his eyes misty, Ted clasped his hands together. "Let's bow our heads."

Both children folded their hands. Elizabeth glanced at Henry. From behind his fist, the toddler peeked at her, sporting a drooly grin and guileless, sparkling eyes.

The small flame of Henry's friendly face melted a tiny portion of Elizabeth's frozen heart. She grinned back.

After the prayer, Ted cut up one half of a cheese sandwich for Henry, then gave the other half to Anna. He dumped the cooled vegetables on Henry's tray and chopped them into manageable pieces. The little boy dug right in, picking up a piece of corn with amazing agility and popping it in his mouth.

Anna slurped the soup from her spoon. "This doesn't taste good like Mama's soup."

"Well, it tastes better than mine." As if to prove it, Ted ate heartily.

Elizabeth detected the faintest hint of scorch. Still, the soup fared better than her collar, better than breakfast, and gave her hope she'd wrestle a measure of control over the cooking.

When he finished, as he had that morning, Ted thanked her for the meal, but this time Elizabeth heard a ring of sincerity in his voice. Close to praise. Perhaps she could handle this job of wife. But then she remembered he'd called their marriage a business arrangement. Exactly how she wanted it. Or so she told herself, as the truth sank inside her like a stone.

Anna dawdled over her food then pushed her chair back. "Can I be excused?"

Ted shook his head. "Not until we're all finished."

Anna frowned then slipped into her seat. "Are you going to read me a story after dinner, Daddy?"

"I can't, pumpkin. I have to plow." His gaze settled on Elizabeth. "But I'm sure if you're nice, Elizabeth would be glad to read you a story."

Anna's gaze darted to Elizabeth, then away. "That's okay. I'm too old for stories."

Apparently the price of nice was too steep for Anna to pay.

Ted ruffled her hair. "We're never too old for a good book."

A few minutes later, when Henry had finished, leaving his tray and the floor a disgusting mess, Ted excused himself from the table and headed back to the fields.

Leaving Elizabeth alone with his children.

Anna stared at her, eyes shooting daggers. Henry gave her a curious look like he would a new toy. All around the kitchen dirty dishes sat...waiting.

Every muscle in Elizabeth's body ached. A few feet

away, the open bedroom door beckoned. She'd done enough for one day and wanted nothing more than a nap.

"You gonna wash the dishes?" Anna's eyes narrowed. "Like you're supposed to?"

"Oh, yes, the dishes." Elizabeth sighed. The work never ended. "You're a big girl. Want to help?"

"No." Anna gave her a small smile. "No thank you," she qualified then headed up the steps to the living room.

Elizabeth pursed her lips. A brat, plain and simple. Well, she'd practiced the art most of her life. Miss Anna might not know it, but she'd met her match in Elizabeth Manning...er, Logan.

Elizabeth pulled herself to her feet with fresh determination, picking up a bowl as she did and affecting an I-don't-care pose. "I'm glad you don't want to help."

Anna stopped cold in her tracks.

"That means I don't have to share."

Anna pivoted back. "Share what?"

Elizabeth swished a bar of soap around in the pan. "Why, the bubbles, of course."

"I'm too old for bubbles, too," Anna said, then stomped out of the room.

Elizabeth dropped her focus to her sudsy hands. Had she made the biggest mistake of her life yesterday? Not only for her, but also for Anna, a little girl who didn't want her here.

She'd done it for Robby, but...what if being here among all this unrest made Robby's life miserable? Once again he'd be living in a house of turmoil. Not a good solution for him.

Or for her.

But what choice did she have?

Across the way, Henry, red faced and bellowing,

jerked against the towel anchoring him to the high chair. Elizabeth rushed over, freed his tether and picked him up. Legs pumping, arms flailing, he resembled a windup toy gone berserk. She held him at arm's length until at last his spring wound down. Yawning, he rubbed his eyes with dimpled fists.

"You look like you could use a nap. Well, so could I." Not that she'd get the luxury.

After washing him up, Elizabeth carried Henry into the living room. She stood there uncertain what to do, while the boy squirmed in her arms. At this rate, he'd never fall asleep.

She thought of the quiet moments in the nursery she'd witnessed as a fourteen-year-old girl, moments between her mother and Robby. Mama held Robby close, rocking him back and forth, told him one story after another. By the second tale, Robby's eyes would close, but Mama kept rocking, holding him tight. In those moments, even as she held herself aloof from her mother, Elizabeth wished she could turn back the clock, be that child in her mother's arms.

Henry arched backward, nearly falling to the floor. She tightened her hold and hurried to the rocker near the window. Here, she had a view of the fields. In the distance, she could see Ted walking behind his team under the scorching sun.

With Henry on her lap, she rocked, but he stiffened his legs, refusing to settle. Why would he fight a nap when she'd love nothing better? She needed a story. *Children's Bible Storybook* lay open on the table beside the chair. Perfect. Elizabeth turned to the middle. "Oh, look, Henry. Noah and the Ark. That should be a good story for you." As Elizabeth read the first page, Henry climbed over her like a monkey at the zoo. "You'll never get sleepy if you don't sit still, you little octopus."

Anna marched in from her room. "He wants me, not you," she said with seven-year-old disgust, then plucked the book from Elizabeth's hands and stuck it under her arm. She raised her hands to Henry. Her brother tumbled into them, looking as content as a debutant with a full dance card.

Apparently Elizabeth would sit this one out. Well, she couldn't be happier. Her feet hurt, anyway.

Without a word exchanged between them, Elizabeth rose from the chair. A terrible heaviness pressed against her lungs, weighing down her movements. This wasn't the nursery at home. This wasn't her family. She couldn't even get a toddler to accept her in this house. She was failing as a homemaker. Failing as a mother. She blinked hard against the tears welling in her eyes, refusing to care.

Plopping Henry on the cushion, Anna quickly took Elizabeth's place, pointing to the picture. Two blond heads merged as one over the page, as close as Mama had held Robby. Just like then, Elizabeth stood watching. If she'd known how to forge the breach separating her and Mama—the stubbornness of a teen too young to understand her mother's need to put a happy spin on Papa's gambling trips, though Elizabeth had known what was going on—maybe she'd know how to connect with Anna.

Or might she have to face the unfaceable herself? That Ted's daughter might never accept her. Now Elizabeth understood her mother's dilemma. Bringing something into the open didn't change it. And might make it worse.

"What does a duck say, Henry?" Anna said.

"Quack, quack!" Henry settled against his sister.

"That's right." Anna shot Elizabeth a smug smile. *Well.*

Anna had established her territory, making it clear she considered herself the lady of the house and Elizabeth an interloper to be ignored like a fly on the ceiling of her life.

Back in the kitchen, Elizabeth attacked the dirty dishes, a lump tightening in her throat. Why hadn't she realized this wouldn't work before she married Ted? She didn't belong here.

She sighed. But Robby did. He needed this. No matter what, for him, she'd make this work. But how?

As a small child, she and Mama had been close. They'd shared many happy times playing dress-up and with dolls, reading, drawing and performing at the piano. She'd recapture those moments and give them to Anna and Henry and, in time, her brother.

Her mind wrapped around a fresh resolve. Elizabeth Manning Logan wasn't going anywhere. Wasn't giving up. Not that easily. Not until she had given Robby the one thing all children deserved. Security.

Her lungs expanded until she felt light, almost buoyant. Once Robby joined them, she'd have an ally in this house, someone who'd look at her with acceptance, with love. Then she'd be content.

She would.

From the living room, in a sweet voice Elizabeth barely recognized, Anna sang a lullaby. Elizabeth dried her hands on her apron and slipped to the doorway. Anna cradled her brother on her lap. Henry's eyes closed, yawning around the thumb in his mouth. In no time, the tot's head drooped.

Anna looked up and found Elizabeth watching her.

"Daddy says I can't lift him into his bed." Pink dusted her cheeks, as if embarrassed by the admission.

Perhaps sharing this moment could be the first brace in building a bridge between them. "Glad to help, Anna." Elizabeth gathered Henry from his sister's arms. He curled against her body, his wispy hair soft against her chin as she carried him into his bedroom and lowered him in his crib. Lying there asleep, he looked angelic.

But looks were deceiving. She mustn't get caught in this trap. Her parents' love for each other had ran the gamut from high hopes to despondency, as Papa let his family down time and time again. The pain of it all settled inside her, adding to her resolve. She wouldn't make the mistake of opening her heart to Ted and his children, only to get it stomped on.

She tiptoed out of the room. Anna sat on the top step leading down to the kitchen, sucking her thumb. The little girl looked tired—or maybe sad. Seeing Elizabeth, she jerked her thumb away.

"You're a hard worker, Anna."

Anna's expression revealed the battle going on inside her, fighting between accepting recognition for her efforts and the desire to shut out Elizabeth. "Thank you," she said finally.

"Your mother would be proud of you."

Anna's face clouded. She rose and slipped out onto the porch, letting the screen door slap behind her. Elizabeth heard the squeak of the swing, then a soft sob followed by another.

Her breath caught in her lungs. Though she hadn't meant to, she'd added to Anna's pain. Unsure what to do, Elizabeth stood there, thinking of all the times she'd wept since Mama died. Perhaps a good cry would help

Anna. If she tried to comfort her, Anna would most likely resent her efforts.

The sobbing stopped. Elizabeth tiptoed to the door. Anna lay curled on the swing, sound asleep, her breathing even, her little-girl face tranquil.

Elizabeth swallowed against the sudden tightness in her throat, then turned toward the kitchen to finish cleaning up and make preparations for the evening meal.

Later, the chore behind her, she dropped onto a living room chair, relieved to get off her feet. Earlier Ted had popped in with the excuse of refilling his water jug, when he could've easily gotten it at the pump. He was no doubt making sure neither she nor Anna had drawn blood. He'd smiled when he'd seen Anna snoozing on the swing.

Whatever the reason for Ted's appearance, she'd welcomed his presence. The walls had begun to close in on her. Those few minutes of conversation with an adult had kept her going.

She yawned. Closing her eyes, she leaned her head against the back, so tired her body molded into the chair.

A soft babbling from his bedroom announced the end of Henry's nap. Elizabeth groaned as Anna raced past on her way to her brother. She pulled herself to her weary feet and followed, expecting to lift Henry from his crib. Instead she found Anna tugging the toddler over the bars. Evidently house rules changed with Henry awake.

Elizabeth watched while the little girl deftly changed Henry's diaper. She obeyed Anna's orders—handing her a diaper and disposing of the wet one in the lidded pail Anna indicated. An odor of ammonia smacked her in the face. Elizabeth's stomach tumbled. She dropped the diaper inside and slapped the lid on after it. What would her stomach have done if the diaper had been more than wet?

Was motherhood, even to Robby, a role too big for her to handle? So much to do—the stories, the naps, the meals, the dishes, the diapers, the laundry—the list was endless.

"Don't forget to wash them. I'm not doing it," Anna announced.

Elizabeth fought the urge to stick out her tongue at the little girl's bossy face. Instead she glanced at Henry, now exploring his nose with a finger. My, babies had the manners of Reginald Parks.

She scrubbed Henry's hands then followed the toddler out of the room. As he staggered about the living room, darting from one thing to another, she held her breath, hovering, arms out, ready to grab him.

Barely missing hitting his head on the corner of the end table, he kept going and tripped over the rocker of a chair, landing hard on his bottom. Immediately he pulled himself to his feet then almost crashed into the desk. He yanked at the knob on the desk drawer. Her heart lodged in her throat as she made a grab for him.

When the drawer didn't open, he tugged the corner of a magazine, pulling the entire pile to the floor, then plopped down to tear the cover from an issue of *Prairie Farmer*. Drool dripping on the pages of the magazine he ripped to shreds, Henry remained in one spot. That was well worth the sacrifice of a magazine. Elizabeth heaved a sigh of relief.

Then as if she'd conjured him up out of sheer panic, Ted appeared. Hair and forearms damp from washing up at the pump. Elizabeth could've hugged him. Finally, someone in the house who'd know what to do with a mischievous toddler.

Looking at his son, Ted gave a gentle smile, his face tender. "Hi, my boy."

Squealing with joy, Henry scrambled on all fours to his father. Ted gathered his son in his strong arms and kissed his cheek, then turned to Elizabeth. "Where's Anna?"

"She was here a minute ago." Elizabeth looked around the room for Anna, her heart skittering like a crab. Had she run off somewhere? Was she hiding? Hurt?

"I'll find her," Ted said calmly.

Hinges creaked. Anna stood in the doorway of the living room, her face pinched, hands hanging limp at her sides, her soft blue eyes bleak, like the sky before a rain.

"I was about to look for you, Anna," Ted said.

"I was in your bedroom." In her fist, she clutched a handkerchief. "Was this Mama's, Daddy?"

Ted passed Henry to Elizabeth then walked to Anna, knelt before his daughter and touched the corner of the hankie. "Yes, pumpkin."

"Can I...can I have it?"

Ted tucked a curl behind his daughter's ear. "Of course you can. Your mama would've liked you to have it."

He pressed the linen to Anna's hands, then kissed his daughter on the cheek. Anna's lips trembled in an attempt to smile that failed, tearing at Elizabeth's resolve to remain detached. Without a word, Anna carried the hanky into the bedroom she and Henry shared and closed the door.

Ted remained where he crouched, head bent, shoulders slumped, as if in prayer. The sight of that hurting child, this strong man's dejection, seized Elizabeth's throat. She choked back tears. She knew grief, had felt that blanket of pain. But she didn't know what to do.

Finally Ted rose and turned toward Elizabeth, his forehead etched with worry. "Anna hasn't been herself since Rose died. She loved her mother, misses her terribly," he said, his voice hoarse, raw with emotion.

"I know how she feels," Elizabeth said softly. "My mother died two years ago. I ached for her. Wanted her back, for one more talk, one more hug." For one more chance to make amends.

Ted's worried expression softened. "I'm sorry you lost your mom."

How little they knew about each other. Yet the desire to help Anna united them. Ted's daughter needed their support and compassion.

"I thought by now..." His words trailed off.

"It's...something you never get over. Not really." She cleared her throat. "Anna's young to lose her mother. She misses her touch, her smile, her scent. Her very essence. No one else will do."

Ted nodded. "Not even me." Swallowing hard, he took the chair beside her, propping his forearms on his knees and hunching forward with his attention on the floor.

"You're wrong. She loves you, Ted, so much she can't stand sharing you."

"When I decided to marry, all I could think about was keeping the children near, making sure they had good care. I didn't consider how that would affect Anna." He ran a hand through his hair. "That's not true. I did, but I chose to ignore it. I thought I had a good reason, but—"

"What choice did you have, really?"

He lifted his gaze to hers, holding it as if the link was a lifeline. "You see that I never wanted to hurt Anna or you?"

She gave his hand a squeeze. "Of course."

"I'm sorry the brunt of her anger falls on you." His expression turned wary. "How did it go this afternoon?"

Elizabeth refused to add to his load. "Good," she said brightly.

The grim smile he gave suggested he knew she'd tempered her response. "Once she's gotten used to you…"

"My presence upsets Anna. She sees me as trying to take her mother's place."

"But only for a while, until she feels more comfortable."

His words might ring with confidence, but his eyes held the unspoken fear he might be wrong. Ted was a good father. He did all he could to meet his children's needs, even marrying a stranger to give them a mother.

The truth settled around Elizabeth's shoulders, as heavy as chain mail. That solution had blown up in his face.

So why did Ted keep looking at her with such hope in his eyes? He'd have about as much success with pinning his hopes on her as seeing rain in a fleeting, fluffy cloud during a drought.

She couldn't fix the unfixable. She wouldn't even try.

Chapter Nine

Ted tucked his children in for the night. Not easy with Anna clinging to him, tattling about Elizabeth's every move, no doubt hoping he'd toss his wife out like a busted toy. He'd tried talking to his daughter about her attitude, but the stubborn tilt of her chin told him he'd wasted his breath.

At last Anna's eyelids drooped and she slept, still hanging on to Rose's handkerchief. Ted tucked the sheet under her chin, then rested his elbows on his thighs and lowered his head to his hands.

Had he made a mistake remarrying? Had he misread the freedom of choice God gave His children, seeing Elizabeth as God's will for them? And added to Anna's unhappiness? Made Elizabeth's life miserable? The fear of failing his children and his new wife weighed him down, all but crushing him.

"Lord, mend Anna's broken heart. Help my children accept Elizabeth," he whispered. "Bless this marriage."

As he laid his burdens at the foot of the Throne, several Scriptures came to mind, precious promises of God's gift of wisdom, of His provision. The Father could bring good out of bad. Buoyed by renewed hope, the burden on his shoulders lifted.

God would help them, was helping them even now. He'd expected too much too soon. Establishing harmony in his house would take time. Adjustments had to be made. He'd keep his expectations on an even plane, his usual course, and the wisest.

He and Elizabeth might not be the typical couple, might never fall in love, but with God's help, they could make this family work.

With one last glance at his children, their faces peaceful in slumber, Ted left the room, prepared by his time with God to bolster his wife. This surely had been a difficult day for her.

In the living room, he found Elizabeth at the desk, leafing through a cookbook. Her hair had pulled loose from the pins and curled around her face. At odd moments like this, he'd glance her way and that beauty would sock him in the gut.

The dejected look on her face now tore at him. Anna wasn't the only miserable person in this house. He hoped, in time, Elizabeth would find contentment.

But life had taught him happiness wasn't a guarantee in this world. He'd give anything if he'd been able to protect his children from that truth, but Rose's passing had introduced them to the harsh reality of death. He'd explained to Anna that her mother now resided in Heaven, but that assurance didn't stop her from missing Rose on earth.

Time. Healing would take time. Accord would take time.

He dropped into a rocker near the potbelly stove, stretching out his legs toward the warmth of the fire.

As he stared into the window at the flames, thinking how difficult childhood could be sometimes, his mind catapulted back.

Fire and brimstone. Exactly what his father had preached at those revivals. Men and women rushed to the altar to lay down the load of their sins. But behind his father's fiery demeanor lived a liar. Even as young as five, Ted had known his dad pocketed the offering, laughing at the stupidity of those he bilked. Not a preacher at all, but a charlatan who stole money to gamble.

When the gaming tables had taken his last dime, he'd put down the cards and pick up the garb of a preacher again, until he'd swindled another stake from trusting souls in another town.

The flames flickered, but Ted barely noticed the dancing oranges and yellows. He saw an endless parade of towns, filled with faces his father had betrayed. Ted had sat on the front row, throat tight with shame, and waited…fear crawling up his spine, sure God would strike his father dead on the spot. But God never did.

The flames began to ebb, but the heat remained. Much like God's love. God didn't kill sinners—He loved them. Even men like his father.

Even men like him.

"Ted."

"I'm sorry, what?"

"How long…since Rose…?" Elizabeth glanced away, evidently too uncomfortable with her question to finish it.

"Rose died thirteen months ago, one month after Henry's birth."

"I'm sorry. I can't imagine the joy of a baby shattered by his mother's death."

"Rose had one goal, to give our baby life." He swallowed hard. "If only we hadn't decided to have another child—"

He refused to finish. Elizabeth had enough to deal with, without taking on Rose's death and the guilt he'd felt but had finally released to God.

He got up from the chair and walked to the side door, eager to change the subject, searching for a way to lighten the mood. "Clear sky tonight. Lots of stars. A full moon."

Keeping her distance, Elizabeth peered out. "It's serene."

He turned toward her. Her eyes widened, filling with uncertainty. "More serene than you."

"Why would you say that?"

"You tiptoe around me like you're afraid I'll bite."

She lifted her chin. "I do no such thing. I'm not the tiptoeing sort."

"Is that right?" To prove his point, he reached out a hand and she jumped. He grinned then sobered. "Things are difficult now, but once Anna adjusts, we'll find an even keel, a way to coexist amicably."

Elizabeth's brow wrinkled. "Is that your goal, Ted? To just coexist?"

She made accord sound dull, boring. But to him, a tranquil life sounded perfect. His father's example of Bible-thumping preaching, his zeal for gambling, had taught Ted to shun fiery passion. When he'd left the riverboat and his "Hold 'Em" Logan existence, he'd promised God he'd make a new start. From that point on, he based his life on God's Word, not on unreliable feelings and bursts of emotion.

"Calm waters, a cool head, looking to God for wisdom—that makes for a happy home."

She gave him a wan smile. "If so, we're failing."

"Don't underestimate God's authority in this, Elizabeth. Give it time. Pray about it. God is faithful."

"No doubt God listens to you, a churchgoing man."

The words she didn't say spoke volumes. "You don't believe He's listening to you."

"I don't rely on God to solve my problems."

If God intended Ted to heed His call, why had He given him a wife with shaky faith? Or was that somehow part of God's plan? "Perhaps He already has," he said, studying her.

Looking unconvinced, Elizabeth merely shrugged.

Somehow Ted suspected his wife's problems referred to more than Anna. Was she talking about him or something else? "No one besides God is worth relying on."

Their eyes locked. All those unnamed problems fell away, leaving just the two of them. Something wounded and raw in Elizabeth called to him. He wanted to protect her. To give her whatever he possessed. Whatever she needed. But he dared not push her. Though he'd pray for her daily, she'd have to find her way. With Anna. With him. With God.

Standing this close, alone in the quiet house, sent his skittish wife to the couch. "Where did Anna and Henry stay last year during planting and harvest season?" she said, deftly changing the subject.

"After Rose's parents returned home, the children stayed at the Harpers' during the day and here in the evening. Anna hated being separated from me." He sighed. "She'd like to follow me around the place while I'm doing the chores. It's not safe."

"Anna's lost one parent. Naturally she wants to keep an eye on you."

He rubbed the back of his neck, stiff from hours behind the plow. If only he could soothe his hurting daughter as easily. "I'm sure you're right."

"How long have you lived in New Harmony?"

"Nine years." She looked at him expectantly, clearly fishing for information. Maybe if he gave her some, she'd be satisfied. "We moved here right after Rose and I married."

"That's when you bought the farm."

He nodded. Rose had desired nothing beyond a simple existence living off the land. Exactly what he wanted... or so he told himself every day. Though at times the life chafed against him like new wool long johns in winter.

"The work is endless, but I'd appreciate it if you found time to read and play with the children each day. That was Rose's way. They're used to some attention."

"Anna's the little mother around here." Elizabeth laughed but Ted didn't miss the lack of humor in the sound. "Not me."

Ted cringed. He hadn't missed his precious daughter's bossy, belligerent behavior with Elizabeth. "Anna's conduct will improve once she gets to know you," he said with all the assurance he could muster.

"Are you trying to convince me or yourself?" She smiled. "Don't worry. I can handle Anna. I wasn't an easy child. I know all the tricks."

"Why doesn't that surprise me?" He chuckled, and then sat beside her on the sofa.

Close enough to notice the curve of her cheek, the length of her lashes and the silky texture of her skin.

Though she'd tried to tease about her behavior as a child, the pain of her admittance clouded her pretty blue eyes.

Lord, please free Elizabeth from whatever's bothering her. Help me to make her feel at home here.

Though, surely his stinginess at the mercantile yesterday hadn't helped matters. "If I acted like I begrudged you the fabric and garments, I apologize. I hate to go into debt but that's the way of life for farmers. If the harvest's good, the bills get paid. If not..."

"If not, you work harder the next year."

"That's farming."

"It's honest work," she said. The admiration in his citified wife surprised him.

"Yes, and that's what matters. But some days I feel like a mule pulling a plow through the mud, that I'll never reach the other side of the field." He paused, forcing a laugh, then sobered. "But I do. I have to."

"What did you do before you took up farming?"

The kitchen clock struck the hour. "This and that," he said, rising. "It's late. If Anna or Henry wakes, don't hesitate to fetch me."

Elizabeth hugged the armrest like a long-lost friend. "My presence is inconvenient. You probably won't sleep well in that drafty barn."

"No, your being here means I can plant and keep my children with me. That's all that matters."

A flash of something he couldn't read streaked across her face. She quickly smoothed her expression. Had he hurt her? If so, he hadn't meant to, but even if the truth hurt, it didn't change the facts. Anna and Henry were his priorities.

He hadn't lied when he'd called their marriage a business arrangement. Perhaps in time, they'd come to mean more to each other. Ted felt far more comfortable in the world of friendly coexistence—two people living together, working toward a common goal—than in strong attraction. Though every time Elizabeth came near, she made him question that opinion.

Worse, she questioned him. Tried to figure out what made him tick. He couldn't let her unearth his past and risk his children's future.

He ambled toward the door. "Before I turn in, I'll find those boots. Can't have you working in your party best."

"Even a mule deserves to be well shod." Elizabeth's steely eyes held not one shred of humor.

"I hoped you knew that taking care of my household wouldn't be easy. I didn't try to mislead you."

She glared at him. "Just once, try putting yourself in my place, Ted Logan. Stick your feet in those boots you promised and see if the fit's comfortable." She left the room in a huff.

He'd intended to mend the fences his daughter had broken, but instead he'd driven a wider wedge between him and Elizabeth.

Perhaps that was for the best.

If they got close, she might discover the truth about him, and soon the whole town would know. All havoc would break loose.

And destroy the way of life he'd made for his children.

Ted must be feeding his hens molasses or something equally sticky. Their eggs stuck to a pan like shy debutants wedged together at a ball. When Elizabeth tried to turn one over, half the white stayed behind while the yolk spewed out, a yellow stream navigating the cast iron, as if two hens went to war in the pan.

So much for her plan to start the morning off on a good note, thinking a well-cooked meal would be a way to ease into the "Oh, by the way, I have a brother" discussion. Instead, once Ted saw the meal, she'd be fortunate if he stayed at the table, much less let Robby join them there.

"Bam! Bam!" Henry beat his spoon on the tray of the high chair. Oatmeal flew, landing on the floor with a splat.

"Henry Logan, I don't have time to clean up the mess you're making. So stop that. Please."

"Bam! Bam! Bam!" He did it again, this time laughing at his cleverness. The last bang sent the spoon clanging to the planks.

If he knew the trouble she'd had making that oatmeal, he'd treat the meal with more respect. Elizabeth bent to retrieve the utensil. "I asked you nicely. Flipping oatmeal is nasty."

No sooner had the words left her mouth, than something plopped on her head. She reached up and grabbed hold of one oatmeal-coated, chubby hand and looked into Henry's grinning face. "Good thing you're as cute as a bug's ear, young man."

"Bug!"

"You're a boy, not a bug."

"Bug," he said, then whacked her square on the nose with an oatmeal-loaded fist.

"Ouch." No wonder Mama had taken her breakfast in bed. The kitchen was a hazardous place. A woman could languish under a mountain of oatmeal and pasty eggs. She wanted to be mad, but found herself running a finger along his cheek.

Henry giggled, ducking his head.

Whenever she saw the mischief in his eyes, part of her softened like butter on a sultry summer day. "I won't be swayed by those dancing eyes, young man."

She walked to the door and whistled Tippy inside. He gobbled the oatmeal and licked Henry's extended hand for dessert before Elizabeth herded him back outside. If Tippy could master a dust mop, he could get a job as a maid.

The smell of smoke brought her nose up in the air. Something was burning. "The toast!"

She raced to the oven. Using a towel, she flung it open and yanked out the pan. Their closest neighbor to the south had sent over a loaf of fresh-baked bread with her oldest son and she'd destroyed the gift. Her eyes stung. She'd been counting on the toast, at least, to be edible.

How would she ever convince Ted to allow her to bring Robby here if she couldn't handle the work she already had?

The back door opened and closed. Anna wrinkled her nose. "I smell smoke."

"How's breakfast coming?" Ted asked.

From across the kitchen, Elizabeth shot him a scowl.

A crooked grin tugged at the corner of his mouth. "Guess I don't have to ask."

He washed his hands and asked Anna to do the same, then took the toast from Elizabeth's hands. "Better check your hair before that lump of oatmeal dries." He scrapped the burned crumbs into the sink.

"That lump is a gift from your son."

Ted chuckled. "He's a generous boy, like his father."

Rolling her eyes, she whirled toward the mirror hanging near the sink and plucked at the oatmeal, shaking it off her fingers into the slop jar, then dabbed at the gooey spot with a damp towel, avoiding Ted's gaze.

"You, ah, missed some." Ted came around her, took the towel and with a gentle touch, wiped at the mess. He stood facing her, mere inches away, close enough she could feel the heat emanating from his skin. She remained motionless, for surely if she took a step, she'd find herself in the comfort of his arms.

"Your hair is beautiful." Husky and quiet, his tone rumbled with something intimate. "Like sun-kissed wheat." His gaze locked with hers, sending a shiver down her spine.

Elizabeth had received dozens of compliments over the years, but never had one left her reeling. She pressed a palm to the mass of curls she hadn't had time to tuck into a chignon. "My hair's a mess. I'll put it up later—"

"Don't. I mean, you needn't worry. You look…good as new."

"I do?" She ran her fingers through her hair, searching for another chunk of Henry's breakfast, while her wayward heart hammered in her chest. "I doubt that."

"Never doubt a man's compliment. They don't come easy for most of us."

Across the way, Anna watched Elizabeth and Ted with narrowed eyes, her mouth thinned in disapproval. Hadn't Elizabeth watched her parents as Anna watched them now? Not out of jealousy or pain as Anna surely did, but with hope.

Time and time again, she'd seen Papa sweet-talk his way back into the good graces of his disgruntled wife. Those moments of affection between her parents hadn't lasted. The inevitable letdowns had sent her mother to bed and her father to the gambling tables.

Elizabeth fingered her mother's cameo, the only piece of jewelry that hadn't been sold to pay the bills.

Her thumb roamed the face of the cameo as she thought of another necklace. A strand of shimmering pearls. Papa had swooped in at breakfast and draped them around Mama's neck. "Happy anniversary! You get prettier with every year, Amanda. As young as the day we married."

Mama had giggled at the claim.

"You don't believe me." He pointed to the mirror hanging over the buffet. "Look at yourself."

With her cheeks flushed with pleasure and her eyes sparkling, Mama was beautiful, regal like a queen. Standing at her side, Papa was her crown prince, tall and imposing. The perfect couple—or so they appeared.

Then Papa danced Mama around the room. She'd thrown back her head laughing, her face glowing like the morning sun.

"I've made reservations for dinner," he said. "Afterward we'll stop at the club."

Mama paled. "Not the club. Not tonight."

He kissed her cheek. "I'll win enough to buy the matching bracelet and earrings. Wouldn't you like that?"

Watching them leave, Elizabeth had never seen a more enchanting couple, looking as if they'd stepped out of a fairy tale. She'd waited up to see them come home. A little after midnight, Mama came in alone. The next day Papa arrived home, and rushed back out again to sell a painting and Mama's pearls to pay a debt.

As always, Mama had smiled, but that smile was a little dimmer, her face a little more shadowed. She and Papa never danced in the breakfast room again.

Her mother might've pretended the Mannings lived

in a rosy world, but she hadn't fooled Elizabeth. A hundred times over in her parents' lives, she'd witnessed Papa charm his way into Mama's heart one minute, then break it the next.

Their happiness had been as fleeting as a shooting star. Love led to shattered dreams and broken hearts. Elizabeth's throat tightened as her hand fell away from the cameo.

Don't. Don't get close.

Don't get wrapped up in Ted and his compliments.

She needed to forget about her parents, forget about Ted's flattering and concentrate on finding a way to ease into the subject of Robby.

Resolute, she turned to the stove. Oh, my, now all the eggs were cooked hard, the river of yellow solid. She sighed and scrapped three of them on a plate, added four slices of bacon and set the dish in front of Ted, who gifted her with a smile.

Ignoring that smile, she returned with a bowl of oatmeal and a glass of milk for Anna. Last she brought the toast, slapped it down at Ted's elbow and then filled his coffee cup.

Ted waited for her to sit, and then bowed his head for prayer. When he'd blessed the food, he grabbed a spoon and scooped oatmeal into his son's open-like-a-baby-bird mouth. Henry grabbed the spoon, playing tug-of-war, and then gave up on the contest and fed himself with his fingers.

Elizabeth should rush over to wash Henry's hands, but that meant tattling on Tippy and on her. Besides, a little dog-lick wouldn't hurt a perpetually grubby boy like Henry. Would it?

"Daddy lets me milk Nellie and Bessie on Saturday," Anna said between bites of oatmeal.

"You're Daddy's helper." Ted tugged one of Anna's braids, and then dove into the hard-cooked eggs.

"Me and Daddy saw you let Tippy inside," Anna said in an accusing tone.

Elizabeth smiled. "Tippy is better at mopping than I am."

"She said Tippy mops." Anna chuffed. "He can't hold a mop, can he, Daddy?"

"Well, evidently he has other ways of cleaning up." He motioned to Henry. "With this guy around, I can see the advantages of bringing Tippy inside upon occasion." Ted's eyes roamed over her face, sending Elizabeth's pulse skittering. "Wish I'd thought of it."

He reached out and brushed a crumb from her lip. Elizabeth gulped as heat flushed her cheeks. This man did strange things to her insides that she wouldn't trust.

She shot up from the table and grabbed a cloth to wipe up Henry. The little boy wailed in protest, shaking his head back and forth with a speed Elizabeth couldn't match.

Anna slipped in between them, took the cloth out of Elizabeth's grasp. Trapping Henry's chin in one hand, Anna sang a tune about scrubbing in a tub and cleaned the cereal from her brother's face. Then, smirking at Elizabeth, she strolled toward the back door.

"Anna, you need to ask to be excused," Elizabeth said without thinking.

"I don't have to, do I, Daddy?"

"Yes, that's the polite thing to do. I've been negligent about our table manners."

With her lower lip protruding, Anna returned to her seat, eyeing Elizabeth. "Can I go, Daddy?"

"Yes, you may."

Anna walked past Elizabeth. "Was your mama as mean as you?" She raced out the door, letting it slap behind her.

Ted sighed.

Elizabeth swallowed hard. She'd tired of her mother's focus on etiquette, while under that facade of perfection their world tumbled out of control.

Did Anna feel the same?

She forced a laugh, but even she could hear the wobbly hurt in it. "Maybe I was too tough on Anna."

"I'm sorry about Anna's behavior. Since Rose died, I haven't had the heart to discipline her. It shows."

"I understand that." She was very aware of the ramifications of losing a mother.

To smooth her relationship with Anna, she'd overlook the small things that didn't matter to children. And leave the training of his daughter to Ted.

She glanced at her husband. Ted's attention had drifted away. He'd gone somewhere else, somewhere far from his kitchen. "It can't be easy, stepping into another woman's shoes," he said at last. "It's not easy for me, either. I try to be a good father, but I'm failing Anna when she needs me most."

The anguish in his tone banged against Elizabeth's heart. "I'm not sure men occupy the same role as women. Some women are born mothers." She didn't bother to add she was not one of them. Ted already knew.

He brought his gaze back to her. "True. My mother... wasn't."

That pause said a lot. Elizabeth wanted to ask, to

probe, but she wasn't here to be Ted Logan's confidant. She was here for Robby.

"What kind of a mother was yours?" Ted asked.

"Loving." She sighed. "I was strong willed and she didn't know what to make of me." Amanda Manning could no more stand up to her daughter than she had her husband. "Martha arrived when I was five and laid down the rules."

"You must've been more like your father."

His assessment stung. But she couldn't deny it. "Papa laughed at the antics that put Mama in a tizzy. He'd say, 'Leave her alone, Amanda. She'll never be bedridden by life.'" Elizabeth swallowed hard. "I realized later they were talking about each other, not about me." She clasped her hands in her lap. "It was never about me."

"I'm sorry." Ted brushed his fingers along her cheek. "You're a precious child of God. Don't let anyone's assessment, even your own, determine your worth."

Tears brimmed in her eyes. She turned her face away. "I'm sorry I was too young to understand her. To understand the battles she fought every day. If only I could ask her forgiveness."

"Nothing Anna and Henry could do would stop me from forgiving them. I'm sure your mother felt the same."

Could Ted be right? Could Mama have forgiven her, even without Elizabeth asking for absolution? "I hope so."

Ted stretched out a hand, taking hers in his firm grip. "If you ask Him, God will forgive you anything. And give you the peace about your mistakes that you need. That we all need."

She gave a wry smile. "You sound like a preacher."

Disquiet flitted across his face. He withdrew his hand.

"I'm glad you're in here fixing breakfast when I'm out at the barn. I can't thank you enough for taking care of us and for watching my children."

She shrugged as if it was nothing. But in truth just making eggs was a formidable task. Yet nothing compared to the demands of taking care of Ted's children.

"Maybe some women aren't born to be mothers," Ted said. "But they can *become* good mothers."

"If you're thinking of me that would take a miracle."

He studied her, his eyes dark, penetrating, as if he wanted something from her that she couldn't give.

Elizabeth rose, gathering the dishes and carrying them to the sink, but for the life of her, she couldn't remember what to do with them.

Behind her she heard the scrape of a chair, then felt the heat of Ted's body as he closed the gap between them. "I hope…"

She turned toward him, waiting. "Hope what?"

He leaned nearer until he stood mere inches away. The solid comfort of his presence slid through her. With his cupped hand, he lifted her chin. Her pulse kicked up.

Would he…?

Would he kiss her?

"I hope in time you'll be happy here," he said. "In every way."

Then he turned and left.

They'd opened up to each other, given a peek into their worlds. And she'd gotten sidetracked from raising the subject of her brother.

Instead of planning her next step toward accomplishing that goal, she slumped onto a chair, reliving that almost kiss.

Feeling the oddest sense of relief.

And disappointment.

the thin cloth, she slumped onto a chair, curling into

feeling the rudder's gentle sway after

hint of apprehension.

Chapter Ten

Even from yards away, the odor of the place hit Elizabeth harder than a belch from Reginald Parks. She shoved the egg basket at Ted. "I'll, ah, wait out here."

He arched a brow. "You're afraid of a few chickens?"

"I didn't say I was afraid." Elizabeth put her hand over her nose. "It's just…they stink."

He bent down and chucked her under the chin. "You *are* afraid." He laughed. "I can see it in your eyes."

She couldn't let him know he was right, not with those teasing eyes daring her to act. These smelly birds would pay for her and Robby's tickets. She dared not refuse to gather their eggs. "Fine, I'll do it…if you go with me."

"I'll show you how it's done." He touched her scarf looped around her head. "If you plan on getting along with the hens, you might want to remove that red kerchief."

"I can't go into that nasty coop without covering my hair."

"Still, you'd better—"

She fisted her hands on her hips. "Ted Logan, you're always telling me what to do."

"Fine. Do it your way."

He opened the door and she slapped a hand over her mouth and nose and stepped inside with Ted on her heels. As the door closed, the henhouse exploded with activity—squawking hens, flapping wings. Chickens streaked across the wooden floor. Flew to perch on the rafters.

Heart pounding, Elizabeth turned to Ted. "These birds are wild! And you suggested I come in here without a kerchief. My hair could be caked with lots more than oatmeal."

He opened his mouth, but she shot him a look and he clamped it shut. *Good*. He'd gotten the message. Finally.

She turned back to the peevish hens, determined not to let her disquiet show. "Haven't you seen a lady in pants before?" she crooned. "Only difference—your pants are made of feathers."

The chickens clucked. Ted joined in with a soft chuckle. Finally the henhouse quieted. Elizabeth inched farther into the coop, letting her eyes adjust to the dim interior.

Two chickens, unruffled and serene, remained in their straw-stuffed boxes. They didn't look all that scary.

She approached the first box on her left, overflowing with a fat, white hen. "Can I have your egg?" The hen blinked at her and squatted farther into the straw. "Please?" She shooed the bird but the stubborn creature didn't budge.

"Slip your hand beneath the hen, real easy like, and pull out the egg," Ted said.

But when she reached, the hen turned one beady, ferocious eye on her, a warning she'd heed. She took a step back. "Keep it, if it means that much to you."

"Here, I'll get it." Ted retrieved the egg without incident. He met her gaze and shrugged. "They know me."

"Too bad I left my calling cards in Chicago." Gripping the egg basket, she ignored Ted's laugh and edged down the row, plucking eggs from the vacant nests. As she approached the next sitting hen, the bird hopped aside to reveal a pristine egg.

Elizabeth smiled. "Now, that's more like it." She stretched out a hand. In a flash, the hen pecked the top. "Ouch! You'd better watch it or you'll end up as Sunday's dinner."

Not that she could kill that bird...unless looks could kill.

"Let me." Ted tried to step between the hen and her, but Elizabeth would not give way.

She reached again. The hen pecked again—harder. Elizabeth let out a shriek. A bird flew from its perch on the rafter into her face. Blinded, her heart lurching against her chest, Elizabeth jerked away, stepped into a water pan and staggered backward, dropping the basket.

Ted caught her before she hit the floor. "Are you all right?"

"I'm fine." But she wasn't. She fought back angry tears. She loathed this farm and all the smelly, scary, noisy beasts living on it. Right now that included Ted.

But in truth, she wanted him to put those strong arms of his around her. Make her feel safe. Secure. Tell her everything would be okay, even though it wouldn't.

"I'm sure you have more to do than watch me make an idiot of myself," she said.

"I tried to tell—"

"I'm tired of you telling me what to do and how to do it." Her eyes stung. She would not let Ted see how overwhelmed she felt. "I'll learn. Maybe the hard way, but I'll learn."

"Fine with me." Ted stomped off in the direction of the barn.

Fine with her, too. She didn't need Ted. Or his help.

By the time Elizabeth reached the pump, the tally favored the hens. Twelve eggs broken, four intact and one very rattled egg gatherer badly in need of a bath.

At this rate, she'd never get Robby here.

As she turned to rinse out the mess in the basket, she caught sight of a wagon pulling into the barnyard. A little girl cuddled against the woman driver. She had company. Until that moment, Elizabeth hadn't realized how lonely she was for female companionship.

From the other side of the screen door, Anna came running.

Elizabeth looked down at her attire. Men's pants and a cast-off, frayed shirt. Too late now. This woman had seen her unusual outfit and still waved a greeting.

By the time she reached the wagon the girls chattered away. Holding a tiny bundle, the visitor dropped her gaze to Elizabeth's attire but the smile never left her face. "I'm Rebecca Harper, your nearest neighbor. Hope you don't mind us dropping in."

Elizabeth smiled. "I'm glad for the company."

"This is our Grace." Rebecca nudged her daughter forward. "Say hello to Mrs. Logan." Grace mumbled a greeting. Rebecca motioned to the baby. "And this is our Faith—eight weeks today."

"How nice of you to pay a visit." Elizabeth reached out a hand, spotted the slime from the broken eggs and pulled it back. "Sorry. The hens and I got off on the wrong foot."

Rebecca grinned, leaned over and pulled a piece of straw out of Elizabeth's hair. "They can be nasty little boogers. Though I'm sure that red head scarf didn't help."

Elizabeth's gaze darted to the barn. "What?"

"Chickens are easily frightened. Red promotes turmoil."

Ted had warned her to not wear the scarf. If only she wasn't as easily riled as the hens whenever he gave her an order, maybe more eggs would've survived.

Anna scooted to her side and peered into the basket. "You broke the eggs? Papa's going to be mad."

"A hen flew right into my face and I dropped the basket."

"You musta upset the hens. I'm going to tell—"

Elizabeth sighed. "Your father knows. He was with me."

"No point in tattling, now is there?" Rebecca gave Ted's daughter a stern look. "I would've expected better of you."

Anna toed the ground with her shoe. "Sorry."

Rebecca turned back to Elizabeth. They exchanged the smiles of conspirators and Elizabeth knew she'd found a friend.

"You're forgiven." Rebecca ruffled Anna's hair. "Now you girls go play while we have a visit."

"Do I still have to watch Henry?" Anna tugged at Elizabeth's shirt. "Me and Grace wanna make a clothespin doll."

Two days ago Elizabeth didn't even know what clothespins were. "Go ahead. I'll listen for Henry."

The girls raced across the yard to the line.

Rebecca smiled. "I'm embarrassed I didn't get over sooner, but Dan didn't finish planting until yesterday.

He agreed to keep the boys so we could chat in peace. That is, if you've got the time."

Elizabeth glanced down at her clothes. "Being caught wearing these, I'm the one who's red faced."

"Are those Ted's pants?" Rebecca asked.

Elizabeth hitched up the rolled waistline. "I'm afraid so."

"Are they comfortable?"

"They're too long and wide but until I get something else to wear, I'm stuck with them."

Rebecca chuckled. "Since I had Faith, I can't even button my dress at the middle." She flapped the skirt of her apron. "This covers the worst of it."

"Oh, I think you look beautiful." And she did. Rebecca all but glowed with happiness. "Go on in. I'll just be a minute."

Elizabeth pumped water over the eggs, picked out the broken shells and tossed them behind the lilac bush, her thoughts scrambling like crabs at the beach.

What should she do to entertain a visitor? Martha served tea and scones. Tea would be an easy task. Scones she didn't have. But maybe she had something else Rebecca would find palatable. Biscuits. She had plenty of those.

Inside, Elizabeth set the egg basket on the floor and scrubbed her hands. "Henry is down for a nap so we can have some peace and quiet. Would you care for tea?"

"Love some." Rebecca laid the sleeping baby in the rocker, pulling back the blanket from around her tiny face.

Elizabeth supposed it wouldn't be polite to ignore the baby, not with her mother standing over her, proud and smiling. She walked over to take a peek. And promptly fell in love. Such a sweet little thing. With lots of dark hair, long black lashes and a bow-shaped mouth.

Elizabeth reached out a finger and traced a line along the sleeping baby's cheek. "She's gorgeous."

How could she feel mushy over a baby when she knew perfectly well babies grew into messy toddlers who exhausted you, then older children who defied you?

No, babies weren't for her. Nor marriage, either, and yet here she was married and drooling over a baby. She'd been cooped up too long. A feather drifted off her clothes to the floor. Cooped up in more ways than one.

Rebecca took a seat at the table. Elizabeth got out the teapot and prepared tea. "Would you care for a biscuit? There's a few left from breakfast."

"Thanks, I'd love one."

"Really? That's so nice of you."

"And here I was thinking how nice it was of you to offer."

"This batch is crumbly," Elizabeth apologized as she set out a plate of biscuits and compote of jam.

Rebecca spread a layer of strawberry jam on top. Though a chunk of the biscuit fell away, she managed to take a bite. "This is delicious."

Elizabeth beamed her thanks. Maybe she was making progress. She returned to the table with cups and saucers.

"So, has Anna declared war yet?"

"Well, if not war, definitely a skirmish." Elizabeth went back for the pot, set it on a hot pad to steep then plopped down in her seat. "Anna resents me for usurping her mother's place. Or so she sees it. She's taken the role of little mommy to Henry and helper to Ted with no intention of giving up her territory."

"Anna's one determined little girl."

Elizabeth poured the steaming amber liquid into their cups. "Kind of like me." Her gaze slid beyond the living room to the children's bedroom door. "Now Henry, he's like a windup toy. Keeping up with him wears me out until he slows down. Thank goodness he takes a three-hour nap and goes to bed early. It's the only time I can cook and clean."

"Boys are more rambunctious, but all three of mine together are less trouble than Grace."

Elizabeth added sugar to her tea. "How old are your boys?"

"Jason's the oldest. He's seven. Mark is four and Calvin, two. Enough about my children. I'm here to get to know you." She took a sip from her cup. "So why did you give up dresses for pants? Is this some new French fashion that hasn't made it to the cornfields?"

Elizabeth grinned. "The one dress I have isn't comfortable to work in."

"One dress? Shame on Ted."

"It's a long story and not at all Ted's fault. He bought material to make three, but…"

"Let me guess. Between the baking, egg gathering and laundry, you haven't had time to make them?"

Avoiding Rebecca's eyes, Elizabeth toyed with her cup. "Truth is I don't know how to make a dress."

"Oh. Sounds like you could use some help."

"I doubt Ted's thrilled with me wearing his clothes."

Rebecca grinned. "From the way you look in those pants, I suspect Ted doesn't mind."

Glancing at Ted's old jeans, all Elizabeth could see was rolled waist and cuffs, frayed ends of twine dangling from her makeshift belt and pieces of straw sticking here and there.

She plucked them off and tossed them into the stove. "I look like an old faded scarecrow."

"Not from behind." Rebecca laughed. "But, before you fall on your face, let's cut some length off those pants."

Ted might not like that, but then the hems were worn and he had more, so why not? In minutes, Rebecca had whacked the jeans down to fit using the large shears she'd found hanging in the pantry.

"There, now we can get started sewing up a dress."

"I can't let you do that." Then Elizabeth held her breath, hoping Rebecca would do that very thing.

Rebecca drained her cup. "It'll be fun. I haven't made anything new in ages."

Elizabeth sent a sidelong glance at Rebecca's dress. The cuffs at her wrists had frayed, but it was pressed and clean. "All right, but only if you'll accept material for making it."

"Oh, no, I couldn't." Rebecca blushed. "I'm glad to help." She carried her dishes to the sink. "I can't let a neighbor of mine wear pants to the ice cream social."

"A social?" Elizabeth clasped a hand to her chest. "Oh, that sounds like fun."

"We hold sack races and horseshoe contests. The men crank freezers of ice cream. The women bring a favorite cake to share."

Favorite cake? She had to bake a cake? Wouldn't biscuits do? Oh my, she'd better get practicing.

Rebecca checked the baby, sleeping peacefully. "Time's a-wastin'. Let's make that dress while the youn-guns nap."

In no time, Rebecca devised a pattern from newspaper. Satisfied it would fit, she cut out a dress and then ran it up on the sewing machine. As Rebecca guided the fabric beneath the metal foot, the soft whir of the wheel accompanied the thump of the treadle.

Hoping to learn something about sewing and her new husband, Elizabeth pulled up a chair. "How well do you know Ted?"

"The way he cared for Rose when she took sick and his kids tells me all I need to know about Ted."

But Elizabeth had questions.

"Why do you ask?"

"No special reason. Ted doesn't say much about his life before he came to New Harmony. Almost like he has no past."

Or one he's hiding.

"All I know is he and Rose showed up at church the Sunday after they moved in. We were mighty glad to see them bring life to this house."

"Were you and Rose friends?"

Rebecca nodded. "She was a sweet woman. Quiet. Thoughtful."

The exact opposite of Elizabeth.

"I recall Rose saying they married in her home church about twelve miles west of here. Their search for a farm brought them to New Harmony."

"Wonder why New Harmony?"

"The Martin place sat empty after Paul died. Reckon the price was right. And close enough for Rose's parents to visit. Often."

Something about Rebecca's tone didn't flatter Rose's parents. But that wasn't her priority. "Does Ted have family?"

"None of his people came to the funeral. Why not ask him?"

Elizabeth forced a laugh. "Now why didn't I think of that?"

Rebecca stopped pedaling and snipped the thread. "What about you? You got any family?"

The question ended her speculation about Ted. She couldn't lie, exactly… "Yes. My father lives in Chicago."

"You must miss him."

Elizabeth swallowed against the sudden knot in her throat, a result of her deceit. "Yes, I do."

Rebecca lifted the skirt from the machine and held it and the bodice against Elizabeth. A dress. Something Elizabeth had taken for granted but now seemed a monumental achievement.

As Rebecca pinned the skirt to the bodice, she glanced at the clock. "Feel free to start supper. I'll have to feed the baby soon."

Perhaps Rebecca's presence in the house renewed her energy or maybe she had finally figured out how to handle that black monster of a stove, but Elizabeth fried up a slab of pork with a minimum of difficulty, peeled potatoes, only nicking her finger once, and put on a pan of sauerkraut. The food bubbled away on the stove, filling the house with heady scents. For the first time, she felt optimistic about the meal.

Back in the bedroom, Rebecca still hunched over the sewing machine. She nodded toward a packet of buttons. "Found those in one of the sewing drawers. They're perfect for this dress."

Lovely mother-of-pearl buttons gleamed in the afternoon sun streaming in the window. Probably Rose had planned to put them on a dress. The thought dampened Elizabeth's mood.

"How did you know how much material to buy?" Rebecca asked.

"Mrs. Sorenson told me."

"The Sorensons are good-hearted. The best. Allow farmers to run up a bill till harvest. Poor Hubert can't keep up with his accounts and his wife has no head for figures."

"I love math."

"Really! Well, God knows what He's doing when He passes out our gifts."

Elizabeth had never thought of her skill in math as a gift from God. How often had she ignored what God had done for her and instead focused on the disappointments?

Rebecca grinned. "I'd sooner eat grubs than face the Sorenson ledger."

"I'd rather swallow earthworms than take shears to fabric."

Giggling, Rebecca taught Elizabeth how to do a blind hemstitch, the topic of math forgotten.

For the second time Elizabeth had heard the Sorensons needed help with their books. Soon as she could, she'd talk to Mr. Sorenson about a job.

Once she'd mastered the hemstitch, Rebecca showed her how to attach the buttons to the bodice. "I'll come back to make the other dress," she promised.

Elizabeth didn't know why Rebecca had done all this for her, but her new friend waved away her thanks, saying it was the Christian thing to do. Elizabeth didn't know much about Christians, but one wore the name Rebecca Harper.

After much convincing, Rebecca had agreed to take the fabric in exchange for making two dresses. When

Rebecca, Grace and Faith pulled out the lane, the pink twill stretched across Grace's lap.

Elizabeth hoped Ted wouldn't be angry with her for giving away the material.

"Smells good in here." Ted scooted past Elizabeth as she stood at the stove. Apparently his wife had gotten over the run-in with the hens, by the refreshed, even happy look on her face. "Did I see some familiar fabric in the living room? In the shape of a dress?"

Elizabeth's eyes lit. "Rebecca made a pattern, cut out a dress and seamed it up all in one afternoon. It fits perfectly."

"Rebecca's a generous woman."

"She is. I don't know how she managed to get away from her brood long enough to help, but she did."

"Probably has to be fast with five children under seven."

"I like her."

"Figured you would. She helped me out with Henry and Anna more times than I can count."

"Ted, I gave Rebecca the pink material in exchange for making two dresses."

He touched her cheek, smiling into her troubled eyes. "I'm glad."

"I thought you might be upset."

"For being generous? Never." His hand fell away. "Rebecca and Dan are struggling right now. Keep them in your prayers."

"I will."

"Are two dresses enough?"

"Yes." She cocked her head at him, a saucy look in her eyes. "I've decided I like wearing pants."

"Now that, dear wife, is very good news." He pulled her close, inhaled the scent of soap with the faintest hint of roses. Sweet Elizabeth.

Face flushed, she pulled away. "We had a good visit."

Ted put himself in her line of vision. "So what did you two talk about?"

"Nothing really. Just the usual lady talk."

But the wariness in her eyes told Ted the topic had likely been about him. Or perhaps Rose. Had she pumped Rebecca for information about his past? If so, she'd been disappointed.

No one knew his secrets.

Chapter Eleven

Sunday morning Pastor Sumner welcomed Elizabeth from the pulpit. The topic of his sermon wasn't deceit, as she'd feared. He never mentioned she'd switched places with Ted's mail-order bride and the lies that entailed. For that kindness Elizabeth paid close attention as he spoke on God's love.

One verse in particular stuck in her mind. *Love is not easily angered. It keeps no record of wrongs.*

A love Elizabeth lacked.

Deep inside, she harbored a terrible anger toward her father. Papa only cared about gambling, putting his family at risk. Killing Mama. Not with a weapon, perhaps not even intentionally, but Elizabeth didn't doubt for a moment that Papa had caused her mother's death.

Her heart squeezed. Truth was she'd even been angry with Mama. For pretending all was well while their lives fell apart. For hiding in her bedroom rather than taking a stand with Papa. On the surface her family appeared typical, but Papa's gambling whipped up wild waves of misery while underneath the surface, strong currents carried them further and further apart. All the while Mama never lost her smile. Papa never lost his bravado.

Until Mama's failing health kept them home, Elizabeth had accompanied her mother to church. But most of Elizabeth's attention centered on the latest fashions and liaisons of her peers, not on the sermon. Except for an occasional stab of fear that Papa would wind up in hell, Elizabeth had given little thought to pleasing God.

But now, during the altar call, a deep longing for such a love brought a lump to Elizabeth's throat. A lump formed by the memories of withholding affection from her mother.

She wouldn't find this Biblical love with Ted. Not when keeping up her end of the bargain they called their marriage was all that mattered.

But maybe here in this church, in the Bible Ted shared with her in the pew and at home, she'd find the answer for the empty ache she carried and the anger devouring her peace.

One final song and the service ended, leaving Elizabeth with an odd sense of loss. But she didn't have time to examine her feelings. Parishioners flooded the aisles, greeting her like a long-lost friend instead of a newcomer.

Outside the wind had come up, blowing the women's skirts and lifting Anna's bangs off her forehead. Spying Grace Harper across the way, Anna took off at a run.

"Did you enjoy the service?" Ted asked.

"Yes, very much."

The pleased expression on his face revealed his desire for a wife with strong faith instead of a backslider like her. He leaned close. "Henry only called out twice during the sermon. Anna created a racket kicking the

back of the pew only once. A good service all in all."
He winked. "If we swapped the kitchen chairs for pews,
maybe Anna would behave better."

Ted's attempt at humor told Elizabeth he didn't blame
her for Anna's attitude. But he'd blame her for keeping
Robby's existence from him. If only she had the courage to inform him about her brother. She would, as soon
as she earned money for their tickets. This morning,
she'd look for an opportunity to speak to Mr. Sorenson
about a job.

Rebecca caught up to them with Faith draped over
her arm like a rag doll. "Have you finished hemming
your dress?"

"Not yet, but when I do, I'll wear it to church."

Before Elizabeth could ask if Rebecca had found time
to make her own dress, the womenfolk of the church
surrounded them.

Lydia Sumner and Lucille Sorenson greeted her
warmly while Elizabeth scrambled to keep the names
straight of the women she'd met inside. Gertrude
Wyatt—buxom with flawless skin; Ruth Johnson—tall,
willowy, wearing jet bead earbobs; Carolyn Radcliff—
petite with sun-streaked hair.

"Why, I'd heard Ted got himself a wife," Ruth Johnson said, giving her wide-brimmed, bow-bedecked hat
an adjustment, setting her earbobs in motion.

"Is that a new hat?"

Ruth beamed. "It arrived yesterday from the Mont-
gomery Ward Catalog."

"It's lovely," Elizabeth said. "Perfect for the shape
of your face."

"Ted's new wife's a dear," Lucille Sorenson interrupted. "Bought all her niceties from me." She flashed

a look at Ruth. "Not like some folks who feel the need to order from the catalog."

Mrs. Radcliff frowned. "You really should stop broadcasting people's shopping lists, Lucille."

A blush dotted the proprietor's cheeks. "It's good for business."

"The Sorenson Mercantile stocks everything a farm wife could want," Elizabeth said, trying to ease the sudden tension.

Ted shot her an amused glance; he then leaned close and murmured in her ear, "The hens are clucking their approval. Appears they've welcomed you into the coop."

Elizabeth coughed to cover a burst of laughter. Someone patted her on the back.

"Mrs. Logan, are you from these parts?" Gertrude said.

"I'm from Chicago."

"Chicago!" Gertrude clasped her hands. "Such a grand city. Will's cousin, Mary Beth, lives there. She's married to a slaughterhouse man name of O'Sullivan. Wouldn't it be something if the two of you knew each other?"

"O'Sullivan? Uh…"

"Oh, you could hardly miss noticing Mary Beth." Gertrude waved a palm. "Red hair, freckles, a pretty girl, but she's let herself go since the babies started arriving."

Carolyn patted her friend's arm. "Chicago's a big place, Gertie. You can't expect Elizabeth to remember Will's cousin even if she's the size of Orville's prize Angus."

Gertrude's face fell like an underdone cake. Martha's only cooking disaster, according to her nanny. "I thought it would've been lovely if they'd met."

Elizabeth pursed her lips. "I bumped into a woman once with more freckles than a hive has bees, but the only words we shared were an apology."

"That's gotta be her!" Gertrude exclaimed. "Imagine that. Why, we're practically family."

Across the way a knot of young ladies giggled. A few days ago, Elizabeth would've fit that group. Now she mingled with married women. Odd how she didn't fit anywhere.

"Where did you and Ted meet?" Ruth took up the slack. "Far as I know he hasn't left town."

Ted shifted the weight of his sleeping son and widened his stance, obviously uncomfortable with the question, but Elizabeth saw no point in hiding the truth. "At the depot."

"Well, of course, but when was the *first* time you met?"

"That was the first time."

Lydia Sumner beamed. "Isn't that romantic? She and Ted married in our parlor the day she arrived."

"You're saying you never laid eyes on Ted before that day?" Carolyn Radcliff's eyes went wide with shock.

"Elizabeth is what I've heard called a mail-order bride," Lydia Sumner explained.

Gertrude gaped. "Well, I do declare. I'm speechless!"

"Well, however you two met, congratulations, Elizabeth. You've accomplished something the single women of New Harmony hadn't been able to do," Rebecca said with a wink.

Ruth Johnson frowned. "Why would you marry a stranger?"

"Ted never seemed like a stranger, not from the minute we met. Why, his greeting nearly swept me off my feet." True enough. Ted's talk about milking cows and strangling chickens had all but made her swoon.

Ruth Johnson waved a finger Ted's way. "As the saying goes—still waters run deep."

Ted coughed, amusement dancing in his eyes.

Rebecca laid a palm over her baby's face and took a step back. "I hope you two aren't coming down with something."

"Your dress is lovely, Mrs. Logan," Ruth said. "A collarless dress must be new."

"Ah, quite new."

A puzzled look came over Lydia Sumner's face. "I distinctly remember that dress having a collar."

"I'll have to remove the collars from my dresses." Ruth fingered the lapel on the front of her frock. "I can't keep up with fashion."

A dark-haired woman, her bonnet covering her face, walked past, herding four children in front of her, glancing neither right nor left.

"I'll be right back." Lydia Sumner hustled after her.

Elizabeth watched the pastor's wife put an arm around the woman. The two put their heads together. "Who is that?"

Gertrude frowned. "Lois Lessman. Most likely her husband Joe's over at the saloon. His gambling's going to put his family in the poorhouse."

"I hate gambling," Elizabeth whispered, her voice trembling with emotion. "Can't you close down the saloon?"

All eyes filled with speculation and darted to Elizabeth.

Mumbling something about finding Anna, Ted trudged toward the group of girls playing on the lawn.

Elizabeth's heart thudded in her chest. She'd revealed too much, raising the ladies' suspicions. How would they feel—worse, how would a religious man like Ted feel, if he discovered her father was a gambler?

"It's a dirty shame. Lois takes in ironing and laundry, cleans for the Moore brothers. Does everything she can to see to it that her boys don't go to bed hungry."

The attention of the group turned back to the Lessman family and off her, easing the tension between Elizabeth's shoulder blades. Perhaps here in this town, she could find a way to ensure gambling split no family apart.

"So how do you like New Harmony, Elizabeth?" Gertrude asked as Lydia Sumner returned to the circle.

"This is only my first trip to town since our wedding."

"It's a good place to live." Rebecca's gaze dropped to the ground. "Just hope we can stay."

Lydia Sumner slipped an arm around Rebecca. The pastor's wife must wear herself out ministering to the women of the congregation. "Are you thinking of moving?"

"We don't want to, but if this drought doesn't end, the decision may be out of our hands."

Her new friend's struggles pinched at Elizabeth's mood.

"Let's not borrow trouble," Lydia advised. "Remember God's in control and we've got His ear."

"Well, it's April. We normally have had lots of rain by now," Rebecca said softly.

The group grew quiet. Elizabeth supposed everyone had a stake in the weather. If the farmers did poorly, the whole town suffered. "Perhaps we should all wash our windows. That always brought rain in Chicago," Elizabeth said brightly.

Five troubled faces turned to her then eased into smiles.

"Yes, and we could keep our laundry on the line," Gertrude declared with a chuckle.

"Or plan a picnic," Carolyn offered.

Lydia patted Elizabeth's arm. "You're good for us, my dear."

"In the meantime," Elizabeth said, "we can work on getting the streets ready for all that rain. From what Ted told me they'll turn into a muddy river."

"What a good idea! What do you suggest?"

Mrs. Radcliff waved a hand at a group of boys tumbling in the yard. "Before we solve all the problems of New Harmony, our youngsters are getting restless."

The ladies broke up, moving off to gather their children.

Gertrude turned to Elizabeth. "I can't wait to hear more about your life in Chicago. I've never been to a big city."

A rocklike weight settled to the bottom of Elizabeth's stomach. What if these women really knew her? Uncovered her secrets? They wouldn't think much of her then. Suddenly the privacy of the farm sounded good.

Elizabeth hustled to the wagon. Across the way, Mr. Sorenson stood talking. Asking him about keeping his books would have to wait until the next time she came to town.

Ted helped her onto the seat, handed the still-sleeping Henry into her arms, then swung Anna aboard and scrambled up beside her. His humor-filled gaze met hers over Anna's head. "I'll be the laughingstock once the men hear I nearly made you swoon at the depot."

Elizabeth squirmed. "Well, at least the men won't be removing their collars merely because I scorched mine," she said, eliciting a chuckle from Ted.

Her heart skipped a beat. And the women won't be quizzing you about your life in Chicago the next time you meet.

Elizabeth stood on a chair in the kitchen, trying not to fidget, while Ted held a yardstick against the skirt of her new dress and pinned the fabric for a hem. To keep from giving in to a crazy urge to run her fingers through the golden hair on his bowed head, she clasped her hands tightly in front of her.

Perhaps Ted prayed as he pinned. The man talked to God at every opportunity.

She couldn't shake the feelings of remorse the pastor's sermon had surfaced that morning. She'd tried to lay all her regret for hurting Mama at Papa's feet.

"You're awfully quiet," Ted said. "Something wrong?"

Everything. "Nothing."

"You sound like something's bothering you."

She sighed. "I've made a lot of mistakes."

"Haven't we all." He rose to his feet and dropped the packet of pins on the table. "I hope I didn't make a mess of this. I measured every few inches and it looks straight, but—"

One look at her face and he lifted her off the chair. "You're not talking about housekeeping, are you?"

"No." Tears filled her eyes.

He tilted her face up to his. His tender expression tore at her. "We all have regrets, Elizabeth." He motioned toward the yardstick. "God doesn't love us according to a measure of our goodness. Or withhold His love by calculating the number of our sins. Whatever we've done, He'll forgive us. All we have to do is ask." He squeezed her hand. "Have you asked Him?"

Unable to speak, she nodded. Countless times she'd asked God for His forgiveness.

"Then He has. Psalm 103:12 says, 'As far as the east is from the west, so far hath he removed our transgressions from us.'"

If only she could share Ted's confidence, his strong faith. But she didn't feel forgiven.

"Trust God, Elizabeth. He'll never let you down."

Perhaps she could trust God. But could she trust Ted? What would he do when he learned she had a brother and intended for Robby to live here? Would he forgive her for keeping the truth from him the way he promised God would?

Ted took her hand in his, his firm grip warm, soothing. "You're my wife. I don't want to let you down, either." His callused thumb slid over the top of her hand.

She fought the comfort of his touch. "I'm a housekeeper, not a wife, with two children to care for and every imaginable chore to do."

"Being a wife is hard work." His attention dropped to her lips. She forgot to breathe. He leaned closer and closer still, until she could see every eyelash. She'd never noticed that narrow circle of silver, stunning against the black of his pupils. "But I could name some benefits of the job."

Before she could ask for a list of those benefits, his hand encircled the back of her neck. With gentle fingers, he tilted her face to his. She got lost in his intense gaze, asking permission. As with a will all their own, her eyelids fluttered closed. A feathery touch of his lips, gentler than butterfly wings, caressed her lips. The kiss grew, deepened, sending tremors to the core of her.

And a sense of rightness she refused to accept.

Love had destroyed Mama.

She clasped his hand and removed it. "Let's get one thing straight. You were the one who called our marriage a business deal. I may be a substitute bride, but a business deal doesn't include love." She took a step back. "Or kisses."

His eyes turned stormy. "What do you have against affection? I'd hate to live the next forty years without it."

"I'd rather be hitched to a team of oxen than yoked by that burden."

"That can be arranged, wife," he muttered.

Elizabeth spun on her heel and raced to her room, matching the speed of her pounding heart, taking with her a void she didn't know how to fill.

She closed the door and leaned against it, sliding her fingertips over her lips, reliving his kiss.

Her demonstrative father had kissed Mama as often as she'd let him. Elizabeth had always known Mama loved Papa. Loved him to *death*. Kisses meant nothing. She'd put no trust in Ted's.

Elizabeth was grateful for the time alone while Ted drove Anna and Jason Harper to school. Well, not exactly alone with Henry in the house, but somehow she managed to read the Bible for a few minutes, hungry for words to guide her. She'd just breathed a prayer to God to help her handle each day when behind her the door creaked open.

Ted's gaze lit on the Bible, then her. "I'll set up the laundry for you," he said.

"I'd appreciate it."

She took Henry from his high chair and plopped him in the pen Ted had fashioned from chicken wire while Ted lugged laundry tubs and carried water to fill them. All the while he avoided her eyes, obviously still angry over last night's stalemate. Having fulfilled the role of a good husband, he said goodbye and then walked to the barn.

Watching his retreating back, Elizabeth sighed. Except for providing the roof over her head and the food on his table, she dared not count on Ted. He needed a mother for his children. The reason he'd married her. She needed to give Robby a home. The reason she'd married him. Assuming Ted agreed to bring Robby here, they'd both get what they wanted.

So why did she feel so hollow?

Sleeves rolled up to the elbows, Elizabeth pushed the first load of clothes under the sudsy water. An hour passed, maybe more. Elizabeth arched her back, then blew out a puff of air and once again bent over the wash-tub. Ted had called this warm, sunny, breezy weather a perfect laundry day. She couldn't imagine doing this chore when the weather turned cold.

Lois Lessman washed clothes and took in ironing to pay the family's bills. If only Elizabeth could help her. Surely if the proprietor of the saloon understood that gambling was damaging a family in town, he'd put a stop to it.

She chuffed. How likely was that when it came to bringing in business? But even if it were, Joe Lessman would find a game somewhere else. Hadn't Papa?

Her sore knuckles struck the ridge of the scrub board. Elizabeth grimaced. Washing Henry's diapers had rubbed them raw. "I hope you're grateful, young man."

Henry hung over the fence, gnawing on a wooden spoon, showing no appreciation for the pain he'd caused. Poor tyke probably had enough of his own with those teeth pushing through.

She boiled the diapers, and then dropped them with a stick into the rinse water. At the line, she used one clothespin to fasten the diapers together, saving time and pins. Anna had made a family of clothespin dolls, decreasing her supply. Flapping in her face, the diapers smelled fresh, clean.

She refilled the tub with clean water for another load. The time dragged by as she stirred, scrubbed, pinned. She fished in the tub and pulled up Ted's white shirt, his Sunday best.

Now pink!

Something was definitely wrong. But what?

With all her might, she scrubbed the shirt on the board but the new color remained.

Heat zipped through her veins. Her dress. Her *only* good dress! She shot a hand into the washtub and yanked it out.

Her beautiful dress was streaked with shades of maroon. She moaned, dropping it into the rinse water, then brought up her head scarf, now faded. Under the suds, the water was red.

Tears stung her eyes. She had to get far away from all this hated work.

"What happened to my shirt?"

Elizabeth jumped.

Ted stood across from her, arms folded across his

chest, staring at the pink garment draped over the wash-board.

If she'd had the strength, she'd have thrown her dress at him. Right now, she wanted nothing more than to use that return ticket to Chicago. Even Reginald Parks sounded good.

Ted surveyed the damage to their clothing then the world of hurt on Elizabeth's face. He loped to the house. Nothing could be done about her dress, but perhaps he could save his shirt. He returned with the blueing mixture Rose kept on hand. Gradually the garment lost its pink hue, giving him optimism he'd be able to wear it on Sunday.

Elizabeth whirled to him. "Will that concoction fix my dress?"

"It would ruin the delicate fabric. Next time sort the clothes, darks in one pile, whites in another."

"You've got all the answers, Ted Logan." Her anger at Papa, her concern for Lois Lessman, all of it rolled inside her. She thrust her hands on her hips. "How about figuring out a way to get gambling out of New Harmony? I can't stand the idea of Mrs. Lessman doing this chore every day."

After hearing Elizabeth's emotional remark on Sunday, Ted had no doubt of her hatred of the gambling lifestyle. Not that he approved. He'd seen what compulsive gambling had done to others—the desperation, the lack of any human emotion other than greed. What it had done to him, a man who earned his living at the expense of others. Now Joe's family suffered because he couldn't pass up a game.

He'd try to talk to Joe on his next trip to town. "Cleaning up a man isn't like cleaning up New Harmony's streets, Elizabeth. Shutting down a saloon won't put a stop to what a man's determined to do. The only way for Joe to control his gambling is to repent and seek God's help."

Elizabeth eyed him. "You know a lot about the subject."

Ted's stomach knotted. "I'm speaking about what the Bible teaches, no matter what issue is taking over a person's life." He rinsed his shirt. "I'll talk to him, but if you want to help Lois, help her find a better-paying job."

Elizabeth returned to the line. From here, he could practically see her mind working. His suggestion seemed to pacify her. But what would she do if she found out about his gambling past? His chest squeezed. Most likely leave him.

Not that he blamed Rose for dying, but losing her hurt. He and Anna still grieved. For different reasons. Rose had been the center of Anna's world. Meeting Rose had been a turning point in his.

But he somehow knew that if he and Elizabeth ever found their way in this marriage, they'd share a bliss he and Rose never had. He couldn't forget the experience of holding Elizabeth in his arms, of the feel of her lips moving under his.

Yet she'd shown not one whit of reaction since. What man knew what went on in a woman's mind? If Elizabeth wanted his touch, wouldn't she give him a smile or say something that would tell him which way the wind blew?

He suspected she kept things from him. How could he condemn her? He lived his life doing the same. One day the secrets would come out. What would happen then?

Chapter Twelve

The days rolled by, until one week had passed since Elizabeth had arrived in New Harmony. Each day during Henry's nap, she made those mainstay biscuits. The cookbook had promised that "good biscuits had saved the day for many a housewife."

The *good* had been the tricky part but practice made perfect, or so Papa used to say, so she always made one batch, sometimes two. Much to her surprise, the batch she pulled from the oven was flaky, golden—perfection. She smiled, anticipating Ted's reaction to her success.

At dinner, she carried the bread plate to the table with her head held high like one of the Magi bearing gifts.

Ted took one look at the pile of biscuits and shook his head. "Biscuits. Again?"

"What do you mean *again?*"

"Nothing, I'm just…full."

"How can you be full? You haven't eaten yet."

He looked at Anna, then at Henry, but neither of his children said a word, leaving Ted on his own. Whether he knew it or not, he was heading into dangerous territory.

"I'm full of biscuits," he said, ducking his head.

"These are perfect. Really. They're not burned on the bottom or hard or bitter or crumbly. Try one." She thrust one at him, but he held up his palm.

"I'm up to here with biscuits," he said, indicating his throat. "Sorry, I can't face another one, no matter how good."

"What do you mean, you're sick of biscuits? You said you had hollow legs that needed filling three times a day."

He had the grace to look sheepish. "I do, but you've given me biscuits for breakfast, dinner and supper for a week."

"Well, that takes the cake!"

"Now, cake, that I could eat."

She swatted at him. "I slaved over perfecting the biscuits you're so fond of and now you won't eat one? Not even a bite?"

"I'm sure in a few days, I'll get over it and—"

"Get over it? Well, see if you can get over this!" She dumped three biscuits on top of the mound of meat and potatoes on his plate. "At this table we're having biscuits."

Ted closed his eyes then rose. "I learned long ago when a woman gets in a snit, a man better head for the hills. In my case, the barn works fine." With that, he walked out the door.

Elizabeth folded her arms across her chest. No one appreciated anything she did around here. She opened her palms and rubbed a finger across a callus. Her hands were a mess. Her feet ached from hours at the stove, sink or washtub. She slaved from dawn to dusk—and for what? To be unappreciated and criticized? To give her brother a good life, she'd tried to mold herself into the perfect housewife. But the apron didn't fit.

She didn't fit.

She walked to the mirror and peered at her reflection. A smudge marred her cheek. Tendrils of her hair drooped at her neck. She never had time to primp. She turned away from the face in the mirror, so different from her own that she almost didn't recognize it.

Returning to the table, she grabbed one morsel of perfection and buttered it, but when she took a bite and tried to swallow, it stuck in her throat. Her shoulders slumped. Why not admit it? She was sick of biscuits, too.

Grabbing a couple, she walked outside to the stoop and whistled for Tippy. He came loping from the barn. She dropped the biscuits into the iron skillet that served as his dish. He walked up, sniffed at them and backed away, tail tucked between his legs.

"Traitor."

Back in the kitchen, she found one biscuit lover. Henry. He'd stuffed half a biscuit into his mouth, flinging crumbs on the floor. Of course, Martha had once said babies would eat dirt and drink kerosene; not much of a recommendation.

She plopped into her seat with a sigh.

Across from her, Anna leaned on her elbows, a glum look in her eyes. "Mommy didn't shout at Daddy."

Rose, the saint. Well, Elizabeth was no saint and not the mommy, never would be. Still, she'd grown tired of hearing about the perfect Rose.

Anna turned those light blue eyes on her. "You made Daddy's ears hurt."

Elizabeth guessed Daddy's tummy was empty, too. Just because Ted didn't want biscuits didn't mean he didn't want to eat. She'd riled him into leaving the house without his supper. "I guess I'll have to say I'm sorry."

"Yep," Anna said, then went back to her meal.

Another thing Elizabeth didn't do well. But since she'd been reading the Bible regularly, she no longer could cling to her old habits. And for some reason she couldn't fathom, she cared what Ted thought of her, cared if he forgave her.

Why? She'd never apologized that much to Mama and Papa.

As she forced down her food, never tasting a bite, the realization dawned—every day she lived with regret for not having apologized to Mama. Once she got the chance, she'd apologize to Papa for disobeying him, even though he'd been wrong to try to marry her off for profit.

But Ted was different. Ted was...

Well, she wouldn't think about that now. He was her husband. She'd leave it at that. They needed peace. Peace that came with the price of one gritted out *I'm sorry.*

Elizabeth plopped some blocks on the tray of the high chair then grabbed Ted's plate. "Will you watch Henry for a few minutes, Anna?"

Amazingly, Anna nodded her agreement.

Elizabeth dumped the biscuits on Ted's plate into the slop jar and headed out the door. A man who liked harmony must find living with her unsettling. She met Ted halfway between the house and the barn.

His troubled eyes collided with hers. "I forgot—"

"Your dinner." She motioned to the towel-covered plate. "I'm bringing it to you."

"Thank you." His eyes darkened. "Sorry about the fuss I made over the biscuits."

"I tossed them in the bucket for the pigs. If *they* dare to reject my biscuits, I'll pull their tails."

He peered over his shoulder, craning his neck as if looking at his backside. "In that case, I'll eat whatever you say."

She laughed. "Your food's getting cold. Come on inside."

Stepping around her, he held the door. "You look tired. Get off your feet while I put the children to bed."

Elizabeth *was* tired. Tired to the bone.

Still, she didn't have to make all those pointless calls on people she didn't like. Or wear a tightly cinched corset every single day of her life or feel so bored her skin crawled.

Or sit across from Reginald Parks.

Elizabeth set Ted's plate on top of the cookstove to keep it warm, and then cleaned up the dishes. When Ted returned to the kitchen, she and his dinner sat at the table waiting on him.

"I'm saying it right out. I'm sorry I got mad." She plopped her chin on her hands. "I *have* made a lot of biscuits. Truth is I'm sick of biscuits, too. Even Tippy wouldn't touch them and he usually wolfs down every scrap I give him. Sort of like you."

Ted took his place at the table and smiled. "Was this another example of that teeny temper you warned me about?"

She bit her lip and nodded.

"Seems it's less teeny than you promised."

"Seems you're less of a biscuit fan than you said."

He laughed. "That's what I like about you—you're never at a loss for words." A crooked grin eased the tension between them. "I accept your apology. And offer one of my own." Taking her hand, he ran a finger over her reddened palm. "You've worked hard taking care of us and I appreciate it. I should have eaten the biscuits, even if it gagged me." He chuckled, then sobered, regret filling his eyes. "I've been expecting too much."

She pulled away from his touch, studying the chipped nails on her left hand and the narrow gold band still shiny and new—a symbol of promise. "I'm not one bit like Rose."

"No, you're you—Elizabeth Manning Logan. My wife. And I'm proud of you."

Ted's words slid into the lonely emptiness inside her, balm to regrets she didn't know she carried. What if she started to care about this man?

A chill slid down her spine, an icy reminder not to foolishly put her heart in Ted's hands.

She leaped to her feet and poured a cup of coffee she didn't want, putting distance between her and Ted, vowing not to let her husband get close.

Elizabeth glanced at the clock. Half past four and Henry still slept. Home from school, Anna played on the porch with her clothespin dolls, dressing them with scraps from Elizabeth's new dress. Potatoes bubbled on the stove. A jar of beef and noodles from the cellar simmered away. Peace reigned.

She had time to rearrange the kitchen. The upper shelves were mostly empty, but well within Elizabeth's reach. She cleared the table, putting all the clutter away, and then organized the cabinet and cupboard to suit her.

From the bedroom, Henry set up a howl. Smiling with satisfaction at her newly arranged kitchen, Elizabeth hustled to his crib. For once, Anna didn't beat her. Apparently she hadn't heard her brother.

Arms outstretched, Henry leaned against the rail, grinning at her.

"What a long nap you had, little man." She swung him into the air. He squealed, releasing a dribble of drool onto the bodice of Elizabeth's new dress. Ah, babies. Nasty little creatures. The reason God made them cute.

She changed his diaper, then gathered Henry to her chest. One plump arm cradled her neck, his soft baby face nuzzling her cheek. The feel and scent of him filled her nostrils, putting an odd hitch in her breathing.

"Mama."

Her breath caught.

He said "Mama" again.

Elizabeth carried Henry to the dresser. "*This* is your mama, Henry," she told him, holding up the picture of Rose and Ted.

"Dada." He pointed to Ted with a wide grin revealing six tiny teeth. Raring back, Henry patted her cheek. "Mama."

Elizabeth shook her head. Surely Ted would set Henry straight.

Only a month old when Rose died, Henry wouldn't remember his mother. Still, Elizabeth didn't want the toddler to forget the woman who gave him birth, probably destroying her health with the effort. She replaced the picture, promising to show Henry his mother's likeness every day.

In the kitchen, she put Henry on the floor to play with some wooden spoons and a pan. But within a matter of seconds, he'd crawled to a chair and pulled up, then toddled toward her.

Ted appeared at the door for dinner in his stocking feet, dewy and fresh from cleaning up at the pump. Sniffing the air, he swept Henry into his arms. "Mmm, smells good."

"Better than smoke and burned biscuits." She grinned, moving to the stove. "As soon as I mash the potatoes, we'll eat."

"You're looking mighty cheerful."

"Well, I am. I had a good afternoon."

"Here, let me do that." He walked to the stove, exchanged Henry for the potato masher and went after the lumps, biceps bulging with each stroke.

She swallowed hard. Those potatoes didn't have a chance.

Ted glanced up, catching her watching him, and winked at her. "Tell me about your day."

Anna dashed in the door, and before Elizabeth could tell Ted anything, she prattled on about school, proudly showing him her growing family of clothespin dolls.

"Using straw for hair's clever of you, Anna. Why don't you lay them down and set the table for supper."

Anna put a pout on her face but did as Ted said. He looked over his daughter's head at Elizabeth. "Looks like you finished that hem." His gaze roamed over her. Something about his expression made her insides flutter. "Does this mean you won't be wearing my pants anymore?"

"Only in the chicken coop and garden."

Ted paused in the mashing and gave her a searing look that had nothing to do with fashion. "Pity."

Heat filled her cheeks. She ran a finger around her buttoned-up collar. Gracious, the kitchen was warm.

"Where's the spoons?" Anna asked.

For a moment, Elizabeth had forgotten about Anna. She dragged herself back to reality. "Oh, I put the flatware in the drawer over there."

"Mama kept them in the spooner."

"Well, with everything put away, I don't have to cover the table in case flies sneak in."

Anna folded her arms across her chest. "Put them back."

Elizabeth looked at Ted for support, but his lips had thinned. He took Henry from her arms. "After you add salt and butter, they're ready to eat."

Ted sat in the rocker with Henry on one knee and Anna leaning against the other, explaining how much ground he'd planted in oats, and taking Anna's mind off the argument.

Recalling the disapproving set of his mouth, all the joy of the day slid out of Elizabeth. She'd worked her fingers to the bone taking care of Ted's house, meals and children, but she had no say in anything.

Ignoring Anna's lack of obedience, Elizabeth set the table herself. Why hadn't Ted taken her side with Anna? Was she merely some maid? Well, if so, she should earn a wage.

At dinner, the food was good, and without a single biscuit, but Ted said very little except a polite, "Will you pass the potatoes?" or "Anna, eat your meat."

Anna chattered away while the meal churned in Elizabeth's stomach.

After dinner, Ted told Anna to wash the dishes then went out to the barn to milk and bed down the animals. Elizabeth prepared the dishwater, and then moved aside for Anna. Surprisingly she pulled over a chair and set to work.

"This water is too hot," she complained.

"Put in a dipper of cold."

"You do it," she said in a bossy tone. "My hands are drippy."

Elizabeth added the cold water without comment, too tired to deal with Anna's attitude.

Ted hadn't supported her attempt to make things more convenient, as if she had no right to make changes. Rose lived in the house with them. Elizabeth understood Ted and Anna still mourned her. She felt bad herself about Rose's early death and all she missed, but how long would it be before what she wanted mattered? Five, ten years? Maybe when Rose's children were grown and gone?

Maybe never.

She slumped against the sink. Ted made promises as easily as her silver-tongued father. Empty promises. Why had she believed him?

Everyone should be quick to listen, slow to speak, and slow to anger. She'd read the verse in the Book of James that morning. But didn't that Scripture include Ted?

A moan pushed past her lips. She'd done all she could to make this marriage work. She shouldn't have to feel like an intruder in this house. She'd had it with the chickens and the biscuits. With Anna's belligerence. And her so-called husband's lack of consideration.

Tears stung her eyes. What choice did she have? Robby needed a home. He would love this farm. He would love Ted, would probably follow Ted around like his shadow.

In her entire life, she'd never felt so trapped.

Finished with the chores, Ted returned to the house, put the children to bed and then came into the kitchen, unable to meet Elizabeth's gaze as she wiped the dinner dishes. He could feel the annoyance radiating off her from here.

He rummaged in the cupboard and then slammed the door shut. "I don't know where anything is anymore."

"What are you looking for?"

"My stomach's in an uproar. I'm looking for a peppermint."

Her steely expression said he had only himself to blame. "They're in the pantry." Her tone could freeze the pond in June.

"Why?"

"Peppermints are edible. Everything edible is in the pantry." A smug expression rode her face.

"You've moved things around, taken things off the table—" His gaze swept the kitchen. "Couldn't you leave it like it was?"

"Don't you mean the way Rose had it?"

Hurt pinged off each syllable. Still Ted held his ground, refusing to relent. If he did, before he knew it, she'd change everything. The furniture. The routine. Him.

He crossed his arms across his chest and leaned toward her. "What's wrong with the way Rose had it?"

"I'm taller. I can reach higher in the cabinets. I moved things up, making room for what hid under that tent on the table." She threw a hand out toward the table. "I'm not used to living in a pigsty."

He threw up his hands. "Pigsty?"

"I'm sorry. But burying condiments and flatware under a pyramid made of cloth is just…well, strange."

Ted ran a hand through his hair. In his chest a battle warred. Part wanted to let her fill that hole inside him, the hole left vacant by more than a few changes in the kitchen. And part was tired of dealing with the trouble in this house.

"Put them back."

"You sound like Anna. Why? It's not like you can't learn where things are." She tossed down the dish towel, her icy blue eyes flashing. "It's not Rose's kitchen anymore."

"You may be my wife, but are you forgetting this is *my* house?"

"Yes, I guess I am," she said, her voice shaking. "Before we married, you claimed all you had would be mine." She crossed the room. "But you've made it clear. Nothing's mine here. And never will be."

She stabbed a finger at his midsection. "Well, I've got news for you, Ted Logan. I've got an eight-year-old brother. As soon as I can, I'm bringing him here. Then I'll finally have an ally in this house!"

Ted felt he'd been sucker punched. "What are you talking about?"

"You heard me. My father will lose our house in a couple weeks. I want Robby to live with us."

He glared at her. "You kept the existence of a brother from me? Why would you do that?"

"I was afraid of your reaction." She stepped closer until they stood toe to toe. "But I no longer care. Robby's my responsibility. I won't let him end up living on the streets." Her voice broke. "He wants to live on a farm. That's why I married you! The only reason."

Ted stomped toward the door.

"You're always running."

He stopped and pivoted toward her. "What do you mean?"

"You'd rather run than deal with our problems."

"That's not true." Was it? He ran his fingers through his hair. "I've learned it's better to calm down."

"Ah, yes, anything to keep that even-keel nature you're so proud of."

His long strides swallowed the distance between them. She eyed him like an angry bull, head down, hands planted on her hips, looking ready to go for his midsection.

"Did you stop to consider how bringing your brother here would affect Anna? You're not just changing the cupboards. You intend to change the number of people living under this roof."

"I'm sorry if it upsets Anna, but I have no choice."

Why had he thought he could marry a substitute bride, a total stranger, and make the marriage work? "What we have doesn't fit anyone's idea of marriage. I see no loving or obeying, even *trying* to obey, in this union."

"You were the one who called our marriage a business arrangement."

Ted's shoulders slumped. That agreement favored him and his children. Truth was, he'd expected Elizabeth to take a backseat to his daughter. "When we married, I believed your desperation stemmed from a lack of money, but now I know you switched places with Sally to give your brother a happy home on a farm. This home can hardly be called happy."

"And whose fault is that?"

A weight settled in his chest, squeezing against his lungs. God probably wasn't pleased with him. Much of that lack of contentment in their marriage could be traced to him.

He better spit out his apology. "First off, I was wrong

to give the impression that the kitchen doesn't belong to you."

"It doesn't. Nothing belongs to me. You spoke the truth."

"No, I reacted without thinking. As my wife, this house, this farm, everything, belongs to you as much as it does me." He leaned against the counter, searching for words to make her understand. "Rearrange anything that makes your life simpler. Anna will get used to it and….and I will, too."

"You saw the changes as my trying to wipe out Rose."

He grimaced. "I can't expect you to understand— I don't understand it myself." He took a deep breath. "That's not sensible. Maybe not even sane."

"It's like Anna hanging on to her mother's handkerchief." She swallowed hard. "You both still love her."

He dragged in a breath and looked away. "Rose and I weren't a great love match." He hastened to add, "But we were content."

"If you weren't in love, why did you marry?"

"The timing was right for both of us. I knew a good woman like Rose would make a wonderful mother. I wanted my future kids to have that."

"Unlike your home growing up?"

Ted didn't answer. He couldn't get into his home life. He cleared his throat. "We still need to talk about bringing your brother here."

By the look in Elizabeth's eyes, he'd hurt her by avoiding the question, but when he pulled out a chair, she sat in it. He grabbed another and joined her. "To hear about Robby's existence in the heat of an argument, well, it threw me. I apologize for that. I'm sure you're worried about him and he misses you."

Tears welled in her eyes and she looked away.

He cupped her chin and turned her to face him. "I have some money for emergencies. We'll use it to buy two train tickets back." She would come back, wouldn't she?

She raised a palm. "I won't add to your burdens. I'll use the egg money to pay for the tickets."

Another child in the house would complicate everything. Cost more, too. Not that Ted could refuse a home to Elizabeth's brother. Poor kid probably waited in Chicago, wondering when his sister would come for him, afraid of what the future held.

Hadn't he done the same as a boy?

"With the way the hens are laying and the price of eggs, it'll take forever to save that much. You're my wife. You and your brother aren't burdens."

She laid a hand on his face, her touch gentle on the rough bristle of his beard. "Robby can help around the place." Her expression brightened. "He's a good boy... nothing like me."

He chuckled. "It'll all work out."

"What about Anna? How will you tell her?"

"She'll love a big brother." Ted doubted he spoke the truth, but he couldn't consider the alternative. "You know, I think Anna's softening toward you." He met her incredulous gaze. "No, really, I do. You're making a difference around here, in the children...and in me."

Her hands fell limp at her sides. A look of despair took over her face.

It pinched at his pride that she didn't care about him. Like it or not, he had feelings for her. Not that he'd let her know. She'd made it abundantly clear she didn't want a real marriage.

Where would this end? How long could he go on this way? He wanted peace, not this constant upheaval. A wife to share his life, not fight him at every turn. A man couldn't bed down in the barn forever.

If he didn't know it before, he knew it now. Elizabeth battled their connection.

Perhaps he was wrong.

Perhaps she didn't even feel it.

Chapter Thirteen

At the noon meal, Elizabeth had avoided Ted's gaze, keeping things impersonal. He thought they'd gotten close last night, but then she'd pulled away, running as she'd accused him of doing.

He'd dropped Anna at the Harpers' to play with Grace on this blustery Saturday afternoon then walked the mile back to his house. By now Elizabeth had put Henry down for his nap.

A perfect opportunity to show an interest in his wife.

He found Elizabeth in the kitchen, putting on an apron over his pants, which she still wore from gathering eggs that morning. "Planning on making those delicious biscuits of yours?"

Her mouth gaped. "You want biscuits?"

No point in admitting the thought put a knot in his stomach. "I'm hungry for a batch." He gave her his most innocent look. "Want some help?"

"And you want to help?" She cocked her head at him, a smile tugging at her lips. "In the middle of your workday?"

With one field to plant with corn, he should hitch up

King and Queen, but his suggestion appeared to cheer her. "If you don't mind."

She examined his palms. "Only if you wash those hands."

Well, at least she was touching him. A good sign peace had been restored. He headed for the sink. "Yes, ma'am."

Suspicion clouded her dazzling blue eyes, as if she didn't believe a word he said, but Elizabeth handed him an apron. He didn't hanker to wear it but no point in making a fuss and take a chance of ruining the harmony between them.

She reached for a crock then opened the door that hid the flour bin. "Measure out two cupfuls of flour." She handed him a knife. "Use this to level it."

He fumbled with the cup and knife.

"Do it like this," she said, showing him how, then handing the knife back to him. "Add another cup of flour."

With her standing so near, he could barely absorb her directions but somehow managed to dump the flour into the bowl. By the sparkle in her eye and the smile playing around her lips, she enjoyed bossing him. She looked… happy. Why hadn't he tried harder to give her joy? Why had he expected her to fall into his arms? With the planting and all the chores to do, he'd neglected his wife. He wouldn't make that mistake again.

She thrust a spoon at him. "Add four teaspoons of baking powder."

And so it went with her giving orders and him following directions until he was wrist high in dough, his hands a mucky mess. He shot her a grin. "This is fun, kind of like playing in the mud. Care to join me?"

She rolled up her sleeves and dove in, squishing the dough between her fingers.

"A nice way to take out your frustrations," Ted said.

"Why do you think I've gotten so good at biscuits?"

He chuckled. Within minutes, they were battling with their fingers over territory in the bowl. When she tried to shove him out of the way, he raised dough-globbed fingers at her in a sinister pose sending her into peals of laughter.

Next thing Ted knew, Elizabeth streaked a doughy finger across his cheek then stepped back, grinning at him. Well, he couldn't let that go without a fight. He grabbed her wrist. She ducked and tried to pull away, but he managed to draw a circle on her forehead.

She retaliated with a batter-smeared mustache above his lip. "You look ever so handsome," she teased.

"You'd look mighty good with one yourself." She scrambled out of reach, but he lunged for her waist, twisted her around and smeared the dough above her lip. "Now your face matches those pants you're wearing."

Things went downhill from there, giggling and making a mess even Tippy wouldn't touch.

Trapping his bride in his arms, Ted lowered his head and planted a gooey kiss on her lips. Amazingly she kissed him back, dissipating the humor like shadows on a cloudy day. Leaving them both breathing deep and staring into each other's eyes with the beat of Ted's heart thumping in his ears.

"I had no idea you were so fond of biscuits, Mr. Logan."

"From now on, I'll take my biscuits raw."

She laid her head on his chest, shaking with laughter. Even covered with dough, he relished having her near.

"Anybody home?" a male voice called through the screen door.

The Stevenses. His in-laws. This wacky scene wouldn't improve their already strained relationship. He walked to the door, stepping aside to let them in. "Lily. Richard. What a surprise."

Lily's hand shot to her mouth, her eyes wide with alarm. "Whatever are you…doing?"

"Making biscuits," Elizabeth spoke up.

Lily, all four feet eleven inches of her, continued to gawk at Ted as though she'd never seen a man in the kitchen before. But then she probably hadn't, especially wearing an apron and a dough mustache. "You're looking well, Lily. A little pale. The trip probably tired you."

He scrubbed a hand across his upper lip, then tore off the apron and hung it on the hook.

Wearing a frown, Lily turned her focus on Elizabeth. "Who are you and why are you wearing—"

"The pants in the family?" Elizabeth winked. "Just teasing." She smiled. "I'm Ted's wife."

Lily swayed on her feet. "Richard, get me a chair."

Taking a firm hold of his wife, Richard eased her into the rocker and fanned her face with a section of the newspaper he'd plucked from the armrest.

Ted should've written Rose's parents about his marriage, but he'd suspected the news he'd taken a mail-order bride would give Lily one more reason to question his fitness as a parent.

He turned to Elizabeth and made introductions.

"Nice to meet you," she said, then scurried to the sink to clean her hands and face. "You'll have to forgive our appearance. We weren't expecting company."

"Sorry for…intruding." Richard glanced at his wife,

now pressing a hand to her bosom. "We just got into town and hoped to see our grandchildren."

"Anna's visiting a friend and Henry's down for his nap."

Lily slumped back in the chair. "Thank goodness." Tears sprang to her eyes. "So this is the replacement for our Rose."

"Lily, there's no call for that," Richard said. "The children need a mother."

"They wouldn't need one if Ted would let us raise them!"

Ted planted his feet wide, ready for battle. "I'll never—"

Eyes blazing, Elizabeth stepped forward. "Ted loves his children more than any man I've ever met. He's a wonderful father."

Ted had been about to rehash the familiar argument with Lily until Elizabeth had stepped in.

And defended him.

Described him as a good father.

A loving father.

His gaze connected with his wife's and something new sprang between them. As if she understood how it felt to be judged by a biased jury.

A heavy silence fell over the room. Richard mopped his forehead with a handkerchief. "So, how did you two meet?"

Ted and Elizabeth's gazes collided, but she quickly averted her eyes. Since the day she'd arrived, he'd never known Elizabeth to be quiet, but now, when he needed her most, she had her mouth nailed shut.

He cleared his throat. "Ah, Elizabeth came out on the train for the wedding."

"But when did you meet?" Richard asked.

Ted swallowed. "Well, we didn't actually meet first—"

"You sent for one of those mail-order brides?" Lily shrieked as if he'd made the faux pas of the century. "Married a stranger and brought her in to care for our grandchildren?"

"I couldn't very well bring Elizabeth into my home unless we married first."

Lily eyed Elizabeth again. "We'll have to extend our visit. See how you and the children are getting on."

How dare Lily question their parenting or their marriage! "They're getting on just fine," Ted said. Though in truth, Anna and Elizabeth mixed like oil and water.

One look at the scowl on his face sent Elizabeth to the stove. "Would you like some tea and biscuits?"

Richard smiled. "Sounds like a good idea."

Lily glanced at the mess and shuddered.

"I made this batch yesterday," Elizabeth said.

"Well, in that case, I will try your cooking."

No doubt to criticize it, but if so, Lily would be disappointed. Elizabeth had perfected the art of making biscuits.

He ushered his in-laws to the parlor then helped his wife clean the kitchen that looked as if pigs had wallowed in muck. Come to think of it, he and Elizabeth looked the part of the pigs.

"They said they were extending their visit. How long do you think they'll stay?" Elizabeth whispered as she corralled her tousled hair into a bun.

He grimaced. "They usually stay a week."

"Oh. My." Elizabeth lifted a stash of biscuits from the glass jar and set out jam and butter. "Once I serve biscuits breakfast, lunch and dinner, they'll cut their visit short."

Ted grinned. "I like the way you think, Mrs. Logan." He laid a hand on her arm. "I want to thank you."

"For what?"

"For trying to make me look good with Rose's parents."

She lowered her eyes, dark lashes brushing against her cheeks. "I didn't do anything."

"Oh, but you did." He came closer, reaching for her, but she turned away, out of his grasp.

"I—I—better get the jam."

"It's on the table."

"Oh, of course." Her cheeks flushed as rosy as the preserves. "I'm sorry I had to meet Rose's parents looking like a mess."

He tapped her playfully on the nose. "Their opinion of you can only go uphill from here." But he didn't care what the Stevenses thought of his wife. Though he'd been upset with her last night, he knew she was exactly the right mother for his children. Her patience with Anna astounded him.

He called Richard and Lily to the kitchen. They all gathered at the table and sipped the tea and sampled the biscuits, easing the stiff mood.

Richard wiped his mouth on a napkin. "Your biscuits are delicious, Elizabeth."

Beaming, she flashed Ted an "I told you so" smirk before turning back to Rose's father. "Why thank you, Mr. Stevens. That's one of the nicest things you could say to me."

He smiled, obviously warming to Ted's wife. "Please, we're family. Call us Richard and Lily."

"She's not a member of our family, Richard. And never will be."

"You might want to reconsider that, Lily," Ted warned affably enough, but he saw in Lily's eyes that she'd caught his meaning.

"When will Anna return from the neighbor's?" Lily asked.

"She should be home soon."

No more had the words left his mouth, than Rebecca knocked at the back door and peeked through the screen. "Well, hello, Mr. and Mrs. Stevens." The door opened, Anna entered. "Have a nice visit," Rebecca called through the screen, practically running to the wagon, tugging Grace along after her. The coward.

Lily flung out her hands. "Anna, darling! Grandma and Grandpa are here for a visit."

Anna stepped into the circle of her grandmother's arms, accepting her hugs and kisses, giving a hearty embrace in return. "Who fixed your braids, sweetheart? They've almost come undone."

"Come here, sweetkins. Grandpa's got a nickel for you." He dug in his pockets, coming up with the coin.

Beaming, Anna took the money then kissed Richard's cheek. "Thank you, Grandpa. I can buy some candy at the mercantile."

"Just don't ruin those pretty teeth."

Having her grandparents near had put a sparkle in Anna's eyes. Their presence appeared to comfort her.

A wail sounded from the children's bedroom. Ted rose from his chair. "I'll get him." He changed Henry's diaper in record time and returned to the kitchen.

Lily rose and took Ted's son out of his arms. "Big precious boy!" she cooed. "Oh, look at your shirt. What is that? Oatmeal?" Her accusing gaze traveled to Elizabeth.

Henry wiggled out of Lily's arms to the floor.

As he toddled away, Richard grinned. "My goodness, look at that, will you? Henry's walking."

"Come to Grandma!" Lily called.

Arms stretched out for balance, Henry tottered over to Elizabeth, throwing his arms around her legs.

Lily buried her face in her hands. "Oh, how I wish Rose could see this. She'd be so proud of her little boy." Her eyes brimmed with tears. "And of you," she said, blowing Anna a kiss.

His eyes misty, Richard cleared his throat. "So, Anna, what do you think of your baby brother's walking?"

"He gets into my stuff," Anna groused.

As Henry sailed past Ted's chair, he made a grab for his son. "He's starting to climb."

"Be careful he doesn't fall out of his crib," Lily said.

"So…how long will you be staying?" Ted asked.

Lily's gaze never left Henry. "Long enough to spoil our grandbabies." She bit her lip. "We've been at loose ends of late."

Across from him, Elizabeth's eyes brightened, a smile curving her face. He could almost see an idea plant itself in her mind. What was she—

"I'm glad you're here," Elizabeth said, turning to his in-laws. "You can help Ted look after the children while I return to Chicago…for my brother."

Without a word to Ted, Elizabeth had set her plan in motion. Would she remain in Chicago? No, she'd return for her brother's sake and in obedience to those vows she'd taken. He couldn't delude himself. He was not the draw.

"Richard and Lily, you can take, ah, our room while Elizabeth's away." He cleared his cup to the sink. "I'll sleep in the barn."

Lily clapped her hands. "A change will do us good. Richard can help with the chores and I'll help with the children and the cooking. It'll be fun!"

Elizabeth gave a huge smile. Obviously pleased by the turn of events. While he'd have to deal with Lily alone. And deal with his daughter's reaction to having a big brother.

Elizabeth's plan had nearly come full circle. In a matter of days she'd give Robby the dream she'd promised—a home. On a farm. With a dog. And her open, dependable arms.

As she walked toward the barn in search of Ted, she pictured Robby hugging Tippy, feeding the livestock and trailing after Ted. So why did she feel a twinge of doubt nip at her stomach? Why did she feel this icy shiver slither through her veins?

She tamped down her silly reaction. Everything would be fine. She was sure of it. Things had worked together beautifully so she could go to Chicago, knowing with Lily and Richard in the house, Ted could finish planting without uprooting his children.

Whether Ted would agree or not, the Stevenses' arrival today was the answer to her prayers.

In the west, the sun had dropped to the horizon, the sky awash with soft pink and peach. As if God had dipped a long rag mop into paint and streaked it across the heavens. The quiet, the stillness of the farm enveloped her, filling her with peace. For a moment, she felt happy. At home.

Then from the barn, she heard a cow low and the soft bleat of the sheep, a reminder of all the work left undone.

The sweet scent of hay mingling with the pungent odor of manure drifted through the door. She paused, waiting for her eyes to adjust to the dim interior. Ted was bent over some kind of metal contraption, tinkering with it then pushing a lever. Nothing happened. He tried it again. Again nothing happened. He paced in front of the machine, muttering in disgust, and then gave it a good kick.

Alone in the barn, or so he no doubt thought, Ted had relaxed the tight rein he kept on his emotions. In his hunched shoulders, she saw tension, even hostility.

"That thing causing you trouble?" Elizabeth said.

Ted whirled to her, then he tried a smile that fell flat. "Yeah."

"Looks like you're having a hard day."

A sigh whistled out of him. "Farming's hard work," he said then went back to the machine. "It doesn't help that this planter's clogged."

She watched him fiddle with that lever, his frustration mounting with every passing second. "Hard work wouldn't deter you. It's something else." She laid a hand on his back. Beneath her palm, his muscles bunched. She blinked, startled by sudden insight. "You hate all this."

"If you mean this planter, well, I think I do right now." But he didn't turn around when he said it.

"No, Ted, that's not what I mean." She stepped back. "Why can't you be honest about what you feel? About this life, this farm?"

He stepped away from the planter and leaned against a rough-hewn support post, his gaze roaming the barn. "Maybe I don't have time to feel. I do the work, pray for rain, sun and warm nights. I don't examine my feelings about the job."

His relaxed posture and matter-of-fact tone didn't conceal the rigid lines around his mouth, his lack of eye contact, as if…

As if he had something to hide.

Why would he deny emotions—anger, joy, sorrow, all the feelings she struggled with daily? "You hate relying on something you can't control."

"If that were true, I wouldn't be married to you."

Though a smile turned up her lips, she refused to credit his comment with a reply.

"The Bible teaches God is in control, not man."

Had Ted used the Bible to avoid her questions? Hadn't she read that believers were to share one another's burdens? That should definitely be true of husbands and wives.

Elizabeth looked around her at the sturdy barn, the cows munching in their stalls and sheep curled up in their pen for the night. "What is it about farming that you don't like, then?"

He shifted under her steady gaze. "Reckon you're determined to make me open a vein and bleed my innermost thoughts." He removed his straw ranch hat, swiped his sleeve over his forehead. "I hate breaking my back planting the crop and then a hailstorm, too much or like now, too little rain, undoes it all." He slapped his hat on his thigh. "Not because of the need for control, but for the risk farming is for my family."

"So why do you stay?"

His eyes lost their focus. "I've had a thought…nothing I'm ready to talk about now."

"Well, if I could, I'd leave."

He took a step closer. "Would you? Really?" he said, his voice soft, his eyes compelling as he searched her face.

Had her declaration hurt his male pride? If so, why? He didn't love her. He wanted to coexist amicably, to give Anna and Henry a mother, a good home. Exactly as she wanted to do for her brother. Yet the lump in her throat said she'd miss Ted if she left. Not that she could. The ring on her finger tethered her to a world she didn't fit.

How had he managed to put the focus on her? "Why do you stay?" she persisted, ignoring his question.

"I'm a man who sticks with things. I stick with this farm. And I stick with this town."

"Well, that's just silly. You should like what you do."

"I'm a father, Elizabeth. Fathers don't run off to pursue whatever whim or urge they get."

She looked away, at the hay cascading over the haymow, at the rafters where owls roosted. At anything but Ted. "Sometimes," she whispered, "they do."

Ted cupped her jaw with his hand. "Good fathers don't. I'm sorry if you had a childhood filled with uncertainty."

She jerked away from his touch. "I didn't. It was... fine. Everything was fine."

But it hadn't been. She was playing the game she'd been taught, the one her mother always played. Put on a brave face, pretend everything was all right and eventually Papa would come back home and make it so. For a while.

Oh, why had she asked the question? Why couldn't she have come in here and said goodbye and been done with it?

He frowned. "When will you be back?"

"I'll return with Robby by the end of the week."

"I'll miss you." He raised a hand toward her then let it drop to his side. "This afternoon…making biscuits… I had the most fun I've had in my entire life."

His admission rocked her back on her heels, but she wouldn't let him know how much his words meant. "I liked telling you what to do."

"Never a doubt in my mind about that." He tweaked her under the chin.

She headed to the door.

"Elizabeth."

She circled back.

"I want to thank you."

"For what?"

"For filling a bit of the emptiness this house had."

His words squeezed against her lungs. "I'm glad," she said, her admission a whisper.

He took a step toward her, but Elizabeth strode to the house, eager to get away from Ted and the feelings he brought alive in her heart.

Chapter Fourteen

Ted dropped Anna and Jason at school, and then drove to the parsonage. Holding Henry in the crook of his arm, he knocked at the door, every muscle as tightly strung as a new fiddle. Perhaps talking to Jacob would set him back on his even-keel course.

Lydia ushered them inside, snatching his son from his arms before they made it to the living room. "Jacob's in his study. Go on in." She ran a fingertip down Henry's neck and he giggled. "I'll watch this precious little boy."

Sitting across from Jacob's desk, Ted told his pastor he'd experienced another verification of God's Call. Three different people had told Ted he sounded like a preacher. "But I'm certain I've misinterpreted God." To prove his assertion, he shared every ugly part of his past. When he finished, he said, "No church is going to accept an ex-gambler for a pastor, Jacob, especially this one. Not when my father swindled our church out of the remodeling fund."

Jacob's brow wrinkled. "Though the debt wasn't yours, you made restitution for that swindle." He rose and walked to the window, pointing in the direction of the saloon on down the street. "I believe you're the right pastor for Joe Lessman. He might actually listen to you."

If only Ted could believe that. Whether he believed it or not, The Call got stronger every day. And so did his resistance. For reasons God must surely approve. He had to protect his family. "I've made too many mistakes."

"The Bible's packed with stories of men who failed, yet God used those men in a mighty way."

A few of those men paraded through Ted's mind. Moses killed a man before God spoke from a burning bush and commanded him to save his people from Pharaoh. To hide his sin with Bathsheba, David arranged for Uriah to die in battle, yet David was God's man. Saul persecuted the early Christians, but God gave him a new name and the task of taking the Good News to the Gentiles.

Ted didn't doubt God had used these men and countless others to do His will. Could Jacob be right? Could men like Joe be the reason God wanted him, of all people, to pastor a church?

Jacob perched on the corner of his desk. "I have a story I want to tell you, Ted. About a young man who didn't believe in God. This man made a point of using God's Holy Name in vain. This man snorted in derision at others' attempts to tell him about the love of God. This man committed every sin in the book and then some. I'll spare you the details.

"And he was miserable." Jacob's voice cracked. "One night he met God. Not in some miraculous way, but in the deeds and love of a godly woman." He smiled. "I was that young man, Ted. That woman is Lydia." His brow crinkled. "I'm no squeaky-clean pastor. And yet, God forgave me. For every sin I committed. For every foul word out of my mouth. For every time I jeered His name. After receiving that pardon, I wanted to devote my life to serving and leading others to Him."

Tears filled his eyes. "Amazingly I've had the privilege of sharing with others the joy I've found in the Lord. Not to judge them, but to love them, as Jesus did the sinners in the gospels. As Lydia did in my life. As I know you will here one day."

Ted was speechless, barely able to take in that this scholarly pastor had lived such a life.

Jacob took a deep breath. "I haven't shared that story often. Conversion isn't about me. But upon occasion someone needs to hear that nothing he's done puts him on a list of untouchables, of spiritual lepers. Because of God's perfect love, we all have hope."

Ted stared into Jacob's eyes and saw the humility, saw the awareness of missed years, missed opportunities. But he also saw a man who valued the gift God had freely given him—forgiveness.

"Ted, Lydia's parents are getting old. They need us. And Lydia's home church needs a pastor." He smiled. "I'd be amazed except I've seen God provide time and time again. We'll miss the good folks here, but we've decided to move back home." He studied Ted. "God is calling you to fill the pulpit here. Not because you're righteous. No one is." He smiled. "Though I can name a few who believe they are. But because you've experienced the incredible pardon of Jesus, and you want to lead others to that precious freedom."

Ted shook his head. "It's too big a risk. I'd have to tell Elizabeth and this town about my past. I could lose my wife." *If I haven't already.* "Once people know about my past, they won't allow me to fill the pulpit. I can't blame them."

"God doesn't call a man to a task without giving him what he needs to accomplish it and that includes an open door. You're never on your own when you're obedient."

In his humanness, Ted couldn't see how his past and God's Call could mesh without bringing harm to those he loved. "Don't you see? I can't let Anna and Henry suffer the ostracism I faced as a child."

"Secrets have a way of coming out, Ted."

As easily as a hot knife slid through butter, Jacob's words sliced through Ted's arrogant assumption that he had the authority to protect his family.

"God's in control, Ted. We aren't. He's opened the door. Will you walk through it?"

Elizabeth pushed through the crowd of travelers moving pell-mell across the platform and spotted Robby, riding her father's shoulders and waving wildly to get her attention. Papa's big welcoming smile eased her concern that he'd still be angry at her defiance. By the time she reached them, he'd swung Robby to his feet.

"Hello, princess," he said, wrapping her in a hug then releasing his hold.

Dropping her satchel at her feet, she tugged her brother close, smothering his upturned face with kisses. "You've grown a foot!"

Robby giggled and puffed out his chest. "Papa says I'm his little man."

"Yes, you are." She turned back to her father, noting for the first time that his suit hung on his large frame; lines grooved his once-smooth face. "You've lost weight, Papa."

"About time," he said. "You look wonderful."

She smiled her thanks. "I've gained a few muscles working on the farm." She ruffled her brother's hair. "Oh, Robby, you're going to love all the animals, one shaggy black-and-white dog in particular."

Robby leaped up and down like a tightly coiled spring. "Really, Lizzie? A dog for me?"

"Tippy belongs to Ted, but—"

Papa's brow knitted. "Who's Ted?"

"I'll explain later. Right now, I can't wait to see Martha."

"She asked that I hurry you home." Papa picked up her bag and they moved toward the street where he hailed a hack. Once they'd settled inside, Robby plied her with questions about the farm the entire way.

The hack stopped in front of the imposing portico. Ted's two-bedroom farmhouse would surely fit into the third-floor ballroom. She dug in her purse, but Papa paid the driver. Where had he gotten the money?

They hadn't reached the front door before it opened. Martha stood waiting, a smile as wide as her open arms and a dusting of silver softening her fiery red hair. Trim, tall, with an iron will and a no-nonsense demeanor, Martha let her hazel eyes skim over her, sizing her up in one swift glance.

Elizabeth slipped into the comfort of those arms and gave the nanny a fierce hug. "I've missed you." A few weeks in Ted's household had given Elizabeth new appreciation for all Martha handled.

"This house isn't the same with you gone," Martha declared, leading her inside. "I want to hear all about what's happened since you left."

As they walked through the main hall, their footsteps echoing in the all but empty house, Elizabeth's heart dipped. Even more of the furnishings were gone.

In the kitchen, they enjoyed a simple, delicious meal while Elizabeth regaled her family with stories of her life on the farm. Catastrophes that had hurt her now brought laughter.

After dinner that night, Martha packed Robby's clothes, books and favorite possessions. Elizabeth kissed her brother good-night, then left Martha and Papa to tuck him in one last time.

In her room, she glanced out the window onto the lawn where she'd made her escape a few weeks ago. Though it felt like a lifetime. She filled a trunk with books, shoes and clothing. She'd donate the ball gowns and frivolous things that would be out of place in New Harmony.

On her way downstairs, Elizabeth noticed a light on in her father's study. She rapped on the door then let herself in.

Papa and a stranger had their heads together. From the expression on her father's face, the conversation had taken an unpleasant turn.

"This must be your daughter, Manning."

Her father paled. "Yes."

The stranger strode to her. "Your father and I go way back. I'm Victor Hammer. Most people call me Vic."

That scar, those eyes, her father's demeanor put Elizabeth on alert. Who was this man?

"I understand you've recently married."

"Yes."

"Seymour said you live on a farm. Big change, I'd imagine." When she merely nodded, he turned to her father. "I'm sure you want to spend time with your daughter. I'll show myself out."

Papa walked him to the door. "I'll find a solution."

The man's smile didn't reach his eyes. "I'm counting on it," he said, then left.

Waiting until the outside door opened then closed. Elizabeth released a gust of air. "Who is that man, Papa?"

"No one of importance."

Elizabeth knew her father. He'd avoided her questions about that man. Why? As if an icy finger slid down her spine, Elizabeth shivered.

Papa motioned to chairs near the fire. "Sit. Tell me more about this husband of yours and his children." He grinned. "Guess this means I'm a grandpa."

"I hadn't thought of that, but you are." The streaks of silver in his hair only made her father appear more distinguished. "You don't look like one."

He smiled. "With two ready-made children and your brother, you're going to have your hands full."

A log tumbled forward, shooting sparks up the chimney. Elizabeth jumped. "I'll admit Anna's a handful." No point in disclosing how much. "Taking care of Henry's a full-time job, but Ted's good to me. It'll work out." Amazingly, she believed what she'd said. "Robby won't be any trouble."

"A small farm can't provide much money." He frowned. "Can your husband give you what you've been accustomed to?"

Elizabeth looked around the barren study, stopping at the spot where Papa's desk and chair once sat. Bookcases crammed with leather-bound books now stood empty. What an irony that Papa was concerned Ted couldn't provide for her when his gambling had almost put them in the poorhouse.

But possessions didn't bring happiness. Another lesson she'd learned.

"Don't fret about me, Papa." She squeezed his hand. "I'm living a rich life. I have all I need and more."

Her father jerked toward the sound of a clearing throat.

Vic stood in the open doorway, his eyes bright like a hawk. "Sorry for the interruption. I forgot my hat." He motioned to the wide window ledge. "Ah, there it is."

Papa ushered Vic out, then returned, his composure shaken though he tried to hide the fact under a wide smile. "So tell me more about the farm."

"It's the perfect place for Robby," she said. "He'll love playing with Ted's dog."

A flash of pain crossed Papa's face, probably guilt over the puppy he'd given then taken away. "Take Robby and leave tomorrow on the first train. I'll see to the arrangements."

"I'd planned to leave after lunch." Alarm traveled her spine. "What's wrong?"

"Nothing new. I'm about to lose the house. I want Robby settled with you as soon as possible." Out of his pocket, he pulled a slip of paper and a pen. "Write down your address in Iowa so I can reach you."

Elizabeth did as he asked, then handed it to him. "What will happen to you? Where will you go?"

"I got a job. Imagine that?"

She smiled. "Doing what?"

"A sales opportunity. I'll be fine, as long as I know my children are safe."

Her stomach turned over, a queasy reminder of Vic. "Safe? What do you mean?"

Papa smoothed the lines on his forehead. "You know, taken care of. Content." He looked deep into her eyes. "Are you happy, princess?"

"I'm fine. All that matters is Robby."

Papa had changed. How much she didn't know, but she couldn't bring herself to broach the subject of his gambling.

"I'm sorry I insisted you marry Reginald. I only wanted what I thought was best for you."

"I'll never understand how you could've promised me to Reginald in exchange for the payment of your debts."

He studied his hands. "I did what I had to do to take care of my family."

"I don't agree with what you did, but I forgive you."

"I can't tell you what that means to me." He met her gaze. "I'm sorry about losing the house. It should've been yours and Robby's."

"The house doesn't matter. Robby and you and Martha, that's what matters."

Papa's charming smile firmly in place, he rose and tugged her to him. "I hope your husband knows what a treasure he married."

No need to tell her father that she and Ted didn't have a real marriage. "Treasure or booby prize." She forced up the corners of her mouth. "I'm not much of a farm wife."

He chuckled. "I have trouble picturing that, as well. Is Ted a patient man?"

"Remarkably."

Suddenly tired, Elizabeth stifled a yawn. "I'm going up to bed. We'll talk more in the morning."

Her father wrapped her in a hug and kissed her cheek. "I love you. Sweet dreams, princess."

"I love you, too, Papa."

That night Elizabeth dreamed of her and Ted climbing an endless hill. She wanted to rest, but he towed her along, insisting they'd make it. An odd dream, but perhaps they would.

The next morning, Elizabeth went down to breakfast. Martha gave her a big hug. "You just missed your father. He left for work."

Elizabeth hurried to the window. Papa stood outside talking to a man. The same man she'd met in his study. Vic. Perhaps Martha could give her some insight into the man. "Who's that talking to Papa?"

Martha glanced out, then shrugged. As Elizabeth watched the men go their separate ways, the nanny bustled around the kitchen, making small talk, but Martha's frenzied behavior only increased Elizabeth's uneasiness.

Robby appeared, rumpled from sleep and ready for breakfast.

"I'll never stop missing you two," Martha said, putting out a breakfast fit for a king.

"I wish you could come to Iowa. I could sure use your help with Ted's children." She sighed. "But there's no room in the house and no money to pay you."

"From what you said last night, your struggles with Anna can't be fixed with good meals and fair rules, though those things are important." She took Elizabeth's hand. "Anna needs you to open your heart to her. To love her. Even when she's unlovable. That's what all children need." She smiled. "That's what I gave you."

At Martha's advice, Elizabeth released a shaky breath, knowing getting close to Ted and his children meant inevitable heartache.

She took Martha's callused hand, now much like her own. "When do you leave for your sister's?"

"I've changed my mind about that." Her eyes filled with tears. "I can't let Seymour go through this alone."

Elizabeth noted the use of her father's first name. What had transpired between Martha and Papa? "What are you saying?"

"I've taken a position as a cook in the same boarding-house where your father's taken a room."

Elizabeth studied Martha's damp eyes, the lines etched in her brow. Never once had she seen anything improper between her and Papa. But the misery in Martha's eyes reminded her of an expression she'd seen in her own. "Are you in love with—"

Nodding, Martha squeezed her hand. "Is that all right with you?"

"Yes." Why hadn't Papa mentioned their relationship? Perhaps she'd been too focused on her own life to notice the attraction between them.

"But I won't marry a man who's set on destroying himself. And those he claims to love. I'm praying for him. For you. For all of us."

"Papa broke Mama's heart. Don't let him do that to you."

"I'm not your mother, God bless her. I've lived in this house since you were five. I never once saw her oppose Seymour."

"Are you saying if she had, things would've been different?"

"Who's to say? Seymour and I have talked. He knows where I stand when it comes to gambling, to what he's done to his family. He wants to change, but whether he can…well, that's why I'm staying in Chicago, for now."

Maybe this woman had made a change in Papa. Or perhaps he'd reached the bottom of the abyss and had found the courage to climb out. Or maybe God was working in Papa's life. Whatever the reason, hope latched onto her heart. Maybe God would perform a miracle where Papa was concerned.

Martha accompanied her and Robby to the depot, and waved goodbye from the platform, tears streaming down her cheeks.

Elizabeth wiped Robby's tears as the train pulled away, tugging him close. "You're going to love the farm."

Her brother would find happiness in Iowa. She hoped Martha and her father would find happiness with each other in Chicago. Without a doubt, Martha was a good influence on Papa.

That Martha and Papa had found something she and Ted might never possess squeezed against her heart.

At least, by marrying Ted, she could give Robby his dream.

Anna blocked the doorway into her room, her arms folded across her chest, her chin thrust to the ceiling. "He's not coming in here."

"Mind your manners, young lady." Ted's stern tone issued a warning, but Anna stood her ground.

"My brother will share my room, Anna," Elizabeth said, wishing she'd thought to settle this before she'd left for Chicago.

Anna smirked. "Daddy doesn't like you and Robby."

"Anna! That's not true." Ted exhaled. "Why would you say such a thing?"

"'Cause you sleep in the barn."

Crimson climbed Ted's neck. "Never mind where I sleep. Elizabeth and I are the adults here. We make the decisions."

Ted's harsh tone crumbled Anna's bravado. Tears

filled her eyes. She spun into her room, slamming the door.

The three of them stood mute. At their feet, Henry clapped his hands, as if he'd witnessed a stunning performance.

Robby leaned into her. "I want to go home." Elizabeth dropped to her knees and drew her brother close. He buried his face against her shoulder. "*Please,* Lizzie, take me *home.*"

How could she tell her brother he had no house to go home to? "It'll be all right, sweet boy. You'll love the farm."

Ted laid a hand on Robby's shoulder. "Do you want to watch me milk the cows?"

Robby shook his head. Tears stung Elizabeth's eyes. Ted was a good man and did what he could to keep things on an even keel. But Robby wasn't some ship passing through rough waters. He was hurting.

"Robby," Ted said, "there are cookies on a plate in the kitchen. Why don't you have a couple before bed."

Robby looked to her. She nodded. "I'll be right there."

Her brother shuffled across the living room and down the steps to the kitchen.

Ted tugged her to the sofa and leaned close. "You're trying too hard, Elizabeth."

"What do you mean?"

"You can't force the children to get along. Give it time. They've just met."

"Would it have hurt Anna to show Robby her room?" she whispered. "She wouldn't even let him look at it."

"She's acting like… Anna." He smiled. "I'll talk to her. But you and I need to relax and give the children time to get used to the idea of being a family. We need to be careful not to pick sides. In the meantime, we'll ask for God's help, then leave it in His hands."

"I'll try."

"I know how disappointing this is for you. Give Robby time to adjust." He patted her hand. "I'm going out to milk."

She walked Ted to the kitchen door. He turned to Robby. "Good night, Robby. Sleep well."

Robby had finished his snack. As Elizabeth led him to her room, she felt a prickle down her back. She'd married Ted to give her brother a home, to give Robby the security he lacked. Never once had she considered that he wouldn't be happy here.

But Anna wasn't about to accept Robby any more than she'd accepted Elizabeth. And her brother missed Martha and Papa more than she'd expected.

But then she remembered Ted's words. She needed to pray. To give it time.

Please, Lord. Work this out for Robby's sake. For Anna's sake. For all of us.

With Tippy loping alongside him, Ted wrestled the slop jar while Robby gripped the pail, not much help, but doing what Ted had asked. His gaze lifted to the sky. Not a cloud in sight. "Looks like another dry day."

Robby nodded.

"Not good for the crops. We need rain."

Robby nodded again, looking jumpy, as though he wanted to hightail it back to Elizabeth.

"You like pigs?"

"I dunno."

From the sad expression on his face, the poor kid must think he was heading to the gallows instead of the pigpen. Earlier Ted practically had to hogtie the youngster to get him to release his hold on Elizabeth's apron strings.

Ted stopped and waited until Robby looked up at him. "Way I see it, you have two choices. You can keep on saying no more than two words to me or you can try and enjoy yourself here."

Robby toed the ground. "I'm probably not gonna stay, anyway."

His words pretty much summarized Ted's childhood. Sympathy rose in his chest. He'd find the same patience he had with Anna. His daughter chose to fight while Robby chose to shrink from connection. He'd do all he could to bring this boy to life.

"My family went from place to place and I know how hard it is to fit in."

Robby glanced up at him, then quickly away.

"I know how difficult it must've been for you to leave your life and family in Chicago to come to an unfamiliar place. I'd like to help you feel at home here...if you'll let me."

Robby didn't say a word, but his eyes glimmered with tears.

He'd no doubt been the pet of the family. Having to share Elizabeth's attention must hurt. But sitting on the sidelines, feeling edgy, lonely and overwhelmed only made things worse. He'd involve Robby in the work on the farm. The best remedy for what ailed him. Time in the fresh air and sunshine wouldn't hurt, either. He'd run the boy ragged.

"This morning, you and I are going to feed this slop to the pigs. By the time we're done, breakfast will be waiting for us. And we'll give those pigs a run for their money." He chucked Robby under the chin. "Now don't

you go telling your sister I mentioned slop and her breakfast in the same breath, or we'll both find ourselves in
the doghouse."

As if against his will, the corners of Robby's mouth
twisted up. "Yes, sir." He cocked his head at him. "Slop?"

"That's what we call what's in this pail. The pigs get
the potato skins, eggshells, every scrap of edible food
left from our table. They love us for it. And we love them
for using our leftovers to grow side meat and chops."

The boy looked puzzled. Better to leave him in the
dark for now. "God knew what He was doing with every
creature He made. Not that we always appreciate them
all. Any animal or bug you could do without?"

Robby shrugged.

At the pigpen, Ted hauled the bucket over the fence,
hopped it and then helped Robby scramble over the slats.
Tippy sat on his haunches, watching. With Robby's help,
Ted dumped the slop into the trough, then stepped back
and called the pigs. "Suey! Suey, pig, pig!"

Ted heard them before he saw them. They left their
foraging in the woods and trotted toward them, snorting,
grunting and shoving toward the trough. Noses plowed
through the mixture, fighting their neighbors for a share.
"They're not much for table manners," Ted said.

"No, sir."

"They remind me of Henry going after your sister's
biscuits."

Robby almost smiled.

"Sometimes you've got to be like those pigs, Robby,
and push your way in." Especially with a girl like Anna.

Ted motioned to the nearby pen. "Never climb that
fence. That old boar isn't above adding boy to the menu."

"Yes, sir."

Back at the house, they washed their hands at the pump. "Better take your shoes off. If you don't, your sister will tan my hide."

Inside, Henry sat in his high chair, smearing oatmeal on his hair. Ted glanced at Robby. "Does my son remind you of anybody?"

"Yes, sir," Robby said, and his eyes almost twinkled. The boy's conversational skills could use work, but the amused expression on his face looked promising.

Whereas his daughter eyed him warily, her mouth turned down as she finished laying out the flatware.

Elizabeth poured the milk. Her questioning gaze met Ted's.

"Your brother was a big help, Elizabeth." Ted glanced at Anna. "With two children to lend a hand around here, the work will get done a lot faster. Perhaps Anna and Robby could handle the egg gathering." Maybe they'd find a way to get past all this timidity and hostility.

Anna crossed her arms across her chest. "I can do it by myself. I don't want his help."

"We all need to rely on others, Anna," Ted said.

"I don't."

Robby's face flattened, his gaze throwing up a wall between him and Ted's family. In the blink of an eye, Anna had undone what little progress Ted had made.

Chapter Fifteen

A vanilla cream cake. What should have been a simple creation. Elizabeth had fretted over the layers as if they were newborn babes. That morning when she'd examined her handiwork, she'd realized she'd created a cake not merely for the Sumner's silver anniversary party, but for her husband.

To show Ted she could master more than biscuits. That she was a wife he could admire. Her heart skipped a beat. If she could, she'd have tossed the cake into the slop jar. Because no matter what that adage said about the way to a man's heart—

She had no intention of letting one vanilla cream cake take her any closer to Ted Logan.

The entire town had been invited to the ice cream social, including Richard and Lily, who'd moved into the boardinghouse and showed no signs of leaving. Elizabeth had been practicing her cake baking on Rose's parents, even learned a few tips from Lily, who delighted in being the superior cook. She and Lily had gotten off on shaky footing, but Lily's willingness to pitch in and her kindhearted treatment of Robby had eased the tension between them.

With the fields planted, the men crouched before ice cream freezers, wearing smiles on their faces, hats shoved back on their heads, eagerly cranking the handles that transformed the glob of eggs, cream and sugar into a luscious treat. Around them, children played kickball, marbles and jacks and giggled their breathless way up and down the hills.

"Looks like everyone is having a good time," Elizabeth said to Ted.

"You look mighty happy yourself."

She gave him a smile, surprised to realize she was. "I love parties. And I'm hoping Robby will make a friend."

With Henry in his arms, Ted reached up to help her out of the wagon. "I'll have to remember your love of parties."

Looking into that handsome smiling face, she marveled that Ted wanted to please her and strived to help Robby feel at home. As he helped her down, the warmth of his touch shot through her. Her insides felt like a cup poured full to the brim, ready to spill over.

Surely this couldn't last.

Anna joined the other children while Robby plodded along with Ted and slouched nearby as Ted set up then cranked his own freezer, with Henry perched on his knee.

Elizabeth carried her basket to a long table covered with a white cloth flapping in the gentle breeze. Women gathered around it, putting out their cakes.

"Hello, Elizabeth." Gertie Wyatt squinted up into the sky. "Not a cloud in sight. All this sunshine gives me the willies."

Ruth Johnson set out a cake frosted with a burnt-sugar icing. "It'll rain, Gertie. Always has." She raised her eyes to the heavens. "Though sooner's better than later, Lord."

Gertie opened her basket, lifted a cake sprinkled with coconut. "Remember when that evangelist came here for a prayer meeting? We had terrible storms all week. But all that rain didn't douse his fire-and-brimstone sermons."

"Yeah, that podium pounding cost us our building fund besides."

"It's the Sumners' anniversary. Let's enjoy the party." Rebecca Harper shifted Faith in her arms. "I hear enough dreary talk at home."

Elizabeth put her basket beside the others and lifted the lid. Inside rested her masterpiece, a towering cake with peaks of white frosting gleaming in the afternoon sun.

Rebecca peeked inside. "What a beautiful cake. You've outshone all of us."

"Don't be silly." Elizabeth looked around at all the marvelous cakes, secretly pleased by Rebecca's appraisal.

Ted came up behind her just as she lifted the cake plate from the picnic basket. The top layer slid toward her. Elizabeth tipped the platter to reverse the momentum, but that only sent the layer toward the ground. She yanked it back and the top layer slid across the bottom, coming to a stop against the front of her dress. "Oh!"

"Let me get a knife," Rebecca said, handing Faith to Ted, then turning to her own basket. Rebecca slipped the spatula under the wayward half and lifted it back in place, then smoothed the frosting over the crack in the top. "There."

Ted eyed Elizabeth's dress. "You look mighty delicious covered with frosting, Mrs. Logan."

The women chuckled.

He stepped closer. "Better even than wearing biscuit dough," he murmured in Elizabeth's ear.

Scrubbing at her dress, Elizabeth's hand stilled. She didn't want her husband drooling over her like she was a confection made only for him.

Winking at her, Ted handed Faith over to Rebecca then wandered back to the men.

Rebecca grinned. "You're perfect for Ted."

"A perfect wife wouldn't be covered with frosting."

"You must not have seen the look in his eye. He's smitten."

Elizabeth's gaze followed Ted. Her heart took a little dive. Did he care about her? What did it matter, really? She wasn't perfect for Ted. She couldn't fill Rose's shoes and was a sorry substitute for Sally. She'd married to give Robby a good home and now that he'd arrived, her brother wasn't happy the way she'd expected. She had no idea why. Or what to do about it.

"Elizabeth Logan, you'd better do something with this girl!" Cynthia Atwater stomped over with Anna, her hand clamped on Ted's daughter's shoulder.

Tears streamed down Anna's face, her eyes wide with fright, her breath coming in hitches. All conversation ceased.

Elizabeth grasped Anna's hand and caught her gaze. "What's wrong, Anna?"

"She took a big hunk out of my cake, that's what's wrong."

Anna shook her head, her body shaking even harder.

Robby tapped Elizabeth on the arm. "Anna didn't do it." He swallowed hard. "I ate the cake."

"Robby, I saw you over with the men. You couldn't have done it." Her brother's bravado waned. But his attempt to save Anna warmed Elizabeth's heart. "Thanks for trying to help," she whispered into his ear.

Elizabeth knelt and pulled Anna into her embrace.

"I didn't do it," Anna said against Elizabeth's neck, her voice soft, pleading with Elizabeth to believe her. "Honest."

This wasn't the Anna with attitude; this child needed a defender, deserved one. Anna had her issues but she wasn't a liar.

"She was right there when suddenly a big hunk of my angel-food cake disappeared. My Betsy saw her take it. Do you have any idea how many eggs it takes to make that cake?"

Elizabeth rose and tucked Anna against her side. "I'm sorry about your cake, but Anna says she didn't do it. I believe her."

Mrs. Atwater's hands rested on her heart-shaped hips. "She's not above a prank like this, I'll tell you. Why, she's got a mouth on her, that girl. Everyone knows it."

Anna hung her head, tearing at Elizabeth's heart. "She's a girl with…opinions. Perhaps at times she needs to express them in a milder way, but she does not lie."

Mrs. Atwater harrumphed. "And what am I going to do with a cake that's half-gone?"

Rebecca marched down the table to Mrs. Atwater's cake and turned the missing part to the back. "It's only missing a chunk. There's plenty left."

"This isn't just any cake. This is a prize-winning recipe."

Elizabeth glanced at Mrs. Atwater's daughter, who

ducked behind her mother's skirts, but not quickly enough. "Are those crumbs on Betsy's mouth?"

Betsy poked her head out and scrubbed a hand over her mouth. "I didn't eat the cake, Mama. I didn't!"

"Let me see that hand, daughter." Mrs. Atwater examined the small palm, dusted with evidence. "Betsy Marie Atwater! You've embarrassed me in front of my neighbors and accused Anna of something *you* did."

"Your cake is tempting," Elizabeth said softly. "Betsy probably couldn't help herself."

Betsy's head bobbed like a small sailboat on Lake Michigan during a storm. "I'm sorry, Mommy."

Apologies were given to all concerned. Betsy and her mother fell into each other's arms, crying. The ladies went back to unpacking their baskets.

Elizabeth felt a tug on her hand. She knelt in front of Anna and ran her palms over the little girl's damp cheeks. "You okay?"

Anna nodded, opened her mouth, shut it again.

"What?"

"You believed me." She leaned close and kissed Elizabeth's cheek, her eyes filled with regret for the trouble between them.

A lump swelled in Elizabeth's throat until she could barely speak. "You're a truthful girl. I had no reason to doubt you."

"I... I say...mean things to you."

"I know how hard it is to lose your mother, Anna. I understand. I understand it all."

As if they'd been given an order, Anna and Elizabeth flung their arms around each other, sharing the pain of their losses. When they pulled away, they shared something else—a new harmony.

Anna spun to Robby. "Want to play with us?"

Before he could answer, she led him to a group of children kicking a ball across the way. Anna glanced back one last time and gave Elizabeth a smile, her gaze filled with warmth, something close to adoration.

Tears pricked the backs of Elizabeth's eyes. Her heart swelled with conflicting emotions that battled for control. What was she going to do now? She cared for Henry and Anna, cared more than she wanted to admit. She'd opened that door to Ted's children leading into her heart.

But she wouldn't open it for Ted. He didn't merely want a mother for his children. He wanted a wife. To kiss. To hold. To share his life. But loving a man could destroy her.

She pivoted, all but running into Ted, who blocked her way.

"I heard you stand up for Anna. I can't thank you enough." He tucked a loose strand of her hair behind her ear. "When I met you at the depot that day, I was afraid you wouldn't fit. But you're a terrific mother." He cupped her jaw with his large hand, his expression intense, full of longing. "A wonderful wife."

Elizabeth pulled away. Ted's words might have meant something if she shared his wish for intimacy. But she didn't.

She wasn't a wonderful wife at all.

Around Ted, neighbors gobbled ice cream and cake, having a good time. Good people doing the best they could with very little other than love and hard work—two things that had been foreign to his family. New Harmony was such a welcoming place. Such a family place. But Ted didn't see the other families. He saw only his own. That Elizabeth had defended his daughter in front of the whole town rumbled through him.

His mother had been an ineffectual woman who'd never taken a stand. Not for her children. Not against her husband. Not for herself. He'd hustled over, ready to defend Anna. Certain with all the grief Anna had given her, Elizabeth wouldn't uphold his daughter. He felt like one penny short of two cents. His wife and daughter might clash at home, but when the chips were down, Elizabeth reminded him of a mother bear with a cornered cub.

"You're looking mighty sober, Ted Logan," Rebecca said. "An ice cream social is no place for that face."

He smiled. "Guess you're right."

"Now what you need to do is ask that pretty wife of yours to join you in the three-legged sack race. Lily can watch Henry and Anna." She took Henry out of his arms and gave Ted a little push toward Elizabeth.

"What about you and Dan?"

"He wouldn't miss the chance to be in the sack with me."

Ted laughed and headed toward his wife. Though he found her surrounded by women, he saw only her. The prettiest, most vibrant of them all.

The ladies stepped back when he arrived, opening a path to his wife. He took her hand and led her aside. "Want to enter the sack race?"

"What do we get if we win?"

He tugged on the brim of his hat, a smile curving his lips. "I heard the prize is a slightly dented angel-food cake."

Her eyes lit with mirth.

Couples donned the feed sacks, not an easy task with the volume of the women's skirts and petticoats. A chorus of giggles and chuckles peppered the starting line.

Ted grabbed a sack from the pile and laid it out on the ground. "Step into it."

Elizabeth did as he asked. "Wish I had on my pants."

Grinning, he joined his left foot to her right then pulled up the sack until it reached her waist and divided her skirts. "I'll hold it while you arrange your skirts. I don't want you to step on your dress."

Everyone lined up. The starter raised his hand.

He tucked her close in the crook of his arm. "Hold the sack with one hand and me with the other."

Her arm inched around his back slowly, as though she expected him to bite. Her gaze slid to his mouth then quickly returned to his eyes. "Which…foot do… we start with?" she stammered.

"Start on the foot in the sack. We'll try to swing them out together." He tucked his arm around her waist and gave it a squeeze. Their eyes met and collided, but only for a moment. "We'll go as fast as we can without falling. If we fall, we'll lose for sure."

The hand went down, a shout went up. In unison Ted and Elizabeth threw out their sacked legs. Gripping each other like their lives depended on it, they lurched ahead. Ted held Elizabeth tight, keeping her on her feet. The Wyatts went down beside them but they kept going, laughing from the exhilaration but never taking their eyes off the finish line. They sped along with only the Harpers in close competition.

At the rope stretched across the ground, Ted lunged, dragging Elizabeth with him. They stumbled over the line, inches ahead of the Harpers, and landed in a heap on the grass, laughing while their neighbors clapped their approval.

Ted gave Elizabeth a quick kiss on her forehead. "We

make quite a team, Mrs. Logan," he said, then extricated them from the sack and tugged her to her feet. "I've never had a better partner."

As he had earlier, he read the panic in her eyes. Why was Elizabeth afraid to get close?

Chapter Sixteen

The woman must have gotten up on the wrong side of the bed. Elizabeth had no other explanation for the harsh expression on the teacher's face as she stood outside the one-room schoolhouse swinging the brass bell. Children formed lines in front of her, girls on one side and boys on the other.

Not that Elizabeth didn't have some sympathy for her, grouchy face or not. She couldn't imagine facing all these children of different ages and intellects every day.

At least no one was telling her whom to marry or where to put the slop. Or pressing to get close. Like Ted.

Jason Harper leaped from the back of the wagon and trotted over to a group of boys while Robby lagged behind, head down, shuffling along like an old man.

Elizabeth tugged at Anna and Grace's hands. "Come along, girls. You don't want to be late."

Anna skidded to a stop. "I don't want to go."

"You have to go to school."

"Why?"

Because Rebecca is watching Henry for the day and

I'm free as a bee on the first day of spring. "Because I said so."

Anna scowled. "That's a dumb reason."

Evidently, regret for past behavior didn't mean Anna wouldn't question Elizabeth's authority.

"Whenever I ask my mama anything she says 'because I said so, that's why.'" Grace rolled her eyes. "Every time."

Well, if Elizabeth sounded like Rebecca, then she must be doing something right. She retied the bow on Anna's pigtail. "Don't you want to grow up to be smart?"

"Why? To bake biscuits all day?" Anna thrust out her lip in a perfect pout.

She'd hit a nerve, that girl. Exactly the life Elizabeth had now. A biscuit maker, for pity's sake. Talk about lowering her aspirations. "No, so you can teach or be a nurse or a doctor. Education gives you freedom."

Anna arched a brow in disbelief.

"Education gives me freedom—when school lets out," Grace said, with a giggle.

Only six and already as smart-mouthed as Anna. "Well, go on, your classmates are marching inside."

The girls whirled toward the schoolhouse then took off at a run, barreling up the stairs, their boots clunking on each step.

Elizabeth pulled herself onto the wagon seat, vowing she wouldn't be a biscuit maker all her life and clicked to the horses. In front of the Sorenson Mercantile, she set the brake and tied up to the hitching rail. She'd sell the eggs, not much of a career but a start.

When she'd packed Anna and Robby's lunch bucket, she made a sandwich for herself. She couldn't waste money eating in town. Not that she knew exactly what she'd do with her day.

A sign caught her eye on a storefront next door to the mercantile: For Lease

This building was available for someone with gumption. Someone with ideas. Someone like...

Her.

Elizabeth peered through the grimy window into a room littered and dirty and in need of paint. But light streamed in the window, throwing patterns on the plank floor. Cleaned up, this would be a cheerful place. Elizabeth ran a finger down the pane. Here women could gather and exchange books and ideas, find ways to improve the community. For a brief time, free from children and homes and men.

She closed her eyes and pictured it all clearly. In front of the window a table, perhaps on the back wall a bookcase brimming with books and magazines.

Her eyes popped open. She'd collect books for a library, maybe start a book club. Ladies could gather once a week to improve their minds. To instigate improvements in the community.

On the back wall, a door led somewhere—outside or to another room? She hustled around the building and found a window. That meant a back room. Her pulse skipped a beat, then slowed as an idea planted itself in her mind, then bloomed.

This could be a place for her and Robby.

Maybe with just the two of them, she could give her brother the attention he needed. Perhaps get him to admit what bothered him, if he knew.

Even with Anna no longer giving him the cold shoulder, the forlorn expression in his eyes hadn't diminished.

Ted treated her brother like a son, but Robby kept his distance, refusing his overtures, looking lost and miserable. Her brother's sadness tore at her. She'd given him everything she'd thought he wanted. And it wasn't enough.

In a way she understood. She felt hemmed in, suffocated by the demands of her routine. She'd gone from a life of ease to a life of endless responsibility, all thrust upon her overnight, giving her no chance to find her own way.

Ted was kind. Trying hard to get close. Too close. He wanted a real marriage when a business contract was what they'd agreed on. She had to keep him at arm's length. She knew with certainty that if she loved Ted Logan, she'd lose herself. She'd become dependent on his smile, on his affection, on the harmony of their marriage.

Then when he chose to withhold that smile, that affection, that harmony, she'd wind up like her mother... brokenhearted.

This shop was her and Robby's ticket to freedom, a chance for independence right here in New Harmony. Maybe here she'd find some air to breathe, some time to find her way.

Would Ted allow it?

Well, she hadn't promised to obey, only to try. And hadn't she tried and tried and tried? Lily and Richard would gladly help Ted with the children until Robby found his stride. She wouldn't be leaving Ted in the lurch.

She sighed. Ted would be upset, but surely God understood her need to help her brother. Her shoulders slumped. But where would she get the money for the rent? *Lord, if this plan is all right with You, help me find a way.*

"It needs a lot of work."

Elizabeth jumped as if she'd been caught in a criminal act and reeled toward the speaker. Mr. Sorenson stood outside the back door of his store, a broom in his hand. He ambled over.

"Two years ago we rented the place to a lawyer but the folks of New Harmony didn't provoke enough lawsuits to keep him. It's been standing empty ever since. The missus and I've talked about expanding, but we got more work than we can handle now. My desk's buried under receipts and a pile of bills."

"I loved math in school. Bookkeeping sounds like fun."

"Fun? I'd sooner get a tooth pulled. And the missus can't add two and two."

Here was her chance. "I'm sure I could handle your books. How much is the rent?"

"What are you aiming to do with the place?"

"I'd like start a ladies' club, maybe a library, though I'd have to find some books."

He leaned on the broom handle and scratched his head. "Sounds citified." He chuckled. "So it's sure to please the ladies. Normally, I'd charge—" He stopped. "Did you say you could handle my books?"

"I'm sure of it."

"In that case, it's yours for the price of handling our accounts."

"That's all?"

"You'll be doing us a favor."

Elizabeth reached out a hand and they shook. "You have a deal."

"Do you want to take a look around? See what you're in for? It's not locked."

Elizabeth opened the door. A three-inch shadow streaked across the toe of her shoes. She leaped back, pressing her hand to her bosom. "Looks like you already have a tenant."

Mr. Sorenson chuckled. "Mice included at no charge."

She pivoted and spotted dust and mice droppings everywhere. Nothing Tippy could help her with here. She'd wanted to escape the tedium of the farm, not add more work to her load. "Looks like I'll need to borrow that broom."

Mr. Sorenson handed it over with a grin, then thumped the window with a fist and lifted it with ease. "That'll improve the odor in here."

A small stove stood away from one wall. Cobwebs dangled between the chimney and the wall. She swung the broom, bringing down the webs.

"I'll fetch a bucket and some rags. There's a pump out back for water."

They walked to the front. Another small stove. More webs but no sign of mice.

"Will you need a table or two?"

"Yes, and chairs. I hadn't thought about those."

Mr. Sorenson waved a hand. "Got some grates out behind the store that'll make fine bases. Barrel lids will work as tops. I'll ask Cecil to nail them together. Covered with oilcloth, they'll look fine."

"You'd do that for me?"

"Not often New Harmony gets a new enterprise." He grinned. "Besides, the ladies might stop in for supplies once they're done chatting here. And Cecil needs something to do besides hanging out at the store, getting in the way." He rubbed a hand over his chin. "I expect the school will loan you a few folding chairs they keep on hand for programs and such."

"What a good idea. Thank you, Mr. Sorenson."

"Ted's a man I respect. I'm happy to help out his missus."

Would Mr. Sorenson be so generous if he knew her plan to move in here? "Could I trade the basket of eggs out in the wagon for oilcloth to cover the tables?"

"You've got a deal. I'll get them." He turned back. "It's a relief to get that empty store off the missus's nag list."

"Let me take down the sign." Elizabeth hurried to the window and then handed it to Mr. Sorenson.

"You know, Mrs. Logan, you're just what this town needed."

"I am?"

"A breath of fresh air. And a pretty one at that." He tipped an invisible hat, then ducked out the back, the sign under his arm.

Her chest filling with excitement, Elizabeth all but skipped to the front door and opened it, welcoming in the breeze and sunshine. She'd found something of her own, a place to exchange ideas and instigate change.

In her mind, she pictured the women coming in, sharing, laughing—making plans for the town and for themselves. And in the process, she and Robby would find a modicum of freedom, a place to find their way.

Mr. Sorenson cleared his throat, interrupting her daydreams. He put a bucket of water and the rags he'd promised on the floor beside her. "I don't see any more mouse nests, just droppings. The missus sent over a scrub brush and a jug of vinegar to cut the dust. Anything else you need, holler."

"Thank you."

"The missus is jabbering about your ladies' club. With you next door, I'll probably not get a lick of work out of her."

"We'll meet once a week, probably on Saturday. Women may not have much time or interest."

"Once the word spreads, you'll be swamped with members."

Elizabeth grinned. "When can you show me your books?"

"How about early Saturday? I can introduce you to my ledger, get you started. After you get that mess straightened out, I'd say once a week should handle it."

Elizabeth stepped outside with the broom and watched Mr. Sorenson head next door. She swung the broom and sent dirt flying. As Martha had always said: well begun is half done. For once the work didn't feel like a chore. Not when it meant she'd take a role in town.

"Excuse me." A familiar fellow she'd met at the café the night she married Ted appeared at her elbow, wearing a plaid shirt rolled at the sleeves, revealing a glimpse of long underwear. He removed his billed cap and squinted into the sun, deepening the grooves around his hazel eyes. "I hear tell you need tables, missus," he said, plopping the cap on his head.

"Please, call me Elizabeth. You're Cecil, the genius with hammer and nails who's going to make my tables."

A deep red blush moved up his neck and disappeared beneath his cap. "Yep. Cecil Moore's the name, but I ain't never been called a genius."

"A man that handy is a gift to womankind."

"Well, I ain't wearing no bow." He hitched up his pants. "How many?"

Stifling a grin, she took count. "Four should be plenty."

"If Sorenson's got that many barrel lids out back, I'll make 'em for ya. I'll be back."

"Please don't rush on my account."

"I only got one speed, missus. Rush ain't it."

Elizabeth watched Mr. Moore shuffle away. Clearly his one speed was tortoise.

Picking up the broom, she swept the store. Dust flew into her face and she coughed then sneezed, wishing for her red head scarf to cover her nose, especially if it would scare mice as well as chickens.

Oscar, the other Moore brother, appeared at the door. Apparently word was spreading, all right, but not to the ladies.

"Cecil tells me you're going to form yourself a ladies' club, whatever that is."

The brothers didn't resemble each other. Oscar was portly, baby faced and short. Cecil was as thin as a reed, long faced and wrinkled.

"Yes, I am." She returned to her sweeping. If she kept getting visitors she'd never finish before school let out.

Oscar swung his head side to side. "Don't look like much."

"It needs cleaning," she said, ending on a sneeze.

He guffawed. "Yes, ma'am, it surely does." He grabbed the broom from her hands. "You'd better git some air. I'll finish this."

Elizabeth took a look at the man's thick waistline. A little work wouldn't hurt him. She grabbed rag and pail and walked outside to wash the window. When Oscar finished, she stepped inside to clean the other side.

"I hear tell you called my brother a genius," he said.

"Well, *you* are a knight in shining armor for protecting me from all that dust, Mr. Moore."

"Shucks, weren't nothing."

"You kept me from a coughing fit or worse." She smiled. "I don't call that nothing."

The two men might not look alike but they both had blushes that would put a new bride to shame.

"Your brother is making tables out of crates and barrels. Isn't that the cleverest thing you've ever heard of?" she said, rinsing out her rag.

"He fancies hisself a carpenter, but hammering crates together don't make him a craftsman."

Apparently the Moore brothers had a competitive streak.

Oscar surveyed the room. "These floors could use mopping."

She gave the window one last scrub and then wiped a hand over her brow. "As soon as I get a bucket of clean water, I'll get started."

"I'll fetch it. It's too heavy for a dainty thing like you."

"Thank you. Your mother raised good men."

"We raised ourselves, ma'am. Didn't turn out to be Jesse James so I reckon we done okay." Oscar disappeared then returned with the bucket. "Where do you want it?"

"I'll start back here." She dropped to her knees and dipped her rag into the bucket.

"You'll mess up your dress," he said, getting a rag. "Can't hurt these here overalls."

Oscar started in the back and Elizabeth followed behind him, washing the woodwork. Her skirts kept getting tangled up around her. If only she had on pants, though the sight might shock the Moore brothers into apoplexy.

Mr. Sorenson appeared at the door carrying red-checked material. "Here are those oilcloths you wanted. Oh, let me do that. You'll ruin your dress. It's so pretty, too."

"I hemmed it myself—well, with a little help from Ted."

"It's hard to picture Ted with a needle in his hand—"

"He didn't sew—"

"Though I recall watching him stitch up a piglet's leg."

"Oh, my."

"Squealed its head off, but that didn't stop Ted. He clamped that squirming shoat between his knees and—"

Elizabeth gulped. "I've got the picture."

Mr. Sorenson grabbed the cloth and went to work. Elizabeth washed the back window, imagining curtains out front and trying to put out of her mind the image of Ted's pig doctoring.

Though there was one thing she'd learned. Farmers made do. Farmers were jacks-of-all-trades. Farmers weren't squeamish.

Nothing about Elizabeth fit farm life.

Around noon Mrs. Sorenson appeared carrying a tray with three thick slabs of ham between slices of fresh-baked bread and tin cups of hot tea. "Hubert, I left your dinner and the Moore brothers' on the table in the back. Mind the store. I'm eating with Elizabeth." Once they'd left, Lucille smiled at Elizabeth. "I can't tell you what a relief it is to have you handling our books. You've given Hubert a new lease on life."

"I'm getting the better deal." She nibbled on her sandwich. "Would you know where I could get two cots?"

"Well, sure, we've got some nice ones." Lucille frowned. "Why would you need cots?"

She couldn't tell the proprietor her plans. Not until she'd talked to Ted. She owed him that much.

But Lucille didn't leave the subject alone. "Are you planning on moving in here?"

"I might be." She swallowed a sip of water, flushing the food she'd eaten down her suddenly dry throat, and then explained her reasons for bringing Robby there.

"I doubt Ted will think much of the idea. No husband would—" Her gaze turned speculative, but she didn't ask questions.

Once Lucille took her tray and disappeared next door, Elizabeth heaved a sigh. Moving in here would cause people to talk, but helping Robby came first.

With an hour until she had to gather the children from school, Cecil showed up with the tables. "May not look like much but they're solid and won't tip, if'n the ladies put their elbows on 'em."

Elizabeth covered them with the oilcloth, not exactly linen but practical and cheerful. Though smaller than she'd like, the tables were sturdy, serviceable and cost nothing. Something she'd come to appreciate.

By the time she left, Elizabeth's club room shone. Cecil stayed behind, insisting he'd wait to help her with the chairs.

At the school, Elizabeth spoke to the teacher, who assured her the chairs wouldn't be missed until the eighth-grade commencement at the end of the month. Feeling optimistic, Elizabeth asked for twelve. Robby helped the older boys load them in the back while she herded Anna and Grace into the wagon.

Anna twisted on the seat to take a look. "Where are we taking the chairs?"

Elizabeth couldn't very well explain about the ladies' club until she'd talked to Ted. "To a shop next to the mercantile."

Anna looked puzzled but forgot about the chairs when Grace mentioned the upcoming spelling bee.

True to his word, before she'd stopped the horses, Cecil lumbered off the Sorenson porch to retrieve the chairs. "Well, Anna girl, looks like your new mama is opening one of them fancy clubs for ladies."

Anna's eyes grew wide and she scampered down from the wagon and dashed inside the building.

Once she dropped off Jason, Elizabeth would talk to Anna. Ask Ted's daughter to give her a chance to talk to Ted.

About the ladies' club.

Soon to be her and Robby's quarters.

Was she making a mistake? Did God approve of her decision? He'd opened that door Ted talked about. Still, doubt nagged at her. She wasn't ending the marriage, but with every day packed with chores and children, she never had a minute to examine what she wanted. But if not for Robby's unhappiness, she wouldn't take this step. She had to find a way to restore his joy, even if it meant taking drastic action.

If she hadn't taken action in Chicago, she'd be married to Reginald Parks and Robby would be in boarding school.

A sense of peace surrounded her, as if God Himself had given her permission to flee. Would Ted see it that way?

Chapter Seventeen

The minute Elizabeth drove in with the children, Ted took one look at her and knew something was up. He said nothing, not through supper, nor while they shared the task of putting the children to bed. But now as they sat at the table drinking coffee, separated by inches but miles apart, he had to know her plans. "Looks like you had a good day."

"Why would you say that?"

"You're different. There's a glow about you." She'd never looked more beautiful. "It's becoming." He took her hand. "What happened today?"

Her eyes lost their sparkle, becoming guarded, even wary. As a gambler, he'd mastered the nuances of expression. She locked her gaze with his. In that moment, Ted knew that he wouldn't like whatever she had to say. He squared his shoulders. "Tell me."

"I've found something of my own, something that will make me happy."

"You're unhappy here." It was a statement, not a question.

She removed her hand from his grip. "Not unhappy

exactly. Just not happy. It's not your fault, Ted. Or the children's."

"Then what is it?"

Biting her lip, she looked away, a furrow between her delicate brows. "It's hard to explain." Her fingers trembled on the handle of her cup. "I need freedom."

He could barely get the words out, but he had to know. "You want a divorce?"

She shook her head. "I made my promise to you before God."

Weak with relief, he slumped against the back of his chair. But if not a divorce, then where would this conversation lead?

"I've jumped into this marriage. I tried to handle your and the children's expectations, but the truth is I don't know what I want, who I am. I need the freedom to find out."

"Doing what?"

"Mr. Sorenson will let me use the empty building next to the mercantile in exchange for taking care of the store's books. I plan to form a ladies' club."

"So your head for figures will pay for this adventure."

"I used to want adventure." Tears filled her sapphire eyes. "Now I just want…me." She sighed. "I'm confused."

Well, she wasn't alone in that. What did she want? How would a ladies' club give it to her? Where would her quest for freedom take her? His heart sank. No doubt farther away from him. Ted picked up his cup. "So what's your plan for this ladies' club?"

"Women need a tranquil place to enjoy one another's company and exchange ideas, find ways to improve their minds, the town."

"There's quilting bees and church functions—"

"No, not merely what they can do but to explore who they are." She laid a hand on his arm. "This isn't about other women. Not really. I'm doing this for me." She folded and refolded her napkin. "And for Robby."

"How will a ladies' club help Robby?"

"I have to figure out why Robby can't adjust and how to help him. Anna has accepted him. Tippy follows him around. You're good to him. Yet my brother's miserable. Maybe he needs time with me. Like me, time to find his way."

"I've tried everything I can think of—"

"I'm not blaming you. I'm not blaming anyone." Her mouth tightened. "Except maybe my father for forcing us into a new life."

Ted cringed. Elizabeth had been forced to marry him.

"Robby misses Papa and Martha, but he can't go back to Chicago." She sighed. "Maybe alone with me, Robby will speak freely. So…we're moving out."

A lump lodged in his throat. He set down his cup with a clink. "The children need you. I forbid it."

Her chin jutted, her eyes narrowed, her mouth thinned.

He might as well have waved a red flag in front of a bull but he couldn't stop himself. He didn't want her to leave. And it wasn't only the children who needed her. She'd brought life into the house. Into him. He cared about her. Yes, at times she rubbed him the wrong way, like rough sandpaper against his skin. But she also captivated him.

She rose. "You can't stop me."

He gave an imitation of a laugh, a scratchy sound. "Guess your escape from Chicago proves that." He stood and stepped toward her. "Have you forgotten we're married?"

"You're the one who called our marriage a business deal."

His fingers curved around her cheeks. "It's no longer a business arrangement to me." If he told her how much he'd grown to care for her, she'd get that haunted look in her eyes. Like a trapped animal facing execution. Why didn't she know he'd never hurt her? "But if it were, by leaving, you're breaking the contract."

"Robby and I need this. I won't give it up." She pushed his hands away. "I'm sorry."

"Have you prayed about this?"

She gave a gentle smile. "I have. I know it's not what you want, but in my heart, I believe I'm doing the right thing."

A part of him wanted to beg her to stay, but the other part understood the need to examine whether the path you'd chosen was the right one. Or if you had what it took to change course.

But why did he keep feeling God's Call to ministry when a pastor's wife didn't solve problems by leaving her family? He'd have to trust Elizabeth enough to let go, to let her find her way and help her brother find his. "I don't like it but I'm trying to understand."

She walked past him. "Tomorrow morning Rebecca will drop me off at the shop after she takes the children to school."

"Sounds like you've got it all worked out."

He heard the bitterness in his tone. Well, why not? Hadn't she wormed her way into all their hearts and now would be leaving a hole as big as Gibraltar? He slowed his breathing. Tried to get a handle on his resentment. Keep that even keel he prided himself on.

Numbers 35:6 popped into his mind. "This ladies' club may be your city of refuge. For a time."

She gave him a beautiful, happy smile. "Thank you, Ted, for understanding how I feel."

Lord, how can I show her I care?

"Elizabeth?" She raised her gaze to his. "I'll ask Hubert to open an account for you and credit it with the egg money. For food or whatever you need. I wish I had more."

"You'd do that for me?" she said softly. "Help me when I'm leaving?"

I'd do a lot more if you'd let me. Instead he said, "I'm sorry for trying to make you stay. I was wrong." He took her hand. "You need to do this."

He understood how tired she must be of feeling forced into things. Of not getting to choose what she wanted. Not her path, not her husband. The only way she'd know if she'd made the right choice was to leave.

Tears flowed down her cheeks. "No one has willingly let me decide anything. Ever. Thank you." She rose on her toes and kissed his cheek.

Though Elizabeth pointed to Robby, he suspected the main reason for her departure came down to their marriage of convenience. He should've seen this coming. She'd married him to give her brother security, a happy home. That plan had failed.

Would their marriage also fail? Divorce wasn't the only way for a marriage to die.

Ted's pulse kicked up a notch. By giving her money, he'd made her flight easier. She might not miss him, but he counted on her missing his children. So much she'd come back. Soon.

Watching his wife retreat into the bedroom, he hoped their marriage would survive this test.

In his entire life, he'd never taken a bigger gamble.

Elizabeth slipped her and Robby's clothes and toiletries into the satchel while Robby slept curled up in the bed, unaware that tomorrow they'd move to town.

By leaving, she was adding to Ted's troubles. But she had to go. Or one morning she feared she'd wake up hating him.

He'd said she had a glow about her. The exact words Rebecca had said earlier when Elizabeth had dropped off Jason from school.

Only, Rebecca had asked if she was pregnant—the biggest irony of all. She and Ted had no real marriage. Her leaving was merely an inconvenience for Ted, maybe an embarrassment. But with Lily and Richard still in town, he'd find a way to keep his life on that even keel he prized.

Elizabeth slipped out of her clothes and into her nightgown, and then crawled into the double bed beside her brother. Bunching up her pillow, she buried her face in it, her thoughts on Ted. She'd miss him. If only he'd court her, make her feel that he hadn't bought her with the price of a train ticket. She was so confused. If only—

No, what mattered was Robby's happiness. With God's help, she'd teach him to trust God, to build a foundation that would help him cope. Yet at the back of her mind a niggling suspicion plagued her. Her motives for leaving might not be as selfless as she pretended.

She and Ted were getting close.

A ragged breath heaved out of her. She had to leave before she got even more entangled with this man and his children.

Heaving a sigh of relief that Lydia hadn't questioned him about Elizabeth's whereabouts, Ted thanked Jacob's wife. Though he suspected that she and half the town probably already knew his wife slept at the ladies' club. What kind of a picture did that paint of their marriage?

At the open study door, Jacob looked up, a broad smile on his face. "Just the man I want to see."

"Guess that means you've heard my wife and her brother moved to the ladies' club."

"I heard, but I don't think things are as dire as you look." He grinned, motioning to the chair across from his desk.

Ted took the seat, trying to gather his thoughts to explain, not that he understood his wife. "I'm trying to give her time...."

"Have you told her about your past?"

"No."

"You know you have to."

Ted studied his hands. "If I do, she's gone for good."

"You're underestimating Elizabeth."

"I don't know why, but she hates gambling. I suspect gambling is behind the reason she married me."

"Ted, I don't believe in coincidence in the lives of believers. You prayed for a wife and God brought you two together. You are a perfect complement for each other."

He chuffed. "How do you figure that?"

"*If* she was hurt in some way by gambling, you've both taken action to start a new life. But, Ted, you've got to be honest with her." He rose and put a hand on

Ted's shoulder. "I watch Elizabeth while I preach. She's softening to the Lord. I can see it."

"She's grown in her understanding of God, of His love, but something's holding her back. If I knew what to do—"

"Change yourself before you try to change Elizabeth."

Ted wobbled back in the chair. Jacob's words packed quite a wallop.

"She's got to sense you're hiding something. It's time to live what you believe. Trust God. He demands obedience. If you obey, He'll walk you through the consequences."

Ted met his pastor's gaze. "Now's not the time. Elizabeth has enough to handle."

"Don't wait too long," Jacob said, his words a warning.

Elizabeth opened the door of Agnes's Café, then hustled Robby outside. Their meal had been interrupted several times by friends coming over to say hello. Ducking his head, Robby appeared shy, uncertain, but his sweet smile won everyone's heart. Elizabeth hid her insecurity under flippant words and a spirited demeanor—far more like Anna than her brother.

Taking his hand, they walked to the nearby park not far from town, something they'd done every evening after dinner since they'd arrived four days ago. They sat on the swings and pumped toward the heavens, laughing as they sailed through the air.

Here Robby came alive, behaved like the boy she knew in Chicago, not the hesitant, downcast child he'd become at the farm. Why hadn't he adjusted when he'd practically begged her to live on a farm? Why hadn't the life met his expectations?

Later, sitting on a bench, the two of them leaned against the back. The sun, a bright orange ball, lowered in the sky. If she'd been on the farm, Elizabeth would've spent part of the day working under that glare. Hanging laundry. Picking lettuce or weeding the garden.

Ted, undoubtedly, tended the fields, the animals, all of them needing constant care, a wheel he could never stop turning.

She should be there.

Guilt panged in her chest. An impossible choice—her brother or her duties as Ted's wife. But to see Robby now, smiling, laughing, she'd made the right one.

"I like this park."

"Me, too." She sighed. They couldn't stay in New Harmony forever. She'd made a promise to Ted, to his children, to God, and she had to honor that promise. "Robby, we need to go back to the farm."

"I like it here." His face wrinkled up. "I don't want... Why can't we just stay here, Lizzie? Just you and me?"

"Ted needs me. I'm married to him, Robby. We're a family."

"I want our family to be just us." He swung his legs, scuffing the grass beneath the bench.

"You have Anna, and Henry will be fun to play with when he's older. And Ted will teach you lots, if you'll let him."

"Anna doesn't like it."

"Why do you say that?"

"Her eyes are sad when Ted's nice to me."

"Well, Anna's been through a hard time. Losing her mother hurts. You and I know how much. She doesn't like to share her father and her brother. But she'll get over it. And if you give the farm a chance, it will—"

"No. I want to stay here."

Elizabeth pivoted toward him. "Why? You've always loved being outdoors. The farm's a perfect place for a boy like you."

He bit his lip and shook his head. Mute.

"Tell me. What's bothering you?"

Robby said nothing. Elizabeth waited, sensing he needed time. Space. He kept scuffing lines in the grass, watching the blades flatten beneath his shoes. "What if… what if Ted loses all the money and the farm's all gone?"

In that instant, Elizabeth realized why Robby had refused to connect with Ted, Anna or Henry. Why he hadn't fallen in love with the land, the livestock, the dog. He'd learned in his short life how quickly those things could disappear. In the flick of a card, the flip of a coin.

"Oh, Robby." Elizabeth drew her brother near, until she could smell the soft-scented soap blended with the little-boy scent on his skin. "That won't happen. Ted isn't that kind of man. Everything will be there. Tomorrow and the next day, and the day after that."

He lifted his face to hers, tears filling his blue eyes. "Even…even the dog?"

She smiled, and her vision blurred. "Yes, even Tippy."

He burrowed closer to her, and she could almost feel the weight lifting off his shoulders. "Lizzie?"

"What?"

"Can we go home?" When he turned his face to hers again, the setting sun kissed his cheeks. "I wanna see the chickens go to sleep."

Elizabeth nodded for a moment, her heart too full to speak. "Tomorrow, Robby, after the first meeting of the ladies' club. We'll go home tomorrow."

Chapter Eighteen

Ted had given Elizabeth five days to come to her senses, but she and Robby hadn't returned. He'd handled his household himself. To ask his in-laws' help would expose his wife's defection and give Lily another excuse to harp about raising his children, as if he couldn't handle the job.

He dropped Anna and Henry at Rebecca's on his way in to town, hoping she'd give them a decent meal while he dealt with his wife. Elizabeth shouldn't play socialite while he worked himself into an early grave. And, while she was at it, make him the laughingstock of the whole town.

His children had capsized his even-keel boat. Henry tested his patience. Anna opposed his authority. Only by the power of prayer had he met the challenge. Each day left him exhausted. His respect for mothers multiplied. Especially for Elizabeth, who'd managed his children and his household without the benefit of experience or the connection of blood.

When she'd married him, she'd taken on a momentous task. And now she'd run away, leaving him to handle it alone.

He'd planted the rest of the garden—taking on her chores as if he didn't have enough to do—and attended to his children, feeding them…something. Each day things had gotten worse around the house, more disorderly and chaotic.

Now standing outside the parsonage waiting for Jacob to join him, hands hung limp at his sides, he faced the truth.

He missed Elizabeth the way Adam must've missed his rib. Something essential had been ripped from him, draining him of vitality. Every word out of his mouth took supreme effort. If he'd thought he had trouble sleeping with Elizabeth at home, he'd found it impossible now that she'd gone. His decision to act, to enlist Jacob's help, wasn't just about his children.

Jacob opened the door, plopped his hat on his head and strolled toward him, his gaze somber. "Not sure Elizabeth is going to appreciate my interference."

"Probably not, but I'm hoping your presence will carry some weight."

"Have you forgotten she insisted I add *try* to the obey vow?"

"Hardly." He sighed. "I must've misunderstood God's call. How can I pastor a church when I can't handle my wife?"

Jacob laid a hand on Ted's back. "All in God's timing."

"I hope God's timing includes my wife's return. Today."

Jacob chuckled. "You and Elizabeth are an exact match for the other."

"Match? Maybe as in struck and in flames. A man can get burned."

"I suspect this situation with Elizabeth is providing something you need to learn before you lead a congregation."

"Well, her absence is teaching me plenty." He stopped in his tracks. "You won't believe this. The gossip must've reached Agnes. She drove to the farm yesterday, bringing my favorite cherry pie and offering her condolences on my broken marriage."

Ted would've liked to refuse the pie but it meant something edible for supper. Besides, he couldn't blame this disaster with his wife on Agnes.

Jacob shook his head. "Shame on Agnes for trying to tempt a man when he's down."

"Worse, Henry toddles around the house, looking for Elizabeth, calling 'Mama.' Anna cries at the slightest provocation. Even Rose's hanky no longer consoles her."

Well, he wouldn't let his children continue to suffer. He strode down the street, itching to settle things with his wife.

"Don't look so grim, Ted. You're attracting attention."

Sure enough, a flock of neighbors were converging on them. Why hadn't Ted remembered today was Saturday and the streets would be crowded? He lengthened his strides, eating up the ground on Main Street, trying to outrun them.

"If you expect me to help get your wife back home," Jacob said, panting, "you'll have to slow down."

"Sorry." Ted shortened his steps, moaning when the others caught up faster than a pack of starving wolves.

Jim Johnson skipped backward in front of them.

"Where you going in such a hurry, Preacher? Did Mrs. Mitchell pass?"

"No."

"Where, then?" Jim persisted.

Jacob shot Ted a look of apology. "We're on our way to the ladies' club to try to convince Ted's wife to come home."

Ted gaped at Jacob. When a man shared a confidence, shouldn't he expect his pastor to keep it private? But no, Jacob had blabbed Ted's personal life to this mob. Not that any of these men had overlooked the fact his wife would rather sleep on a cot in one tiny room than stay home where she belonged.

Orville Radcliff whooped. "Yessir. The mare leaped the fence and moved on to greener pasture."

Will Wyatt guffawed, clutching at his belly. "Can't handle your woman, Ted, without bringing in the clergy?"

"Appears she's got a new man in her life."

Ted stopped in the middle of the street. He and Elizabeth might have their problems but she'd never get involved with another man. He shot a glare at Orville.

Jim scratched his head. "Who'd that be, Orville?"

"Not sure which, but one of the Moore brothers. Leastways they hang around her like flies on horse dung."

Ted wanted to slug someone, hardly God's way. But these men were having themselves a good old time, at his expense. And smearing Elizabeth's good name. Well, he wouldn't tolerate it. "Don't you have business to attend to? Supplies to buy? Milk to sell? Instead of making a nuisance of yourselves?"

Orville grinned. "Shore do, but this showdown's gonna be a whole lot more interesting."

"I'm going along because I want to know what my wife is doing at that club," Will said.

Great. Ignoring the occasional elbow jab in the ribs, Ted strode on, determined to keep his life from falling apart. In front of the shop, now whitewashed brighter than a baby's first tooth, he turned to the men. "I'd like to speak to my wife alone. Well, with Jacob here, but otherwise, alone."

Will folded his arms across his chest. "Reckon that's a decision for the ladies."

Ted opened the door. Women gathered at the tables while his wife stood at the podium, unaware of his presence. The ladies had come as Elizabeth had predicted. And from all appearances, they were enjoying the meeting. Elizabeth had captured their hearts just like she'd captured his.

His gaze swept the room. Shelves on the back wall displayed a few books. Red-checked cloths covered small tables with wooden folding chairs decked out in red-and-white-striped bows at the back, fancied up for a party of their own. A pot of violets sat in the middle of each table. White curtains fluttered in the breeze. The room was cozy and clean, with a smidgen of style that shouted Elizabeth.

His breath caught. Why hadn't he grasped how much she meant to him?

Wearing one of her new dresses, the blue gingham, hair coifed like the first time he'd laid eyes on her, Elizabeth made a fetching sight. His treacherous heart skipped a beat. Beautiful—and devious—that described his wife.

He walked in, the pastor on his heels. The room, abuzz with chatter, quieted. Doffing hats, the men crowded in behind him.

"Why, Ted. How nice of you to show an interest in the club," Elizabeth said, polite and sweet, as if she hadn't left him a week ago. "But this isn't a convenient time. We're in the middle of a meeting."

Heat scorched Ted's neck. "I'm sorry, Elizabeth, but this was when I could get away." He spun his hat in his hands. "I'm here to ask you to come back home. Jacob's along to remind you our vows said 'till death do us part.' There's no ladies' club escape clause in those vows, right, Jacob?"

Jacob nodded. Couldn't he at least thump the Good Book for emphasis? The man was worthless at spreading guilt. By now, his pa could've had Elizabeth on her knees. His lungs squeezed. Not that anyone should pattern himself after John Logan.

Ted surveyed the tight-lipped women. By the looks they shot him, he'd already ruffled their feathers. He was on his own with his rebel wife and a roomful of supporters eager to have his hide.

"Who are these men?" Elizabeth motioned to the crowd that had followed him. "The Break-the-vows posse?"

Cecil hooted and slapped his leg. "Ain't she something?"

The rest of the men chuckled. Ted clenched his jaw. It appeared Cecil and Oscar spent more time with his wife than he did. He gave the group a scowl. With a final snicker, they quieted.

Orville Radcliff cleared his throat. "Reckon you could call us a posse. It's got a nice ring to it." He hitched his pants up a notch. "Say the word, Ted, and we'll hog-tie her for you."

"That won't be necessary." Though the idea had

crossed his mind. Ted took a step closer. "I can handle this on my own."

Elizabeth strode from behind the podium, eyes glaring. Had she read his thoughts?

Oscar snorted. "You're in for it, Ted." He plopped a foot on the rung of a chair. "Mercy, my bunion's killing me."

Elizabeth held up her hand. "Don't take another step." She parked her fists on her hips. "I won't have your dusty clodhoppers messing up our freshly mopped floor."

"It's time they gave a thought to the work they make," Gertrude Wyatt agreed.

Ted yanked off his boots, first one then the other, then stood there feeling like a fool in his stocking feet, his big toe poking through his sock. He covered it with the other foot, but not soon enough, from the smile on Elizabeth's face.

The other men complied and then fanned out against the wall in their stocking feet, all except for the pastor. His shoes gleamed, as if dirt didn't dare cling to his footgear.

"I worked hard on those floors," Cecil grumped. "But Elizabeth's biscuits are worth it. Why, I'd scrub the streets for a daily batch."

Ted's gaze darted to his wife. She was cooking for other men?

"I told you it was one of the Moore brothers," Orville said. "They may be getting up in years, but they ain't dead."

"Who said I was dead?"

Elizabeth patted Oscar's shoulder. "You're not dead. Not the way you eat biscuits."

"I see the womenfolk's point, gents," Cecil said. "You

traipse in here without a thought to the mess you're making. As the man in charge of the town's streets, I have my hands full, I'll tell ya. I can sympathize with the ladies."

Elizabeth nodded. "A point well taken, Mr. Moore."

Cecil scratched his head. "What are you saying, missus?"

"I said you make a good point. As the street maintenance supervisor, you've seen the thoughtless behavior of your gender." Elizabeth gave Cecil a big smile. "The women of New Harmony are in your debt, sir."

Cecil puffed up like a rooster. "You can count on me." Then he scratched his head. "Now that gender part, I'm not sure—"

"She's referring to men, Cecil. Shouldn't you be on our side?" Jim said.

"I'm on the side my biscuits are buttered on." Cecil patted his stomach.

"What I want to know is why my wife's sitting instead of getting our supplies at Sorenson's?" Will Wyatt said.

Gertrude stood with her hands on her hips. Mercy, they all acted like Elizabeth. "I work hard all week, taking care of you and the children. I need time away. Like you—hanging out with the men, playing checkers and telling those tall tales of yours—only we're actually using our minds to solve the town's problems."

Will's eyes about popped out of his head. "I've never known you to speak to me that way."

Suddenly the men and their wives stood toe to stocking toe, ready for battle, except for Cecil and Oscar who had no wives, only bunions to keep them company. The whole thing had gotten out of hand.

If Jacob was right and God intended him to learn something from this standoff, He'd given Ted a whole series of sermons on marriage. But right now, Ted wanted life to return to normal, when the house had been peaceful—well, if not peaceful, interesting.

Ted edged closer to his wife. Her cheeks were pink, her eyes shining. His stomach knotted. Maybe keeping her on the farm was unfair. "Can I speak to you alone?"

Her eyes softened.

Around them couples argued. Ted could barely think above the din. A piercing whistle shrilled, shutting down every sound. All eyes swiveled toward his wife.

Elizabeth removed two fingers from her mouth. "Let's adjourn the meeting and serve refreshments," she said demurely. "Mrs. Johnson made the cake."

Soon the men joined their wives, sipping tea. Ted took a chair at an empty table. Elizabeth finally made it to his side carrying a slice of cake and cup of tea. She set them in front of him then took a seat.

He cleared his throat. "Where's Robby?"

"Over at the mercantile, helping unpack supplies."

"How's he doing?"

She smiled. "Oh, Ted, Robby's better. He's been afraid the farm, the dog, everything would disappear like our house in Chicago. I reassured him. He still misses Martha and Papa and grieves for Mama. But he's able to talk about his feelings now."

"I'm glad." He took her hand. "You were right about that. Right about a lot of things." He sighed, hoping he could make her understand how her leaving had turned his world upside down. "Anna and Henry miss you. A lot."

Moisture gathered in her eyes. "I miss them, too."

Hope for his marriage filled him, swelling in his chest until he wanted to shout with the joy of it.

"What about you, Ted? Do you miss me?"

He missed her, all right. More than parched ground missed rain and the grass missed the morning dew. He missed her like he'd lost a limb, a piece of his heart.

But he couldn't tell her that with Oscar and Cecil at the next table hanging on his every word like hungry dogs waiting for a scrap to fall.

"Of course I do. Last night's dinner was a disaster, worse than any meal you fixed."

She pursed her lips. "I can't tell you how much better that makes me feel."

"I'm sorry. That came out wrong." He lowered his voice. "I miss you. More than you could imagine."

Jacob appeared at their table. He clapped a hand on Ted's back. "Well, looks like you two are working it out. I'd better get back before Lydia sends out a search party."

In accordance with the pitiful help the pastor had been, Ted felt like subtracting a chunk from Sunday's offering.

He took Elizabeth's hand. It felt right in his—soft, feminine. Inside that delicate frame resided a strong, intelligent, vital woman. Already she belonged to the town more than him. He knew she could do anything she set her mind to.

He drew little circles on her palm with his thumb. "Hubert mentioned you're doing an excellent job managing his books."

"He did?"

"Yes." He chuckled. "He also said you bartered with him over the price of eggs."

"It wasn't all that hard. He's a softy really. And worn out handling the store."

Ted nodded. "He's talked about selling but can't find a buyer."

She flashed a smile. "He likes you."

"That's nice but I only care what you think of me."

"I think you're a good man, Ted Logan. A good father. A good citizen. But you don't know much about women."

"I know I'm proud of the job you're doing for Sorenson. I know I'm proud of your plans to improve this town. I know I want you to come home with me."

I know I want to hold you in my arms. But he wouldn't admit that when Elizabeth showed no sign of readiness to hear it.

She studied his face. She rose. "I'll go with you."

The weight on Ted's shoulders vanished. Leaning back in his chair, he watched his wife promenade around the room, speaking to her friends. He liked the way she moved. He liked the tendrils of hair teasing against her neck. He liked her smile, brighter than the summer sun.

The front two legs of his chair hit the floor with a thud.

His heart pounded inside his chest. He was in love. Deeply and totally in love with his wife. The knowledge scared him silly.

He watched Elizabeth chatting as if nothing of consequence had just transpired. Oh, how he loved her. Nothing and no one would keep him from his wife.

She went into the back room and came out carrying her satchel then stopped in front of him. "I'm coming home with you. Robby's doing better and we both miss Anna and Henry. And that cot's killing my back."

Not exactly the reasons he wanted to hear. Yet the softness in her eyes gave him hope she hadn't told the entire truth.

"But I'm not giving up this club." She raised her voice

so all could hear. "We'll meet every Saturday. You ladies can count on that."

Cecil hung his head. Oscar toed the floor. "You, too, Oscar and Cecil."

The brothers' heads snapped up and smiles took over their faces.

"I'm ready, Ted, to pick up Robby and head to the farm. I hope you're up to having me around."

Ted opened the door. As she marched through, he glanced back at his neighbors. They grinned at him, as if he'd lost the battle. His wife was coming home with him.

He'd won, hadn't he?

Chapter Nineteen

~

That night Ted sat beside Elizabeth on the swing, the soft squeak of the chain the only sound, pretending nothing stood between them. He knew otherwise. "There's something I need to say."

She turned toward him. Even in the dim light, he could see her eyes glistened. Were those tears? Neither of them would have any peace until they got things settled.

He cleared his throat. "That freedom you're looking for, Elizabeth. It isn't in a place. It's here." He laid a hand over his heart. "Inside you." He waited for her to speak. When she didn't, he pushed on. "I want you to be happy. What do you need from me?"

"I need to feel I'm worth more than how well I handle a list of chores."

"You think my opinion of you hinges on how well you run our household?"

She sighed. "I'm very different from Rose."

Was Rose at the root of Elizabeth's problem? Some false notion she didn't measure up to his deceased wife? He'd probably planted that seed. Not intentionally, but he was to blame.

"I won't pretend you haven't had struggles in areas where Rose excelled. But Rose never got involved with anything outside her family and church." He squeezed her hand. "I'm proud of the person you are. Proud of all you've set in motion to make New Harmony a better place to live."

She touched his cheek. "Thank you for listening and really hearing what matters to me."

"I like that you have thoughts on things." He grinned. "On most everything."

"I must drive you wild."

She did, but not in the way she meant. But if he admitted he loved her, she'd run. He didn't understand why his wife didn't trust love, but pushing her wouldn't work.

"You're vibrant. Fun loving. Smart. This town wants what you have. Needs it. Why, Cecil and Oscar are in love."

"With my biscuits." She chuckled. "Jealous?"

"Of the Moore brothers? No, they're old enough to be your father. But I am jealous of what you've shared with them. How they've helped you while I've stood back—" he swallowed past the lump in his throat "—hoping you'd fall on your face."

The motion of the swing stopped. "You did?"

"I thought if you succeeded at the club, you'd stay away."

"I'm your wife. I couldn't stay away permanently."

"I wasn't sure what you'd do. You're not exactly predictable." Ted pulled her to him, giving her a squeeze in the crook of his arm, then kissed her gently on the forehead.

She stiffened and pulled away. "I'm tired." She got

to her feet, taking her scent, the warmth of her skin, the essence he craved.

A second longer and he'd have kissed her the way he wanted to. He plowed a hand through his hair. Exactly the reason she'd gone inside. He'd thought he had his wife back, but she was as absent as if she'd stayed at the club. What could he do to ease the gulf between them?

As the Logan wagon pulled into church, Rebecca scurried over to meet it then took Elizabeth aside. Giving them privacy, Ted herded the children into the sanctuary.

"Valera Mitchell lost her mother yesterday," Rebecca said. "We knew she didn't have long. I thought we…"

As Rebecca talked about providing food for the wake, Elizabeth could barely concentrate, but nodded at whatever plan Rebecca suggested before hurrying off to join her family.

Elizabeth recalled once again the pain of losing Mama—her shallow, reedy breaths; the last gasp; the final goodbye. Closing her eyes, she tried to block the memories, but tears leaked beneath her lids. Now Valera was going through the same suffering.

Swiping at her tears, Elizabeth forced her feet toward the doors to the sanctuary. Mere feet from the door, she caught sight of Valera coming toward her, wearing black and a serene smile. Though she yearned to avoid Valera's grief, she waited to offer her condolences, her heart beating wildly in her chest.

When Valera reached her, through her clogged throat Elizabeth mumbled something about the sorrow of losing a mother.

"Thank you, Elizabeth. I'm at peace, knowing God was right there with my mother till the end. I'll always

miss her, but it comforts me to know she's with God."
She smiled. "Why, right at this moment, Ma's probably
singing soprano with the choir of angels welcoming her
into Heaven." She patted Elizabeth's arm, offering comfort instead of receiving it. "I'm grateful for my church
family, especially at times like this."

Somehow Elizabeth made her way to the pew where
Ted and the children waited. Henry reached for her and
she tugged him onto her lap while Anna nestled close to
her father and Robby leaned into her. As the song leader
led the opening song, all Elizabeth could think about was
Valera's peace with losing her mother.

If only she'd been close to God when she'd lost Mama.
If only she could've leaned on Him, not just then, but
during her troubles since. But her faith had been shaky,
immature. She hadn't been convinced of the existence of
Heaven. So much had changed. Now she accepted God's
Word as truth. Now she believed God's promises. Now
she recognized only God could fill this hole in her heart.

Since she'd come to New Harmony, Elizabeth had
absorbed Pastor Sumner's words like parched ground
soaked up rain. He'd spoken about God and His love. To
think of God as a loving Father both startled and com-
forted her. Tears filled her eyes. God loved her even now.
He knew what she needed. Knew she sat in this pew each
week hungering for forgiveness, hungering for a clean
slate, hungering for the peace only He could give. And
He gave it freely. All she had to do was answer His Call.

Until now she'd hesitated to give Him her life. Perhaps
pride stood in the way. Perhaps fear she'd embarrass Ted.
Perhaps her struggle with obedience—something she'd
fought her entire life.

When the congregation sang "Jesus is Calling," something inside Elizabeth softened. Her barren conscience bloomed in her chest, cultivating a desire to rid herself of that long list of her sins. She yearned to be forgiven. She yearned to be washed clean. She yearned to start anew.

Passing Henry to Ted, Elizabeth rose and walked toward the front, her legs moving of their own accord, tears streaming down her face. Before she reached Jacob, Ted had found a lap for Henry and joined her there. He took her hand and squeezed it, his eyes glowing with happiness while Pastor Sumner took her other hand. Standing between them, Elizabeth declared her faith in God's Son and accepted Him as her Savior.

After the final song, friends and neighbors gathered round, smiling and hugging her. They were her family now.

Her heart skipped a beat. One day she'd see her mother in Heaven. No matter what had transpired between them, she knew Mama had loved her even when Elizabeth was most unlovable, just as Mama had loved Papa. Perhaps Mama's hope for Seymour would one day be realized. For after today, Elizabeth understood something she hadn't before. God never wasted love.

She no longer carried her burdens alone. She felt her heart would burst with the joy of that knowledge. Peace and a sense of security filled her. She no longer had to scramble to keep her footing.

To control the uncontrollable.

To fix the broken.

To fear tomorrow.

She had only to lean on God. To love Him. To love others.

Whatever happened between her and Ted and the children, God was in control.

* * *

With the children in bed, Ted and Elizabeth stood washing the supper dishes in the kitchen. He scrubbed the plates until they shone, until they reflected his wife's face as she dried them. She looked like the plates, washed clean. Shiny. Like new.

"You can't stop smiling," he said, and he couldn't stop looking at her.

"I'm happy."

He handed her the last plate. "You know we're united now. Not just by that marriage license, but by the love of God."

She met his gaze. "You've mentioned your Call to ministry. You know the Scriptures. You're an excellent speaker. You care about everyone in this town. All to say, you'd make a terrific pastor." She swallowed hard. " What's keeping you from answering? Am I standing in the way?"

How could she believe that? He opened his mouth to speak.

"Please let me finish." Her forget-me-not blue eyes brimmed with tears. "I'm assertive. Outspoken. Independent." She grimaced. "I don't even know all the Books of the Bible."

"You'd be your own kind of pastor's wife, Elizabeth, the best kind. You may not realize it but people are attracted to you." He smiled. "Your confidence in me makes you the perfect pastor's wife."

"So why do you hesitate?"

"The water's gotten cold." He grabbed the teakettle and added hot water. He could let her see a small part of his childhood. "My father was an evangelist. Our family traveled from town to town, holding revivals."

He paused, wanting to share why this town, this church meant so much to him, yet uncertain of her response.

"Really? That must be where you get your love of ministry."

"Pa had the rhetoric." He almost couldn't speak the words. "Then we'd disappear in the middle of the night with the collection he'd promised to share with the host church, leaving behind a passel of confused Christians."

"Oh, my. That had to be hard."

"Most of those anonymous towns my father bilked mixed together in my mind, but one town stuck. New Harmony, Iowa."

Squeezing his arm, she met his gaze. "That's why you landed here."

"As improbable as it seems, Pa believed in God. He'd justified his stealing by saying he had no home church to support him. Conveniently overlooking many a preacher worked another job and rode circuit on Sundays."

As the memories crashed into him, he scrubbed the bottom of a scorched pot. Again and again, trying to remove the stain, but he couldn't. Any more than he could remove what his father had done to so many other towns.

Elizabeth laid a hand over his arm, stopping him, sending a shiver up his arm. "Thank you for telling me about your father."

He had to tell her that his gambling also stood in the way of accepting that Call. That nothing would make him happier than serving this congregation. But they'd never allow him to step into the pulpit if they knew how he earned his livelihood before he met God. If they knew his pa had cheated them out of the offering all those years ago.

If only he could find the words to tell her, but she glowed with her new faith. She had no idea her husband wasn't the man she thought he was. He'd tell her, but not tonight. He couldn't bear to see that joy vanish from her face.

"But, Ted, your father's actions shouldn't keep you from answering God's Call. I'm sure a congregation would understand you had nothing to do with his actions."

Her attention flitted to a space beyond his right shoulder. Something bothered her, but what? She gave a weak laugh. "I'm a fine one to talk. You're not the only one with a parent you're ashamed of. When you asked how my family lost their money, I sugarcoated the truth, spoke of bad investments. But now that you're considering the ministry, I have to tell you." She cleared her throat. "Papa spent Mama's inheritance gambling. She watched him risk and lose everything she held dear— her money, her heritage, her position—and that slowly killed her."

Ted felt the blood drain from his face. *Why, God? Why did You answer my prayers with a woman whose life had been destroyed by gambling?*

"Why does a man do that, Ted? Why does he take such foolish risks again and again?"

His focus dropped to his sudsy hands. Hands that had made mistakes, now like these suds, covered by God's forgiveness, but would that appease Elizabeth? "It's hard to say. Probably different reasons."

"Maybe if Mama had stood up to him, had taken over the money…"

"Maybe, but dredging up the past can't undo it."

She nodded. "I'm trying to let go of things." She smiled. "I'm grateful I'm married to a godly man."

Her words slammed into his gut, twisting and carving him up with guilt. If only the past could be undone. If only he could bare his soul to Elizabeth. He would. But not now. Not tonight.

"If you think the church could handle my father being a gambler and your father being a hoax, then I'll try my best to be a good pastor's wife. God can use us, Ted. I'm sure of it."

He couldn't look at her.

She reached for his face and brought it to hers. "Put your faith in God, Ted. Rely on Him. It'll all work out."

Here he struggled with obedience, his faith in God's plan shaken. Elizabeth's faith was stronger than his. What an irony.

Fighting tears, he tugged her to him, dripping hands and all. This time she melted into him. Oh, how he loved her. But he couldn't say it, not yet. Not until he'd told her everything.

Not until he told her that John Logan had taught Ted everything he knew about poker—tells, how to recognize cheats. There in the saloons, his father was cool, levelheaded, in contrast with the raving, Bible-thumping, hell-and-brimstone preacher in the pulpit both scaring and fascinating Ted.

How could she bear that he'd followed his father's footsteps when gambling had destroyed her family?

Why had he lived such a life? He'd asked himself that question over and over. Why had he done the very thing he'd despised his father for doing? Was it easier than finding his purpose? Had he inherited it like his eye color? Perhaps he'd never know.

The prospect of telling Elizabeth clogged his throat, clamped his belly like a vise until the pain all but doubled him over. He'd told Jacob he'd tell her. But he couldn't find the words.

Tomorrow. He'd tell her tomorrow night after the party he'd planned. He couldn't risk ruining the celebration. He'd issued too many invitations to disappoint people now. But more important, he wanted to give Elizabeth a big party. He couldn't wait to see the surprise on her face.

But after that, he'd tell her about his past. Most likely, she'd honor their vows. But she might also resent him for the remainder of their lives, a prospect he couldn't abide.

If she could forgive him—and how he prayed she would—would his neighbors? Were all the offhand remarks that he sounded like a preacher, his strong sense of God's Call, the open door—was all of this from God? Or merely coincidences?

God, if this Call is truly from You, give me a sign.

Chapter Twenty

With the library hours over, Elizabeth turned the key in the door of the ladies' club, anticipating the meal at the café Ted had suggested that morning. The prospect of a rare meal out put a bounce in her step as she headed toward the familiar team and wagon hitched to the rail in front of the mercantile.

Her breath caught. Could the harmony between her and Ted be too good to be true? Her parents' marriage had taught her not to rely on feelings that could change in the blink of an eye. But Ted was different from her father. She trusted him.

Yet deep inside, in a place she'd learned to heed, she waited for...

For what?

Trouble.

The thought shot through her, landing in her midsection, a cold lump of uncertainty. Her eyes misted. In less than two months, could she really know Ted? Hadn't she glimpsed a hint of guardedness in his eyes, in his manner, as if he held something back? Even last night she sensed he was under some strain.

Lord, please let this relationship be real.

Up ahead Ted emerged from the store with Henry perched on his shoulders, Robby and Anna walking alongside. When the children saw her, Henry's face lit up like a starry sky on a cold winter night. An odd little hitch took Elizabeth's breath away.

Oh, how badly she wanted the love and solidarity of a family. This family. No other would do. Yet, wanting so much terrified her, seized her throat and squeezed until she felt she'd choke.

No, she'd rely on God and ignore the uneasy feelings churning inside.

Anna ran to her. "Look what Mr. Sorenson gave us." She held out a candy stick, already pointed in the shape of her mouth.

"I'm saving mine." Robby looked pleased with his decision. Did he hang on to the good, thinking he might not get another?

Elizabeth forced a smile. "How nice. Did you thank him?"

Anna popped the candy stick out. "Yes. He said, 'You two are mighty sweet, but it can't hurt to add a little sugar.'"

As Elizabeth took in their beaming faces, her smile relaxed and grew. The transformation in the children bordered on amazing. Since Robby had tried to save her from Mrs. Atwater's wrath, he and Anna appeared joined at the hip. Robby now helped with chores, eager to please and do his part. They'd settled into the normal routine of family life.

Anna still had a stubborn streak, but most days she accepted Elizabeth in a mother's role. Most days Elizabeth loved her role. On other days, she wanted to scream. But Rebecca had assured her that was perfectly normal.

Ted stepped toward her, his gaze warm, intimate, only for her. At the tender longing in his eyes, her mouth went dry. What in the world had she been worrying about earlier? This man cared for her. He may not have told her he loved her yet, but maybe tonight...

Oscar and Cecil tromped out of the mercantile. "Howdy." They doffed their hats to Elizabeth. "We're off on our evening constitutional then heading to the café...for supper."

"What's a constitutional?" Anna asked.

"Means, little missy, that we're taking ourselves on our daily walk. Cecil here is checking the condition of the streets but I'm doing it for my health." Oscar patted his stomach. "I'm getting a paunch. Been eating too many of your mama's biscuits."

Elizabeth smiled at the Moore brothers, good friends and an enormous help around the club. "I'd hate to lose my best biscuit eater."

"I believe that's my position, Mrs. Logan," Ted said, running a teasing fingertip along her jaw.

At his slight touch, Elizabeth's heart thumped wildly in her chest. "I thought you were the one who turned that job over to Oscar."

A flash of frustration crossed Ted's face.

Chortling, Oscar slapped his hat on his thigh. "Elizabeth don't mince words." He plopped his hat back on his head. "See you soon...er, later."

The two men shuffled on as they did every evening. They might not have speed but they made up for it with endurance.

"I've got to agree with Cecil. I like a woman who

speaks her mind," Ted murmured in her ear before tugging playfully at Anna's pigtails. "Ready for supper at the café, Anna?"

Too excited to stand still, Anna and Robby ran around Elizabeth's skirts. Henry squealed and clapped his hands at their antics. "Looks like we're more than ready," Elizabeth said, knowing full well that she withheld all the confusing feelings reeling in her head. But how could she harbor these doubts when all she had to base them on was the feeling Ted kept a secret?

"Then let's go." Ted shoved his purchases under the seat of the wagon then returned to the boardwalk.

In front of the café, Rebecca, Dan and their brood pulled up in their wagon. Their children scrambled down, two of the boys swatting at each other along the way. Rebecca clutched the baby to her bosom as her husband helped her down. "Sorry. We're late."

Elizabeth looked at Ted. "Late for what?"

"Why, ah, late for…spring. Here we've come to town to celebrate the first day of spring and we're a week late."

Elizabeth didn't believe a word of it. "What's going on?"

"Good job, wife," Dan mumbled, as he whisked Henry off Ted's shoulders, then herded his wife and all the youngsters into the café.

Alone on the street, Ted's large hand swallowed up hers and tugged her close. The gaze he turned on Elizabeth was tender, filled with hope and dancing with excitement. Lost in his silver-blue eyes, she held her breath, waiting for what he had to say. But instead he lowered his head and kissed her until her heart rat-a-tatted in her chest.

"Today is the two-month anniversary of our marriage. We didn't have a proper wedding so I invited our friends and neighbors to the café tonight to share in the celebration."

Tears gathered in Elizabeth's eyes. Ted had done this for her? How could she have doubted him? "I don't know what to say…" She rose on her tiptoes and kissed his cheek. "Except thank you."

"You deserve a party for all you've done for us, for all we've put you through." He grinned. "For the pain of flopping, pecking chickens, for a smart-mouthed daughter and damaged silk shoes—to name just a few."

He hauled her to the café door and opened it. A cheer went up. Half the town had gathered in the café, grinning and clapping. Robby and Anna darted toward them. The Moore brothers had cut their walk short, the Sorenson, Sumner, Wyatt, Radcliff, Johnson and Harper families—everyone who'd befriended her, gathered round, thumping Ted on the back and giving Elizabeth a hug. Lois Lessman and her husband stood on the fringes smiling. In the far corner, Lily and Richard even beamed their approval.

Elizabeth pressed a hand against her mouth. "I can't believe this!"

Ted touched her cheek. "I know how hard it's been, being away from the city, away from the polite society you've been accustomed to." He tucked a curl behind her ear. "I want to show you how much…" He paused. "How much—"

"You've become an important part of this town," Lydia Sumner broke in. "Not just by marrying Ted and giving that man some joy, but by starting our library and rallying us ladies to make changes in town. And you know what? That's made some lovely changes in us, as well."

"Oscar brought his fiddle and I got my harmonica," Cecil said, and both produced the instruments to prove it.

Like a mother hen with outstretched wings, Rebecca shooed the children in front of her to a table along the back wall. The group dispersed, moving toward their seats, laughing, no doubt, at the shock still lingering on Elizabeth's face.

"And I knew it wouldn't be a proper celebration without your family," Ted said, and then opened the door. There in the opening stood Papa and Martha. "Your father wired me while you were staying at the club and asked to come here."

Her heart leaped into her throat. She ran to them, throwing her arms around them, nestling into the warmth of Martha's girth, drinking in the love in their eyes, inhaling the familiar scent of Papa's aftershave on his handsome, smiling face.

"Princess, I've finally grown up." Her father's smile faltered. "I'd like to start over in this town if it's all right with you. To give you and Robby the love I was too... preoccupied to give."

"Only if you stop calling me princess!"

When she finally disentangled herself, Elizabeth noticed Martha had stepped back into the circle of Papa's arm and the two of them stared into each other's eyes, like love-struck youngsters.

That's why Papa finally understood love. He shared it with Martha. Elizabeth couldn't stop smiling. She hoped the temptation to gamble wouldn't take Papa over and ruin what he and Martha had.

Bubbling over with joy, Elizabeth introduced Papa and Martha to Ted.

Her father extended his hand. "Good to meet you at last, Ted."

Ted shook hands with Papa then took a step away. "We should get seated. Agnes has lots of food waiting on us."

But Papa hadn't released Ted's hand. "I know you from somewhere."

"Me? No." Ted pulled his hand out of Papa's. "Let's—"

"I remember now." The friendly look dropped from Papa's face. An ominous huff slid from his lips. "You're that gambler."

People pivoted their way, quieted. Watching. Listening.

"Sir, I'm—" Ted didn't finish.

Elizabeth grabbed hold of her father's arm. "You're mistaken. Ted's no gambler. He's a farmer."

Papa snorted and draped a protective arm over her shoulders. "Then he's bluffed you. You're not married to Ted Logan, farmer." He paused, his gaze connecting with Ted's—cold, hard, accusing. "You're married to Ted 'Hold 'Em' Logan, a no-account riverboat gambler!"

A collective gasp rose from their neighbors. Rebecca gathered the children and ushered them out of the door, shooting one last glance at Elizabeth.

The words tore through Elizabeth with the impact of a gunshot. The blood drained from her head and she staggered. Papa kept her on her feet.

Ted took a step back, his face pale beneath his farmer's tan. Their gazes locked. The repentant look in his eyes said it all. Bile rose in Elizabeth's throat, choking her as hope for their future drained out of her.

She'd been right. She couldn't trust this man.

Will Wyatt scratched his head. "Ted's a riverboat gambler? You must be mistaken. Why, he's a pillar of the community."

Jim Johnson slapped his hat against his leg. "Ted's lived in New Harmony for what, nine years? Never left except'n to pay a visit on Rose's folks and that ain't near no river."

A knot of pain settled in Elizabeth's chest, squeezing against her lungs until she fought for air. Her husband, the man she'd given her heart to, was just like Papa. Ted might not have gambled in the past two months while she'd lived in his house, but what did that mean? Two months was nothing.

Her father had stopped on occasion, each time promising a new start. But in the end, he chose the thrill of risking everything over his family. That craving had killed her mother. Ruined their lives. Driven her to marry Ted.

At the irony, a harsh laugh left her lips, the sound bitter, defeated. Ted reached for her. She slapped his hand away.

"Elizabeth, you have to believe me. That's in my past."

"Why should I believe you?"

"I thought you knew me," Ted said.

"I thought the same." Tears spilled down her cheeks. "After everything I told you, how could you hide this from me?"

His pale blue eyes filled with misery. A calculated bluff, no doubt, to win her sympathy. Well, she wasn't stupid.

"I was afraid of your reaction. Afraid of what it would mean for the children if the truth came out. Please believe me. I'm not the man your father remembers."

Seymour gave her shoulder a squeeze. "I wasn't the father I should've been, but I won't let you remain under this man's roof. You and Robby are coming home with me. I know better than anyone—a man like that can't be trusted."

"Just where would home be, Papa?"

Her father looked as if she'd slapped him, gnawing at her conscience. But Elizabeth was sick of all this posturing. Papa. Ted. They'd both caused her enough pain to last a lifetime.

"I'd thought it would be here in New Harmony. But home will be wherever we make it. Martha, Robby, you and me," he said.

Richard Stevens pointed a finger at Ted. "Did Rose have to live with that burden? It must have hastened her death. Lily and I aren't inclined to leave our grandchildren with a gambler."

Soon neighbors surrounded them, all taking sides. Pastor Sumner waved his hands, trying to calm the crowd while Lydia's lips moved in silent prayer.

"Stop it! This isn't your fight." Elizabeth turned on Ted. "I've been such a fool, worrying that a *godly* man like you, a man called to *preach* wouldn't understand my father's compulsion."

She snorted. "You told me once that the truth sets a man free. Every word out of your mouth was a lie!" She pounded her fists on his chest, watched him flinch, but he made no attempt to stop her. "Did you find deceiving me amusing?" Her hands fell away. "Well, I won't be fooled again." She wheeled on her father. "Not by any man."

She looked around the room, so quiet she could've heard a pin drop. "I'm sorry for flinging our dirty laundry in your faces. There will be no celebration, but please, stay, have dinner. It's all part of the show."

With that, Elizabeth strode out of the café on wooden legs, holding herself together with her fury, and walked the short distance to the ladies' club. Her hands shook so badly, it took three attempts before she could get the key in the opening. Once inside, a moan escaped her lips. She clamped her jaw, then sank into a chair, numb, sick to her stomach.

Tears slipped past her cheeks. She swiped them away with a hand. Why cry? Why mourn the loss of a man she never knew? Even as she thought it, her heart shattered. She thought she'd found love, home, family.

Why had she fallen in love with her husband?

Look where love had gotten her. She knew better. She knew the risks. She knew she couldn't trust him. But no matter how much she'd kept expecting that shoe to drop, the reality hurt. Hurt more than she'd ever imagined.

Now she lived Mama's life.

Well, she wouldn't take to her bed. But what would she do? Where would she go? She was caught in the same trap as Mama.

"Elizabeth, can I have a few words with you?" Hat in hand, Pastor Sumner stood in the doorway. "I'll only take a minute."

"I don't want a lecture on forgiveness."

"I've learned hurting people need a good meal or a helping hand or maybe just someone to hold their hand. What they don't want is advice. But I can't seem to stop myself. I apologize for that in advance."

"You're right about all that, you know." She sucked in a breath. "So what's your advice? Besides to forgive.

Besides submitting to my vows until the marriage destroys me?"

"Marriage is a holy bond. And yes, forgiveness is a command. We're forgiven as we forgive, but there's something else I need to say."

She raised her head, daring him to sermonize when her world had turned upside down. Yet she wanted an answer, a way to get through this mess. "What?"

"A couple weeks ago, Ted told me about this strong Call to ministry, certain he'd misread God's will. Then he told me why. I wasn't as shocked as he'd expected. You see, I've got a past I'm not proud of."

He let that statement hang in the air between them.

"I pointed out that many men God used in the Bible had done shameful things. Yet God used those imperfect men. In fact, He handpicked them for His service."

Elizabeth didn't speak. She didn't trust her voice or the words shoving to get out of her mouth.

"There's a story in Luke's seventh chapter of the sinful woman who washed Jesus' feet with her tears and wiped them with her hair. The woman proves that those who are forgiven much love much. Ted's a grateful, changed man. I believe him, Elizabeth. Ted gambled in the past. He's not a gambler now."

He peered into her eyes. "Can you find it in your heart to forgive him?"

"He's lost my trust. He could return to that life. My father did time and again."

"Do you really believe Ted would return to a life that would put his family's security at risk? Do you believe he loves gambling more than he loves his family? More than he loves God?

"You're strong, Elizabeth. Lydia said she'd never have

had the courage to leave her home, her family and travel alone without money to marry a stranger. But you have more than courage, Elizabeth. You have God. He'll get you through this. Talk to Him."

"Why didn't Ted tell me?" The words ripped from her throat. "Especially after I told him about my father's gambling."

"Ah, that would be fear. Fear of losing you."

"Ted doesn't care enough about me to hold such a fear. Our marriage is a business arrangement, a convenience for us both."

"Oh, Elizabeth, I wish you could've been there when Ted asked for my help to convince you to come back home." Pastor Sumner patted her hand. "Let me pray with you." He bowed his head and beseeched God to give her wisdom, strength, all she needed. "God will reveal the truth." He opened the door to leave. "Will you talk to Ted?"

What was the point? Papa's gambling had taught her how easily the dice could flip. "I'll talk to him, but I won't be taken in by his promises."

Pastor Sumner nodded. "Pray, Elizabeth. Talk to God. He loves you both," he said, then closed the door behind him.

Feeling drained, she rose and walked to the back room where she and Robby had stayed. She'd stay here tonight until she could think. She looked out the window at the creek running along the edge of the property, low from the lack of rain.

On past the mercantile she glimpsed a man sitting on a rock, hunched forward, his elbows resting on his knees and his hands dangling in front of him, staring down into the creek. Even from here those powerful shoulders and that windblown blond hair told her the man's identity. Ted. Probably praying.

Tears streamed down her face. Ted's arms had come to mean acceptance. Home. Joy.

How could she ever trust him again?

What did God think about all this? As Pastor Sumner said, she needed to talk to God. Then she'd talk to Ted.

Though talking to Ted would be a waste of time.

Ted rose from his position on the rock and Elizabeth stepped back from the window, not ready to talk to him. Yet.

Papa wanted her. Martha, too. But had Papa changed, really? "Lord, I don't know what to do. Show me the way."

A gloved hand clamped over her mouth, stifling the scream pushing up her throat. Rough hands hauled her back against a man's chest.

Fear gripped her and confusion muddled her thoughts. Who had her? What did he intend? Nothing good.

Heart pounding and tasting blood, she thrashed against him. Failing to get free, she bit the gloved hand covering her lips but didn't reach skin.

A mouth lowered to her ear. "If you're smart, Elizabeth, you'll forget about God and take orders from me."

Adrenaline shot through her. She twisted, turned, battled against the viselike grip, lurching until she heard the sound of ripping fabric. Pins fell from her hair, clinking against the wooden floor. *God, help me!*

She smashed her heel into a shin. Her captor cursed, then slammed her to the floor and pulled a bandanna between her lips. Dragging her into a sitting position by her arm, he shoved her hands behind her back and bound them with a length of rope he'd tugged from his jacket. Then, smirking at her, he tied her feet.

Her efforts to scream sucked the fabric into her mouth, gagging her. The man scrambled to his feet and pulled a gun, a snarl on his face. "Shut up that bellyaching! You're making my trigger finger jumpy."

She quieted.

"That's better, doll face," he said with an ugly smirk. "Now I can introduce myself proper like. I'm Vic Hammer, remember? We met in Seymour's library in Chicago. I'm here to collect the gambling debt your pa owes me."

Heaving for breath, Elizabeth eyed her captor warily, a little snake of a man, full of self-importance. Anger. Greed. By the shabby clothes he wore, he, and most likely his family, paid a high price for his habit.

Ted had rubbed shoulders with such a man. Rubbed shoulders with her father, a man blessed with every material advantage, yet for some reason had been determined to throw it all away. Rubbed shoulders with every sort of a human being who believed a life of ease could come from the turn of the cards.

Vic walked to the window. "Just what I need—a messenger," he said then slipped out the door.

Ted stared into the creek. Much-needed rain would fill it to overflowing but only a trickle of water ran through it now. He felt numb. Just when he and Elizabeth had gotten closer, everything good he'd tried to make of his life had blown up in his face. Not that he blamed Seymour. It was his fault for not telling Elizabeth before this. His throat clogged. The town would never accept him as a pastor now. And Elizabeth…

He'd lost his chance with her.

She fit him, her shape, her lively mind and her energy. Everything about her fit him perfectly, as if God had ordained their marriage.

Last night he'd come close to telling her he loved her. But knew he couldn't until he'd told her everything. He dropped his head into his hands. From the look in her eyes as she learned about his past, all her feelings for him had been shattered. He'd deceived her, given her half-truths, omitting things he'd feared she'd discover.

How had he fallen into this trap? The same trap of deception his father had lived? He'd told Elizabeth truth would set a man free. Yet he hadn't behaved as if he believed it. He'd kept silent to protect what he had, a dangerous motivation.

Why had he taken the same path as his father and turned to gambling to earn his way? He hadn't intended to. He'd hired on to the riverboat as a deckhand. But one night he'd sat in on a game and won. Then he competed every night, getting little sleep. Unlike his father, Ted had a knack for sensing when to hold and when to fold. He lost, sure, but the money piled up.

One windless night his life changed forever. He'd left the game, walking along the upper deck toward his quarters, listening to the raucous laughter from the gallery, the faint call of an owl on shore, the soft slap of the paddles as the boat moved through the murky waters of the Mississippi.

He heard footsteps behind him. Smelled whiskey. Then felt the end of a barrel in his back. "Hand it over, all of it. Or give me the great pleasure of putting a bullet in you."

Ted whipped around, caught the man with an elbow

to the throat, tossing him against the hull. The gun clattered across the wood as Ted trapped him against the side of the boat. In the faint glow from the half-moon, he recognized Alex, the red-haired, mouthy kid who'd lost every dime—then accused Ted of cheating.

"Go on to bed, Alex. We'll forget this ever happened."

"You ruined me!" He sprang at Ted, hands reaching for Ted's throat, coming full tilt. The intoxicated young man stumbled and teetered to the right. Before Ted could get hold of him, Alex tumbled over the rail and sailed down the side, arms and legs flailing. Down, down, down into the water. In his nightmares, Ted still heard the boy's screams. Still felt the whisper of his shirt as he tore out of Ted's grasp.

Ted grabbed a life preserver, tossed it to the river, then dashed to the deck below and dove into the water. Time and time again, he dove, searching. But Ted never found him.

Weak with exhaustion and shaking from the cold, he'd been forced to give up, barely making shore with the last ounce of his strength. He was certain Alex had gotten entangled with the paddlewheel and died.

He collapsed on the bank of the river. As he sputtered water out of his lungs, half-frozen, Ted did what he'd never done before. He prayed. Under the stars, weary with guilt and grief at the terrible end of this young man's life, Ted pleaded for God's forgiveness. In a moment of total surrender, he felt the peace of God wash over him. He met God that night and knew he'd never be the same again.

The next morning, Ted made it to the nearest town and heard from a shopkeeper that a young man named Alex had arrived half-drowned after falling overboard.

God had brought this second miracle into Ted's life. He hadn't caused the young man's death.

Sick at how close he'd come, Ted boarded the riverboat one last time. He packed his belongings and got his money from the safe. He'd found Alex huddled over the rail and returned every dime he'd won from him, reminding him that gambling had almost cost him his life.

From that moment with God the night before, he made a clean break from his existence as a riverboat gambler and gave his life to the Lord and never looked back.

In one of the many towns he'd traveled to, looking for a new beginning, he'd met Rose. She wanted the same thing he did. To work the land. To rear a family. To love God. He'd been drawn to her goodness and proposed. He'd found a farm he could afford in New Harmony and a niche in the community. A chance to give back what his father had stolen from the good people of this town.

He and Rose had been content, something he prized. He'd seen little evidence of it in his father's life and among the gamblers he'd known. He'd grieved when Rose's life had been cut short. He cared for her and she'd believed in him.

But then gambling hadn't destroyed Rose's family as it had Elizabeth's. Whatever feelings Elizabeth had for him, he'd destroyed them now.

He hurled a small stone into the water. It skipped across the creek then disappeared beneath the surface. Waves flowed out in ever-growing circles wherever the stone had touched. Ted's silence had produced ramifications that rippled outward, affecting the good folks in this town, all three children but most of all Elizabeth. If only he'd admitted his past.

Well, he couldn't change that now. Could he and Elizabeth get beyond all the lies? Start anew?

There was only one thing to do.

Chapter Twenty-One

The rope was embedded in the skin of Elizabeth's hands and feet, cutting off her circulation. She battled against the fear tingling in her limbs and despair clawing up her throat by reminding herself God would protect her. God would save her.

But as she looked into the dark, ominous eyes of her captor, doubt whispered in her ear. Victor Hammer—Vic—demanded money Papa didn't have.

As he checked her bindings, she caught the sweet scent of whiskey on his breath, the thick stench of sweat, and something more—an odor of desperation oozing off him in waves.

She'd felt that same desperation when she'd come here. Knew it now. The hope fluttering in her chest a moment ago ebbed.

Vic stepped back. He was short, stocky, with a scar that carved like a scythe along his cheek, ending at his downturned mouth. She'd never forget the man or his appearance. That he didn't hide his face now could only mean one thing. Nausea climbed her throat. He didn't intend to let her live.

He paced the room, his steps calculated like a panther circling its prey. With each footfall, the gun in his hand beat against his thigh. Tap. Tap. Tap.

She wanted to scream. To run. To do something. But he had all the power, and she...she had nothing.

No, she had the power of prayer. Closing her eyes, she raised her head and sent an entreaty to God.

"What you doing? Praying?" He snorted. "Waste of time. I ain't letting you outta here. Not until I get paid. I don't care if Gabriel and his hoard of angels come for me. I need that money. All those riches you're enjoying are about to be mine." He snarled. "Your father thought he'd hold me off forever. That ain't smart. You're my bargaining chip, to bring in what I'm owed. All of it this time."

Elizabeth shook her head, fought at the gag, trying to explain they had no money, but her words caught behind the muslin.

Vic smirked. "I don't care 'bout your problems. Got enough of my own." He planted his hands on the wall alongside her head, the gun clattering against the plaster. "If I don't get this money, my family's tossed out on the streets. All because your brainless father wagers money he don't have."

Papa had done this to them. A heavy weight squeezed against Elizabeth's chest. No, she'd brought this trouble to Ted. To this town.

Lord, help us. Please. Before it's too late.

Ted gave his children a kiss then plopped Henry on Dan's lap and helped Anna scramble into the bed of the wagon between the Harper brood. None of the children appeared to grasp the significance of what had happened at the café. Thanks to Rebecca's quick action, they hadn't heard much. "Thanks for taking Anna and Henry home with you. If it's not too late, I'll pick them up later."

"Wait until morning. Give yourself a chance to…"

Had Dan been about to say, *to repair your marriage?* If so, Ted couldn't see how. But he knew God could change his wife's heart, as he'd changed Ted's one momentous night.

Rebecca patted Ted's arm. *Give her time,* she mouthed.

He nodded and tried to smile, but his lips wouldn't cooperate. He waited until Dan turned the wagon and drove north toward the Harper farm. Once they were out of sight, he strode to the mercantile where Seymour waited.

He'd asked Elizabeth's father for a chance to talk to him. The Sorensons had offered their store as a meeting place then gone home. Ted dreaded facing Seymour's wrath. Not that he blamed him. If Anna ever married a man with Ted's past, he'd feel the same.

If only he could talk to Elizabeth. But both Jacob and Rebecca had suggested he give her time. "Let her calm down," Jacob had said. Ted had seen that chilling anger in her eyes. She hated him. Was it already too late for them?

A man who loved God should know better than to deceive. He was a fallen man, a miserable creature who failed God at every turn. What made him think he should pastor a church?

God had.

Well, if God wanted him to pastor, Ted needed His power to resolve this mess.

One step in the mercantile door and Seymour started in on him. "You aren't worthy to lace my daughter's boots, Logan! I want you out of her life. Out of Robby's life." He jabbed a finger into Ted's breastbone. "You hear me? Before you destroy my children—"

"Like you did."

There, he'd called a spade a spade. Not to retaliate, but to push Seymour Manning to face the truth. To face how his conduct, the mistakes he'd made had wounded his family.

Ted's gaze swept the back wall hung with every imaginable tool, many used to dig, to break up, to cultivate the soil. The time had come to examine the choices he and Seymour had made, even if that excavation unearthed a shovelful of regret.

Seymour paled. "I've changed."

"Then why can't you believe I've done the same? Nine years ago, I made a clean break with gambling. I won't go back. Once Elizabeth's had a chance to calm down, I'm hoping she'll find it in her heart to trust me." He swallowed against the lump forming in his throat. "But, even if I lose her, lose everything—I won't go back to that life."

If only he could get Seymour to understand God could change a man overnight, as He had Ted. "I love God, Seymour. I want to obey His teachings. I want to do His will. I want to fulfill His purpose for my life."

Seymour scowled. "Why should I believe a word out of your lying mouth?"

"Why would I want that life? I have my children, my—" his voice caught "—wife. I cherish them. I don't want them to be ashamed of me, as I was of my father, as I was ashamed of myself for following in his footsteps."

Ted leaned his hands on the table. Before him lay the bolts of material Elizabeth had selected that first day. He smoothed a hand over the blue gingham, seeing her in that dress, and then paused at an unraveled bolt of black stripe. "Except for God, nothing is more important to me than keeping my family together," he said quietly.

Seymour rubbed a shaky hand over his eyes. "You're right." He sighed. "All these years, I've hidden from the truth. It's far easier to bluff." His distant gaze filled with regret. "I blamed you and all those I lost money to," Seymour said. "It was easier than blaming myself. Now my children are paying for my mistakes."

"I believe God has a plan for us, a purpose."

Seymour snorted. "What purpose?" His hardened face dropped away, and a whisper of vulnerability wavered in his eyes, like a man searching for something.

Peace? Forgiveness? Grace? Exactly what Ted had craved before he'd found God.

"You think a man like me has a God-ordained purpose?" Seymour said. "After everything I've done?"

Ted laid a hand on Seymour's shoulder. "I think everyone—"

The door of the mercantile slammed open with the impact of a gunshot. Ted and Seymour jerked toward the sound.

Red faced with exertion, Cecil Moore leaned against the frame, panting. "Someone's got Elizabeth!"

"Who?" The question echoed from Ted's and Seymour's lips.

"A man." Cecil sucked in another breath, a third. "Says he wants money to free her."

Someone has Elizabeth. *Oh, God, no.* His heart twisted. His wife was in danger. His mind scrambled to make sense of the threat. "Money, what money?"

Cecil turned to Seymour. "Said you'd know how much."

The color drained from the older man's face. "It's Vic," he said, his words a horrified whisper.

"Who's Vic?" Ted grabbed Seymour's arm. "What's this about?"

"Vic's someone I..." The pallor of Seymour's face gave way to crimson, then resignation. He dropped into a chair and appeared to collapse into himself. "I did this. I..."

And then Ted knew. This was about a debt—a big one. How many times had he witnessed these disputes? How many men had he seen lose their shirts, their horses, their homes? But this involved his wife.

Ted wanted to shake Seymour, demand how he could be so foolish as to lead this Vic to New Harmony, to practically lay a breadcrumb trail to Elizabeth. But Seymour's eyes had filled with pain, regret and bone-deep worry.

Ted reined in his anger. For now, he and Seymour were on the same side—

The side that would save Elizabeth.

Lord, protect my wife. Show me what to do.

Ted met Seymour's gaze. "Vic's here to collect?"

Seymour nodded. "I have nothing to give him. There's nothing left." A sob tore from his throat. "He'll...hurt her."

Not if Ted got to him first.

The *tick, tick, tick* of the wall clock chipped away at the tenuous hold Ted had on his composure, an unnerving warning that, while he and Seymour talked, Elizabeth was in peril. He turned to go then stopped, as a memory hit him. "Seymour, what's this Vic look like?"

"Swarthy, short..." Seymour hesitated then turned toward Ted. "Oh, and he has a scar on his face."

"Right about here?" Ted traced a finger along his left cheek.

"That's him."

It had been years, but some men stuck in your mind. Ted could still picture Vic as clearly as if it were yesterday. "Victor Hammer. Gambler, small-time operator."

Ted had thought him more pathetic than frightening. But get him mad enough and Vic was capable of anything.

He'd once seen him knock over a table and pull a gun when the cards hadn't gone his way. But Ted wouldn't say that aloud. Not to Cecil. Not to Seymour. Not to himself.

Seymour slumped forward. "If only she'd married Parks."

Fire shot through Ted's veins. Didn't he care that Elizabeth despised the man? "What does that have to do with any of this?"

"Vic threatened my children if he didn't get his money. I had to do something to protect them. When Parks agreed to pay the debt in exchange for Elizabeth's hand—"

"What kind of a father would barter his daughter?"

Seymour jerked to his feet. "A frightened father! Do you think I'd force my daughter to marry that old codger unless I had no other choice?" He threw up his hands. "Wouldn't you do anything to protect your children?"

"I would do anything *but* put my children's lives at risk." Ted shook his head. "I'm sorry. We're both worried and my temper—"

"No, you're right. I gambled away everything that mattered."

"It's not too late for a second chance." Ted laid a hand on Seymour's shoulder.

Seymour's face crumpled. "I pray to God you're right." Tears flowed unchecked down his cheeks.

Ted gave Seymour's shoulder one last squeeze then turned to Cecil. "Where's he got her?"

"In the ladies' club." Cecil paled. "Ted, he's got a gun."

Ted's mind sped through possibilities. "If I bust in on Vic, he might panic. Hurt Elizabeth."

Seymour paced the room. He paused and veered toward Ted. "Where are your winnings? Surely you have some of that money left."

If only he did. "It's tied up in my farm."

"Once Vic realizes he's getting no money, he'll kill her. He'll kill my daughter!"

"Not as long as I'm breathing," Ted vowed. "You and Cecil round up as many men as you can. Have them arm themselves—handguns, rifles, shotguns, whatever they've got—then cover the exits to the ladies' club. Don't shoot unless I give the word."

Ted clamped on his hat and strode to the door.

Cecil trotted alongside him. "Where are you going?"

"First to the church to ask Jacob to gather everyone he can to pray. Then to the ladies' club."

"You ain't facing him without a gun, are ya?"

God keep her safe.

She needed—they all needed—a miracle. "I've got the power of prayer, Cecil," he said, opening the door. "And the weapons God gave me."

Ted's long strides ate up the distance from the church to the ladies' club. Around him, neighbors took up positions behind a wagon, from a rooftop, alongside a barrel. The town had turned out to help, either to offer up prayers or carry a loaded gun. As Ted knew it would.

Seymour crouched not far from the entrance, holding a pistol. Ready to do whatever he could to save Elizabeth. Even Cecil and Oscar carried shotguns, looking ready to blow Vic to smithereens. Ted's stomach twisted. He prayed it wouldn't come to that.

God, I love my wife. Help me get her out of there.

And he was sure that somewhere someone loved Vic. But if not, God did. *Let no harm come to anyone, Father. Not even Vic.*

Ted prayed his plan would work. A sense of calm eased the tension in his limbs. With God's help, he would not fail.

He thought of all he knew about Vic. The man was a wretched gambler. He couldn't sustain a poker face during a bluff. Or read tells—all the expressions, mannerisms and intonations that gave people away. But that hair-trigger temper of his posed a threat to his wife. He dared not underestimate the man.

Elizabeth's life depended on it.

Ted banged his fist on the door of the ladies' club. "Open up! It's 'Hold 'Em' Logan.'"

Ted caught a glimpse of Vic at the lone window in the front of the clapboard building. But he couldn't see Elizabeth. He covered his eyes with a hand to block the glare of the late-afternoon sun on the glass, searching for his wife. His stomach lurched. Where was Elizabeth?

"That's my wife in there, Vic. Let her go."

The man cursed. "Do you have the money?"

"I want my wife. I'm not showing my hand until I'm sure you're playing fair."

A pause. Ted's heart dropped ten times in that moment.

"Guns are aimed at the exits, Vic. The men behind them aren't in the mood to jaw. Now open up."

More cursing from inside. Vic sounded close to losing control. *Lord, calm Vic. Show him another way.*

Armed men and a sense of God's protection surrounded him. But where was Elizabeth? His heart stuttered in his chest. Had he hurt her? "I'm unarmed." He'd speak the language Vic understood. "Face it, Vic. I'm the only game in town."

Slowly the door inched open. Ted looked down the barrel of a revolver. "It is you," Vic said. "Raise 'em."

Holding up his hands, Ted stepped inside. While Vic checked him for weapons, Ted's gaze swept the room. An overturned chair. The podium askew. Then he saw her.

In the corner next to the window, Elizabeth hunched on the floor, gagged, feet bound, hands tied behind her back. Her dress was torn and a section of her hair hung loose from its pins, covering part of her face, but praise God, she didn't look hurt.

Frightened eyes locked with his. He yearned to run to her, to hold her in his arms, to tell her he loved her. But that would turn Vic's attention onto Elizabeth instead of on him.

Vic found the deck of cards Ted had borrowed from the saloon. He cackled. "Looks like you're prepared."

"You all right, Elizabeth?" He'd tried to put all of his feelings for her in his tone, in his gaze, hoping she'd see and hear the depth of his love.

She nodded, made a sound he couldn't understand.

Ted wanted to slap Vic silly for abusing his wife that way, for reducing his outspoken wife to grunts or nods.

Why hadn't he told her he loved her before this? The truth rammed his gut. Hadn't it all come down to his expectation that she'd leave him? Wasn't that the real problem? One way or the other everyone, except God, had left him.

Vic finished his search. "I ain't hurt her. Yet."

Scowling, Ted leaned toward Vic, towering over him, every muscle geared to pounce. "If you've got a brain in that skull of yours, Hammer, you won't take that gamble."

Vic looked wild eyed, desperate, his fear palpable, though he tried to hide it with a smirk. "I'm not leaving till I get my money."

Ted had bluffed Vic successfully before. Meeting Vic's gaze with a steely one of his own, Ted crooked up the corner of his mouth. "Why not make this interesting?"

"Interesting? How?"

"You of all people should know what I'm talking about."

"A game."

Ted nodded again. "I haven't played in, what? Nine years? But I reckon it's like riding a horse. I'll put up the thousand that's owed you. And match it with another thousand. The bank's just down the street."

A crafty smile slid across Vic's face. "Winner takes all."

Elizabeth rocked her body, shooting daggers at him with those dazzling blue eyes of hers, now the color of stormy, wind-tossed seas. If he'd deceived his feisty wife into believing he'd returned to gambling, maybe he could do the same with Vic.

Struggling against her restraints, Elizabeth screeched,

the sound muffled. Her eyes burned into him and her jaw worked against the gag, preventing her from giving him a piece of her mind.

If only she knew how much he loved her.

If only she knew she could trust him.

If only his plan worked.

Vic slammed his hand on the table and jerked Ted's attention from Elizabeth to him.

"I ain't got all day, 'Hold 'Em'!"

Lord, help me divert Vic's attention from the game to You.

"You're right, Vic. Your time's running out."

Cursing, Vic's gaze darted to the door of the ladies' club. "What do ya mean? 'Cause if you've got a trick up your sleeve—"

"You worry too much." Ted leaned back, crossing an ankle over his knee, trying to appear calm as every inch of him wanted to cross the room and help his wife.

If Ted hoped to succeed, he'd have to remember every ploy he'd used as 'Hold 'Em' Logan. Keep voice calm, demeanor nonchalant, gaze nonemotional. Vic must never suspect Ted had no money. That the only contest would be a battle for his soul. That was the only way to get through to Vic and to rescue Elizabeth without bloodshed.

Vic scrubbed a hand across his drawn face.

"You look tired, Vic."

His right hand danced near the gun's handle. "Not too tired to pull this trigger."

"Don't you get weary of courting Lady Luck?"

Vic snorted. "Luck ain't no lady."

God, give me the words. "So why do you do it? Why risk everything on the hand you're dealt?"

"Same reason as you," Vic said, glancing over his shoulder at Elizabeth.

Ted tensed, then relaxed when Vic swung his attention back to him. "I don't gamble anymore. Lost my taste for it. Why not give it up? Find a new path."

Vic hooted, the sound high-pitched, nervous. "Easy for you to say. You was a winner." He toyed with the deck but didn't deal. Could Ted dare to hope Vic was listening?

"I may've won pots, but I lost far more."

Vic chuffed. "Like what?"

"My self-respect."

"Crazy talk." Vic waved the cards in Ted's face. "I'd swap my good name, if I had one, for one big pot."

"I did that," Ted said. "I wouldn't do it again."

"Yeah, you say that now with the winnings in the bank."

"You ever look a man in the eye after you've taken his last penny? Watched a young man fall apart right in front of you?" Ted shook his head, trying to dispel Alex's face as he'd come after him. "The gamble isn't worth the price you pay."

Ted could see the wheels turning in the other man's head. He leaned forward, rested his elbows on the table. "You're losing far more than you're winning, am I right?"

Vic's focus shifted to the floor. "Maybe. Still, this life's better than what I had growing up, which was nothing."

"You had a hard childhood?" Ted hoped the casual question would spur more from Vic.

Tapping the cards on the table, Vic stared into space.

"Hard don't even describe it." He shook his head. "My parents came to this country full of dreams. Worked like dogs twelve-hour days, six days a week. For what? A single room in a dingy, drafty, decaying firetrap of a tenement with a single spigot on each floor and a bath down the hall?" Vic's mouth turned down. "My parents died as poor as they lived."

Ted eyed that gun. Still too close for comfort. He glanced at Elizabeth. She leaned toward them, listening to every word, probably praying. He wanted this over for her sake. But he couldn't rush things. "Any good times growing up, Vic?" he said, hoping to soften Vic's mood and get that gun out of Vic's reach.

A smile played around his lips. "Yeah, we had some good times. Everyone was in the same boat. Neighbors would pitch in occasionally, pooling their food. And music." He grinned. "Pop had the voice of an angel."

Ted heard the nostalgia in Vic's tone. He'd try to build one more bridge. A bridge two men could find common ground to stand on. "You got a wife? Kids?"

"Don't everybody?" Vic's glistening eyes belied his tough-guy tone. "Four boys and two girls. They're the reason I'm here to get what's owed me."

"I'm guessing they'd prefer your presence over a hefty pot. I've lived the life, Vic. I know how much you're gone, how much of your kids' lives you're missing."

Vic looked away. "You sound like my old lady's nagging."

"She cares about you. If you want to be a winner, place your bets on something that earns a wage, instead of paltry odds." He leaned closer, locking eyes with Vic. "Live a life. Not a bluff."

"I'm sick of your gibberish." Vic slammed a fist on

the table, then picked up the gun and raised the barrel to Ted's chest. "I'm not here to talk. I want that money now!"

Worry gnawing in his gut, Ted's gaze flickered to Elizabeth. He prayed for words to restore the calm. To save his wife. "You don't want to use that," Ted said, motioning to the gun. "You shoot me and you'll get yourself hung."

"So what?" But the words shook as they left Vic's mouth.

"So what happens after that? After you die?" Ted raised the ante. "I'll wager your parents taught you where that leads."

Alarm slithered across Vic's face. Only for a moment, but long enough for Ted to know the man didn't relish hell. He cursed. "What did you do? Turn into some blasted preacher?"

"Not yet," Ted said. As the words slipped past his lips, a peace slid through him. "But if the town will have me, I will."

Not that anyone could stop a plan of God's.

Vic's jaw dropped. "Why? Why choose that miserable life when you could go back to gambling?"

"I've found bigger riches in a life led by God. That life my children can respect. That life lets me hold my head up.

"Truth is, I didn't always win. But when I did, others lost. I saw the harm that caused. After a while, that eats at a man." Ted jerked his head toward Elizabeth, every muscle ready to pounce. "You've got a defenseless woman tied up, threatening her life." He leaned toward him. "Do you think God's going to smile on that?" He lowered his voice. "You're not a bad man."

The words hung between them, heavy in the air. Just when Ted thought Vic wouldn't respond, he saw a twitch in the other man's jaw. A slide of his Adam's apple. A few rapid blinks.

He reached across the table, connecting with Vic's forearm, a light touch for some strong words. "God loves you, Vic."

Vic shook his head, resisting the comfort, the grace. But then his face crumpled and the walls between him and God began to break. "God can't stand the sight of me."

"You're wrong there. God never stops loving us. He'll forgive us most anything. I know. He did for me. But He expects us to change."

"And do what?"

Lord, soften him. Help me get through to this man. "God gave you something, some talent you've overlooked. Farming isn't really mine. I'm going to put my hand to the plow, but this time it'll be to cultivate the hard ground of people's souls."

Vic's eyes widened. "You ain't kidding. You're a preacher."

A preacher. Ted smiled. He'd asked God for a sign. That sign was Vic's softening. He'd answer God's Call. Preaching was what he was meant to do. "I'm a man forgiven. God changed me. He'll do the same for you. Return to your family. Give your children another legacy. Show them another way. Before it's too late."

Vic picked up the gun by the barrel and handed it to Ted, then gave a weak smile. "I am tired. Those riches you're talking about sound a lot more reliable than these." He knocked the deck of cards to the floor. They scattered at their feet.

The door burst open. Dan Harper came in first followed by most of the men in town.

Someone handed Ted a rope. "No need for that. Mr. Hammer's had a change of heart," Ted said.

Ted ran to Elizabeth's side, weak-kneed and shaken now that the standoff was over, praising God no harm had come to his wife. The idea of losing her tore through him. It would be like losing his own heart.

He untied her gag, then her hands and feet and tugged her to him, holding her tight, never wanting to let her go. "Oh, Elizabeth, my brave wife. I'm sorry you've had to go through this."

She pressed into him. "I'm sorry that for a few minutes there, I thought you'd returned to your old life."

"I'd never go back to that life, Elizabeth. Not when I have everything—everyone—I want right here in New Harmony." He kissed her. "You."

Chapter Twenty-Two

Elizabeth's nightmare was over and Vic Hammer had a new beginning. Thanks to Ted and thanks to God.

"I'm sorry for treating you like that, Mrs. Logan. It weren't right," Vic said, then clapped Ted on the shoulder and headed out the door, a glow on his face. Looking as joy filled as Elizabeth felt when she'd found God.

She walked to Ted, smiling up at him. "You did it," she said softly. "You saved his soul."

"I had a lot of help..." Ted glanced heavenward. "From the Good Lord." When Ted had asked for a sign from God, he'd had no idea what he was asking for.

"You talked to Vic in a way he understood. By using your past, you got through to him. If I ever had a doubt, I don't now. You should become a preacher."

Ted took Elizabeth's hands in his. "Are you all right with that? Being a preacher's wife isn't an easy life."

She grinned. "It can't be worse than skirmishing with the chickens."

The joy of a new future shining in his eyes, he brought her clasped hands to his lips and kissed her scraped knuckles. "It's so much better, Elizabeth, so much better."

Outside, half the town gathered, waiting for Ted and Elizabeth to emerge from the ladies' club. But they'd have to give them another minute. She had one more thing to say. "I think I always knew about the gambling."

"How?"

She searched for the words to explain her hunch that he hid something. Something big. As she'd grown to love him, she realized that if he did, he kept that secret from her for a reason. A reason she couldn't face. So all these weeks, she'd pushed those feelings aside, until her father had arrived and forced her to face the facts.

But that was in the past. They had a new beginning. It no longer mattered. She smiled. "You married me, didn't you? That was the biggest gamble of all."

He laughed, then sobered. "You have every right to be angry. I kept my past from you. I was wrong. I was… afraid. Afraid I'd lose you."

Leaning into the strength of his arms, into the sanctuary of his broad shoulders, she smiled into his eyes. "You couldn't lose me, Ted Logan. Remember those vows we took? I'm here to stay."

He nuzzled her hair. "I love you, Elizabeth Logan."

Heart soaring, joy burst in her chest and she threw her arms around his neck. "I love you!"

The door opened. Papa and Martha crowded up beside her, followed by Rebecca and Dan with their children and Robby, Anna and Henry in tow. She caught a glimpse of all the good folks of New Harmony who'd been praying at the church heading to the ladies' club. These were her friends. Hers and Ted's.

As they entered, the men doffed their hats, looking

proud of themselves while the women clung to their husbands and babies as if they feared a big gust of wind would blow them away. Vic Hammer's redemption had to surpass Ted's gambling, the town's biggest news until now.

Turning toward their neighbors, Ted's intense gray-blue eyes drifted from one friendly face to another. "It's time for all of it to come out. Past time. I remember someone commenting on my name when Rose and I moved to town." His gaze settled on Oscar Moore. "I believe it was you, Oscar." He let out a long breath. "Does the name 'John the Baptist' Logan ring a bell?"

Oscar's brow furrowed. "That no good swine—"

"Was my father."

The silence tore at Elizabeth. Her heart ached for the man who stood before them stripped bare, all the masks ripped away. Shocked, confused, people looked from one to the other, then at Ted.

Oscar scratched his jaw. "You're *Logan's* boy? That phony preacher who stole the church remodeling fund?" He shook his head. "I can't see it."

"Nope, you ain't his," Orville Radcliffe said. "You may carry his name, be his by blood, but you're nothing like your pa."

Will Wyatt moseyed over and laid a hand on Ted's shoulder. "You're one of us, Ted. Everyone in this town respects you. The way you took care of your younguns after Rose passed. The helping hand you give when it's needed. Why, you're someone folks come to for a dose of God's wisdom."

Pastor Sumner stood beside her husband. "Ted, it's time they knew." He turned to his parishioners. "Where do you think the money to rebuild the church came from nine years ago?"

Folks surged forward and pumped Ted's hand, slapping him on the back.

Ted held up a hand. "I've talked to Dan. He's willing and able to handle my eighty acres for a half share until I can get a buyer. You were right about that, Elizabeth. I'm no farmer." Ted tugged Elizabeth close and tucked a strand of hair behind her ear. "You were right about a lot of things," he said softly.

Elizabeth looked deep in his eyes. "And wrong about so many others."

"Never wrong. Different. Different is refreshing." He studied her face. "Once we sell the farm, I want to help Seymour repay Vic."

Unable to speak, Elizabeth hugged Ted, her eyes brimming with happy tears.

"Ted, as the chairman of the elders," Will said, "I'm here to ask you to fill the pulpit this next week while Jacob's off preaching at their home church."

Onlookers smiled and cheered their approval. Through the open doorway and windows, thunder rumbled off in the distance. Every eye and ear tuned in to the sound of the promise of rain, bringing smiles to their faces.

Papa stepped closer, tugging Martha alongside. "Ted, I can't let you repay Vic. It's time to take some responsibility for my debts. I saw the transformation in Vic. I know the only way I'm going to live the life I want with Martha, here, is if I stop living for myself. Stop trying to bring in easy money, hoping to be a big man."

He motioned to Hubert Sorenson. "I've talked to Sorenson. The store's too much for him and he's willing to sell it on contract. As soon as the paperwork's completed, Martha and I will own Manning Mercantile." He gave her a crooked grin. "Along with a series of payments for the rest."

"Papa, you and Martha are staying?"

Seymour tugged Martha close. "I think we can make a go of the place, especially with a smart bookkeeper of a daughter to keep us on track."

Elizabeth nodded and squeezed her hands together in a voiceless plea. Had Papa stopped gambling?

Seymour grinned. "We'll take ownership of the store as soon as we get back from our honeymoon."

Elizabeth enveloped them in a big hug. "I'm so happy."

"Speaking of weddings—" Ted ran a palm down her face. "Sometimes I marvel that it was you who came to New Harmony, the one woman in the universe who fits up against me perfectly. Who makes every plain day an adventure and treats my children like they belong to her. I'll admit you came to me in the strangest maze of circumstances." He chuckled. "Neither of us was exactly excited about the ceremony."

She laughed. "I marvel how God brought me into Sally's path when she lost her nerve."

"You were never the substitute bride. Elizabeth, you are the genuine article."

"I marvel that the man waiting at the end of the line, sight unseen, has given me more happiness—and grief—" she added with a laugh "—in the past two months than I've had in the lifetime before I met him. I love you, Theodore Francis Logan."

Ted raised her chin and looked deep into her eyes. "I love you, Elizabeth Manning Logan. I've got one more thing to say—"

"Get on with it, Ted. My bunions are killing me," Oscar grumbled. "I never heard a man go on so."

The room erupted with laughter.

"I will if our friends will hold their horses." He bent down on one knee and took her hand. "Elizabeth, will you do me the great honor of renewing our wedding vows?"

Tears stung her eyes. "Yes. I'll even agree to obey this time."

"And why is that?"

"Because I know you'd never ask anything of me that wasn't for my good and in obedience to God." She laughed. "Though I hope that vow won't go to your head, 'cause if you turn bossy—"

"She'll put you in your place," Oscar finished.

Ted grinned. "I'd never try to boss a woman who wears the pants as well as you do." He laid a tender hand on her cheek. "No more lies between us."

"None." She pursed her lips. "Well, almost none."

Ted rolled his eyes heavenward. "What now?"

"I'll speak the truth, except for the number of meals that go into the slop jar."

He chuckled and gathered her in his arms. "Jacob and Lydia are waiting at the church, ready for the ceremony as soon as we can get there. The café is decorated. After one false start, Agnes is expecting us to gather in for our reception. So if you haven't any objections, I'd like to renew our vows now."

"I'm not thrilled with my dress, Ted Logan," Elizabeth said. "Ripped cotton twill is hardly the stuff of weddings."

Rebecca grinned. "I finished that second dress I owed

you, Elizabeth. It's yellow dimity, not a true bridal gown, but right pretty."

Elizabeth smiled. "In that case, Mr. Logan, I'll marry you again. Today."

"You've made me the happiest man in the world!" He lifted her off her feet and swung her in a circle until she was breathless and a bit dizzy.

Lightning streaked in the sky and the first real downpour in months soaked the ground. Rain meant the crops would grow.

With a smile on her face and her children crowding around her, Rebecca opened the door wide, letting in the sight and scent of rain. "A rainy day is the luckiest day for a wedding," she promised.

Elizabeth knew luck had nothing to do with it. "Thank You, God," she whispered, smiling through her tears at Ted. "Thank You for answering my prayers."

"And mine," Ted said, glancing to the sky.

Then for all the days they'd shared and all the days to come, he sealed their love with a kiss.

* * * * *

Florida native **Carla Capshaw** is a preacher's kid who grew up grateful for her Christian home and loving family. Always dreaming of being a writer and world traveler, she followed her wanderlust around the globe, including a year spent in China, before beginning work on her first novel.

A two-time RWA Golden Heart® Award winner and double RITA® Award finalist, Carla loves passionate stories with compelling, nearly impossible conflicts. She's found inspirational historical romance is the perfect vehicle to combine lush settings, vivid characters and a Christian worldview. Currently at work on her next manuscript, she still lives in Florida, but is always planning her next trip…and plotting her next story.

Carla loves to hear from readers. To contact her, visit www.carlacapshaw.com or write to carla@carlacapshaw.com.

Books by Carla Capshaw

Love Inspired Historical

The Gladiator
The Duke's Redemption
The Protector
The Champion
Second Chance Cinderella

Visit the Author Profile page
at Harlequin.com for more titles.

THE GLADIATOR

Carla Capshaw

And we know that all things work together for good
to them that love God, to them who are the called
according to his purpose.

—*Romans* 8:28

Dedicated to:

My son, Deverell—my best blessing.

My parents, for their constant love and
encouragement.

My sister, Nikki.
A talented, savvy woman-of-all-trades.
You're the best friend a girl could have.

My critique partners, Sheila Raye,
Paisley Kirkpatrick, Stacey Kayne and Jean Mason.
What would I do without you? Thank you for
not only reading my stuff, but for being amazing
friends who also happen to be awesome writers.

My agent, Michelle Grajkowski
of Three Seas Literary, for believing in me even when
I insisted on writing "unpopular" time periods.

My editor, Melissa Endlich,
for taking a chance on a new author.
Your patience with this newbie won't be forgotten.

And last, but most, thank You, Lord.
You never fail me. Your inspiration is endless.

Chapter One

Less than a day's journey from Rome, 81 AD

"Look around you, Niece. The gods are punishing you."

Pelonia raised tear-swollen eyes from her beloved father's lifeless face. From where she sat on the ground, her uncle Marcus towered over her, his mouth twisted in a snarl of contempt. Blood oozed from a gash at his temple.

Dazed by his cruel words, she watched him limp toward the torched wagons and pillaged tents of their once wealthy camp. Black smoke stretched toward the heavens. Its sharp stench singed her nostrils, burning her lungs until the fetid air promised to choke her.

Her father's head in her lap, Pelonia stroked his weathered cheek with trembling fingers. Was Uncle Marcus right? Was she being punished? Had her father been wrong to reject the old ways and teach his household to embrace the Christ?

Everywhere she looked, destruction sweltered in the morning's rising heat. All of her family's accompanying servants lay massacred along both sides of the stone-paved road. Only she and Marcus survived.

Pelonia looked toward the cloudless sky. Birds of prey circled overhead. Their hungry cries echoed in the still-ness, mocking her as though they sensed she would join the corpses before she had time to bury them.

On the horizon, a cloud of dust marked the direction of their attackers' retreat. The marauders had struck be-fore first light. She'd heard their battle cry from down-stream where she'd sneaked away to bathe in private. By the time she ran back to camp, they'd taken flight. The demon's spawn had stolen everything of value—animals, spices meant as a gift for her cousin's wedding in Rome, and chests packed with rare purple cloth.

Worst of all, they'd murdered her father.

A wail of anguish rose in her throat, but she bit her lip to keep from surrendering to her grief. Her father would want her to be strong. She couldn't bear to disappoint him. Instead, she bent over his precious body and bur-ied her face in his tunic, begging her Lord to restore his life, just as He had once done for Lazarus.

Long moments passed. No miracle came from heaven, only silence.

She sat up and brushed the graying hair from his brow. Bowing her head, she rocked gently, clinging to her composure when pain threatened her sanity.

God, oh God, her heart cried out. *How could You allow this? Why have You forsaken me when I have served You from my earliest days?*

Her uncle's hulking shadow loomed above her. "Hurry up, girl. There's nothing more we can do here."

Pelonia's head snapped up. "We can't leave our dead exposed! Already the vultures circle above us. Soon the wolves will come. Will you have our loved ones ravaged by both fowl and beast?"

Marcus kicked a rock with his sandaled foot. "I care not. I didn't pretend death and elude our attackers to die of thirst in this glaring heat."

"You pretended death? How could you not aid my father or defend—"

"Cease," he growled so close to her nose his stale breath made her shudder. "Someone knocked me unconscious. When I awoke… Why should I have sacrificed my life for nothing?"

"Because it is your *duty* to defend your family. And to see the dead properly cared for."

"Don't lecture me, girl!" Color ran high across his cheekbones. "I won't suffer your guilt when all but your father have traveled to Paradise. They won't know if their flesh is left to rot, nor will they care."

Pelonia adjusted her father's tunic, wishing she had clean linen to shroud him and the others before placing them in the ground. "Father's spirit is in heaven, Uncle, as are the rest of those who've died here."

"Then their bodies are of no consequence." His upper lip curled with ill-concealed scorn. "According to your religion, your God will give them new ones."

Pelonia winced. Marcus clung to his pagan beliefs, despite her father's years of prayer and good example. She lifted her gaze and squinted at the sun glinting over his shoulder. "How can you be so cruel? Except for me, Father was your last remaining kin."

His hawkish eyes narrowed. "Pelonius is dead, but I continue to breathe. Soon scavengers will see the smoke. We won't be safe once they come to investigate. Unless you wish to join these unfortunate wretches, we must leave *now*."

"No!" She eased her father's head to the damp earth and stood, bristling with defiance. "I won't abandon him or our servants. It's indecent and disrespectful. I won't do it."

His hand jerked up to strike her, but she didn't flinch. Jaw flexing with unconcealed rage, he dropped his fist back to his side.

As though he couldn't bear the sight of her, Marcus glanced to a point down the road. Her instincts warned her to look, but she didn't dare take her eyes off her uncle. He'd proven on many occasions to be as crafty as the Evil One himself.

After a long moment, his mood shifted and much of his hostility seemed to evaporate. He gave her an odd smile. "Then you're a fool, but I'll help you bury them."

Surprised by his capitulation, she swayed on her feet, light-headed with relief. She glanced down the cypress-lined road. A single horse and rider traveled in their direction, but remained at a distance. He didn't look threatening, but wariness pricked her, instilling a new need for haste. She hoped the newcomer proved to be a friend, but after the events of the morning, strangers weren't to be trusted.

Her attention returned to Marcus. "Thank you, Uncle. I couldn't finish this sad task without you."

He grunted. "You speak the truth for certain. You're even smaller than your mother, and she was tiny as a fawn."

"I wish I'd known her." Pelonia hurried toward the charred remains of their camp. Her mother had died giving birth to her seventeen winters past. With her father taken from her, she was an orphan. The thought penetrated her mind like the point of a sword. Her head ached. Loneliness crushed her. She and her father had always been close. He'd treated her as well as any might treat a favored son, let alone a daughter.

Her steps slowed near a destroyed tent. Using a tree branch, she poked through the smoldering ruins, searching for anything that might aid with the burials.

Finally, she found the iron head of a spade, its wooden handle nothing but ashes among the scorched stones and broken shards of pottery. With the end of the branch, she pushed the tool from the embers.

Once the metal cooled enough to touch, she picked it up and headed to the shade of an olive tree. She knelt and began to dig, breathing in the pungent aroma of rich, black earth. Here she would bury her father, her dearest friend and protector. Her chest constricted with the thought of leaving him all alone along this barren stretch of road. Silent tears streamed down her cheeks, despite her best efforts to contain them.

She licked the salty moisture from her lips and dabbed her eyes with the back of her hands. Knees sore, her lower back aching, she finished the shallow grave at last and returned to her father's body. She grasped him under his arms. He was so heavy. Her muscles strained to drag him toward the tree and place him in the grave.

As she straightened his limbs, she thanked God for blessing her with a loving parent, even as she questioned why he'd been ripped from her so brutally.

She caressed his cheek one last time, then tore away the cleanest piece of her tunic's hem. Covering his face with the linen, she choked back sobs. Her entire body shook with sorrow as she placed the dirt over his remains.

"Pelonia, are you not yet finished?"

She patted down the last handful of soil. "Yes, Uncle, I'm done."

Not far away, Marcus waited beside a shallow grave he'd dug with a second, larger shovelhead. She covered the short distance and joined him. "I'll try to be quicker and be of more help. Perhaps if you dig, I can move the bodies and cover them."

The jingle of metal and distant voices carried on the morning breeze. She glanced down the road, brushing her dark hair from her eyes to get a better view. Much closer than before, but still at a distance, the rider continued his path toward them. A large caravan followed several paces in his wake.

From her vantage point, she saw the wagons were too close for comfort. Some covered, some exposed, many were rolling cages filled with people or exotic beasts. Near-naked men, most bound in chains, walked listlessly in the glaring sun.

"A slave caravan, Uncle! We must hide until it passes."

"They won't pester me. I'm too old to be of value and my tunic verifies my rank. *You,* on the other hand, are a prize."

Pelonia blinked in disbelief. Her heart throbbed with fear. She knew slave traders legally bought and sold men, women and children at markets throughout the empire. Ravenous for profit, they often preyed on the weak, prowling the byways in search of free stock.

The morning's events had made her one of the weak. She was the daughter of a prosperous Roman citizen, but this far from home she held no proof of her status. None of her wealth remained to buy protection. Her household had been destroyed. Even her luxurious clothes had been stolen or burned, leaving her with nothing but the simple linen tunic she'd worn to the river.

The feral gleam in her uncle's eyes spread a chill across her skin. "You cannot mean to sell me."

"Why not? You're cursed. I have no wish to invoke the gods' displeasure by protecting you. Besides, I'm your guardian now that your father is gone. I have a legal right to do with you as I wish. After the robbery this morning, I need funds to see me home. You're a comely maiden and will fetch a fair price."

"You're mad!" She darted away, panic pumping through her veins.

His fingers curled around her long hair. He yanked her back, almost snapping her neck and ripping out some of the strands.

His thick arm banded about her throat, pressing the back of her head against his shoulder and exerting enough pressure for her to hold still or choke. "The gods have sealed your fate, Pelonia. I knew it the moment I saw the scout riding this way. I only had to keep you here until he came close enough to claim you."

Terror exploded in her chest. She kicked and twisted, realizing she should have suspected treachery when he agreed to help her bury the dead. Reaching above and behind her, she clawed at his face. Warm blood tainted her fingers. She bit his arm.

Marcus howled and let go. She ran, but he grabbed her elbow and spun her to face him, striking her hard across the side of the head. Her ears rang. Her jaw stung with pain.

Another blow. White specks of light burst behind her

eyes. She tasted blood. He backhanded her left cheek. She fell to the ground, jarring her bones. The back of her head bounced against a rock. Agony lanced through her skull. Marcus's enraged countenance blurred above her. The edges of her vision dimmed, began to turn black.

"Please, Lord, help me," she whispered, just before the life she'd known ceased to exist.

As the orange glow of early evening settled over Rome, Caros Viriathos stood at the arched second story window of his bedchamber. His battle-scarred fingers stroked the smooth head of his pet tiger.

Torches lit the large walled yard below where a dozen of his best gladiators trained with a variety of weapons, perfecting their skills with each other and several wild animals.

While Caros listened to the clang of clashing metal and the roar of angry lions, his gaze traveled from one pair of opponents to another. He studied each fighter's footwork, his speed, every sword thrust and jab of a trident. At sunrise, he would speak with each man in private, point out his flaws and demand perfection. Death might be inevitable, but it could be postponed. And sending men into the arena untrained was a waste of life and capital.

He knew from experience. For ten brutal years, he'd fought in the games, a slave ripped from his Iberian home and forced to serve a cruel master. As an unrivaled champion, he'd won the mob's fickle affections. They rewarded him three years ago by demanding his freedom as the prize of a particularly bloody competition. Since then, he'd begun his own training grounds, the Ludus Máximus, and amassed a fortune. Even his former master acknowledged no one prepared gladiators more suited for combat than he.

He should have been pleased with his life, or at least his comfortable situation, but deep inside, he yearned for peace.

By day, his work kept him occupied, his mind focused on the task of teaching his men the art of battle. But it would soon be dark and the silence of night allowed the Furies to torment him for his past.

Fists clenched, Caros leaned against the marble windowsill. The aroma of roasting meats signaled the dinner hour. His men had finished training for the day. Their teasing gibes and easy laughter replaced the clash of weapons as they disappeared into the cookhouse. After the evening meal, they'd seek out their beds in the barracks, exhausted and ready for slumber.

Wishing his sleep came as easily, Caros had given up hope of ever winning the battle that waged in his head. For years, he'd fought the riot inside him, arguing with his conscience that he'd been forced to kill in the ring or be killed. He'd sampled every diversion Rome offered in an effort to distract him from the guilt gnawing at his soul. Nothing soothed him. Everything he'd tried proved empty until he had more and more difficulty suppressing the cries of all those he'd slain.

The tiger's tail swished on the mosaic-tiled floor, the only sound in the evening's stillness. Footsteps approached in the corridor, drawing his attention and a low growl from Cat.

A fist pounded on the door. "Master," Gaius, his elderly steward, called through the heavy wooden portal, "a slave caravan has arrived. There are a few good prospects. Do you wish to have a look?"

Eager for a distraction from his thoughts, Caros left his post at the window. He'd lost four men in the ring the day before and needed to replace them. "I'll be down in a moment, Gaius. Tell them to wait."

Caros pulled on a fresh tunic and reached for a weighty bag of coins on his desk. Moments later, he joined Gaius in one of the long side yards that ran the length of the house. The stench of animal dung and unwashed bodies made him grimace.

The slave trader, a stout man, paced the straw-covered stones next to a swaying elephant.

In the torchlight, the newcomer came to an abrupt halt when he noticed Caros approaching. He flashed his rotten teeth and his eyes sparkled with the thrill of a probable sale. He stepped forward, sweeping his stubby arms wide to prove he carried no weapons.

"Sir, I am Aulus Menus. You are known as the Bone Grinder, no? It is an honor to meet you." The slave trader bent at the waist in a flamboyant bow. "I saw you fight once four years ago. You took down five gladiators without a single wound to yourself. I can still hear the crowd chanting your name. It is easy to understand why your reputation as Rome's greatest champion is hailed far and wide."

"I'm sure you exaggerate." Unimpressed by the trader's flattery or the odor wafting from his person, Caros hoped the man visited one of the city's baths at the first opportunity.

"I assure you I don't exaggerate. I've heard your name praised as far as Alexandria. Some even hint you're a son of Jupiter. They whisper your name in hallowed tones and—"

"Enough. If you seek to gain my favor with compliments, be warned, you will not. I'm in need of four able-bodied men, no more. The taller, stronger and healthier the better."

"No more than four?" Some of the gleam left the slave trader's eyes. "I have thirty such men."

Caros looked toward the row of ragged beggars on offer. Sitting in the dirt, most appeared too weak to stand. Others sat beside them, skinny, dejected, already defeated. A few slightly stronger ones leaned against the wall. None of them would do. "Are you trying to swindle me? I need men for gladiators, not lion fodder."

In the torchlight, Aulus's face grew red, as though he sensed a hefty profit slipping through his fingers. "This is not my best merchandise. Follow me and I'll show you a host of potential champions."

Unconvinced, Caros nodded and followed anyway. Aulus carried a torch as they walked past the wheeled cages filled with reeking animals and all manner of degraded humanity. The sight of dirty, hollow-eyed children clenched his stomach. A youth sitting beside them reminded him of his own capture and sale into slavery. His loving mother and sisters had been tortured that day, then crucified while he was forced to watch.

Caros pushed the nightmare away. Resigned to the ways of the world, he hardened his heart and continued after Aulus.

"Here we are." The trader halted beside a wagon. He held up the torch, giving Caros a better view into the small prison where a score of men stood packed like fish in a net.

With a practiced eye, Caros considered them. Swathed in loincloths, all were healthier than the wretches in the first lot, but only two or three had the makings of a fighter.

"I told you, no?" Aulus flashed a confident grin. "Any one of these men could be your next champion."

Caros snorted. "How many champions have you trained?"

Aulus's smile faded. "None, but—"

"Then let me be the judge." He pointed to the three best men. "I'll take them if you offer a decent price. Otherwise be on your way."

"Seven hundred denarii each," the trader said without a blink.

Caros laughed. "You *are* a swindler, Aulus. These slaves aren't worth two hundred. You'll have to do better."

"Five hundred, then."

"Two-fifty."

"Four-fifty."

"Two-sixty," he said, enjoying the barter and the slave trader's increasing dismay.

Aulus glanced at his wares, obviously weighing his costs. "Four hundred."

Caros walked away. Several wagons ahead, he saw Gaius inspecting a pair of giraffes.

"Wait!" Aulus sounded pained. "You didn't let me finish."

With a glance over his shoulder, Caros raised a brow and waited for the price.

"Three-fifty."

He sensed the other man's defeat. "Two-seventy."

"Three hundred," Aulus said in disgust. "My final offer."

"Done." Caros returned to the beaten man and opened

the pouch he held. Coins clinked into the trader's out-stretched palm as he counted out the correct sum.

While they waited for the new slaves to be released from the cage and led around to the barracks at the back of the house, Aulus counted the coins for a second time. Satisfied, he dumped them into his own drawstring pouch as they started back to the house's side door.

"That's only three men, Bone Grinder. You said you need four. If you won't purchase the men or children I have on offer, would you consider a wench?"

"We have enough women to meet our needs."

"I have one you could train for the ring," the trader persisted. "The mob loves a woman who can draw blood. They'll froth at the mouth when they learn she's a Christian as well as a maiden. I can see it now—"

"How do you know she's pure?" Caros interrupted, impatient. "Have you touched her?"

"Her uncle made the claim, and she's remained un-sullied while in my possession."

"Her uncle?" A frown pinched Caros's brows. "Her own kin sold her?"

The slave trader shrugged. "It happens often."

"Were they starving?"

"Far from it. On a better day, I imagine the old man is quite rich."

"How can you believe a swine who would sell his own family?" Caros asked, the question tinged with disgust.

"He swore it by the gods."

"And why should I believe *you?*"

Aulus laughed. "Do you think I would lie to you when you could crush me like an acorn? Besides, why would I allow anyone to touch her and ruin a chance for greater profits?"

"Because you're a swindler."

Aulus didn't deny the charge. A grin spread across his lips. He stopped beside an open wagon where three piteous women sat chained to the sideboards. He lifted his torch, pointing to a fourth female stretched out on the floor.

Caros's gaze flicked over the sleeping girl. Purple bruises marred her small face. Long dark hair fanned out around her head, shining in the torchlight. "You intend to pawn this child off as a woman I can train for the ring?"

"I assure you she's no child."

"Why was she beaten? I've no need for a trouble-some wench."

"My scout said she disagreed with her uncle's plans to sell her and the fellow disciplined her for it."

"When?"

"Earlier this morning."

"She hasn't woken?"

"Once, not long after midday." Aulus waved a fly from the tip of his nose. "She'll come to, but there's a nasty bump on the back of her head."

Intent on the girl, Caros's heart beat with an unfamiliar pang of compassion. Having been the recipient of the emotion so little himself, he'd almost forgotten it existed.

"I planned to sell her to a brothel, but since she's a Christian, I'm weighing my options." A wicked gleam sparked in the trader's eyes. "I was told the authorities will pay…three thousand denarii for such criminals."

His eyes narrowed on the slave trader. The claim wasn't true. The authorities might send her to the arena if she didn't deny her illegal sect, but they wouldn't pay for the privilege. He knew what the other man was up to. Aulus thought he had designs on the girl's virtue and would pay any price to have her. "I'll give you fifteen hundred for her."

Aulus laughed. "Oh, no, you won't cheat me this time. I'll take three thousand, nothing less."

"*I* cheat you? It will cost me a fortune to fatten up those wretches you sold me. Fifteen hundred is an expected price for any female slave."

"Ha! This isn't just any female. Virtue is rare these days. Three thousand, nothing less."

"Seventeen hundred."

"Three thousand is my final offer, Bone Grinder. Take it or leave it, it matters not to me. I'll have my profit from you or the authorities. Either way, she'll end up in the ring."

The girl moaned, drawing a concerned glance from Caros. A voice in his head warned him not to let her go. "You know the authorities will pay you nothing."

"Perhaps." A triumphant smile tugged at the trader's lips as though he sensed Caros weakening. "If they won't, a brothel will. There are few uses for a woman, but something tells me I'm bound to make a profit off this one."

His pride chafing, Caros realized he'd fallen into the weasel's trap. If he paid the three thousand denarii, Aulus would walk away with the exorbitant amount he'd originally demanded for the slaves *and* a healthy profit from the girl.

After another glance at the pitiful creature in the wagon, he didn't even mind being bested. Why her plight touched him when he was surrounded by a sea of human tragedy confounded him, but he had to have her.

Calling for Gaius, he gave him instructions to fetch the necessary funds. Once Gaius ran to carry out the order, Caros took the torch from Aulus and returned to the wagon. Chains rattled as the other three women tried to scatter from his presence, but he ignored them. His newest slave consumed his concern.

He reached over the wagon's side and caressed the girl's flowing dark hair before examining the egg-sized bump on the back of her skull. With great care, he lifted one of her hands in his, noticing the fine bones and the soil caked under her fingernails.

"Master?" Gaius said, out of breath when he returned with a large bag of coins. "Shall I tell Lucia to prepare a mat for the new slave?"

The slave's hand still in his grasp, Caros nodded. "Tell her to fix one of her herbal concoctions as well. When the girl awakes, she's going to need relief from her pain."

As soon as his steward walked away, Caros heard Aulus's knowing laughter erupt behind him. "You're already besotted with the wench, no? I wonder what she'll think of *you* when she learns the number of Christians you've slain."

Chapter Two

~❧~

Angry, unfamiliar voices penetrated Pelonia's awareness. Floating between wakefulness and darkness, she couldn't budge her heavy limbs. Every muscle ached. A sharp pain drummed against her skull.

The voices died away, then a woman's words broke through the haze. "She wakes. Fetch the master."

Hurried footsteps trailed away, while someone moved close enough for Pelonia to sense a presence kneel beside her.

"My name is Lucia. Can you hear me?" The woman pressed a cup of water to Pelonia's cracked lips. "What shall I call you?"

Pelonia coughed and sputtered as the cool liquid trickled down her arid throat. Swallowing, she grimaced at the throbbing pressure in her jaw. "Pel... Pelonia."

"Do you remember what happened to you? You were struck on the head and injured. You have bruised ribs. From the swelling, one or more may be cracked, but I believe none are broken. I've been giving you opium to soothe you, but you're far from recovered."

Her eyelids too heavy to open, Pelonia licked her

chapped lips, hating the rotten taste in her mouth. Uncomfortable heat warmed the right side of her face.

Gradually, her mind began to make sense of her surroundings. The warmth must be sunshine because the scent of wood smoke hung in the air, yet she heard no crackle of a fire. Her pallet was a coarse blanket on the hard ground. Vermin crawled in her hair, making her itch. Dirt clung to her skin and each of her sore muscles longed for the tufted softness of her bed at home.

Home.

Her muddled brain latched on to the word. Where was she if not in the comfort of her father's Umbrian villa? Where was her maid, Helen? Who was this woman Lucia? She couldn't remember.

Icy fingers of fear gripped her heart as one by one her memories returned. First the attack, then her father's murder. Raw grief squeezed her chest.

Confusion surrounded her. Where was her uncle? She remembered the slave caravan, his threat to sell her, but nothing more. Had Marcus succeeded in his treachery, or had someone come to her aid?

Panic forced her eyes open. Light stabbed her head like a dagger. She squeezed her lids tight, then blinked rapidly until she managed to focus on the young woman's face above her.

"The master will be here soon." A smile tilted Lucia's thin lips, but didn't touch her honey-brown eyes. "He commanded me to call for him the moment you woke."

"Where…am I?" The words grated in her throat.

"You're in the home of Caros Viriathos."

The name meant nothing to Pelonia. She prayed God had heard her plea and delivered her into the hands of a kind man, someone willing to help her contact her cousin Tiberia.

The thought of Tiberia brought a glimmer of hope. Somehow, she must contact her cousin at the first opportunity.

Her eyes closed with fatigue. "How…how long have I…been here?"

Lucia laid her calloused palm to Pelonia's brow. "Four days and this morning. You've been in and out of sleep, but now it seems your fever has broken for good. I'll order you a bowl of broth. You should eat to bolster your strength."

Her stomach churned. Four days and she remembered nothing. Tiberia must be frantic wondering why she'd failed to attend the wedding.

As children, she and her cousin had been as close as sisters. They'd corresponded regularly and maintained their deep friendship ever since Tiberia's family moved to Rome eight years past. When Tiberia wrote of her betrothal to a senator, that the union was a love match, no one had been more pleased for her than Pelonia.

She opened her eyes. "I must—"

Lucia placed her fingers over Pelonia's lips. "Don't speak. Rest is what you need. Now that you've woken, Gaius, our master's steward, says you have one week to recover. Then your labor begins whether you're well or not."

"My cousin. I must…"

"You don't understand, Pelonia." Lucia hooked a lock of pitch-black hair behind her ear. "You're a slave in the Ludus Maximus now. A possession of the *lanista,* Caros Viriathos."

Lanista? A vile *gladiator* trainer?

"You have no family beyond these walls. You'd do well to accept your fate. Forget your past existence. Your new life here has begun."

"No!" She refused to believe all she knew could be stolen from her so easily.

Lucia frowned as though she were confronting a quarrelsome child. Tight-lipped, she crossed her arms over her buxom chest. "We will see."

Heavy footsteps crunched on the rushes strewn across the floor. The new arrival stopped out of Pelonia's view, but the force of the person's presence invaded the room.

The nauseating ache in her head increased without mercy. What had she done to make God despise her?

Focusing on Lucia, she saw the young woman's face light with pleasure.

"Master," Lucia greeted, jumping to her feet. "The new slave is finally awake. She calls herself Pelonia. She's weak and the medicine I gave her has run its course."

"Then give her more if she needs it."

The man's deep voice poured over Pelonia like the soothing water of a bath. Despite her indignation, some of her tension eased. Curious to see the man who had such a unique and unwelcome effect on her, she turned her head, ignoring the jab of pain that pierced her skull.

"Don't move," Lucia snapped. "You mustn't move your head or you might injure yourself further."

Pelonia stiffened. She wasn't accustomed to taking orders. Neither her father nor the tutors he'd hired to teach her had ever raised their voices.

Lucia glanced toward the door. "She's argumentative. I have a hunch she'll be difficult. She denies she's your slave."

Silence followed Lucia's remark. Pelonia's nerves stretched taut as she waited for a response. Would this man who claimed to own her kill or beat her? She'd heard of men committing atrocities against their slaves for little, sometimes no reason. Was he one of those cruel barbarians?

She sensed him move closer. Her skin tingled and her tension rose as if she were prey in the sights of a hungry lion. At last, the lion crossed to where she could see him.

Sunlight streaming through the window enveloped the giant. A crisp, light colored tunic draped across his shoulders and the expanse of his chest contrasted sharply with his black hair and the rich copper of his skin. Gold bands around his wrists emphasized the strength of his arms, the physical power he held in check.

Her breath hitched in her throat. She could only stare. Without a doubt, the man could crush her if he chose.

"So, you are called Pelonia," he said. "And my healer believes you wish to fight me."

Her gaze locked with the unusual blue of his forceful glare. For the first time, she understood how the Hebrew David must have suffered when he faced Goliath. Swallowing the lump of fear in her throat, she nodded. "If I must."

"If you must?" Caros eyed Pelonia with a mix of irritation and respect. He was used to grown men trembling before him. With her tunic filthy and torn, her dark hair rippling in disarray across the packed earthen floor and her bruises healing, his new slave looked like a wounded goddess. But she was just an ordinary woman. Flea-bitten and trodden upon. Why did she think she could defy him?

To her credit, she wasn't a simpering wench. Her resistance reminded him of his own the day he'd been forced into slavery. Beaten, chained by his Roman adversaries, he'd sworn no one would ever own him. He'd been mistaken, of course. This new slave would be proven wrong as well.

"Then let the games begin," he said, his voice thick with mockery.

"Games?" she asked faintly. "You think...this...this is a game?"

The roughness of her voice reminded him of her body's weakened condition—a frailty her spirit clearly didn't share. Crouching beside her, he ran his forefinger over the yellowed bruise on her cheek. She didn't flinch as he expected. Instead, she closed her eyes and sighed as though his touch somehow soothed her.

Her guileless response unnerved him. The need to protect her enveloped him, a sensation he hadn't known since the deaths of his mother and sisters. As a slave, he'd been beaten on many occasions in an effort to conquer his will. That no one ever succeeded was a matter of pride for him. Much to his surprise, he had no wish to see this girl broken, either.

"Of course it's a game." He lifted a strand of her dark hair and caressed it between his fingers. "And I will be the victor. I live to win."

"It's true." Lucia moved from the shadows. "Our master has never been defeated."

Defiance flamed in the depths of her large, doe-brown eyes. She didn't speak and he admired her restraint when he could see she wanted to flay him.

Challenged to draw a response from her, he trailed his fingers over her full bottom lip. "You might as well give in now, my prize. I have no wish to crush your spirit. I own you whether you will it or not."

She turned her head toward the stone wall, but he gripped her chin and forced her to look at him.

"Admit it," he said with no pity for her loss of pride. "Then you can return to your sleep."

She shook her head. "No. No one owns me...no one but my God."

He dropped his hand away as though she'd sprouted leprosy. "And who might your god be? Jupiter? Apollo? Or maybe you worship the god of the sea. Do you think Neptune will leave his watery throne and rescue you?"

"The Christ." For the first time, her voice didn't waver.

So, she admitted following the criminal sect. Caros studied her, wondering if she were a fool or had a wish for death. "Say that to the wrong person, Pelonia, and you'll find yourself facing the lions."

"I already am."

He laughed. "So you think of me as a ferocious beast?"

Her silence amused him all the more. "Good. It suits me well to know you realize I'm untamed and capable of tearing you limb from limb."

Her fingers clutched at the dirt floor. "Then do your worst. Death is better...than being owned."

Lucia scoffed under her breath, drawing Caros's attention to where the healer waited by the window, the noonday sun coursing through the open shutters.

"What foolishness." Lucia came to stand by a rough-hewn table littered with the bottles and bowls of her medicines. "I warned you the girl would argue, Master.

I'd wager she deserved the thrashing she received if all she did was quarrel."

"The slave trader did mention she'd been beaten for a disagreement with her uncle." Caros's attention slipped back to Pelonia, who'd grown pale and weaker still.

Concerned by her pallor, he berated himself for baiting her, for depleting her meager strength when he should have been encouraging her to heal. Without pausing to examine his motives, he reached down and lifted her into his arms, prepared for her to protest.

When she sagged against his chest without a fight, her acquiescence alarmed him. She weighed no more than a laurel leaf and it occurred to him she'd eaten nothing more than tepid broth for the last several days. In her weakened state, had he shoved her to the brink of death?

Holding her tight against his chest, he whispered near her ear. "Tell me, Pelonia. What can I do to aid you? What can I do to ease your plight?"

"Find… Tiberia," she whispered, the dregs of her strength draining away. "And free me."

Chapter Three

I will not weep.

Pelonia paused in weeding the kitchen's herb garden and wiped perspiration from her brow. Scents of basil and mint mingled with the sweetness of wild jasmine. A small fountain's splashing water and the aroma of fresh-baked bread reminded her of home.

The garden's rich black dirt stained her fingers, resurrecting painful reminders of her father's burial less than a fortnight ago. Fangs of betrayal bit deep. How could a loving God allow one of His most kind and humble servants to suffer so heinous a death?

Why had God delivered her to this gladiatorial training ground, this disgusting den of violence, to serve as a slave? How did He expect her to face Caros Viriathos on a daily basis when each sight of her captor filled her with resentment and simmering rage?

She ripped a weed from the dirt and flung it into a basket beside her. The *lanista* didn't have a right to imprison her here! In the week since Caros carried her from the slave quarters, he'd provided for her needs and seen her cared for, but his vow to rule over her kept him from finding Tiberia. His adamant refusal to contact her cousin, regardless of Tiberia's certain anxiety, stoked her frustration and her fury.

She sneered at the garden wall that marked the boundary of her prison. Caros Viriathos had stolen her life and she would see it returned. In a few days, her injuries would be completely healed and the occasional blurring of her vision would disappear the same as the knot on her head.

She would escape and find Tiberia, who wouldn't hesitate to buy her freedom. It didn't matter that a runaway slave faced the penalty of death. She couldn't abide the abysmal future she faced living as less than someone's chattel.

The weeds she'd discarded drew her attention. Bitterness bloomed until she tasted it. That's what God had done to her. Uprooted her from the flourishing soil of home and cast her aside as if she meant nothing. How could she trust a God who delivered her into such a deep chasm of despair?

The snap of a twig startled her out of her grim thoughts. A low growl directly behind her raised her hair on end. She froze, her breath lodged in her chest. Why hadn't she sensed the animal's approach? She'd heard the roar of big cats and sounds of various game in the training yard, but was the beast here?

Her heart stopped when warm, moist breath caressed her neck and a large wet nose sniffed her hair. From the corner of her eye, she saw the orange-and-black-striped head of a...*tiger.*

"Cat!" Caros's deep voice boomed across the garden. Pelonia's heart raced as though it meant to escape her chest.

"Cat!" he called again, his swift steps crunching dried leaves along the garden's path. "Come, before you terrify my new slave to death."

The tiger sniffed Pelonia's hair once more before he returned to his master. The animal's long, curved tail flicked her in the face as it sauntered off.

An eon seemed to pass before she took an even breath. Her muscles unlocked and she almost pitched forward into the herbs, her hands shaking with latent fear.

Caros's long shadow stretched across the herb bed in front of her. From her seat on the ground, he seemed as tall and formidable as a colossus.

He crouched beside her, his intense blue gaze riveted to her face. "Are you well or did my pet scare you speechless?"

Not wanting him to see her tremble, she tightened her fists and tried to ignore the tiger's golden eyes fixed upon her. "Your pet? Are you insane?"

He shrugged. "Some claim so."

"I agree with them." She pulled another weed. "Only a lunatic would allow a tiger to run loose in his garden."

"He wasn't actually free. He yanked his lead from my hand. It's your fault. You were in his domain and he wished to inspect you."

She gave him a level stare. "It's not my will that keeps me here. I'll gladly go to my cousin's home if I'm making the beast ill at ease."

"Beast?" Caros stroked the tiger's wide head and ignored her statement. "Hardly. He's as placid as a lamb with people he tolerates. He didn't kill you, so he must find you acceptable."

The powerful animal rolled to his side and Caros began to scratch his chin. Pelonia marveled at the sight of the huge contented cat. Sensing the affection between master and pet, she couldn't help but smile when Cat's eyelids began to droop and his body relaxed. Within moments he was stretched out in peaceful slumber.

"See? As placid as a lamb." Caros grinned. "His snoring will begin any moment."

As if on cue, a low rumble emanated from the sleeping creature. She reached out her hand, then drew back. "Can I touch him?"

"Of course," he said. "Move closer so you don't stretch and hurt your ribs."

His thoughtfulness continued to perplex her. She brushed the excess dirt from her hands and did as he said. Hesitant at first, she stroked the top of the animal's head, surprised by the softness of its fur.

"Have you ever seen a Caspian tiger?"

She shook her head. "Sketches only. My father took me to a menagerie once. There were lions and a panther, but no tigers. Have you had this one long?"

Caros continued to watch her. "Three years, since he was a cub. He was the runt of his litter. My old *lanista,* Spurius, refused to feed him since Cat was sickly and he doubted he'd grow large enough for the ring. I fed him part of my rations and when I won my freedom a few months later I took Cat with me. As you can see, proper care has made him as healthy as any of his kind."

"You were freed? You were a slave once?"

He plucked a sprig of mint from a plant at the path's edge. "For ten years. From the age of fifteen, I fought as a gladiator."

She reached for a clump of basil to divide and replant. "Then you've lived the horror of having your freedom ripped from you and your life pitched on end?"

His face darkened. He nodded.

"Did you enjoy being a slave?"

"Why ask foolish questions? Who would *enjoy* being a slave?"

"Perhaps you liked killing for sport in the ring?"

His eyes narrowed. "I killed because I didn't wish to die."

Then how could he enslave others? The injustice of his actions soured her stomach with disdain. She tossed the basil into the dirt and rose to her feet, wincing at the twinge of pain in her ribs.

The tiger opened his eyes, instantly alert. Wary of the predator, she stepped away, but her temper burned too strong to completely curb her tongue.

"You're a hypocrite, Caros Viriathos. How can you buy and sell flesh when you know firsthand of its brutality?"

Dropping the mint leaves, Caros stood, his stance suggesting he was ready for battle. "Think before you insult me, slave. Have I not been kind to you? Perhaps I've been *too* kind if you believe you can question me like an equal when you are not."

She chafed at the reminder of her degraded status.

"You're my property," he continued with confidence. "Remember your place."

Hot with indignation, she stared at him, silently defying his ownership. Eventually, she admitted, "I'm your prisoner, but once I find my cousin, I *will* buy back my freedom."

"You aren't for sale." His fists clenched at his side, his eyes turned the color of a stormy sea. "You are my *slave* and will be until I tire of you. Remember I hold your life in my hand. If I choose to see you dead, it will be so, but you won't be sold."

Inwardly, she trembled at the power he held over her. Tension crackled between them like a growing blaze. Cat sprang to his feet and began to pace with restlessness.

She took a step closer to Caros, a part of her wishing for death to end the misery she'd endured since leaving home. "My God alone can grant you the power to take my life. Should He do so, I will rejoice. Not only will I be free from you, but I will see my father in heaven and be face-to-face with my Savior."

"Your savior?" he scoffed. "You mean Jesus, the Jew the Romans crucified? He's dead. Even if He weren't, why would He want a shrew like you to pester Him for all eternity?"

The blood leeched from her face. His barb struck like the sting of a lash. Her father had taught her to live as an example of Christ's love to others. To trust that God held her in His hand and had a purpose for her life.

Since she'd buried her father, she'd refused to cry. She'd known he would want her to be strong. Shame replaced her anger. She'd tried so hard to please her earthly father, but what had she done thus far to please her *Heavenly* one?

The gate's creaking hinges sliced through the weighted silence. Pelonia glanced in the direction of the kitchen. Gaius, Caros's short, elderly steward approached, his face red from his hurried stride.

"Master." Gaius held up a roll of parchment. "I have word from Spurius concerning tomorrow's games."

Caros raked his hand through his thick, wavy hair. Releasing an exasperated sigh, he met the man halfway.

While he and his steward discussed the news, Cat lay down in the shade of a lemon tree.

Pelonia watched the tall, arrogant man in front of her, a war waging within her heart and mind. Resentment battled with the knowledge that Caros was a man in need of God's love. A lifetime of teaching had impressed her to forgive, to be an example of compassion. But how could she be a light in this gladiator's brutal world when her own spirit felt cloaked in darkness?

Gaius retreated from the garden. Caros returned to her, his angular face an inscrutable mask. "Where were we?"

"At an impasse," she reminded him.

"Ah, an impasse." A devious smile formed about his lips. "Then I believe I have a solution to our dilemma. Apologize for your barbed tongue or I will take your silence to mean you understand your place here and have come to accept your fate."

Praying for patience, she took a deep breath to fortify herself, then slowly released it. "I've accepted nothing. However, I'm an honest woman, so I will be fair and tell you now my plans remain the same as they have been. As soon as I'm able, I will escape from you, find my cousin and see my freedom restored. Until then—"

"Say no more, slave. Perhaps you're unaware runaways are hunted like dogs and dispatched like rodents?"

"I'm aware of it," she said, refusing to be intimidated.

He shook his head, clearly bemused by his inability to cow her. "You're a unique woman, Pelonia. I've never met your like."

She raised her chin. "My father used to say the same."

Caros moved a few steps to the fountain and dipped

his hand into the sparkling water. "What happened to him?"

The question stung like vinegar in a festering cut. Renewed sadness lodged a ball of pain in her throat. "God saw fit to take him home."

"When?"

Pelonia crossed her arms over her chest. She tried to make her voice emotionless. "On the road to Rome eleven days past. We were attacked by marauders. My father and our servants were killed. Everything of value was stolen. Only my uncle and I were left alive."

His eyes brimmed with compassion, awakening a desperate need for comfort. "How did you survive?"

Her eyes burned with unshed tears. She turned her back on him, nearly tripping over the basket of weeds by her feet. "I'd snuck away before dawn to bathe in the river. My father had told me not to go. He said it was too dangerous, that I and the other women could seek out one of the bathhouses once we reached Rome."

Her voice cracked. "We were so close, you see. Less than a day's journey to my cousin's home on the Palatine. But I didn't listen. I hate feeling unclean. My maid would have come with me, but I didn't want her to face my father's displeasure if he discovered my absence, so I went alone. I was in the water when I heard distant screaming. I tried to return with all possible haste. I would have given my life to save any of them. I would have. Honestly, I would have."

In two steps he was beside her, his arms banding about her shoulders. "I believe you. How did you escape?"

Enveloped in his strength, she allowed herself to forget they were enemies for a moment. She pressed her face to his chest, accepting the comfort she craved. "The thieves were gone by the time I arrived. They struck like lightning, unexpected and gone like a fast-moving storm."

"Why did your uncle beat you?"

Her eyes slipped closed. She inhaled the hint of spice on his skin. "I insisted he help bury the dead. He agreed because he'd seen a scout for the slave caravan approaching. When he told me of his plan to sell me, we argued and I tried to flee."

Caros's arms tightened around her. "I'm sorry, *mea carissima*. No one deserves to know such tragedy. Accept your life here, and I promise you will be treated with nothing but kindness."

"Your kindness is no worthy replacement for my freedom." She pushed his arms away, untangling herself from his embrace. "I can't accept a life of slavery. I'd shrivel up and die if I did. For whatever reason, God has seen fit I serve you for now. I'll do my best for His sake, but I won't promise to stay here forever."

Caros's eyes glittered like chips of blue glass in the sunlight. A nerve ticked in his jaw. "Then I make no assurance either, slave. You shall have neither my protection nor my sympathy and we shall see how well your God defends you."

Chapter Four

Caros snatched up a *gladius* and pointed the sword's sharp tip toward his best gladiator. "Alexius, join me on the field. I need to spill blood."

Alexius, a *Mirmillo* specifically trained to fight with a straight, Greek-styled sword, chose his favorite weapon and followed Caros across the sunbaked sand.

At the center of the elliptical field, Caros rolled his shoulders, loosening his muscles.

Alexius settled into a defensive posture, a hint of his usual humor dancing in his dark eyes. "To what do I owe this honor, Bone Grinder?"

Caros tensed, his encounter with Pelonia fresh in his mind. All senses fully alert, he could feel her presence in the garden, tugging at him. He almost returned to her until his temper flared. He was a fool. She'd repaid his kindness with constant rejection. His grip tightened on the sword hilt.

Alexius raised his shield. "Hail, Master. Greetings from one about to die," he said, mocking the adage gladiators chanted to the emperor before battle.

Caros swung his sword and lunged forward, slicing

the other man's upper arm. "Don't test me today, Alexius. I'm in no mood for your humor."

Gaping at the stream of blood on his arm, the Greek grew serious, a state he reserved for the ring. He kicked sand in Caros's face, then thrust his blade with the speed of a whip. "And I'm in no mood to perish."

Blinking the sand from his eyes, Caros sidestepped the blow and plowed forward, whirling his weapon with the swiftness and force of a storm. Alexius fell back.

The atmosphere erupted with excitement. The other gladiators stopped training and cast lots on the victor. Voices cheered from the sidelines. A few slaves poked their heads from the upstairs windows, eager to witness the entertainment.

Caros's *gladius* struck the other man's shield. "A gladiator is always prepared for death."

Alexius plowed forward. His face contorted, his muscles straining against the force of Caros's attack. "I have an appointment with one of my admirers tonight. If I must die in my prime, I'd rather it be tomorrow."

As his sword sparked against the Greek's blade, Caros shook his head, almost amused. Unlike him, Alexius had rejected freedom when offered it. The Greek preferred the life of a gladiator, unaffected by its lowly status when women of every social standing practically worshiped him as a god.

The thought of women revived thoughts of Pelonia. Her huge brown eyes and her mouth made his pulse race, even as her defiance enflamed his displeasure. Worse, he disliked how his heart leaped at each new sight of her.

How could so contrary a female wreak such havoc on his senses? Mystified, Caros thought he'd conquered his emotions years ago. A quick temper usually meant a speedy death in the arena. Only cold efficiency kept a fighting man alive.

Why, then, couldn't he control his reaction to one impudent, albeit beautiful, slave?

With renewed irritation, he focused his energies on the fight at hand. Up and down the training field, the two warriors matched each other blow for blow.

The sun beat down on Caros's shoulders. Bloodlust pumped through his veins, releasing the aggression Pelonia stoked in him.

His sword flashed in the sunlight and caught Alexius on the leg. He smiled at the other man's look of disgust and shrugged. "A wound for your lady to tend tonight."

"I best not mark *you,* then. One more scar and your horde of beauties will run for Campania. You're ugly enough as it is."

"Ha! One of these days, I'm going to tire of your witless tongue and cut it from your insolent mouth."

Grinning, Alexius swung his shield at Caros's head. "Then again, the new slave Lucia mentioned this morning has no choice except to serve you. Perhaps you can force her to meet your needs."

Caros ducked from the shield just before it struck him and rammed his shoulder into the other man's middle. Frowning, he fumed at Alexius's suggestive tone. Had Lucia told him of Pelonia's rebellion?

Caros landed a fist to Alexius's stomach, then another. The other man groaned as he broke away.

The Greek recovered quickly and jabbed with his sword, catching Caros in the ribs. The cut stunned the breath from his lungs.

A smug expression crossed Alexius's face. "You're

growing slow, Master. Perhaps you're getting old for this sort of play?"

"Think again," he said, his side stinging, "and leave delusions to your women."

Caros's free hand shot out. He caught Alexius's sword hilt and yanked. Alexius stumbled forward and fell to his knees, astonishment etched on his features.

Had they been in the ring, Caros could have delivered a deathblow with ease and been done with the match. But he wasn't fighting to the death—at least not with Alexius. His instincts warned Pelonia was another matter and he was in danger of losing both his will and his heart.

Caros eyed his fallen champion, dissatisfied with the fight. His sparring with Pelonia had offered far more interesting sport. Her fearlessness impressed him. "I'm not slow or old. I'm bored. I'd hoped you'd provide more of a challenge."

"I doubt even Mars could have bested you today." Alexius massaged his jaw and laughed, his good humor returning with ease. "Tell me, Bone Grinder, has your temper been appeased or do you still feel a need for blood?"

Caros glanced over his shoulder toward the garden behind the cookhouse where he'd last seen Pelonia. "I fear what I need most can't be solved with weapons."

Alexius's face twisted with confusion. "What is there if not battle?"

Peace. The thought beckoned him, tempting him with the idea of a different way of life. A way of life he'd known in his youth, but abandoned hope of ever finding again.

His desire to see Pelonia too strong to ignore, he left the field without answering Alexius. Before another hour passed he planned to make amends for how he'd treated her. Why drive a wedge between them when he wanted to know her better?

Pushing through the circle of men offering praise for his victory, he handed his *gladius* to one of the guards. He swiped a fresh tunic off a bench and pulled it over his head as he walked toward the cookhouse.

Without examining his need for haste, Caros returned to the garden. A breeze rustled the fruit trees and water splashed in the fountain, but there was an unnatural stillness that made him ill at ease.

"Pelonia?" His steps echoed along the walkway. He noticed Pelonia had done a fine job completing her task. Not only were the weeds gone, but the herbs were trimmed and the paths swept clean.

"Pelonia," he called again, eager to see her face once more.

The gate swung open. A wave of relief died the moment he turned and saw Lucia.

"She's not here, Master." The healer shifted a basket from one hip to the other. "I was on my way to find you. I've looked everywhere, but she's gone."

Tiberia left her plate of uneaten fruit and paced the family quarters of her new husband's Palatine home. Her fingertips brushed the marble top of a writing desk as she walked from one end of the large room to the other. Even the fragrant scent of incense did little to soothe her.

Marcus entered the chamber from where he'd been relaxing in the courtyard. A breeze followed him, rustling the gossamer drapes at each side of the tall doorway.

Taking a seat on the silk covered couch, he picked

up a dish of honeyed almonds from a nearby table and stuffed several into his mouth.

Tiberia pitied him. The horror he'd suffered on his way to Rome was too vile to contemplate. Marcus had arrived the day after her wedding, told her of the attack and his brother's murder. How Pelonia had been kidnapped.

Tears formed in her eyes when she thought of her cousin. Poor Marcus had reluctantly shared how he'd fought for Pelonia's freedom, done everything in his power to keep her from being stolen. If not for his injuries, he'd said, he could have saved her.

"Are you well, my dear?" Marcus asked.

"It's Pelonia. I can't believe she's lost to me forever."

Setting the almonds aside, he cast his gaze to the woven carpet. "We must accept what the gods will. It's not for us to question."

She folded into a chair, feeling weak and far from her usually tenacious self. "I know. I'm just grateful I've had Antonius to lean on. I don't think I could have endured this without him."

"Yes, Fortuna has blessed you." He knelt before her. "You must remember that and focus on your new life. You're a senator's wife now with many responsibilities."

"How can I when I feel as though a hole has been gouged in my heart?"

"I understand, my dear. Who feels the loss of Pelonia and her father more than I? You and your husband are all the family I have left in this world and even that connection is solely by marriage."

She chose a linen square from the table beside her and dabbed her eyes. "No, Marcus, you must think of yourself as our true family. I may have been related to Pelonia through her mother, while you claimed paternal ties, but if blood cannot bind us together, surely this shared misfortune makes us kin."

"You are most kind." Marcus lowered his head. "If only I'd been able to save my brother and precious niece."

Her heart broke for the grieving man. Guilt washed over her. Had it not been for her wedding, Pelonia and her household would still be alive.

Vowing to do all she could to help Pelonia's last paternal relative, she patted Marcus's shoulder. "I should never have invited our loved ones to see me wed. Iguvium is too far north and the journey is perilous. Had I not, they—"

"No, you mustn't blame yourself." Marcus's hand strayed to her knee. "It's tragic to be sure, but my brother and his household courted punishment. What other fate could they expect when they turned from our ancestors and forsook our gods? I believe I yet live because the gods protected me."

Discomfited by his familiar manner and harsh opinion of his brother and Pelonia, Tiberia left the chair and walked to the window where a kestrel balanced on the edge of the sill. For years Pelonia had written about her faith in the crucified Jew, Jesus. She'd often feared her cousin would be found out and sentenced to suffer some heinous punishment. Perhaps the gods *had* taken matters into their own hands after all.

Marcus came to stand close behind her. His knobby fingers clutched her shoulders. "I apologize if I upset you. Let us speak of it no more and remember my brother's house with nothing but fondness."

"Agreed," she said, oddly alarmed by his nearness.

"Good. You're very amiable." He fingered a curl by

her temple before moving back to the bowl of almonds. "I can see you will make a fine senator's wife."

"Thank you." A glance over her shoulder revealed the old man's intense scrutiny. She tightened her shawl around her shoulders, willing her husband to return home quickly. "Excuse me, I must see to the evening's meal."

"By all means." He patted the seat beside him on the couch. "Then return soon and we shall reminisce for a time."

Hurrying from the chamber, Tiberia shuddered and hoped with all her heart she'd only imagined the lust flickering in the old man's eyes.

Chapter Five

Pelonia pulled open the door of the storage room she'd been ordered to clean. Dim light filtered through the slats in the closed shutters, exposing a mountain of dirt and clutter.

Stepping into the narrow cell, she leaned her broom against the wall and set down her bucket of water. She stretched the tight muscles of her back, her ribs burning from the day's strenuous labor. This room was her last. As soon as she finished, she planned to seek out her pallet before Lucia concocted more aimless chores for her to do.

With a fortifying breath, she adjusted her tunic, detesting the coarse brown material scratching her skin from her neck to her ankles. She longed for the soft linen and brightly colored silks she'd always worn at home. Hoping a breeze would alleviate the itching discomfort of her slave's garb, she went to the window and threw open the shutters.

Positioned on the upper story, the storage room provided a lofty view of the training field. Below, Caros shouted at the men gathered around him. His sharp hand motions and livid countenance testified to his fury though the distance between them kept her from discerning his words.

Had some calamitous misfortune befallen them or did Caros Viriathos entertain a perpetually black mood?

No, that wasn't fair. Over the previous week, he'd shown his capacity for kindness by having her cared for while she recuperated. He hadn't turned vicious until she'd refused to accept his ownership.

As the group of gladiators disbanded, she rejected all benevolent thoughts of the *lanista*. She couldn't afford to soften toward him. Caros had declared war against her in the garden. He'd threatened her, frightened her, ridiculed her.

Hate, an emotion she'd never sampled before coming to Rome, crept into her heart. In that moment, all the lessons she'd learned about faith and compassion rang hollow. How could anyone possibly follow all of Christ's commands? Would she ever be able to forgive and love her enemy?

She watched Caros return indoors. As though a violent tempest had passed, an atmosphere of calm descended. The gladiators returned their weapons to the guards and filed into their quarters.

She picked up a rag she'd brought with her and began to dust. A vision of Caros plagued her. No one had ever affected her quite like the gladiator. When she looked at him, she saw a compelling, world-weary man, too proud for his own good. Worse, the sense of helpless fascination she experienced in his presence mortified her.

If she were the righteous person she ought to be, she'd pray for him, but the faith to pray eluded her for the first time in her memory. Never before had God seemed

so distant. The wrath marking Caros's face when he'd
mocked God's ability to protect her filled her with fear.
What if Caros were right? What if her heavenly Father
could no longer protect her? What if He simply chose
not to?

Exhausted from wrestling with unanswered questions, she finished cleaning and headed downstairs. At
the end of a long corridor, she came to a partially opened
door. She knocked hard enough to push it wider. The
room was empty, but something about the restful space
drew her inside.

A wooden sword hung prominently on one wall. Small
ancestral statues, three women and a man, sat atop a
shelf beneath it. A couch and two chairs crafted of rich
wood and the finest, deep blue coverings partially hid
the mosaic masterworks of various animals and lush vegetation that covered the floor. On the wall opposite the
sword, a fresco of mountains against the backdrop of a
fiery setting sun, lent the space a haunting, solitary air.

Crossing to the window, she admired the house's inner
atrium with its decorative columns and trio of fountains.
Climbing red roses perfumed the air with a sweet scent
that reminded her of her own flower garden at home.

An older man shuffled into the courtyard carrying a
hoe and woven basket. When he saw her, she waved in
greeting. A toothless grin flashed across his aged features before he tottered back the way he'd come.

How odd for him to retreat without a single word to
her. She shrugged. What did she know of Caros's servants? Perhaps they were all as strange as their master.

She began to leave a moment before Lucia raced
across the threshold. "Where have you been and what
are you doing in the master's private room?" she de-

manded an octave higher than necessary. "If Servius hadn't seen you from the garden, the entire household would still be in an uproar searching for you."

"What game are you playing?" Pelonia asked. "You know I was cleaning the storage rooms as you ordered."

"You lie. I looked for you there. You were nowhere to be found."

"How dare you call me a liar? I…" Her words trailed away when Caros appeared in the doorway. The room seemed to shrink and her pulse began to race like a stallion set free.

"Master." Lucia looked to Caros with an eager smile. "I found her."

"So I see." His gaze scorched Pelonia from head to foot. "You may leave us, Lucia."

The young healer looked stricken, then resigned before she turned to go. "Beware of this one, Master. She has the face of Venus, but she's even more deceitful."

Caros didn't comment, leaving Pelonia with the uneasy feeling he agreed with Lucia's poison. Once they were alone, he stepped deeper into the room. "Where have you been?" he asked, his tone as emotionless as stone.

"Upstairs." Her gaze roamed over the large bruise on his cheek, the multiple gashes marring the sinew of his arms and exposed collarbone. How much more damage did his tunic conceal? He must be in pain. She resisted a tug of concern and the desire to tend his injuries.

"What were you doing there?"

"Lucia sent me to clean."

"I don't believe you. She wouldn't assign hard labor when you've yet to fully heal."

"She said you meant to punish me."

"Now I'm certain you lie. I said nothing to Lucia about you."

She looked away from his icy blue stare, irritated enough at being called a liar again to dismiss her concern for his wounds. "Your thoughts are your own. Believe what you will. But if you meant to show me how harsh life here will be without your protection, consider your point well made."

"If you were cleaning upstairs why are you here in my private room? Did you plan to rob me before attempting the escape you threatened?"

"First I'm a liar, now I'm a *thief?*" she asked, unreasonably hurt by his low opinion of her. "If you knew me better, you'd realize you have no need to question my honesty. What have I done to give you the impression I'd steal from you?"

Caros contemplated the question while he steadied his breathing. How dare she stand before him acting as though she was in the right? By the gods, she'd given him the scare of his life. Once he'd discovered her gone, he'd turned the *domus* upside down looking for her. Visions of her fleeing into the wrong spot and encountering his men had him locking them up in the middle of the day.

Unwilling to examine the fear he'd experienced when he thought she'd run away, he hugged his anger to him like a protective coat of mail.

"Well?" she demanded. "What have I done?"

He stepped toward her.

She jumped back, her palms outstretched as though to ward off an attack. "Don't come any closer."

He moved forward, within easy reach of her. "Why should I not?"

She dashed away, positioning herself behind a piece of furniture.

"Do you think a chair will offer protection if I choose to lay my hands on you?"

"Some protection is better than none." She squared her shoulders and lifted her chin. "Even gladiators gird themselves before a match."

"True, but no amount of armor can compare with experience. I've fought for almost half my life. You're as battle hardened as a kitten."

She crossed her arms over her chest. "I admit you're a better fighter than I—"

"Yet I'm not the one who usually begins our skirmishes."

"You blame me for the difficulties between us? I've done nothing—"

"But argue." Most of the anxiety she'd caused him began to melt away now that the shock of her disappearance had begun to wear off.

"I've done no more than defended myself. You're just unreasonable. Your high-handedness begs to be brought down a peg."

"Is that so?" He shoved the chair out of his way and gripped her upper arms before she realized his intent to strike. "If we were equals you might be the woman to chastise me. As it is, you're a slave who'd be wise to keep her opinions to herself."

"And you're a pompous…*gladiator!*"

Caros almost congratulated her. She'd held her ground, though he could see fear lurked in the depths of her soulful brown eyes.

"Why are you smiling?" Her distrust was unconcealed. "Have you devised some new punishment for me?"

He caressed her arms, enjoying the smoothness of her skin. "I thought I might train you to fight in the arena. A woman in the games is a novelty. If this display of temper is any indication, you certainly have the mettle for it."

She escaped from his hold and fled to the window. "Your humor is misplaced, *lanista*. If you trained me with a weapon, you'd be wise to refrain from sleep."

He laughed outright. "So, you'd kill me, would you? Doesn't your *God* frown on murder?"

With a defiant toss of her head, she glared at him. Glad to see her bruises all but gone, he admired the way the window framed her beautiful face and delicate stature. Even the ragged tunic did nothing to hide her appeal.

"Blasphemy is a sin the same as murder," she said. "God might not pardon you for mocking Him, but given your contrary nature, I'm sure He'd understand my actions and forgive me without reservation."

"Perhaps," he said flatly. "But you might be surprised to find how difficult it is to forgive yourself."

Mollified by the horror in her eyes, he turned to leave. "Be warned, slave. Disappear again and you won't like the consequences. If you think dusting storage rooms is punishment, you'll realize it's child's play compared to the tasks I'll drop at your feet."

Outside, the sun beat down on him. He sensed Pelonia was jesting when she spoke of murdering him and her God's forgiveness for such an act, but what if it were true? What if her God were powerful enough to forgive the vilest crime and erase the guilt crippling his soul?

Hope flickered like an elusive flame inside him, then burned out just as quickly. He'd done too much evil to think of receiving mercy. He'd killed countless men, many of them Christians. Why would their God embrace an enemy?

He shook his head, his spirit bleak. He was lost with no way to be found. He should accept his fate and stop longing for redemption. Deep in his heart he accepted he wasn't worthy.

Chapter Six

Pelonia couldn't sleep. She tossed and turned on her
hard pallet, her body begging for slumber, her mind too
conflicted to rest. She kept envisioning Caros's dejected
face when she'd taunted him. How could she have suggested she'd murder him or that God would forgive her
for the crime? Yes, she'd been angry, but such meanness
wasn't her way.

She didn't feel like herself anymore. Her whole life
had changed for the bitter. She closed her eyes and tried
to pray, once again asking for forgiveness and direction. Afterward, her heart was lighter, but God seemed
just as distant.

She gazed out the open window. It would be dawn
soon, but for now an array of stars twinkled in the tar-
black sky. As a child, she'd loved gazing into the night,
memorizing the constellations her tutors had shown her.
A smile curved her mouth as she remembered her father
pointing out different celestial patterns and teaching her
the wonders of God's creation. With true gratitude, she
thanked the Lord for those sweet memories.

Giving up on sleep, she flipped away the light covering and stood. Stiff muscles protested as she crossed the tiny room she'd inhabited since Caros brought her here from the slave quarters eight days ago. She wondered when she would join the other slaves. Surely Caros had better use for the space than to allow her a private chamber.

She rested her palms on the windowsill. The first rose-colored streaks of dawn painted the horizon. A cool breeze ruffled her hair and a dog barked in the distance, the only sound amid the silence.

Steps shuffled in the hall. Someone pounded on the portal loud enough to wake the deepest sleeper.

"It's time to rise," Lucia commanded through the closed portal.

"I'm coming."

"Be quick about it. Find out what herbs Cook needs from the garden and fetch them for him."

Pelonia changed her tunic and wrapped the shawl around her shoulders before venturing into the corridor. A series of lanterns lit the way downstairs to the back of the house. A pair of guards waited at attention by the rear door. With a hurried greeting to the giant, dark-skinned Africans, she crossed outside into the fresh air. The smell of baking bread made her mouth water.

Following the brick path to the kitchen, she glimpsed Caros training with a sword in the peach orchard. A look of concentration etched his handsome face. He didn't see her. Free to watch him without the expectation of conversation, she halted, mesmerized by the power and grace of his movements. He reminded her of music come to life in human form. Even the scar that looked like the swipe of a lion's claw across his chest did nothing to detract from his appeal.

"Don't fall in love with him," Lucia said, slithering up beside her. "If any woman ever claims his heart, it will be me."

Pelonia turned to see the healer fixed on Caros with a hungry gleam in her eyes. "You have nothing to fear from me. The man I choose to love will be the exact opposite of Caros Viriathos."

"How so?" Lucia's gaze never left her master.

"I want my husband to share my faith."

"Husband?" The healer snickered. "You're a slave. Why do you think you'll be permitted to marry?"

Pelonia frowned. "I won't always be a prisoner here. I refuse to believe I'll never have a family of my own."

Lucia snorted. "You should be thankful you're alive and give up your fanciful notions."

"It's not fanciful to have faith. Circumstances can change as quickly as an ocean current."

"Like your fortunes did the day you came here?"

"Yes," Pelonia admitted, stung by Lucia's harsh reminder."Then I can do without your faith. Why serve a deity who finds pleasure in making you a slave?"

For a moment, Pelonia grappled for an answer. Lucia's question echoed the very words she'd asked herself so often since coming here. She glanced away from Lucia's sneer to find Caros had finished his practice.

Her face flushed with pleasure when she noticed him watching her. Embarrassed by her reaction, she sought out Lucia's harsh features like a lifeline.

"My God's ways are a puzzle at times," she said, clinging to her beliefs when she had little else to offer. "But I believe He'll work all for my good if I'm patient and wait for Him to reveal His purpose."

"Then you're a fool. Why wait for your God to cause

you more pain? Why not take matters into your own hands?"

A rooster crowed. Caros went off to the gladiators' barracks. Two other slaves finished feeding the animals and walked past them into the house.

"I could arrange for your freedom," Lucia said once they were alone.

Pelonia's heart quickened. A surge of hope welled inside her as did her suspicion. "Why take such a risk? If Caros found out, he'd punish us both."

Lucia flipped her long black braid over her shoulder. "Isn't it obvious? I want the master for myself. Somehow you've bewitched him. He hasn't been himself since you came here. He's only waiting for your body to heal before he claims you, but I'm certain he'd forget you if you'd just disappear."

Why shouldn't she listen to Lucia? Both of them would have what they wanted if she accepted the healer's help. "When could you arrange for me to leave?"

The morning light gave Lucia's face a reddish cast. She smiled. "As early as tonight if you're willing."

Caros added another ladle of water to the red-hot coals. The liquid sizzled and steam filled the circular chamber of the bathhouse. He leaned against the warm marble wall, sweat beading on his skin.

After the morning's sword practice and another taxing workout in the bath's gymnasium, he hurt all over. Little wonder. His fight with Alexius yesterday had left his ribs bruised and his jaw throbbing. He'd been mad to double his usual exercise. Even more foolish to believe the added work would hinder his thoughts from straying to the unwelcome emotions Pelonia stirred in him.

The steam room's door swung wide. He opened one eye and stifled a groan when he saw Spurius Albius swiping a path through the curling white vapor. As always, Caros's temper flared at the sight of his former master, the man who'd stolen ten years of his life.

"There you are, Caros." Spurius's jowls bobbled as he spoke. "Gaius informed me I might find you here."

"What do you want? I'm on my way to the *frigidarium*. I'm in need of a cold swim before I head home."

"Leaving already?" Spurius hefted himself onto one of the marble ledges, adjusting his loincloth to accommodate his massive girth and stubby legs. "Isn't it too soon in the day?"

Caros closed his eyes and leaned his head back against the wall. "Not since you arrived."

Spurius chuckled. "Then I'll go straight to the point. I want you to fight again."

Caros lifted his head, battling his annoyance. "Why do you insist on vexing me with your endless attempts to drag me back to the arena? I've told you no a hundred times."

"I'm persistent. Besides, it's been a fortnight since you last turned me down."

"And I believe I told you if you asked me again I'd feed you to Cat."

Spurius shrugged. "I'm tough as old leather. He'd just spit me out."

"But he might enjoy gnawing on you first."

"If we were in your home, I might be frightened. But here—" Spurius motioned to the rising steam "—I'm safe."

"Not with me in the chamber."

Spurius used the edge of a cloth to wipe the sweat

from his brow. "I know you hate me, but we both know you won't harm me no matter how much you'd like to see me dead. You were a condemned man once. I doubt you'd allow yourself to return to that lowly state."

Caros grunted, unable to argue with the truth. Ending the worm's life would please him to no end, but it wasn't worth sacrificing all he'd achieved. "Exactly. Neither will I return to the games. Entering the arena requires me to place myself back in bondage. Rome itself will fall before I'll forfeit my freedom or be forced to acknowledge another master."

"You're too proud, Caros." Spurius sighed. "The truth is the mob is easily bored. Every day, it grows more difficult to arrange the grand events the crowd demands. The mob wants *you,* their champion, and the games' sponsors are willing to pay any price for the spectators' continued enjoyment."

Caros tossed another ladle of water on the coals. "I'm retired, old man. If you wish to do business with me, speak to Gaius about Alexius or one of my other champions. Otherwise, distance yourself from my presence. My patience with you is over."

"But think of the riches you'd win," Spurius cajoled one last time. "You're still the best gladiator alive."

"I'm already rich. On the other hand, Alexius's talents are for sale."

Taking the hint, Spurius's shoulders slumped in capitulation. "Since you've brought up Alexius, why can't you be more like him? There's a man who understands and enjoys his place in the world."

"He's a slave by choice. If he wanted his freedom I'd let him have it."

Spurius frowned. "You've condemned me as a villain

because I refused to sell you your freedom when you demanded it. But I ask you, what man would happily give up a gold mine? I was a fool to give the mob its way the day they chanted for your release. In the last three years I've lost ten fortunes for my drunken error."

Caros stood and tightened the cloth around his hips. "You're a fool, old man, drunk or otherwise."

"True enough, but I'm also determined. One of these days I'll tempt you out of retirement. You can be sure of it."

Pelonia sensed Caros's arrival in the garden before she heard him. Perching on tiptoe, she craned her neck for a better view of the herb-lined path. Caros and another man approached. Both were dark, tall and broad shouldered, but Caros moved with a grace that rivaled his tiger's. Breathless, she couldn't take her eyes off him.

He caught her staring and without warning sent the other man away. Without breaking their gaze, he closed the distance between them. "Why are you out here in the heat of the day?"

"Your steward assigned me to garden duty. I understood I'm to work here every day."

"I'll speak with him. There are easier tasks in the house."

"No, this is fine." She didn't want to rile Gaius. The old man could make her life miserable if he chose. "I tended flowers and maintained a large vegetable garden for my father's household."

He crossed his arms over his chest. The gold wristbands he wore glinted in the sun. "If you came from a wealthy family, as you claim, why toil like a slave?"

Disliking the accusation in his question, Pelonia

plucked a low-hanging leaf from the lemon tree and breathed in the citrus scent. "Simply because I enjoy planting something, caring for it and watching it grow."

"I see. And how is it you never married? I'd expect a woman of your advanced age to have children of her own to nurture."

"*Advanced* age? Are you trying to insult me?" she asked with mock severity.

"By the gods, *no.*" He shifted uncomfortably. "But most women wed by the age of twelve or thirteen summers. You've yet to wrinkle, but…how old are you?"

"Seventeen." She bit her lip to keep from laughing at his discomfort. "And you? You have enough wrinkles for both of us, so I'd guess you are…?"

"Twenty-eight." He fingered the faint lines around his right eye. "Are you saying you find me ugly and withered?"

She laughed for the first time since her father died. "Goodness, no, but all the scars were a bit off-putting at first."

He sighed with exaggerated relief and led her to a bench beside the fountain. "Were? Does that mean my scars no longer bother you?"

In truth, she no longer noticed them. Not when the uniqueness of his azure eyes and the male beauty of his sculpted lips claimed all of her attention. "No, they don't bother me."

"Good." His gaze dipped to the ground and she saw the beginnings of a smile curve his mouth. He brushed a thick curl of black hair from his forehead. "But you have yet to answer me. What's wrong with you that you never married?"

She rolled her eyes. "There's nothing *wrong* with me.

My father was an unconventional man. He thought it best I wed the husband of my choosing. I've yet to make the fortunate man's acquaintance."

Caros's laughter filled the garden. "Aha! Another woman in search of a perfect man. I doubt you'll find him."

Pelonia fought her own grin. "I've no wish for a perfect man. Just one who's perfect for me."

"Perhaps you've met him, but don't realize it. What if he were…one of my men?"

"He isn't."

"How do you know?"

She weighed her words with care. "I mean no disrespect, but…but my father would never have condoned my marriage to a man of your occupation."

"I see." His lips firmed into a hard line. "I should have known, but it's easy to forget we gladiators are the scum of the earth when most of the empire worships our every move."

"I didn't mean to offend you."

"You didn't. I know the status of my profession. So, what virtues must this god among mortals possess to win your favor?"

"I want no god other than the One I serve. As for a husband, I pray…"

A bird chirped, filling in the late afternoon's silence while she debated whether or not to share further. Being a pagan, and a man, she doubted he would understand.

"Yes?" Caros persisted.

"There was a man named Paul of Tarsus," she said before she lost her nerve.

"You wished to marry him?"

"No." She shook her head, disconcerted by the sudden malice in his expression. "Paul was the first Jew to teach Gentiles the ways of Jesus. In his letters to the various Christian communities, he taught many truths."

"And for this you admire him? I, for one, would reconsider elevating a teacher who led me down a road to persecution and slaughter."

"On marriage," she continued as though he'd said nothing, "Paul taught a husband should love his wife as much as Christ loves his followers. A man should love her so much he would die for her if necessary, just as Christ died for all of us."

"Little wonder you put such stock in love." He grimaced. "And what did this Paul say a wife must do in return for her husband?"

"She must respect him."

Caros frowned. "A man must die for a woman and all she has to do is *respect* him for it?"

Pelonia grinned.

"Are you certain this Paul wasn't a female in disguise? It seems he concocted the rules to lean in a woman's favor."

She swatted his arm. "Paul was a great man, blessed with vast wisdom."

"So were Aristotle, Plato and Seneca. Why should I believe your Paul over the natural order—that woman is born to serve her husband, wanting nothing more than to bear his children?"

"Little wonder we Christians are persecuted for our radical ideas. Men rule the Empire and few of them want to purchase a slave when they can wed one."

"I purchased you, did I not? Though at three thousand denarii you were less than a bargain."

"Three *thousand*...?" Her mouth dropped open. "Why would you pay such a high price?"

His face grew serious. His eyes warmed in the space of a blink. He engulfed her hand in his much larger one and leaned closer until their lips almost touched. "The slave trader threatened to sell you to a brothel, but I refused to allow it."

Shocked to learn of the degradation he'd saved her from, she grappled for something appropriate to say. She wanted to thank him for his generosity, but her enslavement stole all but the smallest portion of gratitude from her heart. "I...why?"

"I mean to have you for myself."

She eased away from his hold, instantly missing the warmth of his touch. "The slave trader robbed you. He sold you a woman who wasn't for sale."

"My receipt and your presence in my home say otherwise."

"You confuse me. I'm certain you'd find a more willing female if you applied yourself to the task of looking for one."

His lips twitched. "I want only you."

Lucia's cold warning rang in her ears. "Because I'm a challenge? Or because I'm an innocent?"

The crisp air hummed with tension between them. "Neither and both. Truthfully...because there's a peace I feel in your presence that I've felt with no one else."

Mystified, Pelonia studied his angular features. His sincerity touched a chord deep inside her, but she found it impossible to trust him. She stood, eager to find the calm that eluded her in his presence. "After these last weeks, Caros, if you sense any peace left in me it's Christ and Him alone."

"Nonsense. I'm drawn to *you*, Pelonia, no other. From the first moment I saw you I wanted you for my own." His long fingers locked around her wrist, preventing her flight. "I won't relent until I've made you mine."

The quiet declaration confirmed Lucia's warning. She shook off his hold and rushed from the garden, his command to return chasing her down the path toward the house. Once in her room upstairs, she shut the door and flung herself on her pallet. Her whole body trembled from the shock of his admission. Her thoughts whirled as she tried to sort out the revelations in the garden. One moment she and Caros had been conversing, the next...

Her skin crawled when she thought of how close she'd come to waking in a brothel. Her father had shielded her, but she wasn't unaware of the harsh realities a female faced on her own. Shorn of a man's protection, most women fell into prostitution, or like her, were sold into slavery.

Neither was an acceptable choice, but for the moment slavery seemed the lesser of both evils. Had she been sold to a brothel, she would still be a slave, shamed with no hope of returning to her family. As it was, at least she had her virtue and the dream of freedom.

She curled into a ball. Her mind raced. Caros planned to make her his paramour. What had she done to draw his attention? He couldn't possibly be drawn to her disheveled and filthy appearance. She'd fought him at every turn. Surely he wasn't attracted to her less-than-servile nature?

Clasping her knees, she lowered her head. "Lord, where *are* You?" Straining to hear even the faintest whisper of guidance, she almost wept when she met with more silence. She'd already lost her father and freedom, would God allow her virtue to be stolen as well?

Lucia's offer rang in her ears. Any hesitation she'd harbored about the timing of her escape vanished. She'd been given the opportunity to flee and she must seek out Tiberia. If Caros sought to claim her, she had no ability or legal right to stop him. Every moment she lingered in his domain brought her closer to ruin.

She had no choice. She must leave tonight.

Chapter Seven

Anxious, Pelonia paced the shadows of her moon-lit room. Lucia should arrive any moment with further instructions. Through her room's small window she checked the lantern-lit yard for the slightest hint of movement. The trainees had been locked in the barracks at twilight. The guards were nowhere in sight, but her stomach clenched with trepidation. If she were caught, and Caros refused to show mercy, she might lose her life.

A dog howled, lending the blackness an eerie quality that stretched her nerves. A knock on the door made her jump.

Pelonia opened the door to her coconspirator. "I've brought you some vegetable broth," Lucia said once the door was secured. "It was childish of you to skip the evening meal. How do you expect to have strength for tonight if you don't eat?"

"I didn't consider—"

"No, I figured as much, but I used your stupidity to aid us. I spread the seed you're feeling ill. When you don't come down tomorrow, people will believe you're unwell and passing the day on your pallet."

"Who will believe such a tale?" Pelonia accepted the fragrant bowl of stewed tomatoes. "Since when is a slave allowed to shirk labor because of sickness?"

The lamp's glow highlighted Lucia's severe features. "Who *won't* believe it? Everyone is aware you're the master's current favorite."

Pelonia's cheeks heated with embarrassment. "I hate being the subject of gossip."

"You've been nothing else since the moment the master plucked you from the slave quarters and insisted you stay here in the house."

She cringed with mortification. Thankfully, her father didn't have to witness her dishonor.

"The entire household has made wagers to see how long before he tires of you."

Humiliated, she turned away. "When do I go?"

"Soon. First, you must listen and heed everything I'm about to say. When you leave the house tonight follow the street toward the amphitheater. Just before you reach the city gates, you'll come to a large statue of Caesar driving a chariot with winged horses. Once there, look for a man with two lanterns. He's the butcher's son, Pales. I've arranged for him to lead you to your cousin's home."

"You're certain he can be trusted?"

Pausing at the door, Lucia nodded. "Watch for me below your window. I'll give a birdcall to signal when it's time."

Several oil lamps bathed Caros's study with a warm orange glow. His gaze soaked in the wall mural of the setting sun and Iberian mountains. After all these years, he missed his native land and grieved the loss of his cherished kin.

His father, mother, sisters. Each of them held a revered place in his heart. With a fond smile, he lifted the ancestral statue he'd had fashioned to represent his father. Wise, the epitome of fairness, his father was the best man he'd ever known.

He replaced the carving and chose the one of his mother, the heart of his family's home. When Caros closed his eyes, he saw her wide smile, heard her gentle voice instructing him to be a man of peace, of honor.

How disappointed she would be to see what he'd become.

He put back the statue with care, then eased into one of the blue padded seats facing the inner courtyard. The illuminated fountain returned his thoughts to Pelonia, a subject never far from his mind.

He winced thinking of the disaster he'd spawned in the garden. By the gods, she must think him a rapist the way she'd fled. The horror on her face when he'd tried to kiss her made him cringe. In the future, he'd master his lust and nurture her trust, not her resistance.

Seeing Lucia enter the courtyard, he sat forward. Why wasn't the healer abed? He surged to his feet when he saw her look of panic.

"Master!" She ran toward him. "You must hurry. Pelonia, that ungrateful sneak, has fled. I was in my room upstairs when I happened to look out my window. There she was, creeping down the road like a common thief. I told you she'd be nothing but trouble."

Fear gripped him. "Which way?"

"Toward the city gates."

Quick steps took him to the bowels of the house. He strapped on a *gladius* and grabbed up a torch, then raced to the side door and into the night.

The torch held high to guide him, he broke into a run. During the day, Rome was dangerous enough, but after dark the streets crawled with every sort of human vermin.

If anything happened to her... He had to find her.

He picked up his pace. Shouting and bawdy laughter echoed from the street up ahead, but it was the woman's scream that raised the hackles on the back of his neck.

A grimy hand covered Pelonia's mouth from behind and dragged her head back against a rock-hard shoulder. A knife blade pressed to her throat filled her with terror. "Be quiet, wench! Someone'll think you don't like us."

Raucous laughter rippled through the drunken gang surrounding her like rabid dogs. Paralyzed with fear, she felt a trickle of blood slide down her neck. The stench of sour mead made her gag. She frantically searched the darkness. Shiny, inebriated eyes leered at her from the shadows. How many men were there? Six? Seven?

Dear God, please help me!

"I want her first," a deep voice slurred somewhere to her left.

"You'll have to wait your turn," another said, the words thick and muddled. Jeering laughter combined with lewd suggestions echoed through the street.

The pack grew bolder. Groping hands snatched at her clothes, pinched her, yanked her braid. The cloth of her tunic ripped, exposing her shoulder to the damp night air.

She squeezed her eyes shut. Unable to move or defend herself, she begged God for mercy.

The giant tightened his hand on her mouth. The pressure against her teeth cut her lip. She tasted blood.

He reached forward with the knife, the metal flashing in the moonlight between her face and the other wolves.

"All of you stand back," the giant ordered. "The woman promised I could have her first. You'll have to wait 'til I've had my taste."

What woman?

A flurry of drunken curses and outraged complaints littered the night, but the long knife aided the pack's decision to slink backward.

"Such beautiful skin," the giant slurred near her ear. His sour breath churned her stomach. She gagged until she thought she might retch. He moved his hand from her mouth and buried his wet lips against the pulse racing in her throat.

She screamed. Her heel stomped his foot. He loosed his hold and the blade clanked on the stone street. Wild with fear, she jerked free from the drunk and ran.

Threats from her pursuing attackers spurred her onward. Was someone calling her name? Without slacking her pace, she turned a corner, then another and another until she was lost. Too scared to stop running, she pressed on, her lungs burning, her heart pounding.

Rapid footsteps gained ground behind her. The glow of a torch grew larger, lighting the narrow alleyway.

"Pelonia!"

Caros? She faltered, tripped on an uneven stone, felt herself falling.

A strong arm swooped around her middle, hauling her up just as her palms brushed the road. In a seamless movement, Caros turned her around, then pulled her against him. "Are you all right?"

She locked her arms around his waist and buried her

cheek against his chest. Like an angel sent from God, he'd come to save her.

The heat of his torch warmed her skin, but did nothing to ease her chilling terror. He held her while she shivered and shook against him. For timeless moments, he rubbed her back until the tremors subsided.

Caros cupped her face with his free hand and tipped her head back to search for injuries. He ran the pad of his thumb over the shallow cut on her throat. Thankfully, the blood had dried and the wound no longer bled. The image of his woman, a blade held against her jugular, would never leave him. If she hadn't escaped those mongrels, he would have slaughtered them all.

He angled the torch for a better view of her ashen face. His gaze roamed over her, accessed the shock stamped across her shattered expression. "It's over now. They won't find us. Can you walk or shall I carry you home?"

"Home?" Her bottom lip quivered, her eyes filled with tears. "I have no home."

His chest constricted with pity. He tugged her against him, holding her close while sobs ravaged her tiny form. A promise to free her and help find her cousin sprang to the tip of his tongue.

No. His arms tightened around her. She was his. He couldn't let her go.

Once she quieted, he took her hand and began to lead her from the alley. "Come, Pelonia, you'll catch a cold. We must get you indoors."

She tugged free. "Why? So you can finish what those jackals started?"

A brow arched in question, he faced her. Illuminated by a pool of torchlight, her creamy cheeks smudged with tears, her lower lip swollen, she held her head high, daring him to deny her suspicion.

He narrowed the gap between them. "Are you crazed, woman? Haven't you realized by now I'm not going to rape you?"

She lifted her chin. "How can I trust such a claim? You said you meant to have me no matter what and there are rumors—"

"Rumors never cease. This is Rome. There's as much gossip here as there is air to breathe."

"You're a man. And I am your slave, or so you keep informing me."

He frowned, disliking the bitter accusation in her eyes. "Pelonia, if I meant to abuse your body, I would have done so already. You've been in my house, tempting me since the first time I saw you in the slaver's wagon."

Confusion furrowed her brow. She crossed her arms over her chest, as though to protect herself. "And what of tonight? Do you plan to punish me for my escape?"

He clasped her hand, tightening his grip when she tried to break the contact. "I haven't had time to consider it, though the gods know you deserve to be whipped."

"No, I do not. What did you expect after today in the garden?"

"I tried to kiss you, nothing more."

"Where I'm from, a man doesn't kiss a woman unless she's his wife. I've heard—"

"Rumors. Yes, I know. Who is this liar who's filled your head with poison against me?"

She glanced away, feigning a sudden interest in the cracked concrete wall of the building beside them.

He switched the torch to his other hand and flexed

his fist, working the stiffness from his forearm. "Was it Servius? I know you worked with him this afternoon."

"No! He's a kind old man. Other than telling me where to find compost, he's barely spoken three words to me."

He raked his fingers through his hair in frustration. The culprit couldn't be one of his other gladiators, not when he'd been careful to keep her separate from them. "Was it another slave? Was it Lucia?"

"I'm cold." She avoided his eyes. "Can we go back to the house?"

So, it *was* Lucia. He heard the guilt in her voice. It was a harsh disappointment to find the person he relied on most among his servants had become a viper. "Tell me the truth. Was it Lucia?"

"She's in love with you," she admitted after a long pause.

"Her actions speak otherwise. How can a person claim to love someone, then turn around and spread lies about him?"

"She was afraid of losing her place."

"She's done a fine job of it." He took her hand and compelled her to follow. "She'll be sold tomorrow."

"No!" She grabbed hold of his arm. "She helped me and—"

He slowed his pace and stabbed her with a harsh glare. "You mean she helped you escape?"

"I didn't say that."

"She did, didn't she?"

"I—"

"Tell me, woman!"

"Yes, but—"

"Did she send you in this direction on purpose?"

She looked pained, but nodded.

"Then not only will I sell her, I'll have her whipped first."

"Please, Caros, don't." Pelonia refused to walk further. "Why must you always threaten violence?"

"I'm a gladiator, remember? Violence is what I do best."

"I find that hard to believe after the gentle way you held me while I cried and soothed away my fear tonight."

The pity in her eyes was more than he could stomach. "It would be wiser if you did."

"I believe you'd prefer to be a man of peace."

Laughter gurgled in his tight throat. "You believe in a dead God, too."

"Don't blaspheme just because you know I speak the truth. Christ has done nothing to earn your scorn."

Smarting from her rebuke, Caros fell silent. A part of him admired her tenacious faith. Even in what must be the bleakest time of her life, she spoke as though she truly believed her God cared for her.

He tried to pinpoint the moment when he'd stopped believing in anything more than his own abilities. Perhaps it was during the dark days after his family's murder or those first terrifying hours in the ring. It had been so long ago he couldn't remember a time when he relied on anyone but himself.

He cast off his introspection. "You're wrong, Pelonia. Peaceful men don't thrive when forced to live a life of violence as I have."

They walked along the empty alley in silence until Pelonia murmured, "Maybe they do if there's a plan for them."

Would the woman never admit defeat? "What kind of plan?"

"I don't know, but who can determine the purpose of a life or why God allows one man to rise and another to fall. We can only trust Him."

"Trust," he scoffed, "mingles in the same net with love and I've survived with little of either."

"That breaks my heart." She squeezed his hand. "What of your family? Did they not love you?"

Her question pierced his chest like a stake. He'd known a wealth of tender emotions with his family, had trusted no one more than his parents and sisters. Watching all of them perish in the space of day had almost broken him.

One of his men opened the gates in front of the school. Caros led her to the front door of his house. He curved a tendril of her hair behind her ear, touched by her concern more deeply than he'd thought possible. "Don't fret about me or my family. Perhaps one day I'll tell you of my past. For now, I wish to make a bargain in order to avoid another fiasco like tonight."

"What is your bargain?" A hint of wariness crept into her voice.

"I will keep my distance, if you give your word not to escape."

She shook her head. "No, I… I couldn't make such a promise and plan to keep it. I won't run off into the night again. I've learned my lesson on that score, but if another opportunity presents itself, I'll take it."

He didn't know whether to laugh at her honesty or march her upstairs and chain her to a wall to ensure she never left him. "What if I vow—"

"To allow me to tell you about Christ?"

"What?" He'd never dreamed she'd bargain with something ridiculous. "I've no interest in your sect."

"I've no interest in living as a slave, either, but I won't try to leave—for a time—if you agree to give me a hearing."

Intrigued, Caros studied her. Why would she endure a

life she found despicable just to tell him the ramblings of a crucified Hebrew? On the other hand, her offer might be the perfect solution. His agreement would buy enough time to break down her barriers and win her capitulation. He would have his way and what would it cost him to listen? It wasn't as if she were asking for his soul.

He planted the torch in the holder beside the door and cupped her face with his hands. Aware this might be the last time he touched her for what would seem an eternity, he memorized the texture of her soft skin and searched the depths of her earnest gaze. "I'll agree to your terms, for a fortnight, Pelonia. But be warned, my beautiful slave, by the end of two weeks' time I will have won your surrender. You'll never want to leave me."

"You think too highly of yourself, *lanista*."

A wolfish grin curved his lips. "Possibly, but remember, I've never lost a battle and I have no intention of losing this one."

Chapter Eight

Caros stood on the edge of the training field. The early morning sun shone hot and bright, glinting on the golden sand. Amid the clang of metal and grunts of pain, a dozen of his newest acquisitions fought to prove their worth.

None of them impressed him enough to sway his thoughts from Pelonia's escape of the previous night. Unable to sleep, he'd woken Alexius and railed at him for nearly an hour. The Greek had been no help. He'd merely laughed and asked how it felt to be enamored.

He'd almost punched his champion until he remembered Pelonia's disdain for violence. He'd stormed back to his own rooms then, convinced she'd whispered incantations over him. By the gods, he was Caros Viriathos, champion of the ring. A *lanista* surrounded by a sea of brutality. Until she arrived, he'd accepted the carnage that defined his existence.

Forcing visions of her soft brown eyes from his mind, he watched one of his assistants divide the trainees into six pairs. He concentrated on his men, but the bargain he'd struck with his beautiful slave kept luring his attention. Winning her favor dangled in front of him like honey before a starving man. Their battle of wills excited him like nothing he'd ever tasted. Other than granting her freedom, which would ruin his chance to see her, he'd do anything to win her favor.

He wished he'd sought her out this morning to relieve his concerns and determine her state of mind. Instead, he'd given orders not to wake her. After last night's ordeal, he felt she needed rest and tender care. The special meal he'd ordered for her pleasure included the finest food and drink Rome had to offer.

His musings turned black when he considered Lucia and her evil tricks. Justice demanded she be punished. He could not allow a snake to thrive in his home.

Caros picked up a *gladius* and entered the field before approaching a pair of trainees. The moment his shadow touched them, the shorter slave dropped his wooden, practice sword and backed away in fright.

Ignoring the coward, he addressed the taller, better fighter. "You were among the men I bought from Aulus's caravan, were you not?"

The slave nodded. "He bought us from a prison guard in Amiternum just days before our execution."

Typical. Many gladiators began their career in a similar fashion. Either a trader like Aulus bought and sold them for profit or the condemned were carted directly to the gladiatorial schools. Who better to perish for the mob's entertainment than those already sentenced to die? "What is your name?"

The man lifted his chin. "Quintus Fabius Ambustus."

"Why were you sentenced to death?"

Quintus squared his shoulders. "I refuse to worship the emperor."

Another Christian? Was he being surrounded? Only Jews and Christians denied what everyone else in the empire accepted by law whether they believed it or not. "If not the emperor, who do you believe is divine?"

"Jesus, the Christ," Quintus answered with conviction.

Caros's thoughts shifted back to Pelonia. What if she discovered he had another of her kind beneath his roof? After a steady diet, Quintus no longer appeared bone-thin or hollow-eyed. Good food and fresh water had restored life to his face and strength to his body. A woman might even think his dark hair and green eyes were somewhat handsome.

He frowned. What if Pelonia found Quintus appealing? They shared the same religion, something she believed necessary for a happy union. Could that common ground breed a deeper bond between them? What if her heart became entangled with the slave's and he lost all chance to make her his?

Jealousy, an emotion he'd never felt before and one he instantly hated, sizzled through him. He scowled and the Christian wisely backed away. "Whatever brought you here, you're my property for the time being. When you're ready, you'll enter the ring and achieve death or glory. It's up to you, but considering the investment I've made in your scrawny hide, I hope you'll choose the glory."

Quintus began to reply, but one of the guards crossed the sand and interrupted him. "Master, forgive me, but you said to inform you when the woman left her room. I believe she's headed for the garden."

Mindful of the bargain she'd struck with Caros the night before, Pelonia dressed quickly. She hadn't fallen asleep until dawn. Waking moments ago, she'd leaped from her pallet; the angle of the sun telling her it was already midmorning.

Her thoughts consumed by Caros, she hurried down the corridor. How strange the very person she'd sought to escape had been the one whose arms she'd clung to. Now, thanks to her vow, she was bound for a fortnight to give up her goal of freedom.

Strangely at ease with her situation, she grabbed up a wash bucket and clean linen cloth from the pantry before making her way outside and into the herb garden. Perhaps her time here had a purpose after all. Unless the Lord chose otherwise, Caros might never have another chance to hear the Good News.

As she collected water from the fountain, smoke from the kitchen fires mingled with the smell of chicken roasting for the noonday meal. Her stomach grumbling, she cupped her hands under the fountain's flow and splashed her face before quickly cleaning her teeth with the cloth.

Behind her a twig snapped. She picked up the overflowing bucket and turned, expecting one of the house slaves had come to berate her tardiness.

Her heart tripped. Cat watched her from a short distance away. His bright golden eyes studied her, his long, striped tail twitched. With a low growl, the tiger prowled toward her.

The bucket slipped from her fingers. Cold water splashed on her sandaled feet, soaking the hem of her tunic. Her gaze darted to the path that led back to the house. Anxious for an escape route or any sign of Caros, she saw neither.

Frozen with fright, she reminded herself the predator was a pet. Caros was probably somewhere close behind him. Gathering her courage, she stretched out her trembling palm and prayed the huge tiger wasn't hungry. "Hello, Cat. Do...do you remember me?"

Cat sniffed her fingers, then licked her palm with his abrasive tongue. He bumped her hand with his nose and pressed against her, snuggling his large head to her chest. She braced herself against the fountain to keep from falling backward.

Taking the hint, she ran her fingers over his fur, paying special attention to each of his silken ears. Delighted by the experience of being so close to the exotic animal, she combed her fingers through the thick ruff of fur around his studded, leather collar.

"You're as sweet as a babe, aren't you, Cat?" No longer fearful, she remained cautious and scratched his chin, delighted to hear his soft sounds of enjoyment.

Snide laughter drew Pelonia's attention toward the garden entrance. Lucia strolled up the path toward her. The empty bucket she held swayed by her side.

"You've conquered the master, now you seek to tame the tiger, as well?"

Cat's massive body tensed. Pelonia tried to soothe him by stroking his ears, but the tiger remained alert, watchful. "I see you're not surprised I'm here, Lucia. I imagine you were disappointed when you learned Caros brought me back."

"Are you accusing me of something? If so, don't mince words. Speak plainly."

Before she'd fallen asleep last night, she'd come to realize Lucia's true purpose had never been to help her. She felt foolish for not seeing through the woman's plans, but now realized her craving for freedom had blinded her to Lucia's true motives.

"Did you ever believe I had a chance for escape?"

A smirk curved the healer's mouth. Her dark eyes were as hard as chips of jet. "No."

"Then why did you lie?"

"I wanted you gone. But I've accepted you're like the stink of old fish, impossible to get rid of unless the master disposes of you himself."

"Not true!" Her outrage clamored for release. "I wanted to flee. I'd have succeeded if you'd done as you promised and arranged for someone to guide me to my cousin."

"Your plan would have proven worthless in the end." Lucia moved toward the fountain. "Caros is bewitched by you. He would have hunted you down and brought you back unless he became disgusted by the sight of you."

"He might try, but he'd need a legion to drag me back here once I reached my family. My cousin's husband is a senator. Do you think he'd let me rot in degradation when he has the influence to see me freed?"

Her back to the garden, the healer plunged her bucket beneath the fountain's flow. "By law you're the property of our master. If he refuses to sell, you can't be bought. He told you so himself. Why didn't you believe him?"

Because a future with no end to her enslavement was no future at all. "I'm certain he can be brought to reason."

Lucia shook her head. "I've been a slave my entire life. The *lanista's* slave since he opened the doors of this school three years past. I've seen how a man gazes at the woman he craves and I can see how much Caros yearns for you."

"You blame *me* for this?"

"Somehow you've made yourself a challenge to him and he never gives up until he's won."

"I've given him no reason to pursue me."

Lucia's lip curled. "He's drawn to your innocence. I won't accept it's anything more. If I hadn't been ill-used since girlhood, I'm certain I'd tempt him just as you have. My plan would have succeeded if only I'd waited longer to tell him you were gone."

Pelonia gaped, mystified by the bizarre workings of the woman's brain. "You make no sense. If you wanted me gone, why tell him I'd fled at all?"

"If you simply disappeared, he might have become obsessed to find you. As it was, I wanted him to *see* your disgrace. I wished for him to find you in the arms of another man. To have the image seared into his mind so he would never look on you with tenderness again. If you were not so pure, I'm convinced he'd lose all interest and send you away."

Numbed by Lucia's venom, Pelonia watched Cat trot toward the gate. Her breath hitched when she saw Caros beneath one of the olive trees a short distance down the path. He lifted his index finger to his lips, warning her to silence.

Pelonia's gaze darted back to where Lucia stood tangled in her own thoughts, her fingers locked on the lip of the fountain as if her outburst had drained her of strength. "I've waited three years for Caros to love me. With all of my being, I've longed to know the gentleness he's shown you without reservation."

The quiet confession tugged at Pelonia's heart, but the brutality she'd endured was still too raw to forgive the other woman. A light breeze rustled the lemon trees.

Caros moved forward. Her eyes downcast, the healer didn't seem to notice his approach.

"Lucia, a word with you." His icy calm made Pelonia squirm with dread.

Lucia spun toward him, banging the bucket of water she'd placed by her feet. "Master, I didn't see you."

"So I gathered from the conversation."

The color drained from Lucia's face. "I can explain."

"No, allow me," he said coldly. "I rescued you from cruelty and made you an important member of this household. I gave you responsibility and more liberty as a slave than most free women ever dream of. You repaid my generosity with lies, theft—"

"Master, I never—"

"*Don't* interrupt me." The entire garden seemed to cringe from the quiet force of his rage. "You repaid me with jealousy and petty envy. Envy that would have seen a blameless girl raped and possibly murdered without a qualm."

"But Caros," Lucia whispered, placing her hand on his forearm with inappropriate familiarity. "You must listen to me!"

The woman must be insane. Pelonia worried for her welfare. Couldn't she see Caros teetered on the edge of committing mayhem? Why didn't Lucia heed the warnings of his clenched fists or the nerve ticking in his jaw? Why did she just stand there and not run for safety?

Caros cast her hand from him as though it were diseased. "You will be punished for aiding the escape of a slave and for slandering your master. You'll be whipped, then sold. Never darken my door again."

"*Noooo!*" Lucia fell to her knees, tears coursing down her face. "Please don't do this, Master. I *love* you. Can't you see the truth? If not for her, you would have come to *me*."

Unable to watch the piteous sight, Pelonia turned away. Lucia's broken spirit sparked her compassion. When she thought of her own failings, the transgressions that stained her soul, who was she to judge the other woman? Without Christ's boundless love and forgiveness she might be as hopeless.

Lucia's sobs rang through the garden. She called Caros's name, begging him to hear her, but he remained deaf to her pleas. With Cat beside him, he didn't stop except to speak with a set of guards outside the gate.

Once Caros disappeared beyond her sight, she approached the other woman as though Lucia were a wounded animal. Seeing the guards move closer, she knelt beside the healer, unsure of the welcome she'd receive. When Lucia continued to weep, Pelonia eased her into an embrace.

Lucia didn't fight. She cried harder. Her tears soaked Pelonia's shoulder. A hard lump formed in her throat as she stroked Lucia's hair, silent in her attempt at solace.

When the tears subsided, Lucia pulled away, her cheeks blotchy, her eyes lifeless. She wiped the damp rivulets from her face. "Can you imagine the pain I've endured since you came here? I've had to tend your wounds, ensure you lived, while knowing every day the man I worship is falling deeper and deeper under your spell."

Before Pelonia could reply, the guards seized Lucia and shuffled her from the garden, ignoring Pelonia's entreaties to stop. Distressed by the woman's treatment, she tried to imagine the hardship of Lucia's life, the harshness of an existence without affection.

She recalled her own history, the blessing of being raised by a father who cared for her and taught her of Christ's love. Her strength came from the truth she'd learned, the certainty that came from being nurtured in faith even when circumstances made her question God's fairness.

But what of Lucia? A slave from birth, she'd been denied familial attachment and weaned on the uncertainty of their society's fear and superstition. Who could blame her for dreaming of a life with a man of Caros's strength or for fighting for her place when she felt threatened?

Pelonia filled the buckets and carried them to an untended corner of the garden. Somehow she would have to sway Caros from the punishment he'd chosen. But how did she ask for mercy from a man who'd never known compassion? Why would he listen to her when, despite what Lucia claimed, she was nothing more to him than a challenge?

A guard approached and gave orders for her to meet Caros in the house. Eager to speak with him, she washed her hands and made her way to the cool interior courtyard where the smell of fresh bread and a table laden with delicacies awaited her.

Caros wasn't to be found, but the tall stranger she'd seen with him yesterday entered the open air space from the direction of the living quarters. With his hair rumpled and his short tunic wrinkled, he looked as though he'd just risen from a deep sleep. Not wanting to disturb one of Caros's guests, she turned to leave.

"Wait," he said, a Greek accent edging his Latin, "I'm Alexius, Caros's champion. You must be Pelonia, his newest paramour."

"I'm no such thing," she denied hotly.

"Of course you're not." A grin parted his lips, creating a long dimple in each of his lean cheeks. "That's why Caros woke me in the middle of the night ranting about you. It seems you're more trouble than you're worth."

She crossed her arms over her chest. "Is that what he told you?"

He shook his head, the sunlight glinting off his dark hair. "No, my opinion only. Is it true Lucia's to be whipped and sold today?"

"Not if I can stop it."

He moved to the table and chose an oatcake glistening with honey. "You think you can change Caros's mind?"

"I have to try."

"By all means, do. I'd hate to see Lucia sent away. She's an intelligent woman and there are few enough of those."

Pelonia arched a brow. "Perhaps you think so because only dim women will tolerate you."

He laughed, clearly not offended. "Lucia's talented with herbs and other medicines. Whether Caros admits it or not, she'll be difficult to replace."

"Thank you, Alexius. I believe you've given me the solution I need."

"I have? How so?"

"I'll explain later. Do you know where Caros is? A guard told me to meet him here, but…"

"I imagine he's on the field. If you were told to wait here, do so. The sand is no place for a dainty woman like you."

"But I must find him. He may have Lucia whipped at any moment."

"No, the men are occupied. He won't interrupt them with frivolity. The punishment won't begin until after the midday meal when the men are resting and it can serve as both a warning and entertainment."

Pelonia's stomach flipped. "Is Caros always so cruel?"

The Greek chewed a bite of peach and swallowed. "Why do you think he's cruel?"

"Don't *you* think it's harsh to have Lucia whipped for the men's amusement?"

"No. She disobeyed and betrayed him. A cruel *lanista* would use her for target practice."

She shuddered. "I tried to escape. What punishment do you think he has in store for me?"

"Ask him yourself." Alexius tipped his head toward the corridor and stood to leave. "There he is now."

In a few brisk steps, Caros joined Pelonia beside the table. For several long moments before Alexius announced his arrival he'd taken the chance to watch her unhindered. Her tart replies to the Greek amused him as much as her concern for Lucia amazed him.

"Have you eaten?" he asked.

"No, but Alexius seemed to enjoy the fruit."

"Why didn't you sample it? I doubt you've eaten since last night."

"It's not mine and I'm neither a thief nor a guest."

"You can't steal this. It's all yours."

"For me?" She glanced at the arrangement of breads and sweet cream, fresh berries, peaches, and oatcakes glistening with honey. "I don't understand. Aren't you angry with me?"

Her pulse ticked beneath the red gash on her neck. The reminder of the rapist's knife held against her throat stoked his ire toward Lucia. "I'm furious, but not with you."

She wrung her hands, her deep brown eyes widened

with uncertainty. "How can you not be? I tried to escape."

He shrugged. "Every slave runs for freedom at least once."

"Did you?"

"More than once," he admitted.

"What happened?"

"I was flogged."

Tears formed in her eyes. "I'm sorry."

Why the tears? Did she fear he'd have her disciplined in a similar manner? "As you should be. I'll be lenient with you this time, but don't test me again."

"I'm not apologizing for my attempted escape. I'm sorry you were ever abused."

His heart beat faster. It seemed eons since anyone bothered to care if he lived or died, let alone whether or not he'd endured a mere whipping.

He cupped her face, her cheeks smooth and soft beneath his calloused palms. Aware of their bargain, that he was breaking his promise not to touch her, he crushed the urge to gather her in his arms. "Then your apology is unnecessary, *mea carissima*. My back no longer pains me. Unlike my heart, if you seek to leave me again."

Her gaze softened. "Our bargain," she reminded him softly. "I've given my word not to leave for a fortnight."

He brushed his thumb along her full bottom lip, comparing its rich color to the ripe peaches on the table. "By then you'll be mine and leaving me will be the last thing you want."

She stepped away as if rejecting the worst sort of temptation. "I doubt it, Caros. You speak of making me yours, but I'll never willingly give myself to a man who's not my husband."

He smiled, aware he never failed to claim what he set his mind to. "We'll see."

"Yes, we will." She tucked a strand of hair behind her ear and moved a few paces deeper into the shade. "Now, about Lucia."

He dropped his arms to his side and his hands balled into fists. "What about the cursed wench? If I hadn't been looking for you in the garden, I might not have heard her confess her crimes. As it is, I've already arranged to have her punished after the noonday meal."

"Please don't," she said, her eyes pleading. "Alexius told me your plans. Consider what it will mean for you and your men if she's gone."

"How can you, of all people, not wish to see her punished? Have you forgotten the course of sorrow and disgrace she charted for you?"

"I haven't forgotten, but I have chosen to forgive."

Astounded, he grasped for words. "You've forgiven her? Why? How?"

"How can I not? None of us has lived a blameless life."

He'd never met anyone with half her generous nature. Forgiveness was foreign to him. In his world, a man lived and died by the sword where one mistake might forfeit his life. There were no second chances. Once again, her strange way of thinking intrigued him. "Tell me why I should forgive her when she's earned the severest punishment?"

Pelonia prayed for wisdom before she spoke. If she ever hoped to impart the heart of the Gospel to this warrior, now might be her last chance. "I can't truthfully say she doesn't deserve what you intend for her."

He snorted. "I knew it."

"But Christ has pardoned me for the wrongs I've com-

mitted. I owe it to Him to follow His example and forgive others when they wound me."

"You should have told me we were discussing religion." He waved his hand to dismiss the subject.

"No, Caros, we're not." She gripped his forearm to
stop him from leaving. "We're talking about love and
kindness, generosity of spirit. The act of extending
mercy, because…because you understand how much
you need it for yourself."

For one unguarded moment, she saw through his hardened exterior to the place deep inside him that was raw
with need.

Her heart nearly burst with want of comforting him.
She could barely refrain from throwing her arms around
him and holding him until the torment in his eyes disappeared for good.

He glanced skyward. "Few people ever receive mercy,
Pelonia. Fewer still deserve it."

"True, but Christ taught He has enough mercy and
forgiveness for anyone who asks Him for it. You must
only believe in Him."

"You can't fathom the things I've done," he said so
quietly she strained to hear.

She could imagine. A man of his skill in the ring
had probably killed countless people over the years. "It
doesn't matter what you've done, Caros. Christ's forgiveness is a gift. One none of us deserves, but His grace is
extended to all just the same."

"How much will this 'gift' cost me? I used to visit
the temples until the priests kept demanding more coin
to fatten their coffers."

"It's free. You can't buy it or earn it. You must only
believe."

He closed his eyes. An expression of pain marred his features. He shook his head. "I can't believe in grace or forgiveness when everything in my life has taught me there is none."

Her heart sank with disappointment. "You don't have to believe in Him this moment, Caros, but I pray one day you will."

Chapter Nine

Marcus Valerius contemplated his nephew by marriage, Senator Antonius Tacitus, with a healthy dose of respect. Shrewd beyond his thirty years, the senator would be difficult to dupe. Antonius's young wife, Tiberia, might be a beauteous and spirited woman, but her brain rivaled the size of a lentil. Not so her husband.

"Why do you need such a large sum of money, Marcus?" The senator tossed a parchment onto his bronze-plated desk. "As I understand it, you inherited your brother's holdings when the marauders killed him a fortnight ago."

"Yes, but the property is far from the delights and advantages one can find here in the capital. Besides—" Marcus spread his hands and schooled his lips into a cajoling smile "—is it really so large a sum between family?"

The senator's lips thinned. "Five thousand denarii is a large amount between anyone—especially family. What assurance do I have you'll repay me?"

"I'm willing to use the Umbrian estate as collateral," Marcus said, determined to risk all if necessary in his goal of establishing himself as an influential man of Rome. "The vineyards alone are worth ten times as much as I'm asking to borrow. When you consider the additional orchards, wheat fields, livestock, the villa and outbuildings…do you think I'd be foolish enough to risk the place if I weren't convinced of my plans?"

"A good business strategy doesn't ensure success, Marcus. Importing wine from your own estate and selling it here in the city without the expense of an importer sounds profitable, but there are innumerable wine merchants in Rome." Antonius adjusted the lantern light. "According to my wife, your brother opted against this sort of venture, claiming it was too risky."

Marcus gritted his teeth. Opening the wine shop was the first step in a larger scheme to obtain the recognition he craved. Years spent in the shadow of his twice-blessed older brother had left him virtually forgotten, his talents dismissed and his life almost wasted. With Pelonius dead and his troublesome niece sold into slavery, he finally had the means to fulfill his ambitions.

"From what my wife tells me," Antonius continued, "Pelonius turned your father's small farm into a thriving enterprise within a short time of his inheritance. Tiberia's high regard for your late brother and his undisputed financial acumen make me hesitant to go against his judgment."

Marcus hid his contempt for the younger man's lack of vision beneath a placid smile. No man worth his salt let a woman sway his decisions, but whether he liked it or not, he needed Antonius's influence. Once he'd made his own connections, Tiberia and her myopic husband could rot for all the care he gave. Until then, he planned to smile and nod in agreement when necessary, and when the time came, collect apologies from those who'd doubted his talents and superior intellect.

"It's true, my brother was favored by Mercury with his gift of commerce, but I'm equally gifted. It isn't my fault Pelonius inherited before me. If I'd been the elder son and the land passed down to me who knows how great our family's fortune might be."

Elated to find he held the senator's full attention, Marcus pressed on. "You'd be a fool not to loan me the funds. I promise you there's no need to fear you'll lose a single piece of silver. I'll pay you back with interest, of course. If I'm unsuccessful, which I won't be, you'll have the estate. Either way you're bound to profit."

"By the gods, it's a tempting offer." The senator picked up the parchment and studied the proposal with renewed interest. He eyed Marcus over the top of the page like a cat about to pounce on a wounded squirrel. "Very tempting. In fact, maybe I *should* loan you the money, then devise a scheme to make you fail. What better place to escape Rome's summer heat than to my own estate in the Umbrian hills?"

Marcus laughed nervously. Perhaps he'd been *too* persuasive. "As we're kin of sorts, Senator, feel free to enjoy my hospitality whenever you wish."

"That's good of you, *kin,* considering you've been a guest in my home for how many weeks?"

Marcus folded his hands in his lap, irritated by his host's subtle gibe. Adopting a wounded air, he straightened in his seat. "I apologize, Senator, if I've overstayed my welcome. Your dear wife was the first to embrace me as a relative since mine were taken so tragically on the way to your wedding. If, in my gratitude toward her,

I've somehow offended you by claiming your people as my own, I—"

"Enough, Marcus. If you'd offended me, you'd be out on the street, not here in my study trying to wheedle me out of five thousand denarii."

Reminding himself to bide his time, Marcus cloaked his scorn beneath a reverential manner. "I'm glad to hear I remain in your good graces."

Antonius left his desk and went to a cabinet painted with a lush scene of Venus rising from the sea's foam. He opened one of its front panels and removed a bottle of wine. "I'll have an agreement prepared for us to sign by tomorrow's dinner hour."

Marcus fidgeted with excitement. He was on his way. "What rate of interest will you charge me?"

"Only twenty percent. It's fair enough considering the money lenders' price." The senator lifted the bottle of red wine. "Shall I pour you a glass of your family's finest to celebrate?"

Marcus accepted with his first genuine smile in weeks. Without a doubt he'd been right to sell Pelonia and cleanse the family of her Christian defilement. The gods must be pleased with his loyalty to them, for they'd been smiling on him ever since that fateful day.

He stood and accepted the glass Antonius held out to him. "Indeed, Senator, I'm happy to drink with you. There is much to celebrate and I'm confident there is even more excitement to come."

Pelonia had just finished weeding the vegetable garden when Caros's steward found her in the courtyard and delivered new orders.

"Make haste for the kitchen," Gaius said. "The master

has invited a special guest to dine with him this evening. You're needed to help with the preparations."

A ruckus outside the front of the house caught his attention before she could reply.

"She's here!" Gaius bumped into a large potted palm on his swift retreat to the main door. A handful of house slaves scurried after him. Pelonia followed to the edge of the atrium, curious to see who'd set the household on fire.

Positioning herself behind one of the tiled columns lining the covered porch, she had a clear view of the proceedings without being seen.

Near the door, Gaius lined up the slaves in a tight row. The steward took a deep breath, forced a smile and swept open the portal.

Pelonia gasped. The woman who breezed across the threshold was easily the most beautiful vision she'd ever seen. Her unblemished, alabaster skin provided an elegant contrast with her black hair and exotic, kohl-rimmed eyes. Perfectly dressed in a flowing tunic of rare blue silk, she wore a matching *palla* around her shoulders. The shawl, in the same blue as the tunic, was shot through with gold thread that shimmered in the light.

An elaborate gold headpiece held her fashionable, upswept curls in place. Bejeweled baubles, rings and necklaces adorned her slender form from her tiny ears to her rich, blue-dyed leather sandals.

As the guest moved deeper into the house, she gave Pelonia a glimpse of the expensively crafted litter she'd arrived on and the four muscular slaves who'd carried it.

Perhaps the lady was royalty.

"Where is my favorite *lanista*?" the woman asked, quizzing Gaius on Caros's whereabouts. "I rushed here from across the city as soon as I received his message late this morning. Is it too much to expect he greet me at the door?"

Pelonia's interest heightened. Why had Caros invited this stunning woman to meet with him?

"He's due from the baths at any moment, my lady." Gaius helped her remove the shawl, revealing the guest's gold, sapphire studded belt. "He told me to make you comfortable if you arrived before he returned."

The guest seemed unimpressed. "Typical man. Issue a summons, then expect a woman to wait. Normally, I wouldn't tolerate such rudeness. If it were anyone besides my dear Caros, I'd leave this instant."

Pelonia stifled a laugh. She liked the new arrival's spirited manner.

"I'm sure he appreciates your patience, my lady." Gaius handed the *palla* to the first slave before ushering the woman past Pelonia and into a sitting room. The other slaves trailed in their wake.

"May I fetch you a drink?" Pelonia heard the steward ask. "Or would you prefer something to eat? What can I do to provide for your comfort?"

Pelonia peered around the corner. The woman perched on the sofa. Her head tilted at a regal angle, she contemplated the offer. "I suppose a glass of new wine will do. And a selection of those special rolls your cook bakes would also please me. Just make certain he doesn't skimp on the honey."

Gaius clapped and two of the slaves ran to do the visitor's bidding. The remaining two slaves gathered large peacock feather fans from the corner and began to wave them over the woman. Bracelets jangling, the new arrival

folded her hands in her lap and leaned forward slightly
for Gaius to fluff her pillows.

"How long before Caros returns?" she asked, tapping
her fingers on her knee. "You know I bore easily, Gaius.
Perhaps I'll venture to the training yard and take stock
of the newest men." She sprang to her feet.

"My lady..." Gaius threw up his hands in defeat as
she disappeared down the corridor in the direction of the
training field. The steward shook his head and slanted a
glance at Pelonia. "That fireball is Adiona Leonia. She's
one of the richest widows in Rome and was among the
master's first admirers. She's loved him for years."

Her favor toward the widow dimmed and a twinge of
jealousy unsettled her.

Gaius waved his hand as if to erase his last statement from the air. "Forget my rash words. I'm not one to
spread gossip about our master and you're needed in the
kitchen. Widow Leonia will expect her meal prepared
on time and to perfection. The master will be furious if
she's disappointed."

Pelonia headed to the cookhouse. Her brow pleated
with troubling questions. What did Caros want with Adiona Leonia? Was the vivacious beauty really in love with
him? Most likely, but how did he feel about his admirer
in return? Worst of all, had Caros been toying with *her*
emotions when his heart already belonged to the widow?

Pelonia entered the kitchen, drowning in uncertainty.
Heat blasted her. The aroma of cooked meat enveloped
her and she noticed a trio of pigs roasting on a spit above
the flames.

Adjusting her coarse tunic, she remembered the fine
silk of the widow's ensemble, garments similar to the
ones she used to wear every day and took for granted.

She washed her hands in a bucket of tepid water, ignoring a pang of envy. She joined the other four slaves kneading dough by the window. Deep in debate about which gladiator they found most handsome, the girls didn't acknowledge her greeting.

Pelonia's fingers worked the sticky, wheat-colored mass atop the table. The girls' chatter faded as her thoughts drifted back to Adiona. Little wonder Caros found the woman attractive. She was too beautiful by half. Not only was she stunning, but her vibrant energy infused the air around her. She smelled fresh, too, clean with a hint of cinnamon and other fragrant spices.

Pelonia wrinkled her nose, disgusted by the smell of smoked pork clinging to her own body. She hoped Cat didn't mistake her in the dark for his evening snack. With the back of her hand, she brushed the sweat from her brow and, knowing it would make it worse, resisted the urge to scratch the chafed area on her shoulder beneath her tunic.

Her fingers grew idle in the dough as she stared out the window. In less than a month, her life had changed beyond recognition. Her chest ached from holding in her grief. A well of loneliness opened inside her, dragging her into its darkness. She missed her father, her home, her friends. She missed being herself.

With all her heart, she wished Caros had met her as she used to be, not the bedraggled slave she'd become. Perhaps then he would respect her and view winning her affections as something more than a game.

"Stop dawdling!" The girl beside her jabbed an elbow in Pelonia's ribs. "Word is more guests are coming tonight. We have to hurry and get more loaves of bread in the oven."

Rubbing her side, Pelonia bit back a retort and finished kneading her portion of dough, then several others. Heat from the fire made her perspire until the itchy cloth she wore stuck to her back and chest.

What she wouldn't do for a bath. She longed for the soothing comfort of the water, the cleansing ointments on her skin—

"Pelonia?" A male slave called from the doorway. "Are you in here?"

She brushed the flour and bits of dough from her hands before wiping them on a towel. "Yes, here I am."

"The master wishes to see you. He's waiting in the atrium."

She left the kitchen, but didn't rush to find Caros. After all, he had Adiona to amuse him. Bending to pick a sprig of jasmine along the path, she tucked the flower behind her right ear. She breathed in the sweetness, shamefully aware that one small bloom could not hide the odor of her unwashed clothes and person.

Once she entered the house, she straightened her shoulders and held her head high. As she made her way into the courtyard, she noticed the lack of Adiona's presence and breathed a sigh of thanks.

Caros met her beneath the columned porch. The sight of him stole her breath. He'd had his hair trimmed and was freshly shaven. The thick black waves of his hair curled around his ears and brushed his forehead. His white tunic looked new, as did his leather sandals. She'd never seen him more handsome. Had he gone to such trouble with his appearance to impress his beautiful guest?

He grasped her elbow in a light grip. "Where have

you been? I sent a messenger for you almost half an hour ago."

"Half an hour?" She glanced at the sundial, then schooled her features in an innocent expression. "I'm surprised you noticed the time with such pleasant company to entertain you."

He looked startled. "You met Adiona?"

"I didn't meet her. I saw her when she arrived."

His lips spread in a slow smile. "She *is* pleasant, is she not? And beautiful enough to rival Venus, don't you agree?"

"She's remarkable," she answered, determined to sound congenial. Why, she couldn't pinpoint, but she waited for him to refute any serious involvement with the woman.

No denial came and she restrained herself from shaking one out of him. Jealousy buzzed in her head like an irritating fly beside her ear. She pasted on a smile to save her pride. "I hope the two of you are most happy together."

"Oh, we are," he assured her. "Adiona and I have known one another for years. Unlike you and me, she and I are of similar minds. Our relationship is everything I desire it to be."

She swallowed her heartache and reached up to tuck a stray wisp of hair behind her ear. The jasmine fell to the mosaic floor. Having forgotten she'd placed it there, she realized how pathetic she must seem compared to the luminous widow. With her hair unwashed and lusterless, the feed sack of a tunic she wore and dirt embedded under her fingernails, she was a broken stem next to an artfully arranged bouquet.

Caros bent to retrieve the sprig and handed it to her.

"Is all well with you, Pelonia? You seem a bit disheart-ened."

Careful not to touch him, she took the flower. "If I seem down, it's because I'm confused."

"By what?"

"By you," she admitted. "If you belong to your widow friend, why did you attempt to woo *me*?"

He shrugged. "Why do you care? You're the one who claimed we're ill-suited. You should be delighted I've taken you at your word."

The flow of the fountain filled the silence. A reply froze in her throat. She searched his face, captivated by the deep blue of his eyes, the strength of his jaw, the fullness of his lips.

Her vision blurred with unshed tears. How much loss could she endure? First her father and household, now Caros when she was just beginning to understand how much she cared for him. It was cold comfort to real-ize she'd been right to withhold her heart since his had proven fickle.

She bowed her head. *Please, God, hold me together. Don't let him witness my despair.*

His warm fingers slid around the back of her neck. With a gentle tug, he pulled her toward him, but she re-fused to budge.

Voices carried from the direction of the guest rooms. Caros released her the moment Adiona entered the court-yard.

"There you are, my darling." The widow's bright smile curved her painted mouth. She linked arms with Caros and her amber gaze scanned Pelonia from head to foot. She frowned. "This isn't the one you suggested earlier, is it? She'll never do as a maid of mine. She looks like she hasn't bathed in a week. I might get fleas."

Pelonia's cheeks burned and with as much dignity as she could muster she walked away. Her vanity wounded, her feminine pride shattered, she clutched at the hollow ache in her chest.

"Where are you off to?" Caros called before she could escape indoors. "I didn't dismiss you."

Her steps slowed to a stop. Her mortification fresh in her mouth, she couldn't bring herself to turn around.

Caros watched her intently. Would she carry out a test of wills in front of his guest? He hoped not. It would be an affront he couldn't let pass. He counted to three, then commanded, "Come here, slave."

He saw her wince and regretted the order. He'd meant to make her jealous, not earn her hatred for all eternity.

She turned, her entire manner as stiff as an iron blade. Her dark eyes shimmered with anger…or was it injured pride?

"Yes, *Master?*" she said, her tone so cold, he suspected he'd catch a chill.

Easing from the widow's grasp, he moved halfway to Pelonia. This close he could see the emotion wasn't anger or injured pride in her troubled eyes. It was raw humiliation.

He released a sharp breath. What a fool he was. The one woman he wanted most in life and he was certain he'd just lost her.

Chapter Ten

Pelonia struggled to hide her embarrassment behind a mask of indifference. Aware of the widow's scrutinizing gaze, she couldn't bear for the arrogant gorgon to see how deep her insult cut.

She crossed her arms over her chest, uncomfortable with Caros's probing stare. "If that will be all, *Master,* may I go? There's work to be done in the kitchen."

He raked his fingers through his hair and gave a terse nod of consent. "Go, then. I'll speak with you later."

Her back as straight as a pike, she fled indoors. Once out of Caros's sight she pressed against a wall for support, waiting for her trembling to ease. Her anger burned against Caros and his icy paramour. The woman in her wished for a way to teach the malicious beauty a lesson in humility.

Adiona's husky laughter rippled through the garden. "Amazing!" she exclaimed. "I do believe our undefeated champion has finally met his match."

"Adiona, don't—"

"And a slave girl no less. How delicious!"

Fascinated, Pelonia stilled though she knew she should walk away.

"Leave it." He sounded exasperated.

"No, you must tell me," the widow said with glee. "I'm intrigued beyond bearing. How did you, with women all over Rome vying for your favor, fall for such a scruffy little mouse?"

Pelonia bristled, her dislike of the widow and her mockery growing more intense with each passing moment. She held her breath waiting for Caros's response.

"I've never struck a woman before," he said darkly, "but you're tempting me."

The widow gasped. "There's no need to be cruel. I was jesting."

After a long, tense moment, his heavy footsteps sounded on the tile. "Forgive me," he said, his voice strained. "In my bad temper, I forgot your past misfortune. After all these years, you must know you're safe regardless of my threats."

Pelonia's brow furrowed. Had Adiona been abused once? Perhaps the widow's brusque exterior hid a core of inner pain? If so, she couldn't help but feel a twinge of pity for the woman.

"I *do* know," Adiona murmured, almost too softly to reach Pelonia's ears. "I'm sorry I teased you. Love is an affliction. I've seen the various ways the malady affects its victims and I know you're not the giddy sort."

He grunted. "Leave it, Adiona. I'm not in love with her. The girl's a slave. No more, no less."

A chill settled in Pelonia's bones. The widow spoke, but she didn't hear over the rush of recriminations swirling through her head. *What did you expect of him, you silly idiota? A declaration of undying devotion?*

She bowed her head, distraught to realize some sort of acknowledgment was exactly what she'd hoped for. *Brainless, stupid, foolish...*

Heavy with disappointment, she climbed the stairs to lick her wounds in the solitude of her chamber. With Caros otherwise engaged and dinner preparations reaching their zenith, she suspected no one would notice her absence.

An hour later, a small oil lamp illuminated Pelonia's room. The sun had said farewell and darkness enshrouded the city. She stood at the window. Every fiber of her being urged her to run, to escape the prison of her despair. Yet, she was trapped as much by the guards at every gate as her promise not to flee.

Her fingers gripped the sill until her nails made marks in the wood. She must have been deranged to make the bargain last night. Yes, she wanted to tell Caros about Jesus, but if she were honest with herself she had to admit her capitulation stemmed from other reasons as well. Had it been the tenderness she imagined in Caros's eyes or her own gullibility? Perhaps both had conspired to trick her into believing something more, something precious yet unexplored, existed between her and the *lanista.*

Not that it mattered what she thought. This afternoon he'd been clear in his denial of any affection for her.

The girl's a slave. No more, no less.

His words circled over and over in her mind, scalding her with each relentless pass.

The smell of roasted meats carried on the cool night air. She hadn't eaten since morning. Her stomach grumbled. The banquet would begin soon. She tensed, aware that if anyone noticed her absence it would be during the meal's first few courses. Once the guests were immersed in the party's merriment, no one would care if there were too few servants or not.

Lying down on her pallet, she tried to reach out for God's guidance, an inkling of peace. Instead, her mind tormented her with visions of Caros and his lady love. Jealousy hounded her. How had she come to care for him in such a short time? When had he wormed into her heart so completely?

Lord, how do I pluck him out?

She rolled to her side. The shadows on the walls flickered like evil specters laughing at her misery. She stood and began to pace.

Shuffling footsteps drew her attention. Someone knocked on the door. If she ignored them perhaps they'd leave her be? Another knock, this one more insistent.

"Open up!" a gruff voice demanded. "I have word from the master."

She glared at the portal and the harsh male concealed behind it. She might as well answer; there was no lock. She wrenched open the door…and stared in astonishment.

"The master sent this for you." The short, burly slave nodded to a wooden tub held by two other slaves behind him. Confused, she backed up and let them deposit the large, barrel-shaped container in the corner.

"They'll be back with water," the gruff slave informed as he tossed her a folded bundle of cloth. "You have instructions to ready yourself. The master's guests will be arriving within the hour. You're expected to help serve the meal."

Moments later, the slaves brought water, filled the tub and left. She closed the door and undid the bundle she held. Inside, she found a fresh tunic, a bottle of cleansing oils and two rough cloths to dry herself with. Delighted by the items, she placed the oils and cloths by the tub and draped the tunic over the room's lone chair.

With a sigh, she slipped into the steaming water. It was almost too hot after weeks of bathing in cold, but the glorious sensation of being immersed in sweet bliss relaxed her muscles and lifted her spirits.

Tipping her head back against the rim, she closed her eyes. Why had Caros sent her the gifts? Had Adiona's scorn shamed him enough to be generous? Or did he simply wish to avoid embarrassment in front of his guests? No doubt, his displeasure would soar if she entered his banquet as odorous as a "scruffy little mouse."

She refused to rile her temper with thoughts of the widow or her insults. Whatever Caros's reason for the bath and other gifts, she was grateful.

The water cooled. She reached for one of the cloths and spread it on the floor. Stepping out of the tub, she applied a thick layer of spice-scented oil over her skin and through her wet hair. At the bath complex, an attendant would use a strigil to scrape the dirt and moisture from her body, but in the absence of both helper and implement, she used one of the rough cloths to buff her skin until it shone with cleanliness.

By the time she heard Caros's first visitors arrive, she was rinsing her hair. Clean and refreshed, she wrapped the strands in one of the dry linens and, stalling for time, washed her other garments.

Faint chatter and the muted melody of a panpipe filtered through the open windows, signaling the start of the evening's entertainments.

She'd best hurry. Her hair finger-combed and braided,

her teeth cleaned, she finished dressing, thankful for the new tunic and the softness brushing her body. She slipped on her sandals, tied the laces around her ankles, and headed for the first floor.

Caros noticed Pelonia the moment she walked into the dining room, a pitcher held in each hand. He willed her to glance his way, but she denied him even the slightest acknowledgment. The oil lamps provided a clear view as she made her way toward the low-lying couches surrounding the banquet table.

His longing for her so strong he could taste the bitter sweetness of it, he admired the sway of her hips and her supple, honey-toned skin. In different garments, no one would suspect her slave status. She possessed the bearing of a goddess and her natural beauty put every other woman in the room to shame.

The music shifted tempo. A kithara and lyre joined the panpipe. Had she enjoyed her bath? He wished he'd thought of her needs sooner, before Adiona's mockery had a chance to hurt her. Had his wits been quicker, he might have saved Pelonia a healthy dose of embarrassment.

His gaze followed her as she mingled with his guests. Filling empty glass goblets with fresh water or honeyed wine, she smiled often, speaking when spoken to. The easy laughter that followed her comments added to the party's jovial mood.

She conversed with Alexius, unaware of her effect on many of the males in attendance. Noticing how the eyes of the men lingered on his woman, Caros struggled to contain his temper. Perhaps he should have overcome his need to see her and left her upstairs away from lust-filled eyes.

Adiona moved beside him, her sweet perfume surrounding him like a thick cloud. She linked her arm with his. "It's going well, don't you agree? Marius Brocchus and his mistress are eating all the honeyed figs, but other than that everyone seems happy enough."

He looked down into his friend's kohl-rimmed eyes. "The evening's going as you planned. I'm glad we could help one another."

She rose on tiptoe and kissed his mouth. "You're the last man in the world worth a denarius. I would have sent Lucia to my country villa even if you hadn't agreed to this fete."

He groaned. "You might have told me sooner."

Squeezing his arm, she laughed. "You can admit you're enjoying yourself."

He located Pelonia near the banquet table. As long as she remained in the room he managed to be content. "You know I'm not one for parties."

"Indeed, I do. *Everyone* knows you've been a recluse this last year. I've defended you, but…"

Adiona chatted on. Caros listened with half an ear. He'd stopped his wild socializing when he realized how empty it left him. Without Pelonia's presence even this fine gathering would soon bore him.

He barely noticed when Adiona went to make conversation with Alexius. As the night progressed, he did his duty and spoke with a number of couples and a small group of senators debating the consequences of Emperor Domitian's new policies.

Throughout the night, his female admirers approached

him, but with his attention focused on his slave, he dispatched the women with ease.

His brows pinched together. He'd lost sight of Pelonia again. It wasn't uncommon for drunken guests to claim a comely slave for a night's use and with many of his visitors swimming deeper in their cups, he worried for her safety.

A well-known soloist began a bawdy song. Cheers and applause filled the room. Revelers reclined on the couches, stuffing themselves with more of the delectable food.

Adiona came up beside him. She tugged on his arm. "Why are you frowning when Rome's most-sought-after entertainer is performing for your benefit?" She sighed. "Isn't he wonderful? He was so honored when I sent word you would be here tonight, he cancelled a previous engagement to sing elsewhere."

Another burst of laughter erupted in the far corner. Pelonia had been gone too long. He started to seek her out, but caught sight of her in the open doorway, on a return trip from the courtyard. His anxiety lessened. She must have gone to refill her pitchers or care for the guests sampling the cooler air outside. Either way it was time for her to leave.

"Excuse me," he said, withdrawing his arm from Adiona's grasp.

Pelonia froze when she saw him approach. He smiled and relieved her of the pitchers, handing them to another slave close by. Unmindful of the hush descending around him, he took hold of her hand. "Come with me, *mea carissima.* I believe we've both endured enough for one night."

Chapter Eleven

Uncomfortably aware of the sudden whispers and keen interest aimed in her direction, Pelonia followed Caros from the dining room and down the corridor.

"Did I displease you?" she asked. "Where are you taking me?"

"You please me," he said without slowing his pace. "I wish to walk with you."

"Won't your company be offended if you leave?"

"If they are, so be it. They're Adiona's guests, not mine."

Bemused, she continued beside him, relishing the heat of his large hand engulfing hers. After hours of torture watching him in the clutches of other women, she was both irked and elated he'd chosen to leave alone with her.

Outside, a few widely spaced torches illuminated the stone path. The party's music and merriment drifted from the house behind them, becoming fainter the farther they moved away.

The peach trees rustled in the cool breeze as she and Caros reached the training ground. One of the night guards opened the gate. With a curt nod to the Nubian,

Caros led Pelonia onto the sidelines. The gate clicked behind them as though enclosing them in a world of their own.

They crossed the sand to a bench at the edge of the moonlit field. "Sit here," Caros said. "You look like you need to rest. With all the mayhem tonight, this is the quietest place I could think to bring you."

Her bewilderment deepened. If he had no affection for her as he'd told the widow, why did he treat her with persistent kindness? Where had a man who trained gladiators learned consideration?

Exhausted from a day of labor and a night serving his guests, she eased onto the bench. He towered above her, making her nervous. She craned her neck to see his face in the shadows. "Won't you sit beside me?"

Their sides touched when he took the space to her right. The heat of his body warmed her bare arm and thigh through her tunic. He laced his fingers with hers. Startled by the frisson of sensation that ran up her arm, she stilled but didn't move away. Her fingers meshed with his and an unexpected, inexplicable sense of intimacy cocooned them.

"Did the evening go as you planned?" she asked, resisting the urge to rest her head against his shoulder.

"I didn't plan it. Adiona did. She believes a banquet here amongst my champions will make her the envy of the other city matrons."

Reminded of her rival, she released his hand, but he held firm. A vision of the widow kissing him not long ago reared its ugly head. A desire to send the woman on an extended stay in the wilds of Germania overwhelmed her. She looked toward the empty field and prayed Caros wouldn't see the jealousy she struggled to conceal. "Perhaps we should head indoors."

"Why? Are you cold?" He wrapped his arm around her shoulders and pulled her closer to his side.

Unused to being held by a man, she stiffened for an instant, then gave into temptation and leaned against him.

"Is that better?" His lips brushed her hair. She nodded against his chest. He pointed to a constellation in the northern sky. "Do you see those three faint stars and the brighter one slightly south of them?"

"Yes, I see them."

"Now, follow a straight line north from the single star to that bright one just…there. Do you see it?"

She nodded, loving that he shared her interest in the stars. "The picture is called Cygnus the Swan, is it not?"

"You study the patterns? But you're a woman."

"And being a woman I should have no interest in the heavens?"

His shoulder lifted in a slight shrug. "The women I know are interested in other things—clothes and jewels, and endless adulation."

"I like clothes and jewels. The adulation—" she wrinkled her nose "—I can do without."

She felt the heat of his gaze studying her profile. She pointed to another set of stars in an effort to distract his attention. "Do you know Draco the Dragon?"

He leaned closer and looked in the direction she pointed. "No. I've only learned The Swan, Orion and the Great Bear."

She gave him a sideways glance and grinned. "Then perhaps I can teach you a thing or two."

"By all means, proceed."

"All right. From those four stars, follow south along

his tail." She moved her finger as if tracing a winding river. "It ends there between the Great Bear and its cub. Do you see?"

"I do. It's called the Dragon, you say?"

"*Draco* the Dragon. Don't forget," she teased with mock seriousness. "If you do, he might slither from the sky and eat your tough hide."

His laughter rumbled low and deep. He tugged her back against him. "Am I to take it you wouldn't protect me?"

"It depends."

"On what?"

"On how poorly you'd treated me that day."

He chuckled. "As well as I treat you, you'd have to throw yourself in front of me and beg Draco's mercy."

"Ha! So you think."

"Did I not give you fresh tunics and divert my much needed slaves from the banquet's preparations to fill you a bath?"

"Yes, you did," she said, growing serious. "And I appreciate them both."

"You're welcome," he sounded pleased.

"Thank you for bringing me here. The stars are beautiful tonight."

"Not half as beautiful as you." The compliment heated her cheeks. He cleared his throat and changed the subject. "Most people study stars to worship them or predict their own future. I didn't know your sect—"

"We don't. Why worship created things when we worship the true Creator?"

"Then why your interest? I can see it's keen."

"Yes, it is. It stems from my father. He used to be a deeply superstitious man. He studied astrology and worshipped the stars, the full pantheon, anything to relieve his uncertainty of the future. A few years before my birth, he accepted Christ as his Lord. After that, Creation became a thing of beauty, a testament to God's loving power and he learned to fear no longer."

Her mind sifted through cherished memories and she smiled into the dark. "When I was a child, we used to walk through our fields late at night. Father pointed out the constellations and told me stories." She swallowed the lump forming in her throat. "He told me he loved me as far and wide as the heavens, but even that didn't compare with the depth of Christ's devotion."

"I know you must miss him."

The compassion in his voice brought the sting of tears to her eyes. "More than I can say."

"You always will, but after a time the pain will lessen."

"It doesn't feel like it." Grief weighed on her chest like a box of iron.

"I lost my entire family in the space of one morning. Believe me, I know of what I speak."

Stunned speechless, she searched his face, her eyes wide with shocked dismay. "Your entire family? What happened?"

The moonlight revealed his bleak expression, his haunted eyes. "My father served Galba when he was governor of Spain. When Nero discovered Galba planned rebellion against him, he ordered the governor's execution along with his followers and their families."

Reminders of Nero sent a shiver of disgust down her spine. Even now, seventeen years later, rumor held the insane emperor set the great fire that burned half of

Rome. Later, he'd blamed and persecuted thousands of Christians to mask his own treachery.

"But the plot must have failed," she said. "Galba became emperor a few months after Nero's suicide."

"Yes, the plot failed." Caros glanced away. "Because my father defended Galba with his life. When the killers realized the governor escaped, they marched to my family's door and accused us all of being traitors. I fought them. I was fifteen at the time, a youth against four seasoned assassins. Of course, I didn't stand a chance. They raped my mother and two younger sisters, then crucified them in our atrium, while they forced me to watch."

"Women and children?" Tears coursed down her cheeks. "Dear God, how did you survive?"

A cynical laugh broke from his throat. "My fighting impressed them. They sought to make a few coin and sold me to the local gladiatorial school. They assumed I'd die my first time out. Most gladiators do."

Words failed her. She shifted on the bench and threw her arms around him. He hesitated, then almost crushed her in a tight embrace. "I'm so sorry," she cried against his shoulder. "I can't imagine how you must have suffered."

Caros squeezed his eyes shut and buried his face in her soft hair. Never before had he revealed his family's horrific story. The telling had left him weak and shaken to his core. Pelonia's love for her father and home reminded him of the one he'd treasured so well and lost. How could he stand by, witness her pain and not do what he could to ease her grief?

In sharing with her, wanting to help her, he hadn't guessed how much his own wounds would be soothed by her tears. She resented him as her master and distrusted

him as a man, yet she wept for him as though her heart
bore him the deepest affection.

After years of being surrounded by hate, injustice and
violence, he marveled at the depth of her loving spirit.
The sound of her tears pierced the inner armor he'd fashioned to protect himself. Some of the anger and despair
he'd harbored so long seeped away.

Her sobs eased and quieted. She loosened her steely
hold and sagged beside him. His arm curved around the
back of her shoulders, he allowed his fingers to caress
her upper arm. "Are you well?"

He felt her nod against his chest. She sniffed. "I'm
sorry for taking my bitterness out on you the last few
days, but you seemed like such a stalwart target. Now,
I'm ashamed of myself. As much as I've suffered, you've
suffered three times worse in life."

"It's not a competition. Pain is pain. The next time
you need solace from yours, come to me. I'm strong, I
can bear it. It's true I failed in my past, but I'm no longer weak nor will I fail again."

Pelonia looked into his eyes and for the first time saw
insecurity there. Did he think by sharing his history, by
revealing he hadn't always been the unconquered champion he was now, he'd altered her opinion of him? Did
he think she somehow found him lacking?

May it never be! She cupped his cheek and wished
she could replace the lifetime of tenderness he'd lost.
"You're the strongest man I've ever known. If I thought
it before, after tonight I know it for certain."

"Pelonia, I—"

The gate creaked, forewarning someone's arrival.
Aware there were too many rumors about her already,

she removed herself from Caros's arms and slid to the far end of the bench.

One of the house slaves ran toward them. "Master, the widow Leonia requests your attention."

"Have the guests begun a riot?" Caros asked. "Is the *domus* in flames?"

Panting for breath, the slave shook his bald head, his face pinched with confusion. "No, my master, but she insists—"

"Then tell her she'll have to wait."

The slave didn't argue. He backed away, then ran for the house.

Pelonia stood, disturbed to realize she'd forgotten Adiona's presence not only in Caros's home, but in his life.

Remember he's not yours. "Was that wise? What if the widow ventures out here and finds us?"

"It wouldn't matter. She has no say over me."

She searched the shadowed angles of his face. He seemed sincere. "She acts as though she does."

He shrugged. "Adiona's concerned about the party, nothing more. I, on the other hand, am bored by the whole affair. I'd much rather spend my time out here with you."

A lion's roar echoed from the covered cages in the distance. Arms akimbo, she turned her back to gather her thoughts. Was she being duped? Had the story of his family been the truth? Or was Caros a man like her father often warned about? A charmer who would say whatever worked to bring a woman to heel? Hadn't Caros already promised to win the bargain between the two of them?

Trying to be fair and not suspicious, she recalled their conversation from earlier in the afternoon. He'd implied he and the widow were more than friends. Their kisses this evening confirmed it. At the banquet, he'd flirted with a gaggle of other beauties and she'd seen how he fanned the heat in their eyes with no effort at all.

She conceded he'd done nothing untoward. The women were responsible for their own actions. But was he a man who could never be satisfied with the attentions of only one female? The evidence wasn't strong enough to condemn him outright, but with her heart and virtue at stake, she had to be wise. "I'd like to retire now—alone."

The bench creaked behind her. His footsteps sifted through the sand until she felt his presence at her back. His hands eased around her shoulders as though he feared she might bolt. "I don't want you to go."

"Why, because you're bored with the festivities?"

"No, because I enjoy your company."

She closed her eyes, afraid she might weaken. God forgive her, she wanted to believe him.

"You're trembling."

"I'm cold."

He moved to wrap his arms around her, but she stepped beyond his grasp.

"What's happened here?" He eased her around to face him. "Why are you leery of me again?"

"I can't trust you."

All hint of softness left his face. "Is it because I'm a *lanista?* Just because I train gladiators, just because I fought as one doesn't mean…"

She waited, holding her breath for him to finish.

"Doesn't mean I have no heart."

Her lips quivered with unspoken words of comfort. She forced herself to stand her ground when she wanted to smother him with care. "I know you're not heartless.

In truth, your kindness to me is more than I expected when I awoke to find I'd been enslaved."

"Then why do you run hot and cold? Do you think I'm so untried I can't see you have feelings for me? Why not yield and end this yearning between us?"

Fear shot through her. He spoke the truth. She was entirely too susceptible to his charm. Riddled with self-disgust, she despised her weakness. What was wrong with her that she could be tempted by a man whose question proved his sole motive was to conquer her will and seduce her?

How had she grown so weak, so needy to forget she was little more than a game to him? "I should have guessed what you were up to. It's little surprise you were undefeated in the ring. You don't give up."

He crossed his arms over his broad chest, stretching the fabric of his tunic. "Should I be ashamed of the fact? I assure you I'm not, but what does it have to do with the affection between us?"

Affection? Does he suspect I'm falling in love with him?

"How do you fare?" His expression shone with sudden concern. "Even in this dim light, I can see you've paled."

I don't love him, do I?

She pressed her hand to her queasy stomach, wishing she could deny the truth. She backed away. "I told you I need to retire. I'm too exhausted to match wits with you when I've worked all day with little to eat."

He followed after her. "Let me help you to your room."

"No, there's no need."

"I insist." He took hold of her arm and coddled her to the gate.

No longer able to bear his unsettling touch, she broke

his hold and preceded him back to the house. Somewhere along the orchard's path, her queasiness turned to anger—anger with her own stupidity. They had a bargain. How had she allowed herself to love a man who viewed winning her affections as merely a challenge?

Back inside the domus, the party raged on. The music played louder, wilder. Drunken laughter rang through the house. Pelonia glanced over her shoulder at the same time Adiona latched on to Caros's arm. His intense gaze locked on Pelonia and the look in his eyes guaranteed he would seek her out later.

Chilled by the promised reckoning, she mounted the steps to the second floor. Gaius called her name, but she rushed up the stairs and pretended not to hear him. She'd played the part of a good slave for days, but now she'd had enough. *Let him come and fetch me if he must, but Lord, please prepare him for my ire if he does.*

She entered her room and slammed the door. The lamplight sputtered. The tub was gone. Her wet clothes had been removed as well, replaced by a stack of fresh garments on the chair.

Berating her traitorous heart, she unlaced her sandals and kicked them off. Out of all the men in the empire, Caros was the worst possible choice for her to love. At present, she was his slave and he was her master. When she escaped, and she had to, her family would never accept him or his violent past.

She stopped by the window, choking back her regret. Regardless of her growing affection, she promised to be more guarded, to use wisdom from here on out. No matter her feelings or those of her kin, an even greater wall stood between them. Caros disdained Christ. She had no future with a man who didn't share her faith.

A heavy hand knocked at the door.

"Who is it?"

"Gaius. The master sent me."

She opened the door, ready for battle. Her protests melted on her tongue when she saw the older man held a tray loaded with several dishes of fragrant food. Her stomach cramped with hunger. Why would Caros send his steward to fetch and carry like a common slave?

Gaius pressed past her and set the tray on the floor by her pallet. When he straightened, his dark eyes studied her from under bushy gray brows. "The master said you're to eat every morsel."

She glanced at the tray covered with plates of shredded meat, vegetables, fruits and bread. It was more than she'd eat in two days.

"Tomorrow is market day." He paused at the door. "The master wants you to go with him. He expects you to ready yourself by the seventh hour and meet him in the atrium."

"Why?"

"Who are you to ask why, girl? You will do as your master instructs."

She raised her chin. "And if I don't?"

"Then you're a fool and you deserve whatever you get."

Chapter Twelve

Caros rose early the next morning and dressed with care. The sun was out and the first nips of autumn blew in through the open window. Despite the abrupt ending of their talk the night before, he anticipated a fine day spent with Pelonia. He left to meet her, a smile curving his mouth.

He entered the courtyard and found Adiona perched on a bench instead. His good mood faltered, but he quickly subdued his disappointment and greeted his friend with a kiss on each cheek.

"You're awake early, Adiona. After last night's entertainments, I figured you'd be abed until well after midday."

"Shows how little you really know me, my darling. I'm never one to sleep late." She rose from the bench, her bracelets jangling, her vibrant yellow tunic flowing to her feet. She smiled. "You look delectable this morning. Are you on your way out?"

A quick glance around the atrium revealed no sign of Pelonia. "It's market day. I have supplies to purchase."

"You?" Her eyebrow lifted with amused disbelief. "In

case you're unaware, you have a capable steward. Why not send him instead?"

"Gaius is resting. You and your cohorts wore him out last night. He's not as young as he used to be and I don't want him to die on me."

"Of course not. Good slaves are hard to come by." She linked her arm with his and they began a slow turn around the covered porch. "Yesterday, while I waited for you to return from the baths, I noticed you have several new trainees. One in particular caught my interest. I wonder if you might sell him to me."

Caros eyed his friend with genuine surprise. He'd never known Adiona to notice any man except to slice him with the sharp edge of her tongue. "Which man?"

"One of your trainers called him Quintus Ambustus. He's a condemned man, one I'm sure you wouldn't miss if—"

"What price are you offering for him?"

Adiona shrugged a slim, silk-draped shoulder. "Whatever you wish, of course."

Caros clenched his jaw to keep it from falling open in amazement. Clearly Adiona was trying to hide a powerful interest in his slave. "Did the man insult you or commit some other crime against you? Is that why you wish to buy him, to see him punished?"

"No. What did I say to make you think so harshly of me? Am I really such a cruel woman?"

"To most men, yes," he replied bluntly. "I'm the only man in the city you're civil to."

Her lashes fluttered down, but not before he saw the flicker of shame in her eyes.

"Let's forget I asked about him, shall we?" Her bracelets jangled as she dismissed the subject with a wave of her bejeweled hand. "It was silly of me. Slaves are as easy to come by as specks of dust and I already have a house full of them. The last thing I need is another mouth to feed...or back to whip as the case may be."

"I didn't mean to imply—"

"No, it's quite all right, Caros." All hints of vulnerability disappeared from her manner, but the bright smile she gave him didn't quite erase the chagrin from her eyes. "Let's discuss another matter, shall we? I know you'll find this a trivial one, but the banquet's success last night was even greater than I hoped for. Of course, I have you to thank. Your reputation is still unmatched in Rome. Most everyone came just to catch a glimpse of you."

"Relieving me of Lucia's presence is thanks enough."

"She's waiting outside in a cart as we speak. As I promised, she'll be sent to my country estate tomorrow. If you change your mind and want her returned—"

"I won't want her back. After what she did—"

"What she did was wrong, but understandable. Women can't help but love you."

If only that were true in Pelonia's case he'd be a contented man. As it was, his slave never failed to perplex him. Each time he thought she might waver in his direction, she slammed the door in his face.

"Even I love you, and as you pointed out I detest men."

"Not all of us are like your late husband." He kissed the back of her hand. "One of these days you'll find a good—"

"Don't say it!" She froze to the spot. "If one more *well-meaning* person tells me I'll wed again, I'll scream until the Forum crumbles."

He struggled to maintain a straight face. "Be warned, those who protest the loudest often fall hardest."

"Ha! I'll consider marriage as soon as you break your vow and return to the arena."

His humor evaporated. "I'll never be a slave again."

"Nor will I." She flipped her *palla* across her chest and over her left shoulder. "Slavery is all marriage offers a woman and there isn't a man alive worth sacrificing my freedom for."

Understanding her agitation stemmed from harsh experience and deeply imbedded fear, he plucked a rose from the bush climbing up the column beside them and presented it to her.

Her face softened with a smile that lit her dark eyes. "You're too kind. It's no wonder I can never stay angry with you."

"Be careful of the thorns."

"Don't worry." She lifted the red bloom to the tip of her nose. "I've been pricked so many times in my life, I'm immune to pain."

A movement at the edge of the porch's double doors drew his notice. Dressed in one of the new tunics he'd bought for her, Pelonia appeared at the bottom of the staircase just beyond the doorway. *Finally*.

Adiona followed the direction of his gaze. "Ah, the slave girl awaits."

He looked into his friend's knowing expression and narrowed his eyes in warning. "Remember what I said about being kind. If you insult her again our ties of friendship will be severed once and for all."

She raised her hands in surrender. "Who am I to find it strange the great Caros Viriathos is in love with a mouse."

"Don't make light of what you don't understand, Adiona."

"I understand all too well, my darling. Now go to the fortunate girl. I can see you're desperate to be near her."

He nodded and kissed the back of her hand in farewell. The widow murmured something, but with his interest fixed on Pelonia, he heard none of it.

Passing the porch's columns and potted palms, his quick strides erased the tiled space between them. The closer he came to Pelonia the more distrust he saw in her eyes.

He crossed the threshold and stopped at the base of the steps. This early in the morning, a cooler temperature prevailed in the house. He rested his hand on the banister, his sandaled foot on the first step.

By the gods, she stole his breath. Her skin beckoned his touch. Her mouth was enough to drive him mad.

"Gaius said you ordered me to meet you here this morning."

He nodded. "You're going to the Forum with me."

"So he said."

Why was she acting indifferently when he could see the spark of interest she couldn't quite hide? "Are you ready to leave, then?"

She glanced at Adiona's departing back. "What of your guest?"

"She's leaving in moments. I've already said my goodbyes."

Pelonia's lips thinned, but she descended the last step. "You're the master. Lead and I will follow."

Her coolness rankled. "What ails you, Pelonia? Are you not well rested and properly fed? Is a day at the market with me less desirable than hours here scrubbing floors?"

"Nothing is less desirable than scrubbing floors... except perhaps, scrubbing the latrines."

Was she jesting or insulting him? "It's good to know how high I rank in your estimation."

"If someone's high regard is what you seek, perhaps you should spend more time with your lady love."

"My what?"

"Nothing. If you're ready, perhaps we should leave?"

He hid a smile, pleased by her jealousy. He took her by the elbow and led her outside where the morning's comfortable autumn temperature surrounded them. The street in front of his home was calm with only a few pedestrians and a passing horse cart. A stray dog sat on the corner scratching fleas.

"We're leaving later than I planned," he said.

"Perhaps you should go alone. I might slow you down."

And miss spending time with her? "No, it makes no difference."

He helped her into a waiting chariot and stepped up behind her.

"Your horses are exquisite," she said. "And this chariot has some of the finest wood carvings I've ever seen. The details of these tigers are superb."

Her compliment pleased him. "The craftsman was a friend from India."

"He's a true artist."

With a wave of his hand, he signaled the slave holding the bridles to move away from the pair of black Spanish stallions. Pelonia gripped the chariot's curved front panel before he flicked the reins. The horses whinnied and ambled down the drive, then entered the street at a steady clop.

As the chariot picked up speed along the stone pavers, the movement stirred a breeze that blew strands of her hair against his cheek. He savored the clean scent and its silken texture against his skin.

Unbidden, he wondered what it might be like to have Pelonia for his wife, to wake up with her soft and warm in his arms every morning.

"I've never ridden in a chariot before." She cast a glance over her shoulder, her dark eyes bright with excitement. "We always traveled by litter in town and by cart for longer journeys."

"Where are you from?"

"Iguvium." Her chest ached with a sharp, sudden pang of homesickness. She looked straight ahead. The dirty streets and multistoried living complexes on either side of the wide lane were a far cry from the rolling hills and sun-warmed villas of the Umbrian countryside she loved. "It's a small but beautiful place built up the side of a hill about six days north of here."

"I know of it. I fought there once."

"Did you? When?"

"About five years ago. I saw much of the amphitheatre, but little of the town."

He shifted his stance and his chest brushed against her shoulder blades. She gasped at the unexpected tremor that danced down her spine.

"Perhaps you'll visit there again someday and see its finer parts." Not wanting to encourage more peculiar feelings, she focused on the horses and the expert way Caros maneuvered the chariot through the thickening traffic of horse carts, wagons and other chariots.

"I remember the meadows were abundant with a wealth of red and yellow wildflowers," he said.

She nodded, once again surprised by the gentle spirit beneath his battle scars. For his sake, she wished she could turn back time and regain the years he'd lost to violence.

"You must have been there in summer," she said. "It's a beautiful time, but fall is my favorite. The harvest will arrive soon and everyone will be celebrating…"

"What's wrong?"

Her eyes burned with tears. "I no longer have a home there. My father is gone. All the loved ones of my household are dead. My uncle owns all that my father worked for. Our land, our villa…everything."

"The uncle who sold you?"

She nodded.

His lips brushed her temple. "Again, I'm sorry for your loss, Pelonia. The area seemed a peaceful place. The kind of town where a fortunate man settles to raise a family."

She cleared her throat and choked back her heartache. "Is it a town where *you* might want to raise a family?"

He slowed the horses to turn down an empty side street. "I never planned to marry. Some gladiators do, but I wanted no wife or children to leave behind unprotected if I died in the arena."

"Your sentiments are honorable, Caros. I believe my father would have acted the same in your circumstances." But what of Adiona? Her curiosity got the better of her. "What of these last three years? You've been a free man. Why haven't you wed?"

He shrugged. "Perhaps no one will have me."

"I can't believe—"

"I'm a *lanista* after all. Wasn't it you who reminded me my profession is the lowest of the low? Tell me, what decent woman ties herself to a barbarian?"

Her cheeks flamed. She knew she'd been wrong to judge him. She eyed him over her shoulder, eager for him to see her sincerity. "I misspoke and I'm sorry for my arrogance. The more I've come to know you, the more I think whoever you choose to wed will be a woman truly blessed."

Surprise flared in his deep blue eyes, but he said nothing. He flicked the reins, driving the horses into a faster pace while the road remained deserted. Wind whipped at the fringe of hair around her face and ruffled the edges of her tunic. Aware of his muscled arms around her, she allowed herself to brace against the solid column of his body to keep from falling backward.

His lips brushed her ear. "You're not frightened, are you?"

"I've never traveled this fast in my life," she admitted, a touch of anxiety heightening with the jolt of excitement she felt.

"There's no need to be afraid, this is hardly the races. Perhaps we'll visit the Circus Maximus. With no obstacles to watch for, I could show you the true meaning of speed."

The cloud of sadness lifted from her slim shoulders, if only a mite. "Could we?"

"Perhaps another day." He indulged in the scent of her hair, glad to hear a spark of curiosity in her voice. "I know for a fact the races are on today and you wouldn't want to ride with a charioteer. They're nothing but insanity incarnate."

"As opposed to gladiators?"

He grinned. "We're not sane, either. We're killers, remember."

Her lips compressed into a prim line. "I thank you for the reminder."

He chuckled. "Here, take the reins. Perhaps I can teach *you* a thing or two."

Her hesitant smile told him she remembered saying the same words to him the previous night. She accepted the leather strips in a tight grip. "By all means, proceed."

The back of her head brushed the center of his chest. He drew her closer. His hands covered each of hers. "Hold the reins loosely. Let them ease through your fingers."

The chariot began to veer to the right.

"Caros!"

"Don't be afraid. Take control or your horses will feel your fear. To steer, pull back on the left or right rein like this."

He allowed her to drive unaided through the next few streets until they came to the city gate and the traffic began to back up.

"Thank you. I enjoyed that! For the first time in weeks I've felt free." She handed back the reins and gripped the chariot's front panel.

Her joy pleased him, but he didn't expect the twinge of guilt he experienced for holding her captive. He did have the power to set her free. He wanted her happy just as he was happy, yet to free her was to lose her—a prospect he refused to face.

It had been years since he felt alive—as if there were something valuable to wake up for each morning. He would have to try harder, look for other ways to please her until she no longer sought a life apart from him.

They neared the amphitheater. A gift from the Flavian emperors to the people of Rome, the massive arena had been dedicated the previous year with a hundred days of continuous spectacles. Standing four stories, the white travertine exterior gleamed in the morning sun. The day's first games were in full force. The mob's roar swept across the distance.

He felt Pelonia tense. "What's wrong?"

"We're not going there, are we?"

"Not yet. I have business with the editor this afternoon. I can't avoid it or I would. My business won't take long."

"The editor?"

"He arranges the games." He maneuvered past a cart that swerved to the road's edge, then guided the chariot in a westerly direction toward the Forum. The horde of wheels and horses' hooves clattered on the stone road, drowning out further conversation.

Caros reined the horses to a stop not far from the Via Sacra. People swarmed around the chariots and other forms of transport. "We'll leave the chariot here. I'll hire one of the boys over there to watch it while we're gone. The way isn't far."

He helped Pelonia to the ground. If not for her vow, the milling crowd would provide an ideal cover for escape. Coins exchanged hands. The chariot seen to, Caros led her along the Sacred Way, pointing out sites of interest. "There's the Palatine to our left. And up on the Capitoline there, the Temple of Jupiter."

With no interest in the pagan temple, Pelonia surveyed the Palatine. The hill was overgrown with elegant palaces of Rome's noblest families. Somewhere up there, her cousin Tiberia resided. An eager fascination gripped her. *Which home is it?*

The thought of her kin being so close overwhelmed her with happiness and…unexpected gloom. Her cousin was her dearest friend. Who better to share her feelings about Caros with than her closest confidant? Yet the moment she saw Tiberia again, she would be forced to cut her ties with the man who meant more to her with each passing day.

"Are you tired? Do you need to rest?" Caros' light touch on the small of her back made her realize she'd stopped walking.

"No, I'm fine." She picked up her pace, her turmoil increasing with every step. Their situation was intolerable. Each kindness he showed her made him dearer to her heart, but every day she remained a slave eroded her inner core of strength. How long would it take before she joined the other slaves with broken spirits and nonexistent wills?

"You're too quiet."

She looked into his blue eyes, her heart melting at the concern she saw there. Just a short time ago, she would never have guessed this rugged man capable of such gentleness. "I'm sorry. I have many things on my mind."

"Tell them to me. Perhaps I can help."

She shook her head. "No, I have to work them out for myself."

He wasn't pleased, but he didn't press her. They continued along the road without speaking. The din of the crowd surrounded them. Food stalls lined the street. The smell of spices, roasted nuts and exotic fruits tinged the air.

Caros cleared his throat. "Your unhappiness isn't related to Adiona, is it? She has a wicked tongue. The way she mocked you in the garden yesterday was cruel. I told her so."

More concern for her feelings? "Thank you, but why did you bother? You know I plan to leave as soon as our agreement is finished. I don't want to cause trouble between you."

Anger flashed across his face. He led her to the side of the road, to a quieter spot between a large statue and a laurel tree. "You might as well abandon your thoughts of escape. You won't be leaving in two weeks' or two years' time. I can't let you go."

"Why? What is it about me that can't be replaced? Anyone can weed the garden. I'm almost useless in the kitchen and I refuse to warm your bed. If it's a matter of coin, my family will repay you. If you're in need of affection, why not seek it from…"

"From whom? My lady love?"

"Yes," she snapped, annoyed to have her own words thrown back at her.

"And who might that be? One of my admirers? One of my other female slaves? Why don't you enlighten me?"

"You know very well, it's Adiona."

"Come again? I couldn't hear you over all the racket in the street."

Her hands balled into fists at her sides. "*Adiona.* Considering what I saw this morning and what you told me yesterday—"

"This morning? What did you see?"

"You seemed most reluctant to let her leave."

His brow arched. "And yesterday? What did I say?"

"You said she's pleasant and lovely enough to rival Venus. That unlike the two of *us,* the two of you are of similar minds. That the relationship you share with the widow is everything you desire it to be."

That I'm a slave and nothing more.

His face inscrutable, he pressed closer. She stepped away until the tree trunk scratched her back. He gripped her upper arms and leaned over until they were eye to eye. "Finally a woman who listens. Why did you hear all the wrong things?"

"What do you mean?"

He sighed. "It's true I said those things and none were lies. I also said I think *you're* beautiful and told you of my family—something I've never told anyone else."

She glanced away. "I'm honored you confided in me. I realize you shared with me to help ease my grief. You're most kind for doing so."

"I'm not kind." He released her and raked his hand through his hair. "I told you because you're special to me."

"Special? Will you be more specific? I confess my thoughts are like jumbled string. I've wrapped myself in them until I fear I'll never break free."

"How shall I define it? I've already told you I want you."

"What does that mean? My father warned me of men who *want* every woman they see."

"*I* only want *you*."

Her knees went weak. "Then what are your true feelings for the widow?"

"I care for her, but not in the way you think. She's been an excellent friend who's given me much. When I gained my freedom, she used her influence to help me establish the school. In return, I've been her friend and protector, nothing more."

"Then why did you lead me to believe otherwise?"

"We should proceed to the Forum." He turned to leave. "At this pace, the best wares will be gone and we'll endure second-rate meat for a week."

She grabbed hold of his tunic along with a few chest hairs. He winced but froze to the spot. Her hand dropped away as though she'd touched fire. "Oh, no, we're not moving on until you tell me the truth. As it is, I feel you and your 'friend' have made me the back end of a joke."

"You're no joke to me." He groaned. "Adiona had nothing to do with it. I didn't speak to her about you except to tell her she'd been cruel. She suspects I care for you, but…" He combed his hand through his hair again. "In truth, you've found me out. I encouraged you to believe there was more between Adiona and me because I wanted to make you jealous."

Her mouth fell open. Caught between hot indignation and enormous relief, she realized he'd succeeded without a hitch. "How did you know I'd be jealous of her?"

"I didn't. She came when I summoned her to take Lucia. I had to think of something since you didn't want the wench whipped or sold."

"You amaze me," she said softly, her secret thoughts finding words before she realized she'd spoken them.

His expression warmed with pleasure. "The first time you spoke of Adiona to me, I knew you were jealous."

She felt her cheeks burn. "Only a little."

He chuckled. "I saw it in your eyes. You wanted me to deny all involvement with her. Your reaction gave me hope. After the speech you flayed me with the day before about how unsuited we are—"

"But we are," she interrupted. "Nothing's changed."

He waved away her protest. "Don't travel down that

road again. Whether you acknowledge it or not, there's something unique between us."

She couldn't deny him, nor could she admit she agreed. No matter how much she was growing to love him, she still had to leave.

Chapter Thirteen

Pelonia followed Caros up the hill to the Forum. The pristine weather had lured a rambunctious crowd. Merchants hawked everything from food and plants to boat sails, while street musicians played tunes on various instruments, hoping to earn coins or gifts of food.

She'd never visited the world's capital and everywhere she looked Rome offered something new to delight the eye. The public buildings—temples, basilicas and various monuments outshone any she'd ever seen.

"What's that over there?" she asked, pointing through the milling throng to a unique circular building.

"The Temple of Vesta," Caros said, distracted by his attempts to lead her through the shifting sea of people.

"Where the Vestal virgins keep the flame of Rome alive?"

"The very same."

"You don't *really* believe Rome will fall if the flame burns out, do you?"

As he sneaked a glance at her, his lips curved in a mocking smile. "All good Romans believe it."

"But you're not a good Roman," she said as they

walked up the congested steps of one of the basilicas. "You haven't even adopted a Roman name."

"Out of respect for my father, I carry the name he gave me."

"You said your father served Galba, but did he resent the Romans conquering your homeland?"

"No, he was a citizen, just as I would have been had I not been forced into the gladiatorial trade. That didn't stop him from loving our Iberian heritage or wanting to pass on that heritage to me."

Caros tightened his grip on her hand when they entered the basilica by way of the main entrance. Rows of arched windows allowed light into the magnificent market. Two levels of shops lined both sides of the central pathway. The walls, floor and rows of support columns were all fashioned of polished white marble.

Lilting strains of a pan flute combined with hundreds of voices echoed through the cavernous space. The heavy flow of people jostled Pelonia, threatening to knock her over more than once. Caros steadied her each time and navigated the multitude with ease.

"What a marvelous place," she said in awe.

Caros grunted. "It's crowded."

"It's beautiful. All the craftsmanship is perfection."

"It stinks like a sty."

She laughed. "Who would have thought you'd have such a sensitive nose?"

"You enjoy teasing me, don't you, woman?"

"A slave must find enjoyment where she can."

He chuckled. "As must her master. Remember that the next time I try to kiss you."

The thought of him kissing her no longer unwelcome, she ducked her head to hide a shy smile of pleasure.

Caros cleared the way for her as they entered the butcher shop. The smells of fresh meat surrounded her. Shouted orders and voices haggling prices competed with the bleat of lambs and a few mooing cows. Animal carcasses hung from hooks behind the long counter.

The shopkeeper looked up from a large pile of coins. His eyes bugged when he saw Caros. He swiped the coins into a drawer and hurried from behind the counter.

"You are the Bone Grinder, no?" the shopkeeper asked, his wrinkled face bright with excitement. "By the gods, it is an honor to have you in my shop."

The clamor faded into silence. Gaping mouths and curious eyes turned to stare.

Amazed by the people's reaction, Pelonia studied Caros. She'd never seen him beyond the walls of the school and it was an enlightening experience to find so many people revered him.

"The honor is mine," he said.

The shop owner's face took on a slight frown of concern. "I usually have dealings with your steward. Is Gaius well?"

"He's fine."

Pelonia allowed her attention to wander. Caros let go of her hand once the other customers returned to their business. While she waited for him to arrange deliveries to the school, she meandered around the shop, comparing the costs of various meats with the lower prices she would have paid at home.

Caros joined her near a table laden with buckets of brown eggs. He tucked a wisp of hair behind her ear, sending a shiver through her body when his calloused fingers brushed her cheek. "I was watching you," he said. "Not once did you try to run off."

"You're surprised? We have a bargain and I'm a woman of my word."

He opened the door and ushered her out into the press of patrons. "We do have a bargain. Up to now, I wasn't fully confident you'd keep it if an opportunity arose for you to escape again."

"I assume I passed the test."

He nodded. "You're honest, I'll give you that."

Some time later, Caros finished his business with several other merchants. He led Pelonia into a different shop. Perfume sweetened the air. The skeins of white cotton hanging from the ceiling drew her attention, as did the vibrant bolts of silk lining the walls. Freewomen dressed in lavish tunics and *stolas* admired the feminine wares that covered the counters and shelves.

"I've brought you here because I realize you need certain items. If—"

"Caros!" One of the women, her hair covered in a fashionable blond wig, rushed toward them from a counter full of cosmetics. A delighted smile curved her painted lips and lit her kohl-rimmed eyes. "It's been months since I saw you last."

Pelonia bristled at the woman's too-familiar tone and the way she greeted Caros with a lingering kiss on each cheek.

"Cassia, what a pleasure to see you. I've been working," he said. "I have many new men to train and they've claimed my full attention."

"I missed you at my banquet last week." The blonde pouted as she gauged her effect on him from beneath lowered lashes. "I sent you a special invitation since my husband was out of town."

Pelonia's eyes rounded, then narrowed when Caros

cast a guilty glance her way. Disgusted to find he would dally with another man's wife, she abandoned his side and sought out the counter farthest from him. Hating the ease with which Caros sent her emotions reeling, she forced herself to admire a set of ivory combs while the elegant shop mistress finished her business with another customer.

"I'll see you Sunday," the shop mistress said as she handed the other woman a folded bundle of yellow cloth.

"Sunday," the customer agreed. "At the seventh hour, down by the river."

A bell on the door rang as the customer left. The shop mistress turned her attention to Pelonia. Instead of ignoring her and treating her like a slave as the other merchants had done most of the morning, the older woman offered a pleasant, "May I help you find something?"

"Thank you, but I'm just looking. These combs are exquisite."

"And very expensive," the mistress said, though not unkindly. "I have others over here. They're carved of wood, and not as fine as the ivory, but some are quite nice."

Glancing to find Caros continued his conversation with the would-be adulteress, Pelonia followed the silver-haired shop mistress to the far end of the counter. The other woman pulled out a large wooden box filled with combs and began to pick out the best pieces.

Pelonia stopped her. "Please, don't waste your time on me. There are several customers here who need your help and I have no coin."

"I assumed you had no money." The shop mistress's expression softened with compassion. "I can see you're a slave of the *lanista* over there. You look so unhappy, I couldn't help but wonder if he's hateful to you."

"No, no, he's kind," she hurried to defend him, surprised the woman spared her a second thought. "But thank you for your concern when I'm no more than a stranger to you."

"It's important to be kind to strangers. Even the wicked are good to their friends."

Pelonia wondered if the other woman was a fellow believer. Jesus had taught a similar lesson and it was an uncommon one in a world where few people cared for anyone beyond themselves and their own families.

On impulse, she tapped the wooden counter, drawing the shopkeeper's attention to the spot. Pelonia traced the sign of the fish, a secret symbol Christians used to identify themselves.

The woman looked up, a huge grin parted her lips. She nodded and squeezed Pelonia's hand as though they were long-lost relatives. "What's your name, child?"

"Pelonia. And yours?"

"Annia."

Caros's footsteps warned of his arrival. The shopkeeper released Pelonia's hand and began to place the combs back in the box.

"Do you see anything you want?" he asked. "If so, let's buy it and be on our way. The editor is waiting for me at the amphitheater."

"There's nothing," Pelonia said, reluctant to accept gifts from him. She noted Annia's frown when Caros spoke of the arena. Like most Christians, the older lady would despise the games. Not for their barbaric cruelty alone, but because a multitude of their fellow believers had been tortured in them and slain for sport.

"Are you certain?" he asked. "I thought I saw you admiring those ivory combs. If you want them—"

She shook her head. "I have everything I need. Let's be on our way. I don't want you to be late on my account."

Pelonia shared a lingering glance with Annia. For the first time since her arrival in Rome, she didn't feel quite so alone. It was heartening to find another believer, to feel connected to the body of Christ again.

Outside the basilica, the sun shone brightly. The afternoon heat had erased the morning's fall breezes. Caros took her by the hand and led her quickly through the open market and back down the Via Sacra.

"You seem different since we left the Forum," he said. "Tell me, what did you and the shop mistress speak of?"

Pelonia hesitated. She wouldn't lie, but neither would she confess she'd found another Christian. She didn't think he would report Annia to the authorities. After all, he hadn't turned her in, but she couldn't take a chance with the woman's life either. "We spoke of many things I'm certain you'd find of no interest. And you? Did you and your *married* friend have much to discuss?"

"More jealousy. That pleases me," he said, laughing. "Cassia and I are no more than acquaintances. She's rich and bored. Like many women of her class, she thinks she'll find excitement in the bed of a gladiator. If nothing else, she'll have something to gossip about with her friends."

"And she wants you."

"I'm a champion of Rome. All the women want me."

Pelonia marveled at his conceit until she realized he was teasing her. With a gentle poke at his ribs, she laughed. "They must not know you very well."

"You wound me," he said in a lighthearted tone, but his intense blue eyes grew serious. "Perhaps I should have said, all the women want me, except the one I want most."

Unable to jest when words of tenderness rushed to her lips, she sought sanity in the distraction provided by the merchant wagons along the pebbled path.

As they neared the amphitheater, the crush of people thickened. The roar of the mob inside the gleaming torture palace grew louder, spreading through the air like constant thunder.

Pelonia's stomach rolled with dread. "Can I please wait for you out here? You have my word I won't flee and I've proven I won't break our bargain."

His arm slipped around her shoulders and he pulled her tight against him. "No, it's too dangerous."

His refusal brooked no argument. He ushered her beneath one of the amphitheater's arched doorways, down a flight of concrete stairs and past the guards standing watch at the back entrance. From what she could tell as they walked down a long corridor, they were directly under the spectators.

"This way," he said when they came to a choice of direction. "Those steps lead to the arena."

No one offered Caros resistance when he bypassed the long line waiting outside the editor's office.

Caros pushed open the office door. The occupant barked, "By the gods! How dare…oh, it's you, Caros. Come in and take a seat."

A moment later, a wealthy man, by the looks of his fine white tunic, exited the office and took a place at the front of the line. That he seemed honored to give up his time with the editor spoke volumes of his respect for Caros.

Caros led her inside the dingy office. Large parchments advertising past competitions covered the walls. A barred window near the ceiling allowed noise from inside the amphitheater to filter into the dusty space. She sat on an upended crate in the corner, while Caros took the chair in front of the large wooden desk.

The editor, a rotund, pockmarked individual, lifted a glass and a ceramic jug. "Care for a drink, Bone Grinder?"

"I'll pass, Spurius. Knowing you, it's probably laced with hemlock."

Spurius chuckled. "I admit I'm not above tipping the scales in my favor, but you have no worries from me. As long as there's a chance I might lure you back to the ring, you're safe."

Pelonia tensed. She hadn't considered the possibility of Caros returning to the games. Fear for his safety rushed to the fore of her mind. Lacing her fingers together in a tight ball, she willed away the image of him hurt and bleeding.

"What's this about you contracting forty of my men for tomorrow, then amending it to twenty with less than three days notice?" Caros asked in a quick change of subject. "If you need no more than twenty fighters, so be it, but don't think you won't pay me for the original count."

The mob cheered. Feet pounded above them like thunder on the ceiling. Motes of dust danced in the stream of light allowed by the small barred window.

Spurius hefted his girth and reached to close one of the window's shutters in an effort to muffle the noise. "The executions have gone over long today."

Caros's hands fisted on the wooden desktop. "They usually finish long before now."

"Executions?" Pelonia sat forward on the bench.

Caros turned in his seat. "Thieves and murderers, nothing more."

"And a few deviants." Spurius frowned at Pelonia as though she were a dog who'd dared to interrupt. "They rounded up a group of Christians and the traitors have been pitted against a pack of wolves."

"That's enough," Caros warned the other man.

"The crowd has been wild today." Spurius continued with the undiluted glee of a man who found pleasure in butchery and torture. "The mob loves a good show and I make a fortune when the seats are full."

Pelonia shuddered at each horrible word. The room began to spin.

"What's wrong with her," Spurius griped. "She isn't one of them, is she?"

"No!" Caros snapped. "She has a tender heart. That's *all*."

"Then why is she here? A tender heart is the first thing to die in this place."

She launched to her feet and threw open the door before Caros had the chance to stop her. She pushed through the tangle of bodies blocking her path and ran down the hall.

"Pelonia, come back!"

Deaf to Caros's order, she took the steps he'd pointed out as a passage to the arena. On the first landing, she froze. A strangled cry broke from her lips as her gaze traveled the huge oval theater packed with an ocean of bloodthirsty spectators. The atmosphere writhed with terrible excitement and chants for human death poisoned the air. Never in her life had she seen such horror.

With the floor of the arena out of view, she pressed onward. A guard barred her path. "Woman, you're not permitted here. You'll have to find a place to stand with the other slaves in the top rows."

She ducked under his arm and raced to the rail, ignoring his command to halt.

In the center of the sand a pack of wolves circled a handful of men and one young woman. Terror lined the prisoners' faces, though their lips moved as if in prayer.

One of the beasts lunged at the woman. Raucous laughter swirled through the crowd.

"No!" Pelonia screamed just as a large gray wolf leaped at one of the men.

"You can do no good here," Caros said a short distance behind her.

She spun to face him and the guard standing a few paces behind his left shoulder. Tears coursed down her cheeks. "Please make it stop," she begged, knowing even *his* power didn't extend far enough to end the suffering below.

Caros's face creased with pity. He grabbed hold of her arms and drew her against him. "If I could end this for you I would, but those poor wretches are beyond human help."

The mob's frenzied cries erupted around them. Pelonia squeezed her eyes shut, horribly aware that each new cheer meant another slaughtered Christian.

Chapter Fourteen

Caros swept Pelonia off her feet, holding her tight while she wept against his chest. He'd witnessed numerous executions over the years. The scene below was no different except this time he observed the fray from above, instead of fighting in the thick of it.

The mob's wild chants swarmed like locusts as the last two men in the arena struggled to protect the woman—a woman who could easily be Pelonia if the Fates turned against her.

The thought soured his gut. He brushed a kiss across the top of her head. For the first time in years, fear coursed through his veins. Now that he'd found a woman to love, he refused to live without her. But what if someone uncovered Pelonia's secret and took the choice from his hands? What if someone threatened to throw *Pelonia* to the wolves for her Christian beliefs?

Bile rose in his throat. Anxious to leave, he sought out the exit. A storm of stomping feet pummeled the marble risers and a blast of wild shouting thundered around the arena.

With a last backward glance, he saw two of the wolves

begin to circle the woman. His feet froze. Time faltered and stood still. Riveted by the animals' cunning, Caros felt each of his muscles tighten with dread. He willed the Christian to deny her beliefs and save her life. A simple retraction of her faith would provide a way of escape.

Why didn't she grasp the opportunity and see herself freed?

The pack moved like a troop of gladiators, sizing up the weaknesses of their prey and how best to attack. It wouldn't be long before all of the Christians lay mangled in the sand.

A seasoned predator himself, Caros held his breath as the largest she wolf determined a precise moment to strike. The pack charged as one frenzied unit, downing the last three Christians in a single, simultaneous assault.

An unfamiliar ache took root in his chest. He closed his eyes and pushed the pain away as the mob's triumphant roar erupted around the arena, freeing him from his momentary trance.

Pelonia writhed in his arms and fought to look over his shoulder, but he tightened his grip, pinning her with his superior strength as he carried her toward the exit. "Don't look, *mea carissima*. It's a gruesome sight and we've both seen more than enough."

Neither of them spoke on the journey home. The senseless butchery in the ring disgusted Caros. He'd never enjoyed the public executions, but he'd grown calloused to them.

No longer.

His love for a Christian made all the difference, destroying his ability to look upon their deaths with the same resignation and complacence.

He stole a glance at Pelonia beside him in the chariot, her eyes red and swollen from tears. His breathing grew difficult. Long ago he'd become accustomed to all manner of physical pain, but her quiet sorrow filled him with helpless agony.

Tender feelings and emotions he'd buried years ago to survive the bleakness of his existence rose up like a tide. Guilt for his part in past executions choked him. None of his usual excuses soothed his conscience. By the gods, how would she see him if she learned of his misdeeds? After witnessing her people die in the ring, she was certain to despise him. All hope of winning her affection would be forever lost.

He reined the chariot to a stop a few paces from his front door and waited for one of his slaves to lay hold of the bridle. He jumped from the chariot and offered to help Pelonia down. She alighted without touching him, as though she could see the stain of blood on his hands. Stung by her rejection, he closed his fingers and dropped his fist to his side.

He stepped toward her, but she retreated. Frustration gripped him. Was she in shock or had the few gains he'd made in earning her trust fallen by the wayside? "Come, Pelonia, let me help you. As long as there's breath in my body, I promise you won't be harmed. You must know by now you have nothing to fear from me."

Her glassy gaze rested on his face. "You think not, *lanista?* Why did you bother to stop me from seeing the truth? Do you think I don't realize all of you Romans are cut from the same bloodthirsty cloth?"

Caros held his tongue. Her bleak expression tore at his heart. If it eased her anguish to lash out at him, so be it. "I didn't want you to see your people killed. I suffered when I saw my loved ones butchered. The pain has stayed with me all my life. I hoped to spare you from a similar grief."

"If you wished to spare me grief, you should have thrown me into the ring with those beasts. But then again, you *are* one of the wolves. Why share me with your kin when you plan to win our bargain and have me all to yourself?"

Her bitterness gutted him. She saw him as an animal, a murderer...and she was right. He may not have been in the arena this afternoon, but he'd been a fixture in countless other fights. He cleared his throat. "You're upset and with good reason. Let's go inside before we say something we'll both regret."

Pelonia proceeded Caros through the front door. Gaius met them in the dim light of the entryway. "Master, you have a guest. She arrived a short time ago and asked if she could speak with you. She's waiting in the atrium."

"Who is she?"

"Her name is Annia. She claims to be a shopkeeper at the Forum."

Irritated by Annia's bad timing, Caros made his way to the courtyard. An older woman with gray at her temples sat in profile on the bench in front of the fountain. She stood and faced him the moment his sandals brushed the mosaic floor. He recognized her cheerful face from the shop where he'd spoken with Cassia.

"Good day to you, Madam." He gave a slight bow. "My steward says you wish to speak with me."

"My name is Annia." A smile crinkled the edges of her friendly brown eyes. "Thank you for seeing me unannounced."

He motioned for her to return to her seat on the marble bench and offered refreshment, which she declined.

"I know you're a busy man. I promise not to take much of your time. I met your slave, Pelonia, today in my shop." She adjusted the voluminous folds of her wine-colored *stola*. "She reminded me so much of my own daughter I've come to ask your permission for her to visit me. That is, if she agrees."

"Your daughter?"

"She passed on last year."

"You have my sympathy."

"Thank you." She lowered her gaze. "I know my request is an odd one, but grant my appeal and you'll have my deepest thanks."

Caros spotted Pelonia half-hidden by the nearest column. Her troubled eyes pleaded with him to give his consent. After the events of the afternoon he wanted to please her. Yet he wasn't about to create a situation that might aid Pelonia with her plans of escape.

"No. The streets are too dangerous for a beautiful young woman to walk alone and the many claims on my time make it impossible for me to act as her bodyguard."

"I understand your wish to protect your property, but this is a gladiatorial school. Surely there's at least *one* other man capable of seeing to her safety."

No longer willing to debate the point, he offered Annia one of his most charming smiles. "Perhaps, perhaps not. Either way, Pelonia isn't free to leave these grounds without me."

"I see." Water splashed in the fountain while Annia fiddled with the folds of her *stola*. "Then may I visit her here on occasion?"

Caros considered the perceptive gleam in the shop-keeper's eyes. Normally, he'd dismiss an uninvited guest without explaining himself, but his mother had taught him to respect his elders and this woman's gentle smile reminded him of her. He tried a different tack. "I'll have to consider—"

"Please allow her to visit." Pelonia hurried from behind the pillar, making no pretense of her eavesdropping. Her cheeks held a renewed hint of color and her eyes begged for his consent. Further refusal withered on his tongue. How could he say no to such a beguiling plea?

He gave a slow nod. Her face softened with gratitude and the smile she gave Annia sent a jolt of relief through his veins.

He realized he'd feared she might never smile again. Without another word, he turned on his heel and headed for the training field, in dire need of release from his tension.

Bemused by Caros's abrupt exit, Pelonia watched him disappear down the corridor that led to the rear of the house.

Anguish weighed heavy on her shoulders. She wished she could bite off her tongue. His shattered expression when she'd compared him to the wolves would torment her for the rest of her days. Her cruelty was inexcusable no matter how much the executions distressed her. Caros wasn't to blame for the evil she'd witnessed today. That he'd tried to protect her from seeing the worst of it proved once again what a man of compassion he was.

"Pelonia? Pelonia, child, are you all right?"

She blinked several times as if waking from a dream. "I'm better now that you're here," she said, striding forward. "Your presence is a lift to my spirit."

"I'm glad to hear it. At my shop today, I felt as if we'd known each other all our lives."

"I felt the same."

"I spoke no lie when I told your master you reminded me of my dear Phoebe."

Pelonia followed her friend to sit on the bench, careful not to crease the fine cloth of Annia's *stola*. She clasped the older woman's soft, warm fingers. "I'm sorry to hear you lost her last year."

Pain spread across Annia's gracefully aged features. "The authorities executed her, her husband and my grandson in the arena."

"How horrible! I saw the executions today. I—"

Further words failed her. A vision of the wolves made nausea roll in her belly. A jagged pain knotted in her throat. Annia put her arm around Pelonia and drew her close. "Don't fret, child. They're with the Lord, dancing at the feet of Jesus."

"As is my father," she whispered, resting her cheek against Annia's shoulder.

"What happened to him? Was he executed as well?"

A tear trickled across the bridge of her nose and onto Annia's *stola*. As quickly as she could, she told her friend of the marauders' attack, her uncle's treachery and her sale into slavery.

"My dear girl. How much you've suffered! No wonder the Lord sent me here to comfort you."

"You *are* a comfort. At times, it's been frightfully easy to think God has discarded me."

"Never." Annia patted her hand. "One of the most beautiful traits of our Lord is His ability to create joy from mourning. He always has a plan and it never fails to work for our good. Sometimes we may not like or understand His ways of achieving that good, but in those times our faith is refined and we grow stronger."

She sniffed and wiped her cheeks. "You speak the

truth. My father used to say the same, but I confess I feel my faith is hanging by a thread. I've never been angrier with God or so overwhelmed by bitterness. Even when I repent or do my best to accept His will, I say or think things that make me cringe with remorse. Truly, a part of me wants to rail at Him and demand to know why He took everything of value from my life."

"We must remember our Father never takes what He doesn't return with interest when He owes us nothing at all."

"I know," she said in a small voice. "But how can He return my father or the loving home that no longer belongs to me? How can He return your daughter and your family?"

"I'll see my loved ones again when I join them in heaven, just as you will see your father. As for the rest, it's all part of the mystery that makes His ways a wonder to behold. Wait upon the Lord and let Him renew your strength like an eagle's."

Wiping her tears away, Pelonia sat up and nodded. "I never used to cry. In Rome, it seems I cry every few hours."

"Tears cleanse the soul."

She sniffed and offered a weak smile. "Then mine must be spotless."

"And the *lanista?* What does he think of all this weeping?"

"Caros is ever kind."

"*Kind?* There's a word I didn't expect to hear when describing a man known for violence."

"He's gentle as well. And considerate."

Annia frowned. "Are you besotted?"

Sadness spread through Pelonia like a growing stain. She plucked a small frond from a potted palm beside the bench. "It matters not if I am. Caros and I have no future together."

"That's probably the wisest course of action, but why do you believe so?"

Pelonia wished wisdom could mend a broken heart. "He rejects our faith and I'll never let go of it. He's my master and I can't live as a slave forever. I *will* have to escape. When I do, he'll hate me for it."

"And what if God has planted you here for a specific purpose?"

"He has," she answered with assurance. "He's shown me I'm to be a light in this dark place. Why He chose me, I don't understand. My inner flame is flickering at best. I believe a worse failure would be difficult to find."

"Don't listen to the lies the Evil One would force on you." Annia stroked Pelonia's hair. "Who, in the midst of trouble, ever feels successful or doesn't question God's plan?"

"I suppose no one."

"The important thing to remember is that even when we are weak, our Lord is strong. Just because our prayers haven't come to fruition, doesn't mean the answers aren't already on the way."

Chapter Fifteen

Caros's third opponent of the afternoon landed on his back in a burst of sand. After years of conditioning himself to fight, he knew of no other way to relieve the tension that plagued him. His attempt to find release from the condemnation in Pelonia's eyes had proven futile. Like the tip of a red-hot poker, her accusations probed the raw sores of his diseased soul.

His lip curled at the unconscious gladiator on the ground. Supposedly a champion of more than a year, the Thracian had been a disappointment, and lasted no time at all. Where was Alexius when he required a challenge?

Fingers flexing around the hilt of a *gladius,* Caros searched the field for another man to bring down. His gaze landed on the trainee he'd purchased the same night as Pelonia. The Christian he was certain she'd find attractive if she learned of his presence here.

His eyes narrowed. Even Adiona, a woman known for her hatred of men, had found this particular trainee worthy of interest.

Unreasonable jealousy fueled his displeasure. He lifted his weapon and pointed the bloodstained tip toward the slave. "You there. Quintus, is it not? Present yourself."

Quintus's intelligent eyes darkened with caution, but he made his way from the shadowed sidelines and into the late-afternoon sun.

Caros clapped his iron *gladius* against the slave's wooden sword. "You seem to be taking to a gladiator's life with ease. A few more weeks of training and you might survive a round in the arena."

The trainee kept up his guard. "Whatever God wills."

"God?" Caros swung the *gladius* with more force than necessary. "You think your God has a hand in the ring?"

Quintus blocked the blade with notable speed. "Nothing happens that my Lord doesn't allow."

A vision of the day's execution flashed in Caros's mind. "Then your God is a merciless tyrant."

"I've thought the same a few times myself."

"And yet you continue to serve Him? Would endure being made a slave and cast to the beasts rather than deny Him?"

The slave stayed alert, his sword at the ready. He nodded without hesitation. "I'm here in this pit for no other reason."

The conviction in the slave's green eyes leveled Caros. He stepped back and dropped his weapon to his side. The victims in the ring today had shared the same fervor or they'd have denied their beliefs and saved themselves. Like Pelonia, they believed in an elusive, compelling force Caros wished to comprehend, but couldn't quite grasp.

His thirst for battle drained away. He jabbed the *gladius* point first into the sand and strode toward the sidelines.

Silence fell across the yard. A quick glance over his

shoulder revealed Quintus and the other trainees gawking in astonishment. No one was more amazed by his undisciplined behavior than Caros himself. He pulled a tunic over his head and pointed to the gate that led from the training ground. "Come with me, Quintus. I have a few questions for you."

As he walked to the egress, he ignored the quizzical looks of his assistants and motioned for them to resume training. Crisp orders followed by the clack of wooden swords sounded in his wake. A Nubian opened the gate. Quintus's quick steps trailed him through the arch and onto the stone path.

The gate clicked shut. The tranquility of the peach orchard did nothing to ease Caros's inner upheaval. He raked his fingers through his hair and spun on his heel, pinning Quintus with a terse glare. "I want you to tell me of your God."

Surprise notched Quintus's features.

"How does He command unwavering devotion among His followers?"

"Loyalty is the least we can give when compared to the gift of salvation Christ offers."

Caros scowled. "As far as I can see, the only gift you Christians receive is a shameful death in the arena."

Quintus stood taller. "There's no shame in dying for Christ."

"Have you been to an execution, slave? There's no glory in it, either."

"Compared to what?" Quintus asked, unable to conceal his contempt. "A gladiator who spills his lifeblood for mere sport and a drunken mob's amusement?"

"Gladiators don't die for entertainment." Caros knew

he lied. "When one of our kind dies in the ring he does so to exalt the emperor and reaffirm the glory of Rome."

"Exalt the emperor? A flesh-and-blood man who will return to the dust at his appointed time? I'd rather praise an all-knowing, loving God. One who promises life eternal if I have the courage to live, and if need be, die for Him."

"If your God is as loving as you claim, why are there times when you think He's cruel?"

Quintus hesitated. The muscles along his jaw worked as he sought to control his inner strife. "The trials of my life of late have caused my faith to falter on occasion. But I'm confident the Lord's forgiven me for those weak moments."

"You speak of being brought here?"

"Yes, among other things."

"Yet, you believe your God is good?"

Quintus nodded. "Even when my plight makes me *feel* otherwise, I choose to walk by faith and believe all the trials I face are part of His greater plan for me."

The dinner bell rang in the distance. A gentle breeze blew through the orchard, rustling the branches and scattering the fallen leaves along the path. Caros's skin prickled despite the warmth of the early evening.

The Christians' sincerity impressed him, persuaded him their beliefs held merit. Both Quintus and Pelonia had suffered tremendous loss, yet they continued to believe their God cared for them in a personal way, that He hadn't abandoned them no matter how dark their circumstances.

He longed to experience that kind of peace, but the jeering faces of those he'd slain stomped through his mind like a barbarian horde. An endless parade of regrets condemned him to a life of turmoil. How he wished life had allowed him to chart a different course than one of constant slaughter. Perhaps then he could cast off his guilt and accept that forgiveness existed.

Convinced he was irredeemable, he tried to brush aside his torment. Pride kept him from asking more questions. It was easier to pretend he didn't care about his place in eternity than reveal his deepest fears. "If I believe in your God, I might find myself tossed in with the wolves. Who needs the aggravation?"

A resigned smile touched the trainee's lips. "If *you* ended up in the arena, I'd pity the wolves."

Caros forced a laugh, but his guilt weighed heavier than a slab of marble. The reminder of his experience in the ring returned him to the core of his dilemma. Not only did his past actions stand like a yawning chasm between him and the Christians' intriguing God, but Pelonia would despise him even more if she learned of all the believers he'd killed.

He would just have to keep the specifics of his past a secret from her.

Sitting heavily on the nearby bench, he braced his elbows on his spread knees. He may not be able to accept Pelonia's God, but he would do his best to earn her affection. A difference in religion shouldn't stand between them. She was his match. His heart's desire. At the moment, he represented everything she despised, but there had to be a way to change her mind and win her love. He didn't know how to stand aside and let her go without a fight.

He eyed Quintus through the twilight. The trainee shared Pelonia's beliefs, had read the Christian texts.

Perhaps he understood something she didn't that would allow her to share her life with a nonbeliever.

He stood and paced several steps before wheeling around to find Quintus beside one of the lantern posts. "I have a slave—a woman I purchased the same night I bought you. She's also a follower of your Jesus. She was with me today and witnessed the executions. Indeed, she blamed me for them."

The trainee shook his head, his expression a combination of anger and anguish. "Did my brothers and sisters endure much pain?"

"No," he lied. "They went quickly."

"God be praised." Quintus rubbed a weary hand across his eyes. "Is this woman the same girl whose uncle sold her?"

Caros nodded. "What do you know of her?"

"Very little. I heard a man haggle a price for her. A thousand denarii if I remember correctly."

The slaver had made a tidy profit off him with Pelonia, but Caros felt he'd gotten the better part of the bargain.

"Why did she blame you for the executions?" Quintus asked. "Did you arrange the killing or provide the wolves?"

"No.... Not today."

The hoot of an owl filled the silence as Quintus absorbed the full implication of the statement. The slave's mouth twisted with unconcealed repugnance. "I see."

"Do you?"

"I believe so."

"Then explain it to me."

"It's simple enough," Quintus said. "You're in love with a Christian, but you've killed her kind. Now you're laboring with the question of how to win her affection without having to admit your guilt or share her faith."

Caros flushed at the accuracy of the slave's assessment. Was the trainee some sort of sage? His insight bordered on clairvoyance. "What makes you think I have any affection for Pelonia?"

"I can read the symptoms. A calloused man like you wouldn't be burdened by a woman's bad opinion unless he cared for her."

Caros flinched, stung by the unpalatable truth. Unable to bear the scrutiny in the other man's gaze, he looked toward the remnant red and gold streaks that stretched across the deep purple sky. In no time at all, total darkness would descend, blanketing the city as completely as the regrets consuming his blackened soul.

Footsteps from the direction of the main house pulled him from of his thoughts. A slave ran to him, gasping for breath. "Master, please come quickly! Gaius collapsed. With Lucia gone there's no one left in the household who knows how to help him."

Caros cursed as he ran for the house. What else could go wrong?

While other slaves swept the floor and tidied the kitchen, Pelonia finished stacking the last dishes from the evening meal. Her hands scalded from the water she'd used to wash the trainees' mountain of platters and bowls, she toweled perspiration from the back of her neck and tossed the damp cloth into a laundry basket beside the back door.

Her conscience pricked her. Since Annia's departure an hour before dinner, she'd thought of little except how unfairly she'd accused Caros. The Lord had brought her here to share His light, not add to Caros's guilt or burden him with condemnation. She ached for the brothers and sisters she'd lost to the wolves today, but it did no good to blame Caros for the violence, nor did it aid God's purpose to wound him with her spiked tongue.

Leaving the kitchen, she relished the brisk night air against her heated skin. She arched her back, stretching the muscles made stiff from an eternity bent over a steaming bucket of water and admired the clear sky and bright stars overhead.

Where had everyone gone? The sound of insects hummed through the night, but no human voices. Lanterns glowed in the windows of the house. Torches burned along the path that led to the training field, but the whole place seemed eerily deserted, which was nonsense given the number of trainers, gladiators and slaves living within the compound's walls.

Vowing to apologize to Caros the next time she saw him, she wandered through the orchard, careful to stay in the shadows lest anyone see her. There were enough rumors milling about her already.

A gust of air extinguished two of the torches along the walkway. Tree limbs swayed above her like long arms beckoning her deeper into the night.

She made her way to the marble bench she'd shared with Caros the previous day. Her hand lingered on the spot where his had rested. A bittersweet sensation settled over her. She wished she could revisit their time together on the training field and revel in the unique closeness she'd shared with him as they gazed at the stars. Those few hours alone in his company had been some of the sweetest of her life. If she believed in the Roman gods or were prone to superstition, she might think he'd whispered incantations to steal her will.

Sensing she wasn't alone, she left her seat and squinted into the darkness. A mysterious figure approached from the direction of the gate that separated the orchard from the training area. "Caros?"

"No." A tall stranger stepped from the shifting shadows, his sculpted features strong and handsome in the torchlight. "Don't be frightened. My name is Quintus Ambustus. The *lanista*'s no longer here."

Recognizing a trainee by the cut and coarseness of his belted tunic, she backed away. "Why are you out here by yourself?"

He motioned toward the field behind him. "The gate is locked and the guards have gone to keep watch at the barracks."

She half turned toward the main house, aware it was a mistake to remain in the man's presence unattended. Not only was the situation dangerous, but her instincts warned of Caros's wrath if he found the two of them alone together. "Do you know where your master is?"

His deep-set eyes narrowed with rejection. "I call no man master, but as for the *lanista,* one of the other slaves called him to the house."

With a murmur of thanks, she started back the way she came.

"Wait." He stayed her with a light grasp on the shoulder. "Are you Pelonia?"

She shrugged off his touch. "How do you know my name?"

"The *lanista* said you attended the executions with him today."

A sharp pain cleaved her chest. "Yes," she managed

in a choked whisper. "I'll never forget the terrible sight or the sound of thousands demanding murder."

"I'm sorry." His bright green eyes brimmed with empathy. "I understand you're a Christian."

Her eyes snapped back to his face.

"Don't be alarmed. I am also."

His unflinching gaze convinced her of his sincerity. Gratitude flowed through her from the unexpected gift. "Praise be to God. You're the second believer He's placed in my life today."

The strain eased from his tall frame. "The Lord is good indeed. When the *lanista* mentioned you earlier, I prayed for a way to meet you, and here you've appeared. It seems an age since I spoke with another of our faith."

"Caros told you of my beliefs?"

"Yes, but you needn't worry. Your secret will stay with me."

"I wasn't worried. Caros must be aware you're a fellow believer. He's far from careless."

He nodded. "I've seen little of him in the few weeks I've been here, but I've gleaned the same impression."

"How did you come to be here in the gladiatorial school?" she asked, her curiosity piqued.

"You and I arrived the same night, though I had no idea if you'd been kept here or taken to serve elsewhere."

"The worst day of my life," she said sourly.

"I've enjoyed better myself." His dry tone made her laugh. "In all seriousness, I'm sorry to remind you of harsh memories, but believe me, I understand the trials you've faced. I've endured similar circumstances myself in recent months."

Her brows pinched. "How do you know anything about me? Surely Caros didn't discuss—"

"No, he said very little about you. I was chained in one of the wagons close enough to hear your uncle offer you to the slave trader."

She frowned, still unable to comprehend Marcus's hatred.

"He told the slaver what happened to your camp. The fresh graves spoke for themselves."

"I see." Her throat was tight and scratchy. She didn't want to hear more. She continued to struggle with her loss on a daily basis. Her uncle's betrayal only added to the cauldron of grief and rage that kept her at odds with the life of faith she desired to lead.

"What of you?" She swallowed down her hurt and anger. "How did you come to be here?"

"I was condemned to die because of my faith, but the jailer sold me to the slave caravan."

"I'm sorry." Empathy ran through her. "But as you still live, God must have a plan for you yet."

He glanced over his shoulder toward the training field. "At times the Lord's ways are difficult to understand and accept."

She recognized the pain and thread of ire in his voice. Her fingers tightened around his with sisterly compassion. It was her turn to offer encouragement and comfort, she realized, just as Annia had done for her earlier in the day. How like the Lord to bring each of them a friend to bolster their faith in times of trouble.

"Quintus, believe me, I don't always understand the Lord's ways or means of bringing about His plans, but I do know He's trustworthy. Our circumstances may make us *feel* alone, but I believe He'll never forsake those who love Him."

"I know you're right." He smiled and stood taller. "I said the same to the *lanista* and I believe it in my heart."

"You spoke with Caros about living by faith?"

He nodded. "He asked me to tell him about God. I have a strong suspicion his interest stems from your example and a desire to understand you. We all have a purpose and I think yours at the moment is to win your gladiator."

"Yes," she agreed with growing confidence. "I believe I am, too. I pray for him daily and do my best to share the Good News. I realize some may think I'm an odd choice, but—"

"No, you seem the best choice to me." He squeezed her hand, offering reassurance and friendship. "Anyone with eyes can see you've made a good impression on the man. He cares for you. It wouldn't surprise me if you're the only person in the world capable of piercing the armor around his heart."

Hope warmed her like the sun after a frigid rain. "If what you say is true, then it's worth the loss of my freedom. I'll consider myself blessed that the Lord has chosen to use me."

With his elderly steward resting in comfort, Caros went in search of Pelonia. She wasn't in her room, or the slave quarters, the atrium, kitchen or herb garden.

A nagging fear drove him toward the orchard, the last place he could think to look before he called the guards and began a search within the school and beyond the compound's walls.

If he'd trusted her only to learn she'd duped him long enough to escape, he'd...

His feet ground to a halt. His heart slammed against

his breastbone. The sight of Pelonia holding hands with the one man he didn't want her to meet caused his stomach to heave with a violent need to retch. As he stalked forward, his eyes narrowing on Quintus, he regretted leaving Cat in his cage. It had been a long time since his tiger had had a human to toy with.

"Slave," he snarled at Quintus. "Step away from her unless you wish to find yourself entertaining the lions at first light."

Pelonia whirled to face him, a look of astonishment, or was it guilt, stamped across her expressive features. A sheen of red clouded Caros's vision when the defiant trainee took his time to back away and put a suitable distance between the two of them.

Jealousy shredding his reason, Caros locked fingers around Pelonia's delicate wrist and pulled her against his side. His hostile gaze flicked back to Quintus. "Leave us, worm. If I see you near her again, I'll slay you where you stand."

"Caros, please, let me explain!" She thrust herself in front of him, her small hand splayed against his chest. "You're behaving like a lunatic. I won't allow you to harm him."

Allow? Icy rage slithered through him. "You aren't strong enough to stop me."

"I know, but—"

"Why do you care? Is this slave more than a stranger to you? Have you somehow discovered he's your perfect man in so little time?"

Bewilderment scored her features. She eyed him as though he'd gone mad. "No. I'd try to stop you because tomorrow you'd regret your idiocy and the death of an innocent man. You're burdened by enough guilt as it is. I'd want to save you from piling more on yourself."

Feeling like a cobra in the hands of an expert charmer, he dragged his gaze back to Quintus. "Take this path back to the *domus*. Report to the guard on duty by the back door and have him take you the long way around to the bunkhouse."

Quintus offered no acknowledgment of the order other than to tip his head in a respectful nod to Pelonia. "Good night, sweet lady. I hope the Lord answers your prayers with all possible haste."

Seething at the man's audacity, Caros waited until the trainee was out of earshot. "What prayers, Pelonia? Already my slave knows more of your secrets than I do. Share them with me."

She stroked his chest as if to soothe him. "I can't until you're ready to hear them."

The heat of her palm reached through the thin fabric of his tunic. He lifted her other hand to his chest and held both tight against him, his heart pounding from the powerful effect of her touch.

His anger began to fade though his jealousy continued to roar like a bonfire. He refused to share her or give her up. Every part of his being longed to draw her against him, to kiss her until she agreed to be his woman for the rest of her life. Their bargain could burn Hades' fires for all he cared.

"I'm ready now, Pelonia. I want no barriers of *any* kind between us."

She winced at his tight grip on her wrist. "Let go," she said, softly. "You're holding me too tight."

He relaxed his fingers without breaking the contact.

"Why do you think the idea of you choosing Quintus drives me insane?"

"Quintus? I just met him."

"He's better suited for you than I am," he said gruffly. "He shares your faith. His true occupation is one of a learned and respected man, not death. No scars mar his face or form. He's—"

"Not you," she replied with simple honesty.

His mouth snapped shut. A mix of expressions crossed his chiseled features—astonishment, uncertainty, and finally...hope.

His vulnerability shattered her remaining defenses. His height and nearness surrounded her. The spicy scent of his skin and the night's peach-infused air robbed her of protest as he gathered her against him.

"There's no man I prefer over you."

She felt the last traces of hostility drain out of him. His lips brushed the top of her head. Gooseflesh prickled her skin. She snuggled closer, resting her cheek against the center of his chest. Lulled by the solid thud of his heart beneath her ear, she chose not to examine the oddity of finding so much peace in the arms of such a violent man.

"Must I beg or is your silence how you intend to punish me?" he asked against her hair.

"Punish you?"

He leaned back and waited for her to look at him. "Yes. For being a 'bloodthirsty' Roman."

She flushed with guilt. "I don't blame you for the executions. I regretted what I said to you even before you left me alone with Annia. Now, once again I find I'm in the wrong and needing to apologize for the meanness of my tongue."

"No." His fingers cupped her cheek, then slipped into her hair at the nape. "You did nothing."

"I said horrible things. I wish it weren't the case but I only seem to lose control of my temper when I'm with you."

"You were in shock and I'm not the easiest of men."

"Please don't make excuses for me." The kinder he became, the worse she felt.

He opened his mouth to argue, but seemed to think better of what he planned to say. "You're right. I shouldn't make excuses for you. Your insults ripped through my heart like flaming arrows, causing more pain than I've ever endured. Then, when I could bear your scorn no longer, I searched for you to discuss the matter only to find you sharing secrets in the arms of another man."

Remorse rolled over her in waves. Not for her innocent behavior with Quintus, but for the hurt she'd caused Caros with her angry accusations. Never in her life had she wounded anyone as much as she had him—the one soul she wanted most to see healed.

"Caros, I…" Her voice rasped over the lump in her throat. She lifted her gaze, ready to apologize, to plead for forgiveness and offer a fresh start between them, but amusement gleamed in his eyes. "I…why are you laughing?"

Chapter Sixteen

Caros endeavored to keep a straight face. "I'm not laughing."

"You lie." She swatted his chest and tried to break free of his hold. "Tell me why you're laughing at me or I'll have to twist your arm and make you."

"Vicious woman." He closed his eyes. At the moment she almost escaped, he tightened his arms, not ready to relinquish the exquisite torture of holding her so close. "All right, I admit it. You have a face as easy to read as an open scroll and it makes me happy to see how concerned you are for me."

"Happy?"

"You say the word as though you've never heard it before."

"I've heard it." She burrowed back against him, her arms wrapped around his waist, her cheek pressed against his heart as though she meant to stay with him forever. "You just surprised me, but then you always do."

He stroked her hair, loving the silken tresses that made him grateful he had hands to touch her. "I wouldn't want to bore you."

She grinned up at him, her doe eyes sparkling like the stars above them. "You make me feel many things, *lanista,* but boredom has never been one of them."

He squeezed her until she squealed and merry giggles filled the cool, autumn evening. "If I confessed to the feelings you stir in me, you'd run for the hills in maidenly fright."

Relaxing back against him, she sighed from what he hoped was contentment. "Then confess nothing, for I'm pleased where I am and too tired to run anywhere."

"The woman is finally satisfied." A chuckle rumbled in his chest. "If exhaustion is the ingredient needed to make you stay with me, I'll have to devote more time to thinking up chores for you."

She yawned. "You best hurry, then. Our bargain ends in twelve days' time."

The reminder spiked him in the heart. Despite the tenderness between them, she clung to her plan to escape at the first opportunity. The knowledge hurt more than he cared to admit. "Why do you remain so adamant to leave? Have I not treated you well and shown you as much respect as any man can show a woman?"

She stilled like the night surrounding them. "Let me go."

Cursing the end of what had become an enjoyable evening, he released her. Her shoulders thrust back, she aimed for the bench several paces away. Already his arms missed holding her.

Never one to admit defeat, he decided to double his efforts to convince her of her place by his side.

"My wish to leave isn't swayed one way or the other by how well or ill you treat me," she said, her tone as stiff as her small body. "As I've told you before, I want my freedom because to live as a slave is abhorrent to me. This degraded state is not who I am. Would you be willing to change places with me? To take on a mantle of slavery once more?"

"I swore the day I won my freedom, I'd never lose it again."

"Then how can you expect me to abide the loss of *my* freedom just because you will it to be so?" She kicked a fallen piece of fruit with the toe of her sandal. "It also troubles me greatly to know my cousin must be worried sick…or worse, mourning me if she believes I'm dead. If you felt a tithe of my pain when I think of Tiberia suffering, you'd let me go this instant."

"And what of *my* pain?" he asked quietly. "What am I to do once you leave here? I'm not naive enough to believe you'd return to me if I released you."

Distant voices carried through the crisp night from the direction of the house.

"You're wrong," she said. "I'd come back to you. I want you to know the Lord."

"Of course." He threw up his hands in exasperation. "Why didn't I guess? If not for your absurd need to see me believe in your God, you'd be seeking escape at every possible turn."

"Most likely," she agreed. "But then, without my hope for your soul, there'd be no bargain between us in the first place."

"Without your silly beliefs, you'd already be in my bed and there'd be no *need* for this cursed bargain between us."

"No. My father taught me to be a woman of honor. Christian or not, I wouldn't share your bed without first being your wife."

A bitter laugh erupted from his throat. "Wife, slave, what's the difference? Either way I own you."

Pelonia paled until her luminous skin shone as white as a pearl in the moonlight. "There's a difference, Caros. If you don't realize that simple truth, then regardless of whether or not you believe in my God, there's no hope at all for us."

A rooster crowed, waking Pelonia from a dreamless sleep. Her lashes fluttered open. It was the first day of the week. Three days had passed since the executions, three nights since she and Caros had quarreled in the orchard.

Disheartened by the situation between them, she rose from her pallet, noting the rising sun. The chill in the air reminded her of Caros's attitude toward her. He hadn't spoken to her since they'd argued, but every once in a while she would catch him studying her with a fierce gleam in his eye that turned to ice the moment he realized she'd seen him. She'd offended him greatly and though she was sorry she'd hurt him, she took solace in the fact she'd told him the truth.

Washed and dressed, she made her way to the herb garden. She'd developed a routine over the last few days and found she enjoyed caring for the plants as much or more here than she did at home. Along with pruning the existing plants, she'd marked out a vegetable garden on three sides of the fountain and planted seeds from a variety of root vegetables to see how they'd take in the rich, black soil.

Cat met her inside the gate. No longer afraid of the tiger since the day he almost shoved her into the fountain, she scratched his head and rubbed his ears, laughing when he closed his eyes in contentment and nuzzled her chest with a gratified grunt.

Hearing footsteps, she looked up to find Caros's steward picking his way toward her.

"How is your health, Gaius?" she asked once he stopped a few arm lengths away from her. "The color's returned to your face but should you be up and back to your duties so soon after your collapse?"

The old man offered a grim smile that pleated the wrinkles of his thin face. "I'm well enough thanks to your garlic concoction. I believe the culprit for making me ill was a poorly prepared joint of mutton. It smelled less than fresh when I ate it. I should have known better."

"I suspected as much. Who hasn't suffered the consequences of eating bad food from time to time? I believe the mixture I shared is fairly well-known. I was surprised no one here knew how to fix it for you."

"This is a gladiatorial school. Lucia excelled at gentle remedies, but our physicians are better at binding wounds than mixing potions."

"I'm sorry the healer is gone because of me."

"She was wrong to behave as she did," he said without mercy. "I've found the master to be a wise man who handles situations in the best possible manner. Don't concern yourself any longer. Lucia was sent away because she deserves to be, but she'll be fine."

Pelonia nodded. "I hope you're right."

"I am, but I didn't come to fetch you to make small talk about Lucia. You have a guest."

"Who is it?" she asked, no longer surprised by Gaius's brusque manner.

"Annia, the shop mistress from the Forum." His mouth turned down in clear disapproval. "The master informed me she might visit, but he said nothing of her bringing a mob along with her."

She patted Cat on the head in a quick farewell. "Where did you tell them to wait?"

"In the chamber just off the front entrance," he called as she hurried toward the house.

She found Annia and her companions waiting patiently on the plush couches in the sitting room.

Annia hopped to her feet the moment Pelonia rushed across the threshold. "I trust you don't mind my bringing friends."

"Of course not," she assured her. Annia's soft perfume surrounded Pelonia as she gathered the elegant older woman in a hug.

"Then let me introduce you."

Gaius's "mob" turned out to be two couples—one, a fresh-faced pair of newlyweds dressed in matching shades of yellow, the other a plump middle-aged husband and wife, both with graying hair and dark eyes.

Annia took the older woman by the hand. "You may remember Marcia here from my shop the other day."

"Yes. I believe you mentioned meeting by the river this morning."

Annia nodded, her good mood infectious. "The five of us meet to worship God and discuss the texts this time each week. After I told them of your dreadful plight and that you weren't able to join us in our usual spot, I suggested we visit with you here instead."

"How wonderful." Pelonia beamed with happiness. "You're all an answer to prayer. It's been over a month since I've gathered with anyone to praise the Lord. I couldn't be more pleased you're here."

"What of the *lanista?*" Marcia's husband, Festus,

asked with marked concern. "Forgive me, but it seems strange to worship in the home of a man known to kill Christians. Is he here? Are we safe?"

Pelonia's smile faded. Her first instinct to defend Caros, she tamped down a forceful reply and kept her voice as mild as possible. "What do you mean *known* to kill Christians? It's true the *lanista* trains gladiators, that he fought and killed for several years but he's been retired from the games for a long time now. He's never even fought in Flavian's amphitheater..."

An uncomfortable silence fell over the group. The visitors exchanged uneasy glances. Festus cleared his throat. "Forgive me, dear sister, I spoke out of turn."

"No, I'm certain you didn't. Please don't treat me like an outsider. What has Caros done?"

Festus shifted nervously from one foot to the other. "You're newly arrived to the capital. There's little chance you know of your master's history before the mob demanded his freedom. He was the best gladiator this city's ever seen. Before I chose to follow the Way, I used to enjoy the games. Back before the Flavians built the arena, the editors set up fights in squares, back alleyways, even the middle of the Forum on feast days. The Bone Grinder, as the *lanista* was called then, never failed to rouse the crowds who gathered just to see him kill."

"He was known for his speed and tenacity," Geminius, the other male guest added. "The spectators loved him because no one stood a chance against him, and he rarely showed mercy. He played the crowd and made them dream of being him. Unfortunately the victims included many of our sect who were charged with treason and brought in for execution."

Trembling, Pelonia sank into the seat behind her. Perhaps she'd been naive, but she hadn't allowed herself to consider just how many Christian lives Caros had ended.

Annia coughed and left the comfort of her pillowed chair. "That's enough, men. Can't you see what you're doing to the poor girl? We didn't come here to add to her distress."

"No, we didn't," said Geminius.

"Shall I get you a cup of water, Pelonia?" his young wife, Vergilia, asked.

"No, I'm fine," she insisted, her head throbbing with tension. Her concern for Caros blotted out all rational thought. A distant part of her admitted she was horrified by the number of deaths at Caros's hand, but armed with the knowledge of his past, how could she condemn him? He'd once told her he'd learned to survive under the threat of kill or be killed. Loving him as she did, she was only too thankful he'd been strong enough to live.

"Whatever Caros did, it's in the past." Pelonia met each of the other's uncertain gazes with a direct look of her own. "As far as I'm concerned the past is where it will remain."

"I agree," Marcia said. "No one is blameless. The Lord says to forgive. Like Pelonia, I intend to follow His instructions. Now, perhaps we should pray. We've started off badly. Let's begin afresh."

The others murmured in agreement. Pelonia joined them in prayer even more firmly convinced Caros needed the peace of Christ in his life if he ever hoped to overcome the horrors he'd known.

Dripping with sweat from his morning sword practice, Caros toweled his face and bare chest before slipping his favorite old tunic over his head. As he made his way down the hall toward the atrium, he stopped midstride, caught off guard by the chorus coming from somewhere in the house.

It couldn't be Alexius singing. He heard more than one voice. Besides, his friend sounded like a mule with a cold when he sang. Was it the other slaves? He doubted it. As far as he knew they'd never before felt the need to burst into song.

In the sun-drenched courtyard, the voices grew louder, competing with the splash of the fountain. Discernible words caressed his ears and drew him across the covered porch toward the front of the house.

The Lord is my Shepherd; I shall not want.

Locating the source of the soothing hymn, he crossed his arms over his chest and leaned against the doorframe, wondering if a mirage had sprung up in his sitting room or if a group of Christians really had been audacious enough to gather under his roof.

He makes me to lie down in green pastures.

He leads me beside the still waters.

He restores my soul.

The last words caught him by surprise. He listened more intently, his interest keen to learn who might restore his soul.

He leads me in the paths of righteousness for His name's sake.

Yea, though I walk through the valley of death, I will fear no evil: for You are with me...

His eyes sought out Pelonia where she stood worshipping her God, an expression of intense love and peace making her even more lovely than usual.

As the group continued to sing, Pelonia's eyes fluttered open. Once again she caught him staring at her.

This time he didn't feel angry for being found out or trapped and ashamed by his inability to keep his eyes off her. This time, he felt...welcomed.

She smiled at him, a glorious display that lit up her face and allowed him a deeper glimpse of her beautiful spirit. The hope of reconciliation shone from her eyes.

Stretching out her hand, she beckoned him to join her in front of the shuttered windows. He took a step forward, surprised by his eagerness to share in the atmosphere of peace their worship created.

The song ended. He peeled his gaze from Pelonia to find the other believers gaping at him. He saw in their faces, they knew who he was. Worse, what he'd done to their kind. To their credit they tried to hide their distrust, but the trepidation etched in their expressions severed the tenuous thread reeling him over to Pelonia's side.

The temptation to join them evaporated. What madness to think he could leave his old life behind when everyone except Pelonia knew the full extent of his brutal past.

With a terse shake of his head in answer to Pelonia's invitation, he turned on his heel and left the house.

Pelonia flinched as the heavy stone door closed with an angry thump. Owl-eyed, her companions stared at her in speechless alarm.

"He isn't going for the authorities, is he?" Festus yelped, his voice reed-thin with fear.

"Don't be too anxious," Geminius warned. "If he wanted us dead, he wouldn't bother to contact the authorities. He'd have killed us himself."

Annia and the others launched into an agitated debate about their safety, but Pelonia didn't weigh in. Every nerve in her body demanded she go after Caros. She rushed for the door, nearly tripping on her tunic's hem in her haste to catch up with him. The guard moved to bar her way, but her new friends closed ranks around her, sweeping her past the guard and out onto the front steps. Blinking the sun's glare from her eyes, she spotted Caros just before he disappeared into the thick flow of pedestrians on the street.

Frantic to be heard over the clack of horse hooves and wagon wheels, she called Caros's name as she sprinted down the steps before the guard had a chance to follow her.

Caros whipped around. His eyes flared, then narrowed. Walking back to her, his steely disapproval gripped her by the throat. "How did you get out here?"

"My friends—"

"You mean those fools abandoning you?"

Pelonia craned her neck to see behind her. Wringing her hands, Annia waited by the school's tall, iron gate, but the other two couples fled in the opposite direction.

"Your surliness frightened them."

"Cowards," he sneered, grasping her hand and dragging her back toward the house. "At least your friend Annia seems to possess a bit of courage."

"So do the others." Offended on her friends' behalf, she did her best to pull free. She didn't appreciate his snide attitude or his overreaction. After all, she hadn't been trying to escape. She'd followed him because she'd been worried about his feelings. "It took great courage for them to worship in the home of a *lanista*."

"Great courage or tremendous stupidity?"

Pelonia bit back a tart reply. Marching up the steps, he berated the guard for his carelessness and hauled Pelonia through the front door. Annia close on their heels,

Caros blocked the door with his arm. "You've 'visited' long enough today, mistress."

With a decisive thud, he closed the door in the older woman's indignant face.

Chapter Seventeen

Annia descended the school's front steps, her maternal instincts running rampant. Until now, she'd believed Pelonia's assurance she was well treated, that she felt the Lord had placed her in the gladiator's home for a purpose. She didn't want to question Pelonia's calling, but she feared the *lanista's* anger might lead to violence.

Her mind already forming a plan to help Pelonia, she realized she may not have known the young woman long, but she'd come to think of her as a daughter. Perturbed for provoking Caros's temper, she wished she'd used better judgment and come alone this morning. With the damage done, she had to do something to correct her lack of foresight.

Calling for the litter she'd arrived on, she gave her servants swift orders to be taken to the Palatine hill. Pelonia had mentioned her cousin's marriage as her family's reason for venturing to Rome in the first place. Perhaps her cousin's important husband wielded enough influence to see Pelonia freed from the *lanista's* hold.

Annia hopped from her litter the moment it arrived in front of Senator Tacitus's palace on the Palatine. The huge marble columns and grand portico reminded her of a religious temple. Taking a deep breath, she lifted the hem of her tunic and *stola* enough to keep from stumbling on any of the myriad steps leading to the front door.

At the top of the stairs, she noted the wool marking the doorposts, an indication of the bride and groom's recent marriage. She knocked and breathed a sigh of relief when the palace caretaker allowed her entrance.

Inside the cavernous entryway, she waited, the smoky-sweet scent of incense drifting from the family's shrine in the atrium behind the long blue curtain to her right. She caught her breath at the vibrant frescoes decorating the walls and the numerous busts of the senator's illustrious family lining the brightly hued edges of the mosaic floor.

The curtain parted and a slender young girl stepped from the shadows of the atrium.

Annia surged forward. "Forgive my intrusion this morning, but I must know, are you Tiberia, wife of Senator Antonius Tacitus?"

Her manner severe, the girl nodded. "I'm Tiberia. My caretaker says you have news of my cousin."

Confused by the cold, almost hostile tone, Annia began to question the wisdom in coming here. Perhaps Pelonia bore her cousin more affection than Tiberia returned? Fearing she'd made yet another error this morning, she eased back toward the exit.

"Where are you going?" Tiberia waved her hand and two slaves moved to block Annia's escape. "Do you or do you not have news of my cousin?"

"I believe I may have made a mistake."

"Why? Did you think to come here, demand a reward

for your information and leave without any of us being wise to your deceit?"

"Reward? You misunderstand. I want nothing from you. I wish only to tell you of your cousin Pelonia's whereabouts. I fear for her safety and pray you and your family will be gracious enough to rescue her."

The girl hesitated, her small, slightly uptilted eyes narrowing with indecision. The curtain rustled again. A feminine voice called from behind it, "That's enough, Asa, I'll see to our guest myself."

Annia watched the girl bow toward the curtain and scurry off down a side hallway. The curtain parted again. This time an aristocratic woman stepped into the entry. Appearing slightly younger than Pelonia by perhaps a year or two, the newcomer's red *stola* and white under-tunic gave her a dramatic air that went well with her above average height and patrician features.

"I am Tiberia, the person you seek. I trust you'll forgive my small deception and understand the need for it. When Pelonia disappeared, my husband offered a reward for news of her whereabouts. We've been swarmed by charlatans bearing lies simply to gain a few coins ever since. Now, please," she said urgently, "tell me of my cousin. My husband commissioned the best scouts to find her. They brought news she was dead."

"The scouts were mistaken," Annia assured her, relieved to find she'd made the right decision to come after all. "Her family's camp was attacked by thieves and everyone killed except Pelonia and her uncle. That same day, her uncle sold her to a slave caravan."

"No! I can't believe you," Tiberia said, the color draining from her face.

"It's true, my lady. She was sold to the *lanista*, Caros

Viriathos. She's being held in his compound even as we speak."

"I've been such a fool," Tiberia whispered, staring at the floor. "I believed him."

"Who did you believe, my lady?"

Her full mouth pinched into a thin line, Tiberia shook her head, unable or unwilling to share more. She clasped Annia's hands, her unsteady fingers clutching tightly. "I've been so distraught. I blamed myself for Pelonia's death. Please, you must take me to her this instant. I *must* see her for myself."

"That may not be easy, my lady. I believe you will need your husband to attend with you. The *lanista* is a difficult man from what I can tell. I'm certain he won't let you see her without being forced."

"Nonsense." Tiberia snapped her fingers and called for a litter. "My husband is a senator of Rome. No one refuses me entrance. Least of all a filthy gladiator trainer who dares to think he can keep me from my cherished kin."

Unsure of his status as far as Pelonia was concerned, Caros found her under a lemon tree in the herb garden a short time after the noonday meal. Cat lay stretched out on the ground beside her, basking in the cool autumn afternoon. Deep in thought, her chin resting on her raised knee, she idly stroked the tiger's ear.

Pleased by the peaceful sight of his woman and pet together, he admired Pelonia's courage. In small ways and large, she proved her immeasurable worth. Few people viewed his tiger as anything more than a vicious beast, but she possessed a talent for seeing deeper into a person—or tiger, as the case may be. In less than a week, she'd overcome her initial fear and accepted the animal, treating Cat with as much affection as if he were her own. He lived in hope of the day she would accept him with as much ease and openness. Though why she would ever find him worthy of her was a mystery after the way he'd treated her and her friends earlier in the morning.

Dry leaves crunched beneath his sandals, drawing Pelonia's attention. Her expression unreadable, he continued toward her. The idea of entering a ring full of lions held more appeal than facing her and admitting his guilt.

Unpracticed in offering apologies, he'd spent the last hour devising the best strategy to win her forgiveness for his heavy-handed behavior. Why had he become so unreasonable over a few judgmental glances? Most of society condemned him as next to nothing because of his profession. Why, all of a sudden, did the opinion of a few weak-livered Christians cause him the slightest concern?

Because Pelonia will side with them.

He crouched beside her in the shade, his fingers folding into the short coarse mane around Cat's neck. The quiet disappointment in her regard made him regret his earlier actions even more than he already did.

He rubbed his chin, waiting for her to berate him. When she said nothing, he assumed her silence was meant as some form of feminine punishment. Usually blessed with the ability to ignore a woman's sulks, he found the idea of Pelonia thinking badly of him an herb too bitter to swallow.

"How long do you plan to be angry with me?" he asked, his attention focused on his dozing pet.

"Have you done something to make me angry with you?"

"Don't play games, Pelonia."

"I'm not." She shifted to her knees, then rose to her feet, brushing the flecks of dirt and leaves from her tunic. "Nor am I angry with you. I thought *you* were furious with me."

"No, not in the least," he said, standing.

"I find that difficult to believe. Your fierce looks of the past three days have said otherwise. And this morning—"

"I behaved like a mad dog."

"No, you were hurt and I'm truly sorry for it. Believe me, I'm upset with my new acquaintances enough for both of us."

"You'd side with *me* against your fellow believers?"

"I'd side with you against anyone except God."

Astonishment rattled him to his core. The bright color blooming up her slender throat told him she'd spoken secret thoughts with an unguarded tongue. She never ceased to surprise him. Grateful to find so unique and generous a woman, he thanked her God for bringing her into his life.

"Why do you think I followed you this morning, Caros? To cause another argument between us? No," she answered for him. "I chased after you because I saw your expression when the others judged you. They didn't give you a chance. They should have known better. If they claim to be followers of Christ, they ought to show His love to all of those in need of it."

Astounded by her attitude after the way they'd parted three nights ago and then his harshness this morning, he couldn't believe his good fortune. Even more convinced she was the finest person he'd ever known, he brushed his thumb over her smooth, rosy cheek, loving her more with each passing moment. "I need no one's love but yours."

A startled gasp broke from her lips. More heat stained her cheeks until they glowed bright red. "You're wrong. We *all* need Christ's love and forgiveness. At this moment, you most of all. I believe you're suffering from a strong case of conviction."

He raked his fingers through his hair. "Conviction, eh? Conviction of what?"

"Jesus taught—listen to me, don't shut me out," she said when he rolled his eyes and opened his mouth to interrupt her. She waited until she held his full attention before she continued. "Jesus taught that no person comes to the Father unless the Holy Spirit draws him. The Spirit is drawing *you,* whether you accept it or not. The road to believing in Christ as Savior and living by faith can be a rocky one if a person refuses to follow the truth he knows in his heart."

"Is that why I berated your friends and slammed the door in Annia's face?"

She reached for a lemon leaf and split it into strips. "I think you overreacted out of fear."

"I fear nothing." *Except losing you.*

"That's not true." She stepped closer. "You wanted to join us this morning. Don't deny it. I saw it on your eyes. It wasn't until you noticed the others' reactions that you changed and became defensive. Are you concerned if you turn to Christ the other believers won't accept you?"

Being Romans, her friends knew truths about his past that she didn't. "Their opinion matters to me as much as the dirt beneath my feet."

"If you say so."

"The only opinion I care about is yours."

She pinned him with a knowing look that made him feel she possessed the talent to read his thoughts and divine the secrets of his soul. "Is that why you haven't told me of the Christians you've killed?"

She might as well have kicked him in the stomach. "Who told you?"

"It's not important. Why didn't *you*?"

"Why would I? Especially after your reaction to the executions."

Her soft hand reached up to caress his cheek. "Only now do I comprehend how much my words must have hurt you. I'm sorry."

"Then you don't hate me for what I did to your kind?"

"No! When I heard what happened, I remembered what you said about learning to kill or be killed. I'm just grateful you survived all those years."

He nuzzled her palm, overwhelmed by her sweet spirit.

"I'm ashamed of how I dragged you down the street like a common slave this morning."

Clearly he'd caught her off guard. "Why? Don't you think of me as a common slave?"

"There's nothing common about you." He kissed her fingers. "In truth, I believe I haven't thought of you as a true slave since…the first time I found you in this garden."

Astonished, she didn't know whether to laugh with glee or to screech at him. Her fingers tingling from the brush of his lips, she stepped away. "Then why threaten to bend me to your will and force me to accept my bondage? Why do we have a bargain at all? Why not release me to find my cousin?"

"Because I want you here with me, within arm's

reach. I want you here where I know I can see you every day, every *hour* if I choose."

She turned her back on him, but not before he saw her tormented expression. "What of *my* wants, Caros?"

"I'll give you anything except your freedom."

"Every other gift pales in comparison."

He inhaled sharply, desperate enough to offer all that he had left of himself. He grasped her shoulders and eased her back around to face him. "What if I give you my heart?"

Her lips began to tremble. The muscles of her face twitched as she worked to maintain her composure. Her huge dark eyes watered with unshed tears. "Please don't, Caros. As much as I want to, you know I can't accept any part of you as long as we have no future together."

Chapter Eighteen

Tiberia waited impatiently in the covered litter while one of her slaves announced her arrival and obtained entrance into the gladiatorial school. Surrounded by thick, gray stone walls and a massive iron gate, the school reminded her of a military fortress—perfect for training men to kill or die in honor of the emperor.

Without a hint of softness to be seen from the front street, the formidable compound sent a quiver of unease through her already agitated nerves. Perhaps Annia had been correct when she'd recommended bringing Antonius along with them. A part of her wished she'd listened to the older woman she'd sent home earlier, instead of simply sending word to the senator by way of a messenger.

Her fingers tapped a rapid tattoo on the fat silk pillow she reclined against. Through the thin lavender veil shrouding her litter, she watched the throng of pedestrians scurrying to and fro. If her slave didn't return soon, she feared she might burst from all the restless energy frothing inside her. She couldn't wait to see Pelonia again.

Spying her slave the moment he stepped outside the gate, she held her breath in eager anticipation as the tall Lycian sprinted toward her. It didn't bode well that sweat beaded his upper lip despite the afternoon's mild weather.

She snapped her fingers. Her bodyguard pulled the curtain back and helped her alight. "Well?" she demanded of the slave. "What news do you have for me?"

"The steward, Gaius, welcomes you, but he warns the *lanista's* mood is far from pleasant. He recommends you return another day."

Her lips thinned into an agitated line. "He does, does he? What day does he suggest?"

A trickle of sweat seeped down the slave's temple. "The ides of December, my lady."

"The ides of *December?* That's six weeks away!" Infuriated by the obvious rebuff, she drew her shawl tighter around her stiff shoulders and marched toward the massive front gate, her slave hard-pressed to keep pace with her.

"Open up!" she commanded the guard at the gatehouse. "I am Tiberia, wife of Senator Antonius Tacitus. I'm here to speak with your master."

After much debate, the guards opened the gate, its hinges creaking from the weight of the massive iron piece. The Lycian ran ahead to announce her presence, gaining admittance into the *domus* just as she arrived on the doorstep.

"It's an honor to welcome you, my lady." The elderly steward bowed low as she crossed into the entryway.

"Where is your master? He has much to answer for," she said, biting her tongue to keep from calling the old man a liar. *The ides of December indeed!*

"In the herb garden, my lady." He led her to a sitting room off the atrium. "Please, make yourself comfortable. I'll inform him you're here."

Refusing to be put off any longer, she pursued him at a short distance, careful not to draw his attention to her presence behind him. Leaving the cool interior of the *domus,* they followed a path past the kitchen, through a gate and into a connecting garden rife with lemon trees and an abundant variety of herbs.

The delicate scents of rosemary and mint mingled with the sound of voices emanating from a spot around the kitchen wall beyond her view.

"Pelonia, wait!" A deep male voice sliced through the warm afternoon.

Tiberia ran toward the voice, concern for her cousin pressing her onward.

The sight that greeted her could have been plucked from a tragedy. The *lanista's* hands clutched Pelonia's shoulders like the talons of a great winged beast. An expression of such forlorn agony creased Pelonia's visage, Tiberia felt her own throat close over and her heart pinch from the pain of it.

"What are you doing to her?" Tiberia demanded, racing to her cousin's rescue. "Get your vile hands off her this instant!"

The *lanista* stilled, but didn't release his prey as commanded. Pelonia's gaze darted toward her, her eyes wide with shock. As recognition dawned, her countenance brightened by degrees with elated disbelief. With little effort, she shrugged off her captor's hold. "Tiberia? Is it really you?"

The steward began an immediate round of apologies to his master for not having known she'd followed him.

"Fetch Cat before he frightens our guest," said the gladiator. "He's in the corner beyond the fountain."

Unconcerned about a cat, she held out her arms to Pelonia in welcome. "Yes, dear cousin, I'm here for you. I came the moment I learned of your whereabouts."

Pelonia launched herself into Tiberia's embrace with a jubilant shriek. "The Lord be praised for bringing you here! You can't imagine how happy I am to see you. Marriage must agree with you. You're even lovelier than the last portrait you sent me."

Unwilling to let go, Tiberia held on tighter, tears of thankfulness burning the back of her eyes. "I believed you were dead. I can't thank the gods enough you're alive."

"How did you find me?"

"I…" Momentarily struck speechless, she watched in amazement as the steward led a tiger from behind the fountain and up the stone path. "By the gods, what is that beast doing in the garden?"

"The tiger is Caros's pet. He's fairly harmless."

"Fairly?"

"He *is* a tiger." Pelonia laughed. "You should have seen the look on your face just now."

"And how did you react the first time you saw him?"

"I confess, much the same way. The tiger sneaked up behind me and breathed down my neck. It was a curious sensation to say the least."

Regaining her wits, Tiberia giggled. "I can imagine."

Pelonia linked arms with her, apparently unconcerned by the *lanista*'s black expression. "Now, tell me, how did you find me?"

"Your friend Annia visited me this morning. I didn't know whether or not to believe her at first, but any positive word of you was most welcome. Marcus, that weasel, led us to believe you were kidnapped. I lost countless nights' sleep, I was so worried about you. The scouts we sent to search for you reported you were dead. I've been racked with grief for weeks, blaming myself for—"

"No, no, you mustn't blame yourself. You aren't responsible for anything that's happened," Pelonia assured her. "I'm sorry I didn't send word of my good health. You were never far from my thoughts, but circumstances prevented me from contacting you."

Understanding perfectly, Tiberia narrowed her gaze on the *lanista*. She'd heard stories about Caros Viriathos. Her husband enjoyed the games and was an avid admirer of the great champions. This close to the infamous former gladiator, she could guess why he'd never been beaten. He was a colossus—battle-hardened, massive and formidable. A long scar ran down his cheek and his tunic did little to hide the marks of battle on his arms and legs. She imagined the hostile gleam in his eyes alone had sent many confident challengers into early graves.

Silently reminding herself of her position, that the man wouldn't dare harm a senator's wife, she began to lead Pelonia from the garden.

"Wait," Pelonia said, not so easily led. "I want you to meet Caros."

With no desire to greet the man who'd enslaved her favorite relative, Tiberia wrinkled her nose with distaste, but submitted to propriety for Pelonia's sake.

"Caros," Pelonia beckoned with an outstretched hand. "Come and meet my cousin, Tiberia, my dearest friend in the world."

Struck by the informality between them, Tiberia marveled at the way the *lanista*'s severity softened each time he glanced at her cousin. Was it possible Annia had been mistaken in thinking he'd kept Pelonia as a slave?

"It's an honor to meet you," he said.

Sensing his insincerity, she inclined her head, but didn't return the sentiment.

Pelonia attempted to fill the awkward silence. "Tiberia is a recent bride."

"Yes, Pelonia was to be one of my special guests." She didn't bother to dull the edge of accusation in her tone. "Apparently she was otherwise detained. How long have you had her enslaved?"

"Almost three weeks," Caros replied. "She was unconscious when the slave trader brought her here. I had no way of learning who she was or who awaited her."

"And, of course, you searched for us the moment you learned her true identity?"

He shrugged. "No."

"You honestly planned to keep her as a slave?"

"My plans are none of your concern."

Incensed by his audacity, she glanced at Pelonia, who watched from beneath one of the lemon trees, arms akimbo, her eyes fixed on the *lanista,* her expression unreadable.

"Whatever your plans, you must realize they've been altered," Tiberia said, at the end of her patience. "No relative of mine will be chattel in your possession."

"How do you intend to take her from me?"

"Through the front door, of course."

As though he enjoyed baiting her, he smirked with infuriating calm. "I'll warn you now that's a risky scheme. *If* you make it past me, there are armed guards at every exit who've been threatened with severe punishment if she escapes."

"Don't toy with me, *lanista*." She stamped her foot in vexation. "What kind of fiend are you? You can't honestly hope to imprison her here now that you know who she is and the importance of her family. My husband, the senator, will never tolerate it."

"Obviously, you place more value in your connections than I do. I broke no laws when I bought her—"

"If it's a matter of coin—"

"It isn't."

"I'll gladly repay you with interest."

"I've no need of your money."

"You're just being stubborn!"

Pelonia joined the fray. "That's enough, both of you."

Caros reached for Pelonia and led her to a spot by the fountain, too far away for Tiberia to overhear their conversation. Confused by the gentleness in the brute's manner toward her cousin, she acknowledged there was a stronger tie between the two of them than she'd originally been prepared to admit.

Her lip curled in disgust at the idea of *her* relative being entangled with anyone of the gladiatorial trade. Her friends and neighbors, even her husband, might be consumed with the games and its champions, but only from a spectator's distance. The gladiators were revered for their skills and entertainment value, but they were still lowly slaves and their *lanistas* did little more than pander flesh.

A jewel like Pelonia deserved a man similar to her own dear Antonius, a man of prominence and wisdom who knew how to appreciate a woman of Pelonia's rare qualities and strength of character.

At the first possible opportunity, she'd see that Antonius arranged a proper marriage for Pelonia. Her gentle cousin deserved nothing less than the best.

Certainly *not* an animal like Caros Viriathos.

Still overwhelmed and giddy with happiness from Tiberia's unexpected appearance, Pelonia sat beside her cousin on the long cushioned couch in the house's main sitting room. Warm sunlight filtered in through the open shutters, bathing the frescoed walls and potted plants with a golden hue.

"What did he say to you just now?" Tiberia asked, feigning an interest in the folds of her *stola*.

"Nothing dire, I assure you." In truth, Caros had reminded her of their bargain, that she'd promised not to leave.

"Are you certain?"

"Of course, I…ah, here's Gaius with some refreshments for you."

Gaius placed a glass goblet of spiced wine and a charger filled with oatcakes, honeyed dates and fresh grapes on a low table within Tiberia's reach.

"What's the meaning of this?" her cousin demanded. "Did you intend to insult *me*, or Pelonia when you thoughtlessly brought a single glass?"

"Tiberia," Pelonia groaned. "Don't—"

"I meant no insult, my lady. I'll fetch another."

"See that you do, and be quick about it."

Once the steward left, Pelonia shook her head at the younger girl. "I appreciate you taking my part, but I wish you hadn't berated him. His manner is a bit distant, I admit, but Gaius carries out his tasks with great care. He thinks of me as a slave. Naturally he didn't bring me any refreshment."

"That, my dear, is the crux of the problem." Tiberia reached for one of the smaller oatcakes and placed a fig on top. "You're not a slave. You're the victim of an outrageous misunderstanding. If that twice-cursed gladiator weren't such a stubborn brute, you would have been returned to the protective bosom of your family weeks ago."

Or found myself in a brothel. Pelonia flicked an imaginary piece of lint from her tunic, while Tiberia enjoyed her treat. "Don't speak ill of Caros. You don't know him. He's an honorable man."

"Yes, honorable enough to enslave you and *honorable* enough to refuse your freedom." Tiberia snorted. "I don't understand how you can defend him. Has he threatened you? Or worse, has he beguiled you?"

"Neither," she denied a little too vehemently. "But I've come to know him over the past fortnight and I... I think I understand him."

"Not a difficult task, I'm sure." Tiberia brushed the crumbs from her fingers. "A mindless barbarian can't be too difficult to read."

"Tiberia, stop."

Her cousin shrugged, unbothered by the warning. "What's this about a fortnight? Is the dolt unable to count as well? He claimed you've been here almost three weeks, not two."

Pelonia prayed for patience and tamped down her aggravation. She was finally in the company of Tiberia again. The last thing she wanted was to cause an argument, though she'd forgotten how opinionated her cousin could be. "Caros is a successful man of business. His sums are fine. I don't recall much of my initial time here. Uncle Marcus beat me senseless. I was unconscious the first several days. After I awoke, it took another week to get me on my feet and recovered enough to be useful."

Tiberia's face puckered with remorse. Her fingers clenched the ample folds of her scarlet *stola*. All traces of flippancy disappeared. "Tell me of Marcus's treachery. Annia shared what she knew with me before I sent her home and came here."

Pelonia told her the full extent of Marcus's duplicity.

"I was a fool." Anger radiated off the younger woman. "I believed him when he claimed you'd been kidnapped and welcomed him into my family as a true relative. Knowing he betrayed you into slavery is heinous enough. Realizing he did so within hours of your dear father's murder has me tempted to hire an assassin. I'm certain the world would be a far better place without an insect of his ilk."

Despite the painful reminder of her father's death, Pelonia bit her lip to suppress a chuckle. "I admit the thought of revenge holds a great deal of appeal, especially if Marcus's punishment is slow and painful, but let's leave the matter in God's hands, shall we? I don't want you guilty of murder on my account."

Tiberia sighed and a slight smile played about her lips. "I know you don't mean it. If a fly were dying you'd look to make it more comfortable in its last moments. But it does my heart good to see you've retained some of the playfulness I love most about you."

Not wanting to spoil the reunion with more woeful talk, she squeezed Tiberia's hand. "I'm truly glad to see you, cousin. I don't think I'll ever be able to express how much."

"Of course you are. Even if you didn't love me so well, weeks enslaved in a gladiator *ludus* must have set your teeth on edge. I imagine you'd be pleased to see any unscarred and smiling face."

"You're probably right." A sidelong glance at her cousin's indignant expression made her laugh. "In truth, I've had little exposure to the school. I've helped in the kitchen, but my chores have been contained to the garden for the most part. Caros says it's too dangerous for me to be around the men."

"*Please* don't say any more. I can't abide the thought of you toiling like...like a common *slave!* By the gods, I think I'm going to be sick to my stomach."

More of Pelonia's laughter filled the sitting room. She made a show of examining her cousin's soft, unblemished hands. "Nary a mark in sight. You are a senator's wife for certain."

"I'm glad you're amused, but seeing you in this shapeless rag of a garment is a travesty. The moment we leave this place I'm taking you to the Forum. We're going to replenish your wardrobe with the finest silks available. You always had superior taste. I want your opinion on a new set of *stolas* for me as well. In fact, shopping will be the extent of your labor for at least a month."

"It sounds grand," she said, realizing she lied. Certain she'd be bored senseless without Caros to spar with, she did her best to deny the twinge of panic she felt at the thought of not seeing him every day. She forced a bright smile. "Tell me of your new life. Is marriage as blissful a state as you wished for?"

"It's even better." With a wistful sigh, Tiberia fell against the back of the padded couch. "Antonius is all I've ever dreamed of in a husband. He treats me with honor and more kindness in a day than Father ever gave me or Tibi in a decade."

"How is your sweet sister?" she asked, delighted by her cousin's blessed state. "Tibi must be, what, thirteen or fourteen by now?"

"Fifteen last June." Tiberia scowled. "Honestly, I don't know what Mother and Father are going to do with the brat. When she doesn't have her nose in a scroll, she's spouting philosophy and forever arguing with their houseguests—and mine. She refuses to marry and her reputation has preceded her until no suitable man will risk taking her on. Lately, she's threatening to wear a man's short tunic and cut her gorgeous flaxen hair. I told her, no matter what she does to fashion herself as a son, Father will pay her no more mind than he ever has. Thank the gods, Antonius is a wise and patient man or he'd forbid her presence to darken our door."

"I'll pray for her," she said, concerned for her younger cousin. Having been blessed with the best of fathers, she despised the thought of Tibi suffering from a lack of paternal affection.

"Yes, do. Perhaps your God will succeed with her where mine have failed."

"I'm praying for you, too, you know."

"You needn't bother. I'm pleased with Juno's blessings on my house thus far."

Pelonia nodded, mindful of her cousin's resistance to Christ. Tiberia would come to Christ when she was ready. If she'd learned one thing from her father and Uncle Marcus's relationship it was that a heart commitment to the Lord couldn't be forced.

"Enough about me, Pelonia. I want to hear about you. What is the cause for this queer sensation I get when I watch you and the *lanista* together? He doesn't behave toward you like I'd expect him to treat a slave, yet he claims he owns you and refuses to release you to my care. For your part, you defend him as though he's your lover."

Flushing with embarrassment, she prayed Tiberia remained ignorant of just how much she did love her supposed master. At a loss of how to explain her unusual relationship with Caros, she left the couch and feigned interest in a figurine of a centaur atop the side table. "As I said before, he's a good man. He's treated me well."

"Are you saying he hasn't seduced you?"

She shook her head. Eyeing one of the large ostrich fans in the corner, she wished for one small enough to cool her hot face. "No, he hasn't."

"Nor raped you?" Tiberia asked delicately.

"No! I told you he's an *honorable* man."

"The gods be praised again." Tiberia rose from the couch, her *stola*'s heavy folds of red silk falling to her feet. "Mother told me it was much easier to find a virgin a suitable husband and I believe she's right. With your beauty and the dowry I'm certain Antonius will bestow on you, I've no doubt we'd find a decent man regardless, but I want you to have a husband of the highest caliber."

Pelonia ran her finger down the smooth figurine's cool marble spine. She wanted Caros or no one. "I don't believe I'll ever marry."

"Of course you will. Don't you want children? What of having your own home and social position? You wrote once not long ago telling me how you wished with all your heart to find a loving mate. What's happened to change your mind?"

I've given my heart to a man I can't have.

Gaius passed the sitting room's door. Intrigued by the steward's curiously quick pace, Pelonia stepped out into the atrium. Moments later a deep male voice rumbled across the entryway.

"Antonius!" Tiberia exclaimed, rushing into the atrium. "He must have received my message. I've every confidence he'll see the entire matter between you and the *lanista* resolved in no time at all."

Following her cousin into the entryway, she spied Tiberia's new husband, his white, purple-edged toga proclaiming his senatorial status. A hair's breadth shorter than her cousin, Antonius possessed a lean, muscular frame, a prominent blade of a nose and intense dark eyes. His regal posture and the haughty jut of his chin proclaimed his innate confidence.

Here's a man who can force Caros to free me.

The happiness brought by Tiberia's reemergence in her life began to dwindle. Why, after weeks of praying for a reunion with her family, did she suddenly wish they'd never found her?

"Come, Pelonia. Meet my magnificent husband."

Her legs heavy with guilt from her disloyal thoughts, she did her best to ward off the cloud of dejection descending upon her. As was custom, she inclined her head. "It is an honor to meet you, Senator."

"No, the honor is mine, my lady," he said without a hint of falseness. "My fair wife has been overwrought in her concern for you. To claim Tiberia's high regard is no easy task and I dare say she favors no one higher than you."

"Thank you, Senator, but I must respectfully disagree." She grinned at her cousin who stood with her arm entwined with her husband's. "You are the person she values most in the world. She's sung your praises since last spring in her letters to me and even more so since her arrival here this morning."

The newlyweds exchanged an intimate glance of mutual admiration. Antonius looked back to Pelonia. "From my wife's message earlier, I understand the *lanista* is under a false assumption about you. I've met Viriathos on more than one occasion. I don't think there's cause for alarm. He's a clearheaded and reasonable man. Don't fret any longer. I'll have you freed within the hour."

Chapter Nineteen

Caros prowled the confines of his study, cursing the Fates for delivering Tiberia to his door. Outside, the air grew ripe with the promise of an early fall storm, but the most powerful squall was no match for the tempest of fury and fear swirling inside him.

Like a chain squeezing him ever tighter, the possibility of losing Pelonia threatened to choke the heart from his chest. If the senator's wife had her way, all the vows he'd made to keep Pelonia within his reach would be shattered.

"Ahem."

His steward stood framed in the doorway. The old man's uncharacteristic nervousness knotted the cord of muscle across Caros's shoulders and up his neck. His teeth on edge, not that it took much to irritate him since the invasion of Pelonia's pugnacious cousin an hour ago, he prepared to hear the worst.

"Don't dither like an old woman, Gaius. What have you to say? Has Hades arrived yet?"

His eyes downcast, Gaius nodded. "The senator is waiting in the courtyard, Master. Shall I show him in?"

Caros uttered another fervent oath. A frequent guest of Adiona's lavish parties, the senator and Caros had met on previous occasions. The head of his powerful family since his father's death the previous year, Antonius Tacitus was one of the few men in Rome with enough influence to see Pelonia released whether Caros forbade it or not.

His mouth pressed in a firm line, he threw himself into the chair behind his desk. Once he'd recognized Tiberia in the garden, he'd expected the tall beauty's husband to make an appearance sooner or later.

By the gods! *Why* did Pelonia's cousin and the senator's new wife have to be one and same?

Gaius fidgeted with the rope belt around his waist. "He told Pelonia he'll have her freed within the hour."

Caros's brow arched at the man's gall. "How arrogant of him. And how like a politician to make a promise he can't keep."

"Are you certain he speaks false, Master?"

He wasn't certain at all. He surged back to his feet, his temper as black as the approaching storm clouds. Like all good politicians, the senator could be a crafty swine when it suited him, but in most cases he used his talents for the good of all Romans. His genuine concern for the masses had won him great popularity. He was respected as much by the common plebs as his own patrician class. His marriage less than a month ago had been a grand occasion with much of Rome's aristocracy in attendance.

Caros stopped by his desk and picked up a stylus, rolling the slender writing implement between his palms. The fact that Pelonia was a member of the senator's family and, by rights, under the powerful man's protection, shot a dart of cold panic through his veins.

God, please don't let me lose her.

The stylus snapped between his fingers just as a harsh blast of thunder shook the walls. Wind whipped at the curtains, yet Gaius continued fluffing the blue pillows on the couch as if spring had come to call.

"I trust you don't plan to scrub the floors before you fetch the guest?"

"No, Master." The steward lit a bowl of incense on the mantel.

The sweet aroma invaded Caros's nostrils and made his head ache. "Enough fussing," he snapped. "Fetch Antonius and take that noxious incense with you."

Moments later, Gaius returned with the senator. Caros wondered if the other man had worn his ceremonial toga as a silent means of intimidation. He forced a smile. "Senator, it's been overlong since I saw you last. Allow me to congratulate you on your recent marriage and welcome you to my home."

His eyes shining with excitement, the senator gave a vigorous nod of his head, seemingly oblivious to Caros's less-than-eager manner. "As always, it's an honor to meet with you, *lanista*. You know I've been an admirer of your accomplishments for years."

Caros murmured his thanks.

"Much to the chagrin of my new wife, your champions continue to draw me to the arena much too often. In fact, I ventured to the Colosseum just a few days ago because I thought your men were scheduled to fight. I was disappointed when I found I'd gone the wrong day. To add salt to the wound, the executions lasted longer than usual. I had other unavoidable business to attend to and in the end, missed the afternoon's entertainment altogether."

"I recall the day you speak of." Caros indicated a chair in front of his desk for Antonius to sit down. "I was there for the end of the executions. The mob seemed pleased enough by the wolves and their prey."

"True, but the punishment of a few deviants doesn't excite me. I prefer the combat of trained men. Otherwise, all one has is carnage and what pleasure can be found in common gore?"

"None, I suppose." Noting Antonius considered Christians deviants, Caros waited for the senator to make himself comfortable before claiming his own place behind the desk. "As a *lanista,* I'm gratified to know there are still a few spectators interested in more than raw butchery and blood."

"Of course. A true connoisseur understands a gladiator's greatness is in his technique and stamina. Since you are their teacher, it's little wonder your men are so magnificent to watch." The senator arranged his toga to flaunt its wide purple edge to best advantage. "However, you must know I'm here to discuss an even more important, though less enjoyable, subject than the games."

The rain came down in earnest. He nodded. "I assumed as much."

"My wife says she's spoken to you about her cousin."

His fingers dug into the arms of his chair. "Yes, she's quite adamant I free Pelonia and negate my claim on her."

"It seems only right. You must admit there's been an error concerning her presence here. I assured her you're a reasonable man—"

"You were mistaken...at least where that particular slave is concerned."

"I see." Antonius pursed his lips. "Surely you understand my wife and her cousin are closer than sisters. You must realize Pelonia can't stay here any longer."

"Pelonia is well cared for. There's no reason for her to leave."

"You jest," the senator scoffed in disbelief. "In the absence of her uncle, the girl is under my care, my protection. No member of *my* family will ever serve as a slave."

"The three thousand denarii I paid for her says otherwise. And as I reminded your wife, I broke no laws when I purchased Pelonia. What grounds, other than your pride, do you have for attempting to wrest her from me?"

The senator gawked at him with bug-eyed dismay. "Why so much? Are you mad?"

Caros shrugged. "Perhaps. People have said as much on more than one occasion."

"I believe it." The senator considered the information while he strummed his fingers on the desktop. His previous amicability was replaced with a flintlike gleam in his eyes. With a wave of his hand, he seemed to dismiss Caros's claims. "It matters not. This is a question of family honor and my wife's happiness. I'll pay whatever your price up to double your original cost, plus fifty denarii to reimburse what you've paid for the girl's food and upkeep."

"As much as it pains me to disappoint you or your lovely wife, there's no price worth the loss of Pelonia. She's mine. I intend to keep her."

"She's not a bone for us to fight over like a pack of hyenas," Antonius derided.

"No, she's the fairest prize imaginable."

Dawning flared in the senator's gaze. "You're in love with her, *lanista*."

He didn't deny it.

"You can't marry her," Antonius said, his tone matter-of-fact. "And it's impossible for her to continue on here as if she's a mistress. Her father was a citizen. A woman of Pelonia's stature must wed a worthy and like individual. That is, unless you've prostituted her or passed her among your men."

"What I've done with my slave is none of your concern."

Adopting a haughty air, the senator sat back and glowered. "What have you done to her?"

"I've treated her with respect."

Antonius looked doubtful. "Have you used her for your own pleasure?"

"What do you think?" Caros began to see a way out of the mire. Given time, Antonius was shrewd enough to deduce a girl with a questionable reputation was certain to become a family embarrassment. Pelonia was no matron to be excused of having other lovers. Any man Antonius deemed worthy enough to join his family's ranks would want an untouched bride—or at least one not sullied by a lowly gladiator.

"I suppose it was too much to hope you'd kept from spoiling her. Pelonia is beautiful. What man wouldn't try her if given half a chance?"

Caros gripped the cool wooden back of his chair. He glared in warning. "I assume a happily married one."

"Of course. That goes without saying."

"Of course," he said flatly. "I'll consider this discussion closed. Pelonia is mine and it's easier for all concerned if she stays here with me."

"I wish it were that simple." Antonius shook his head. "I'm afraid I can't abandon her here. Given you're not married, I doubt you'll understand, but I've no wish to fall into my wife's bad graces over an issue as trivial as this."

"It's not trivial to me."

"I'm sorry, but my own comfort comes first." The politician in Antonius rose to the fore. "The simple fact is this. Either you release Pelonia into my care or I'll take you to court. I have many friends there and many favors to call in if necessary. Who do you think will win the case?"

A nerve began to tick in Caros's jaw. The injustice of the threat galled him. He clinched his fists, calculating the ease and swiftness of snapping the senator's neck. "What of Pelonia? A trial will turn into a spectacle. You seem overly concerned by appearances. Have you no care for her reputation?"

"That's rich coming from you." Antonius's snide laugh raised the hackles on the back of Caros's neck. "You have the power to save her name or ruin it, *lanista*. Thus far, no one important knows she's been a slave in a gladiatorial school. If the gods are kind, we might be able to salvage her yet. Force me to take you to court, and…" Antonius shrugged eloquently, then stood to leave. "It's up to you how we proceed from here. Either have Pelonia delivered to my home by tomorrow morning or meet me in court at the ninth hour midweek. If you care for her, as I believe you do, release her into the arms of her family. Allow her to recover from the tragic circumstances responsible for bringing her here and wed the kind of respectable man she deserves."

Antonius swept from the room, leaving Caros to contemplate the pounding rain and his less-than-acceptable options.

* * *

"You can't be serious!" Tiberia wailed in distraught exclamation. "Pelonia *must* leave with us tonight, husband. Who knows what that miserable cur will do to her if she's forced to stay another night in his clutches?"

"I'll be fine," Pelonia said, exchanging an uncomfortable glance with the all-too-perceptive senator. "Caros won't harm me."

"You don't know what he'll do for certain." Tiberia began to pace, her hands gesticulating to stress her point. "He's a seasoned competitor and a violent man. He hasn't faced the threat of losing you before. Up to this point he may have been long-suffering where you're concerned, but who's to say his patience won't snap? We really must see you safe before another tragedy befalls you."

"I think it's best if I leave in the morning," Pelonia insisted, determined to speak with Caros and promise to return to visit him. "The men have come to an agreement. Do you want your husband to break his word?"

"Oh, Antonius," Tiberia said, her face pinched and mournful. A man's word was his bond. "Why didn't you bargain for her release today instead of tomorrow?"

"I thought it best." The senator's voice conveyed his absolute certainty. "If I believed for one moment your cousin faced potential harm, she'd be leaving with us now."

"I don't like it." Tiberia pouted. "How can anyone expect me to leave her here when I've just found her again."

Antonius clasped her upper arms in a soothing manner. "The simple fact remains the *lanista* owns your cousin. You must brace yourself for the worst. If he chooses to meet me in court, Pelonia may not come home for several days."

"He's not that stupid, surely?" Tiberia asked Pelonia.

"He's not stupid at all." She tried not to let Tiberia's constant stream of snide remarks about Caros bother her. Tiberia's vehemence stemmed from loyalty. Her cousin was acting out of love in wanting to see her swift release. The younger girl had no way of knowing her main concern at the moment was not for herself but for Caros and how shaken he must feel.

Guilt snapped at Pelonia for the endless anxiety she'd caused her cousin. By rights, loyalty belonged to her family, not the master who intended to keep her enslaved. She should be as eager to go with them as they were to take her home. Yet, the silken bonds of love kept her more firmly tied to Caros than the strongest iron shackle. Yes, she craved freedom, but the cost of leaving Caros suddenly seemed a precipitous price to pay.

"I think it's time we left," Antonius announced.

"We can't. The rain has yet to die down," Tiberia said grumpily.

"A little rain won't harm us." His firm tone brooked no disagreement. "Tell Pelonia goodbye, my dear. You'll see her tomorrow one way or the other."

With a quick bow to Pelonia, he started for the door, leaving his wife to give her a hasty embrace and follow in his wake.

Once they left the house, Pelonia sank into the chair behind her and dropped her face in her hands. *Dear Heavenly Father, thank You for bringing my family to me, but what am I to do about Caros?*

Lost in his thoughts, Caros leaned against the study's doorway, facing the inner courtyard. The pouring rain had mellowed to mist and drizzle. Light from the lanterns in the interior rooms glimmered on the wet pavers. The twilight air was cool and refreshed, but Pelonia's imminent departure meant darkness was descending on him in more ways than one.

Across the courtyard, he saw Pelonia's tiny form exit the sitting room, her light colored tunic glowing like a beacon in the day's ebbing light. With her head bowed, she didn't see him, giving him a chance to observe her unhindered. The air of melancholy she wore disturbed him, churning up regrets he didn't want to address.

She leaned against one of the pillars and stretched out her hand to catch the rain dripping from the roof tiles. Her beauty held him in thrall. The shine of her hair, her creamy skin, made him long to touch her, even as the loneliness surrounding her lanced him with guilt.

Tiberia's appearance must have caused her to miss her family, freedom and the life of privilege she'd known with greater fervency than usual. What madness had possessed him to believe he'd ever be enough to replace what she'd lost?

He left the doorway, the back of his hand brushing the cool raindrops off a potted palm as he cut his way through the courtyard. Her family's invasion today had shaken him out of his selfish dream world. The money he'd paid for Pelonia gave him the legal right to keep her and he'd convinced himself she would be better off with him because he loved her. But after today's revelations he understood that if she chose him, he had nothing to offer but a demotion in social status and her family's endless disappointment.

He'd made the right decision in the hours since Antonius left. It hadn't been easy to come to terms with losing her, but in the end he wanted Pelonia's happiness above his own.

He heard her call his name. A smile played about her lips. "Caros, there you are. I'd like to speak with you."

"I want to talk with you as well. It's your last night here, after all."

If he hadn't been watching her so intently, he would have missed the way her bottom lip quivered before she steadied it between her teeth, or how she dropped her gaze to hide all traces of her true feelings. Either reaction may have been caused by happiness or sorrow; he couldn't divine which. He had more reason to believe she was elated to leave, but the hope that she possessed even a shred of lasting emotion for him, and wanted to stay, was hard to kill.

The mystery of how best to proceed knotted his tense muscles to the breaking point. He strangled the impulse to shake her until she admitted her thoughts on the matter and probed for answers using a different tack. "I imagine your joy is boundless at regaining your freedom. I made a mistake not to insist Antonius take you away tonight and save us both the hassle of packing you off in the morning."

"Yes, why didn't you? Tiberia was most upset to leave me here." Her eyes sparkled with a glassy sheen in the lantern's light. "I suppose you didn't think of it because it's not *your* back that endures a hard pallet every night."

"I offered to share my comfortable bed, but you declined."

"And rightly so given this sudden wish of yours to be rid of me."

The last thing he wanted was to be free of her. From the moment he'd seen her in the slaver's wagon, she owned him. For the first time since his family's murder, he'd dared to love another. Had he been wiser, he would have dismissed the ardent feelings she stoked in him. Relinquishing her hurt the same as severing his sword arm.

"I took the hint this afternoon when I offered my heart and you denied me," he said, willing his pain not to betray him. "You'll be better off with your family."

She glanced away, but didn't try to convince him otherwise. "Strange how my refusal didn't matter to you until the senator called me kin."

Suspicion rang in her voice. He raked his fingers through his hair. "I admit I chose to ignore the claims you made about your father and the ties you held to an important family because it suited me. I'd have been obliged to return you to your cousin and, at the time, I didn't want to let you go."

Rain dripped on the mosaic tiles as Pelonia considered him. "Because, *at the time,* you were determined to prove your mastery over me."

"You misunderstood—"

"No, I think I understand perfectly. Victory is what you care for most in the world. Admit it, you didn't want to give me up because you were determined to win the pact between us. Even the offer of your heart today was just a ploy to overcome the last dregs of my resistance."

The coldness in her tone was so unlike her, he flinched.

"But you want to lose the senator's goodwill or a court case even less than the game between us," she said bitterly.

He fought the instinct to pull her against him and show her how much he wanted her above all else. "If you believe so..."

Her eyes brimmed with misery and doubt. "I don't know what to believe, Caros. Either you lied to me when you said you cared for me or you're deceiving me now. I came out here with promises of my own…if you cared for me half as much I care for you—"

She gasped as his strong arms banded about her, dragging her against the marble column of his body. His lips silenced her with a kiss that plucked every thought of resistance from her mind. Her eyes drifted closed as his clean, spicy scent filled her senses. Her knees grew weak. Dizzy and shaking from emotion, she locked her arms around his waist to keep from falling.

A tremor ran through the corded muscles of his back. Through the thin linen of his tunic she felt the bumps and indentations of the scars from countless whippings. Her heart bled for the pain he'd endured. She held him tighter, the need to spend the rest of her life showering him with love and tenderness expanding inside her until the ache in her chest robbed her of breath.

The feeling was so intense, so poignant a sob built in her throat and a tear slid down her cheek.

How can I live without him?

He softened the kiss, drawing her even closer. "Look at me," he rasped, his warm breath caressing her ear. "Look me in the eye."

Her lashes fluttered open. His blue gaze burned with a light that singed her to the marrow, branding her his forever whether he chose her or not.

"Don't ever think I don't care for you." He cupped her face in his large palms and brushed her tears away with the pad of his thumb. "You're *all* I care about. I'd forgotten how to love… No, I'd forgotten love existed until I saw you lying there in the slaver's wagon. I wanted to keep you even if it meant forcing you to accept me because life without you was dark and empty. Believe me, I've thanked your God more than once for bringing you here, though now the time has come to let you go."

"You *do* believe in Him."

He shook his head. "It's too late for me, but it's not too late for you to enjoy the kind of life you were born to with the kind of man you deserve."

"*You're* the kind of man I deserve!" Her voice cracked. "If you'd stop being stubborn—"

"No. Today I accepted you have to go. I've nothing to offer you except your family's eternal disappointment and a foreigner's name. If you stayed with me you'd lose your rightful place among the exalted families you'll mingle freely with when you return to your cousin."

"I don't care."

"You will. If not today, then when our children are born and must bear the stigma of having a father who was once a slave. What will you tell them when they ask why people look down on them?"

"The same thing I'll tell them when they ask why we don't visit the pagan temples or participate in the pagan feast days or accept the emperor as a god. I'll teach them we're a people set apart by our Heavenly Father who don't need society's mark of approval."

He caressed a strand of her hair between his fingers. His eyes were soft and tender. "I've said it before and I'll say it again. You are truly a unique woman, Pelonia. I've never met your like. When you leave here tonight and return to your cousin, remember you always have a friend in me. If you or your loved ones need a sword to fight for you, I'm here."

"Tonight?" The cold evening air seeped into her

bones. He spoke with finality, as though he hadn't heard her…or refused to.

He nodded and called for a litter. "This is goodbye, *mea carissima*. There's no reason to wait until morning."

Chapter Twenty

"Don't look," Tiberia said in a hissed whisper. "Adiona Leonia is standing over there by the statue of Mercury."

Pelonia froze in a moment of instant dread, her gaze darting around the Forum's chaotic central market in search of Caros's obnoxious friend.

Her sudden tension palpable, Tiberia latched on to Pelonia's arm. "She's that beautiful creature in the golden tunic. She's rich beyond imagination. My husband jokes that even the gods owe her coin." Her smooth forehead pleated with frustration. "I've given it my all to glean an invitation to one of her parties. So far she's rebuffed and ignored me, but I'm determined not to give up."

"Why is an invitation from her so important?" she asked, her eyes settling on the elegant Adiona and the bright purple *palla* draped around her slender shoulders.

"She's one of the city's leading matrons. Antonius assures me I'll know I've been accepted into the highest social circles once I've been received by her."

"I don't know why you bother. You're lovely in your own right. You have a wonderful husband and home—"

"You don't understand," Tiberia said, clearly distressed. "My husband is a powerful and important man. It's my duty to add whatever honor I can to his house. If I don't, Antonius might think he's made the wrong choice of bride."

"Never." She squeezed Tiberia's hand. "Antonius loves you. As far as the widow Leonia is concerned, *you're* a senator's wife. It seems she'd be the one to vie for your attention."

"Senators are voted in and out of their position, but Adiona—"

"Lingers like an unshakeable cough?"

Tiberia's lips twitched with laughter. "You're too kind. Adiona's more like a plague. Unfortunately, if I don't earn her approval I'll be a social pariah." She lost a shade of color. "*Please* tell me she's not coming this way. I'm not prepared to meet with her."

Pelonia angled in front of her cousin to give the girl time to collect her wits. Her massive bodyguard trailing close behind, Adiona sailed through the crowd seemingly unaware of all the slacked-jawed males and disapproving women she left in her wake. Her kohl-rimmed eyes took on a perceptive gleam of recognition the closer she came.

"What a surprise, Publia, is it not?" The widow's bejeweled bracelets jingled as she came to a standstill.

She felt Tiberia stiffen behind her. "My name is Pelonia."

"Oh, yes, forgive me, will you? I'm rather shocked. It's not every day one returns from a sojourn in the country to find a peacock has taken the place of a mouse."

Refusing to give the widow the satisfaction of seeing her upset, she soothed her palms down the pale blue silk of her own tunic, deriving a measure of comfort from the fact she no longer wore slave's garb. With her hair fashionably arranged and pinned with sapphires, and her skin back to its usual health from a month of daily treatments at the baths, she reminded herself she was no longer the trampled weed she'd been the last time she'd suffered Adiona's presence.

"How is Caros?" the widow asked. "I went by to see him when I returned to Rome yesterday. Gaius told me he ventured to Neapolis a week ago and has yet to return."

"I don't know. I haven't seen him in a month," she admitted once she absorbed the shaft of pain the sound of his name caused her. "I hope and pray he's well."

Adiona's eyes flared with surprise. "You haven't seen him? Judging by your transformation, I assumed he'd made you his mistress."

Pelonia's cheeks burned. Tiberia shrieked at the insinuation, drawing attention to her presence as she stepped to the fore. "My lady, you may not remember me. My name is Tiberia—"

"Yes, I know who you are." Adiona settled a tolerant smile on the younger girl. "We met shortly before your wedding to Senator Tacitus, correct?"

"Yes, my lady. It's an honor to meet you again." She slanted a terse glance rife with questions at Pelonia before returning her smile to the widow. "I really must assure you my cousin was *never* that man's mistress."

"Your cousin?" Her exotic eyes danced with mischief. "How intriguing. My steward mentioned you'd had a relative return from the dead."

"Yes, we're grateful the gods brought her back to us."

"The gods?" Adiona's husky laughter mingled with the din of the milling crowd. "When exactly did Caros achieve divine status?"

"The *lanista* is hardly divine, my lady, but after the way he treated Pelonia, the gods below may want to enlist his help in learning a trick or two."

"Really?" Adiona's manner cooled. "I've never known Caros to mistreat a woman."

"He treated me well," Pelonia said, eager to nip any gossip before it bloomed.

Adiona shifted her gaze to Pelonia as though she'd forgotten her presence altogether. "Marvelous, I'm glad to learn you won't spread lies about him."

"Never, I—"

"We missed you at our wedding." Tiberia quickly changed the subject, drawing the widow's attention back to her.

"I sent my regrets when family matters kept me from attending," Adiona said. "I was loath to miss such a special occasion."

"Thank you." Tiberia managed to look serene. "I did receive your kind regards. Both my husband and I were saddened you couldn't join us."

"I hope you'll let me make it up to you. I'd love to give a celebration in your honor next Tuesday night if you and the good senator are free."

Tiberia beamed, her discomfort obviously forgotten in the face of being handed her dearest wish. "I'll have to speak with my husband, but I'm fairly certain we have no previous engagements."

"Excellent." The widow nodded to both of them as she took her leave. "I'll look forward to seeing all of you then."

"No. Try this," Caros instructed Quintus. "Lunge forward with your right foot. Use the force of your weight to bring the *gladius* through in an even arc, slicing your opponent's face or middle. If you have two opponents and one is behind you, follow through with the swing, careful to keep control of your sword arm. Otherwise get out of the way as though your life depends upon it. Stand around twiddling your thumbs and you'll end up with a blade in your throat."

"Perish the thought!" a female voice burst from the sidelines.

Caros glared at Adiona. "When did you arrive?" As stunning as always, his friend couldn't seem to take her eyes off Quintus. Quintus, on the other hand, didn't look pleased to be standing there in nothing more than his sweaty tunic.

Intrigued by Adiona's continued interest in his slave, he realized the increase in Quintus's breathing wasn't entirely due to the morning's exercise.

Caros shook his head. The trainee was well on his way to becoming another of Adiona's love-besotted fools. "What are you doing out here tempting my men, woman? Do you mean to cause a riot?"

Her husky laughter reached across the golden sand. She cocked her head at a flippant angle; the bejeweled hoops adorning her ears glinted in the sun. Her eyes slid back to Quintus and captured the Christian's gaze. "There's only one man I'd like to tempt into anything."

Quintus turned his back on her, the veins in his sword arm popping from his tense grasp on the *gladius*. A crimson tide of embarrassment rose up Adiona's cheeks. Seeing the hurt in her eyes, Caros groaned under his breath. Her seductive behavior made it easy to forget she wasn't nearly as jaded or wanton as she pretended. A victim of Cupid's arrow himself, he pitied her.

Leaving Quintus with instructions to continue the morning's practice, he dried himself off with a nearby towel and made his way to Adiona. "Let's go indoors. I'll have refreshments prepared for you."

"There's no need," she said as they walked through the gate and into the shade of the peach orchard. "Gaius brought my favorite cinnamon buns and sweet wine before I ventured to the field to watch you."

"Ah, now I understand the intoxication in your eyes when you gazed at Quintus."

Scarlet crept up her neck. "I don't know what you're talking about."

"No? I half feared you were going to pounce on him."

"Nonsense. If I happened to pay attention to him overlong it's because the man's ineptness with a sword is mesmerizing."

"He's much improved."

"Possibly, but I worry he's going to impale himself."

He laughed for the first time since Pelonia's departure. "I see. So it was your *concern* that made you proposition him?"

He held the door for her as they entered the domus. "You're hateful," she said, slapping him on the arm. "I did no such thing. To think I came here as soon I heard you'd returned from Neapolis because I feared you were in the doldrums. Obviously your mouse was right to leave you."

His humor fled. "You know nothing of it."

"Oh, but I do. I saw her in the market three days ago. She looked splendid. I doubt she misses you at all. Truth to tell, I hardly recognized her."

Envy snaked through him. He'd tried, by the gods, he'd tried to cast her from his mind, but Pelonia was embedded in his heart like a thorn he couldn't pluck free. He'd left Rome hoping a change of scenery would help distract him from constant thoughts of her. It did no good. Each night he dreamed of her only to wake restless, unfilled…his heart broken by the weight of his loneliness. "She's a diamond. Exquisite and rare."

"How sweet, a poet gladiator. It's unfortunate you let such a prize slip through your fingers."

His lip curled at her sarcasm. "It wasn't by choice, you hag."

Her laughter grated on his nerves as she preceded him into the inner courtyard. Seating herself on the marble bench beside the largest fountain, she fluffed the generous folds of her vibrant blue *stola*. "The senator must have arranged her departure then. No one else but the emperor has enough sway to force your hand. With Domitian new to power he has more important things to attend to, I'm sure."

She surveyed him from beneath her lashes. "I understand there's a plot to wed her off to Minucius Brutus. Such a pity, considering your high regard for the girl. Minucius is upstanding enough, but as dull witted as the Brutus name implies."

Jealousy chilled his blood. "Where did you hear this?"

"My steward. I quizzed him about the situation after I saw your little mouse at the Forum. You know how he keeps me informed of the city's most interesting tidbits. It seems someone began a rumor that Pelonia was a prostitute in a gladiator *ludus*."

He slammed his fist into his opposite palm. "Who started the lie?"

"I know not. Even if I did I doubt I'd tell you. From the flare of rage in your eyes, I'd be signing a death warrant. I can do without the blood on my hands. It's such a chore to wash off."

"Does Antonius know the deceiver?"

"I don't believe so." She brushed a wisp of dark hair behind her ear. "I suppose anyone who attended the party we hosted might be the culprit. At any rate, it seems there are too few agreeable men willing to wed your slave because of the report. From what I understand the senator had to double the massive dowry he'd originally settled on her before even Minucius expressed an interest yesterday. He's in desperate straits, you know. If you recall, the Brutus family suffered a major financial loss two years ago when their holdings in Pompeii were buried in the ashes."

He felt like Vesuvius on the brink of eruption. The irony of the situation hit him hard. He hadn't returned Pelonia to her family to see her married off to some weakling who wanted her solely for coin. Where was the justice when he'd gladly give half his fortune to see her once more, and the other half just to hear her sweet voice again?

"I'm going after her."

Adiona looked doubtful. "What good could you possibly do? You'll never make it past the senator's front door. You must accept you've lost her."

He sat heavily on the bench beside her, too tormented to care if she saw him in such a low state. "I released Pelonia to Antonius because he promised to find her a husband worthy of her."

"Why didn't you wed her yourself?"

"Don't vex me any more than I am, Adiona. Why do you think I didn't marry her when she's what I want most in the world?"

"I honestly don't know."

Her genuine bewilderment made him angrier. "I'm not good enough for her. Don't you see? I spent most of my life a slave, good for nothing but killing and violence. I have riches, yes, and invitations to the grandest homes in the empire, but only because I'm a novelty, an oddity for my hosts to show off before their friends like some two-headed bull."

She entwined her arm with his and placed her head on his shoulder in sympathy. The water splashed in the fountain beside them as they sat together for long moments without saying a word.

Somewhere in the house a door closed and the smoky aroma of the cook fires drifted in the air. Adiona sighed. "I don't believe in love, but *if* I did and a man loved me as you love Pelonia, I'd give up all that I have and consider myself blessed by the gods to have found him."

A bitter laugh burned in his throat. *Her God is the other reason she won't have me.* "I thought you hate men."

"Oh, I do. In my opinion, you're the last good one and clearly your heart is taken."

"Quintus is a good man, too."

"He might as well be a eunuch for all the notice he gives me."

"I think he notices you too well."

"You do?" She sat back, her expression guarded. "Why do you think so?"

"Because he's a healthy man and you are a fantastically beautiful woman."

Her nose crinkled in disagreement. "You saw him turn away from me."

He debated whether or not to tell the true reason for

Quintus's rejection. Deeming her trustworthy, he shook off her hold and stood. "I imagine he turned from you because he's a follower of Jesus the Nazarene. To Quintus, I imagine, you're temptation in flesh."

"A *Christian?*" She began to laugh uncontrollably. "Leave it to me to fantasize about a deviant!"

He frowned. "From what he's told me, there's nothing strange or perverse in their beliefs."

"They eat human flesh and blood! If that's not unnatural, what is?"

"I asked Quintus why." He leaned against a pillar and crossed his arms over his chest. "He explained they aren't cannibals like so many believe. They have a custom where they take bread and wine as a remembrance of their God's death for them."

"*You've* been asking him about his beliefs?"

He nodded.

"Why? You know their sect is illegal." Understanding dawned in her large amber eyes. "It's Pelonia. She's one of them."

"Yes," he admitted slowly. "It's the main reason she won't have me."

"Stupid woman. She cast aside the man who loves her and for what? Minucius? I assure you he has no Christian bent." She went to Caros and embraced him. "You know I love you as my dearest friend?"

He hugged her back. "Of course. And I care for you as a friend."

"Then I must beg a favor."

He released her and stepped away. "Why is it I've faced hordes of gladiators determined to kill me with less trepidation than I feel when you turn all winsome and womanly?"

"Will you favor me or not?"

"When have I ever refused to help you?"

"Good." She smirked. "I'm having a fete Tuesday night and I'm in need of a two-headed bull to display."

Chapter Twenty-One

The soft notes of a panpipe drifted in from the court-yard as Pelonia reclined on one of the low couches sur-rounding a table laden with the evening meal. Tiberia sat back on her own couch to Pelonia's left, the senator across from them. A variety of boiled vegetables, roasted lamb and salted fish made up the bulk of the dishes.

Tiberia selected a piece of spiced lamb. "Antonius, my love, don't forget we're to be celebrated by Adiona Leonia tomorrow evening. I'm wearing a blue tunic and silver *palla,* so I've had matching garb prepared for you."

"Whatever you wish, my dear, as long as the garment's not fashioned of wool. This heat is enough to blind me." Antonius snapped his fingers and motioned for slaves to wave huge plumed fans to cool the lantern-lit room.

"The warmth reminds me of late summer," Pelonia remarked, disliking the use of slaves, but unable to com-plain when she was little more than a guest in the palace.

"Indeed, but October was comfortable enough. Per-haps it will cool back down and become more season-able in a few days' time." He raised his glass chalice and drank a long draught of sweet wine. Not for the first time that evening, his pensive gaze settled on Pelonia. She picked at a morsel of lemon-seasoned fish, leery of his hesitant manner. Did he have some misfortune to share?

He heaved a heavy sigh. "I've pondered how best to tell you I have news concerning your uncle."

She dropped the spoon she held. Fear winded her as she recalled the last time she'd seen her uncle and his hatred toward her.

"Marcus returned to Rome earlier today and sought me out this afternoon at the Forum."

Pelonia's heart kicked back to life with a jolt.

Tiberia sat up, her knees hitting the table in her haste. "I hope you carted him off to the amphitheater! I'm certain there's a least one hungry lion willing to tolerate rancid meat."

"What did he want?" Pelonia reached for her water and tried to drown the acid rising in her throat.

"The cur was in a fine mood, actually. He has no idea you've returned to us."

"What are you going to do with him?" Tiberia asked. "His villainy can't go unpunished after the harm he caused our family."

"Don't worry, he'll regret his treachery." A sly smile curved the senator's lips and for the first time he appeared to Pelonia as a true politician. "Before he left Rome several weeks ago, he and I struck a bargain," Antonius said. "He borrowed five thousand denarii from me and offered the property in Iguvium as collateral."

"You mean my father's property?" Pelonia asked in disbelief. At the senator's nod, a wave of anger doused her fear with fury. She pushed the dinner plate away as she swung her legs over the edge of the couch and surged to her feet. "How dare he! My father toiled his entire life to make a home for us. And Marcus thinks to squander it? For what purpose?"

"He plans to open a wine shop and make himself a notable man of Rome." Antonius laughed. "It's ludicrous. Can you imagine? As if there aren't enough wine merchants in this city already."

Pelonia sensed she was missing an important detail, but her indignation blinded her. "Many times Father tried to give my uncle business responsibilities, but Marcus proved to be unsuccessful every time."

Tiberia sent her husband a queer look. "If the venture was bound to fail, why did you lend him the money?"

Antonius motioned for his wife to sit back down. "Don't fret, my love. You can trust that all is well. Marcus expected me to introduce him to key buyers and help insinuate him into our social circle. The *idiota* thought to use my reputation and my coin to set him up in grand style, yet he didn't think to offer me a partnership or a share of the profits. He must have taken me for a fool, but he'll soon learn who the imprudent one among us is. Even without the harm he caused Pelonia, I'd planned to teach him a lesson he won't soon forget."

Pelonia sank back onto the low couch. "What do you intend to do? I admit I'm having difficulty not hating him for what he did to me, but you aren't going to have him maimed or…or worse, are you?"

"He deserves worse," Tiberia said with an indelicate snort.

"No." Pelonia weighed her reaction with care, mindful of how she thought the Lord expected her to behave.

"What do you mean, cousin?" Antonius took another drink of wine. "I'd think you'd want Marcus dead after he sold you into slavery."

"I don't want him dead."

"You intrigue me, truly you do. Every other person I know would be demanding Marcus's head on a stake. But not you. Why? What makes you different?"

"I'm not so different. If I were to live by my impulses and feelings alone I'd wish for his death—no, I think I'd help you plan it. But I seek to walk a different path, one not always easy to follow."

"The way of your Christian God?" he asked.

"Yes. I want to serve Him and cultivate forgiveness in my heart."

"Have you forgiven Marcus, then?" Skepticism darkened his hawklike eyes.

"I'm trying." With her temper still blazing, she understood his doubt. "I've asked the Lord to help me, but I've yet to fully succeed."

The music shifted to a softer tempo, carrying on the warm breeze that fluttered the wispy drapes flanking the open doorway to the courtyard.

"Forgiveness is a nice sentiment," Antonius said. "But have a care who you admit your religion to. Being Tiberia's kin and mine by marriage you're safe here, but if you were anyone else I'd be forced to report you to the authorities."

The warning duly noted, she lowered her gaze and nodded.

"The truth is, whether you excuse Marcus or not is of little consequence to me," Antonius mused aloud. "The man is headed down a painful and well-earned road." He chose a round of flat bread from a stack within his reach and tore it in two. "I'm certain you and my dear wife will both enjoy the outcome once my plans have come to fruition."

* * *

With the help of a slave, Pelonia alighted from the litter once Tiberia and the senator stood on solid ground. As her gaze wandered up…and up…and up the wide stretch of steps leading to the palace of Adiona Leonia, she was convinced the edifice was the most lavish structure she'd ever seen other than a few of Rome's grandest public buildings.

Lit by a succession of tall bowl lanterns blazing with fire on every third step, Adiona's Palatine home boasted three stories graced with marble Corinthian columns and artfully arranged statuary. Bougainvillea, deep orange in color from the fire's glow, spilled from the series of arches along the second floor.

In the lush front garden interspersed with statues of Roman deities, jugglers entertained some of the early arrivals, while wandering musicians filled the night with festive songs.

"Isn't this wonderful?" Tiberia exclaimed with pleasure as she tugged on her husband's arm. "Can you believe all of these preparations are for us?"

"I'd expect nothing less from widow Leonia. There's no better hostess in all of Rome." A swirl of laughter, music and merriment surrounded them. "I'm proud of you, my dear. Not everyone is capable of earning the widow's favor, but this grand showing means she must have been impressed by you."

Pelonia drew her sheer white *palla* closer around her shoulders. Numerous well-wishers arrayed in colorful fabrics and sparkling jewels stopped to give their regards to Antonius and Tiberia. Pelonia followed the evening's honored couple, careful not to draw attention to herself. It had been months since she'd attended any kind of social function as a guest. Before she'd come to Rome, she'd always loved a merry occasion, but here she felt strangely out of her depth.

Perhaps she shouldn't have come. Though she tried to accept God's will and learn the lessons she thought He wanted to teach her, the tragedies of recent months had stolen her usual good cheer. She was lonely without her father to talk to and the constant, intolerable agony of missing Caros seemed to increase by the hour.

"Why are you frowning?" Tiberia asked. "This is the grandest of occasions. Please smile, if only for me."

Tiberia was right. The evening was meant to be a triumph for the newlyweds and Pelonia refused to dampen the festivities with any more of her dreary spirits. Determined to be an asset to her cousins, she plastered on a pleasant expression, nodded politely when necessary and made appropriate comments when Tiberia or Antonius introduced her to various acquaintances on their slow progress up the steps.

By the time they reached the final landing, Pelonia was a touch more confident she could put the *lanista* out of her mind for once and maintain her cordial façade—at least until she saw the large fountain twinkling with hundreds of tiny floating oil lamps. Without warning, the arrangement reminded her of the stars she'd gazed at with Caros during the party Adiona hosted at his home. The thought, so unexpected and fierce, overwhelmed her with memories of his arms wrapped around her and the intensity of his kiss.

"How beautiful!" Tiberia exclaimed beside her. "Have you ever seen such a glorious sight?"

Pelonia's answer lodged in her throat. She was floundering in a deep well of pain that threatened to drown her. A hollow ache was expanding inside her until it threatened to swallow her whole. With the exception of her father, she'd never missed anyone as much as she missed Caros. But where her faith promised she'd see her father again one day in heaven, the loss of Caros burned like true death, stealing away all the joy she'd ever know and stretching her life out before her like a lonely, colorless road.

"You're thinking about *him,* aren't you?" Tiberia asked. "You must put troubling thoughts behind you, dearest. You won't have to face him again. The widow Leonia may be friends with that horrid *lanista,* but she knew you were attending with us tonight. I'm certain she didn't invite him."

"Caros Viriathos has been absent from this sort of gathering for more than a year," Antonius added, craning his neck as though looking for someone.

"Except for the party Adiona hosted at his home not too long ago," Tiberia said. They crossed the threshold of the palace. "I confess, at the time, I was jealous. Everyone heard of the fete and I can't think of anyone who wasn't overcome with envy if they weren't invited... By the gods, isn't this stunning?"

Pelonia gulped. The grandeur on display was indeed magnificent. From the flower petals strewn across the mosaic-tiled floor to the sweet scent of incense, consideration had been paid to every detail. But it wasn't the beauty of the large circular entryway with its rare yellow marble or the valuable bronze statues that drew her attention. It was Caros standing in profile just beyond the arched doorway leading to the palace's inner chambers.

She began to tremble. To her starved gaze, he was even more handsome than she recalled. The tallest man in the room, his black, wavy hair curled around his ears and nape. His lean jaw clean-shaven, the embroidered tunic he wore and the gold bands circling his wrists highlighted the deep bronze of his skin. Captured by the undeniable pull of his appeal, she took a step forward.

"Don't go." Tiberia latched on to her arm to stay her. "I'm surprised Adiona invited him tonight. Truly, I believed she'd exhibit better taste. Still, you must stay here. You'll look like a prideless *idiota* if you run to him when he's speaking with that gorgeous dancer over there."

He was talking to someone? Through the shifting bodies of the milling crowd, she strained to see the "gorgeous dancer."

"I've tried to shield you from the ugliness," her cousin continued in an embarrassed whisper, "but the gossip has been rife about you since someone let it be known he enslaved you for weeks at the school. Fortunately, Antonius has found a fine man who's willing to overlook your...past."

Registering the dancer's elaborate wig, heavy cosmetics and transparent costume, Pelonia paid no attention to Tiberia. The sensual delights the beauty's gaze offered Caros knotted her stomach with jealousy. That he seemed captivated by the woman and didn't rebuff the obvious invitation shattered Pelonia and broke her heart.

"Perfect. Our honored guests have arrived." Adiona Leonia approached, her breezy manner one of an accomplished hostess. The smile she wore seemed genuine. She welcomed the three of them with a kiss on each cheek, then clapped her hands to draw the attention of her other guests.

The music and conversation died down. Pelonia forced herself to look interested in her hostess's introductions, though her entire being danced with the awareness of Caros such a short distance away.

When she was finally able to glance at him again, he acknowledged her presence with a slight nod before he turned away. His lack of regard stung the same as a slap in the face.

Pierced through the heart, she lifted her chin in a valiant effort to maintain her dignity. The urge to flee into the night was strong. Inside, she felt herself crumbling. Tears scratched the back of her eyes and her chest locked up, making it difficult to breathe.

Thankfully, the introductions were over and her cousins' attention had been claimed elsewhere. They were too caught up in chatting with other guests to notice her plight. Murmuring her excuses, she sought out a quiet corner of the huge palace to calm her nerves in private.

Blinded by the need for a hasty retreat, she ran into a solid male chest. "Excuse me, I—"

"What are *you* doing here?"

Speechless, Pelonia stared into the livid face of her uncle.

"Marcus," Adiona exclaimed, covering the few paces it took to join them. "So good of you to come when you've only returned to Rome yesterday. The senator will be delighted you're here. He feared you might not make it. I see you've already found your niece."

Chapter Twenty-Two

The sight of Pelonia jolted Caros with a mix of pleasure and pain so intense it almost felled him. After five weeks and two days of missing her, he had to turn away or fall at her feet.

The sound of blood rushing in his ears drowned out the music and flirtatious banter of the dancer who'd approached him. Heart slamming against his ribs, every instinct urged him to toss Pelonia over his shoulder and carry her back to his home where he could keep her all to himself. Half mad with longing, he'd been in torment living without her.

His willpower at an end, the craving to see her forced him to seek her out. In an instant, he located her in the center of the entryway. Dressed in slave's garb, he'd found her beautiful, but cloaked in silks and finery she was a feast for the eyes, an unspoiled oasis to a man dying of thirst.

A pained frown marred her brow. She spoke to her cousin, then pivoted toward the exit. He followed her, his feet carrying him across the tiled floor as though they possessed a will of their own.

He was too far away to stop Pelonia from colliding into the burly newcomer a few steps ahead of her. The man's expression brimmed with recognition. His eyes flared with instant hate, his mouth twisted in a snarl.

Caros abandoned any pretense at politeness and began to shove his way through the thick crowd. From the corner of his eye, he saw Adiona abandon the clutch of guests she was speaking to and rush to Pelonia's side.

"I see you've found your niece," Adiona said at the same time Caros joined them.

Niece? "Marcus?" Caros's right hand balled into a fist.

"Yes, I'm Marcus Valerius. Who wishes to know?"

"If you're the man who abused Pelonia and sold her into slavery—" Caros swept Pelonia behind him and looked down on her worm of an uncle "—then I do."

Marcus's bravado began to fade until he noticed the circle of inquisitive onlookers forming around them. He puffed out his chest, determined, it seemed, to scrape together a show of strength, no matter how meager. "And... and who might you be?"

The music died on a discordant note and the din of conversation faded to shocked whispers. Adiona entered the fray. "You'll have to forgive Marcus, my friend, he's new to Rome." To Marcus, she said, "Let me introduce you to Caros Viriathos, undefeated champion of Rome, *lanista* of the Ludus Maximus—"

"And the man who's going to make you suffer ten times for every hurt you caused my lady."

The bystanders gasped in unison. Adiona snickered. Antonius stepped forward to wrangle Marcus from danger, but it was a halfhearted effort at best. Caros felt Pelonia's cool hand on his upper arm, heard her say his name, but he ignored everything except the maggot in front of him.

With malicious pleasure he watched her uncle squirm, aware that all of Rome's finest citizens would think Marcus a coward if he bolted. Judging by the nervous twitch in his left eye, Marcus knew it, too.

The tension mounted until a shout went up from the crowd, "I'll wager a thousand denarii the old buzzard ends up dead."

Laughter and more wagers broke the brittle atmosphere. "Thank the gods someone has a sense of humor," Adiona muttered. Distracting her guests by calling for more music and refreshments, she exclaimed, "I'll make that three thousand if anyone's game."

Pelonia tugged on the back of Caros's tunic. She was having a difficult time focusing on the seriousness of the situation when all of her senses were dizzy with the delight of being so close to the man she loved. That her uncle was keeping them from a pleasant reunion added to her dislike of him.

"Caros, my darling," Adiona said blithely. "If you must shed blood have a care for my floor and take the violence outside, will you?"

"With pleasure." He caught Marcus by the scruff of the neck and ushered him down a side hall.

"Caros, don't hurt him." Pelonia chased after the two men, vaguely aware of the group of revelers following on her heels.

The corridor led outside to a small garden. A few torches provided enough light for safety's sake, but the simple arrangement of benches and flower beds surrounding a whimsical fountain spoke of a private sanctuary vastly different from the public areas of the palace.

Wasting no time, Caros let his fist fly. Her uncle squealed in pain. Cupping his face as blood gushed from his nose, Marcus fell backward into the fountain, splashing water over the garden's pavers. The scent of blood encouraged the spectators. Excitement whipped through the air. More wagers were shouted.

The Romans' love of violence sickened Pelonia. Caros's bloodlust frightened her. No matter what she tried, he ignored her pleas for reason. Fearing he would murder Marcus and end up in prison or worse, she threw herself in between the two men to beg for mercy just as Caros threw another punch.

His fist clipped her forehead. Pain shot through her skull. She staggered back.

"Pelonia!" he shouted.

At the same time, the crowd heaved a collective groan.

The ground shifted. She felt as though she were spinning. She stumbled and started to fall.

Caros caught her before she hit the pavers. He lifted her, cradling her against his chest. Ashen with regret, his face blurred before her eyes. "I'm sorry, *mea carissima,* I'm sorry."

She rested her head on his shoulder. A feeling of safety, absent since she left him, enveloped her. "I… I'll be all right."

As he carried her through the stunned onlookers, he murmured, "I pulled back the moment I saw you, but you were too close."

"I know. It's not your fault."

"We're going inside. I'll have you more comfortable in moments." He groaned under his breath. "Your cousins are here."

"What have you done to her?" Tiberia screeched.

"Not now, girl."

"She's *my* cousin." Tiberia trailed them down the hall. "You *will* tell me what happened."

Caros walked on without comment, but Pelonia heard Adiona relay a quick report of events.

"By the gods!" Tiberia railed. "You were warned to keep your hands off her, *lanista!* Now look what you've done. I should have known you'd resort to brute force— one of your sort always does. Do you think her betrothed is going to stand still for this?"

Betrothed?

Pelonia felt Caros go rigid. Her cousin must be mistaken. She mused her hearing must have been affected by the blow or else her brain had been loosed from its moorings because she'd made no agreement to wed anyone.

Caros was the only man she'd accept.

"Is it true?" he asked for her ears alone.

She shook her head, sending another blast of pain through her skull.

He relaxed and brushed a kiss across the throbbing spot on her brow. "That's good. You're mine. You won't marry anyone if you don't wed me."

His high-handedness should have irked her, but she snuggled closer. Why be upset when he was simply confirming what she wanted and already decided for herself. If only he would come to believe in Christ…

"If you weren't such a barbarian, this would never have happened," Tiberia rattled on behind them.

"Cease your prattle, girl. You're paining my head," Adiona snapped impatiently. "If anyone is to blame for tonight's fiasco, it's your husband."

"What do you mean?" the younger woman demanded. "I didn't see Antonius assaulting your guests."

"No, but he came to me yesterday and requested I invite Marcus tonight."

A door opened. "Take her in here, Caros. There's a bed she can have for the night," Adiona said.

Pelonia lifted her head long enough to peer over Caros's shoulder and watch as everyone followed them into the room.

"Caros told me of the uncle who'd sold Pelonia, but I didn't realize it was Marcus." Adiona continued with Tiberia's set-down. "Of course, your husband did. I suspect he *knew* something like this would happen, didn't you, Senator?"

"Is it *true*, Antonius?"

She heard the distress in her cousin's voice and hated having a part in the cause of it.

"Yes," he admitted.

Caros tightened his arms around her.

"But why? You *knew* how important this evening was to me. You must have guessed Marcus's presence would ruin it."

"It depends on your definition of ruin, my dear. *You* see bloodshed and a wrinkle in the festivities. *I* see that Marcus has been humiliated beyond repair. All of Rome will shun him for the rest of his days without my having to say a word."

"But how did you know—?"

"I took a chance our hostess would invite Caros and another chance his feelings for Pelonia would demand he act in her defense."

"You're as crafty as Marcus," Adiona condemned.

"Hardly," Antonius said. "However, I am an opportunist. One doesn't become a successful politician without learning how to manipulate circumstances to one's benefit. But unlike Marcus, I'd never sell my own kin into slavery nor lie to them for financial gain."

Adiona snorted. "Perhaps not, but it's clear you'll manipulate and lie to those who *aren't* your kin. What did you plan to do if your gamble failed?"

"I'd have confronted Marcus. This lofty assembly is the ideal place to ruin a reputation. Thankfully the *lanista's* temper is predictable enough I didn't have to do the unpleasant business myself."

Pelonia stopped listening to the others quarrel as Caros placed her gently on the bed. She opened her eyes, grateful for the dim light. He crouched beside her and brushed her hair back from her cheeks. She smiled, loving the gentleness in his eyes.

"I regret all of this," he said. "I'll never forgive myself for striking you. Tell me, why did you throw yourself in front of Marcus?"

"There's nothing to forgive. It was an accident, one I caused. I trust you'd never hurt me, but I thought you were going to *kill* him."

He kissed the back of her hand. "That's what he deserves after he sold you, but I only intended a good thrashing."

She cupped his cheek and allowed her thumb to caress his warm lips. "I admit I don't like how he cast me out, but I'll be forever thankful the Lord brought me to you."

Caros swallowed the lump in his throat. Tenderness washed through him. "I'm grateful He did, too."

"Caros, are you listening to this tripe?" Adiona's inflection strongly suggested he say something. "Antonius has arranged for Pelonia to wed Minucius Brutus. Do you have an opinion you'd like to share on the matter?"

"His opinion doesn't matter in the least," the senator injected. "He has no claim or rights to her."

Clamping his anger, Caros gave Pelonia's hand a reassuring squeeze before he stood to face the other man. "I may have no right to her, but I *have* claimed her. I trusted you to find her a suitable husband. Minucius Brutus is not acceptable. Given your failure to meet the terms of our agreement, I'm taking her back into my care. If she'll have me, I'll wed her. If she won't, then I'll wait until she does. She's mine and no one else will lay a hand on her."

"I won't give my permission for her to wed a *gladiator*."

"Then I won't seek it."

The senator grew red in the face. "How dare you?"

Caros had had enough. He launched forward, grasping Antonius and Tiberia each by the arm. Before they realized his intent, he pushed them through the door and shut the portal behind them. His hand on the latch, he turned to his friend. "Adiona, leave us for a few moments."

"Need I remind you this is *my* house?" she sputtered.

Fists pounded on the other side of the door.

"Need I remind you I can pick you up and deposit you in the hall like I did the others?"

Adiona began to argue for principle's sake, or so Caros suspected, then thought better of it and sauntered toward him. She reached up and patted his cheek. "May Fortuna be with you, my darling, I do believe you're going to need her."

Once they were alone, Caros returned to Pelonia. With great care he removed her sandals and covered her with a blanket before kissing her gently on the cheek. "Go to sleep, *mea carissima*. Tomorrow is a new day and we have much to discuss."

Chapter Twenty-Three

Abandoned by the guests who'd witnessed his disgrace, Marcus berated the Fates. A few jeers wafted back to him, branding him with shame. Soaking wet, he levered himself out of the fountain. The agony emanating from his nose and up through his eye sockets was enough to blind him. Humiliated in front of the very citizens he'd planned to impress, he swore to wreak vengeance on all those who'd ruined him.

Staggering back up the path, he gingerly cupped his swelling face in an effort to stem the slow, yet steady, stream of blood. He'd spent the last five weeks establishing his business. With the money he borrowed from Antonius he'd rented an expensive location in the Forum to set up shop.

It was a natural assumption to think the senator had arranged his invitation to Adiona's tonight to fulfill his promise and introduce him to the influential contacts he needed to lure a wealthy patronage.

Perhaps if he'd stayed in Rome he might have been better prepared to meet Pelonia. As it was, he'd been slow to recognize the trap closing around him.

And it was a trap—a neatly set one. Though Marcus had yet to figure out the connection between his niece and the *lanista,* he harbored nary a doubt that Antonius had engineered the night's events in an effort to avenge Pelonia. Once again the twice-cursed wench and her blasphemous beliefs were the catalyst for all his troubles. He'd thought he'd taken care to remove her from his path, but the gods must be testing him—and his patience—to see if he were truly worthy of their blessings.

Shivering, he gritted his teeth, then winced at the burst of pain behind his battered nose. He'd lost everything. He needed no oracle to see Antonius intended to demand his investment back. With the money spent, his savings gone and no way to make a quick return now that he was a pariah, the property in Iguvium was forfeit.

Soaked to the skin, he ordered a slave to fetch him a fresh tunic and a cloth to dry himself.

The longer he waited outside like a beggar, the more his fury grew. Shamed by how easily his enemies surprised him tonight, he likened Antonius and the *lanista* to a beast he must slay if he ever hoped to regain his pride. Pelonia was its heart. Cut her out and the beast would topple.

Fortunately for him, his niece was an easy target. Rome was an unhealthy place for a Christian.

"Pelonia, wake up!" Tiberia said. "We must get you out of here. Soldiers are at the front door demanding your arrest."

Her cousin's urgency acted the same as a cup of cold water splashed in her face, waking Pelonia from a sound sleep. A dull ache throbbed behind her forehead, but she thrust back the luxurious bedcovers and jumped up instantly, her feet hitting the floor before she even had her bearings. She shook her head to clear the grogginess. "What? Why?"

Tiberia passed her a servant's tunic. "Hurry, change into this. Perhaps you won't be as noticeable. Antonius and the *lanista* are buying you time, but we don't have long before the soldiers surround the palace."

"We stayed at Adiona's," she said aloud, glancing about the room Caros had put her to bed in the previous night.

Now fully awake, the gravity of what was happening filled her with fear. "Why am I being arrested?"

"Can't you guess?"

"Marcus told the authorities I'm a Christian."

Tiberia nodded. "I left to warn you before I heard the full story, but it seems he reported you for sedition."

Exchanging the silks she'd worn the previous night for the tunic, Pelonia hurried to tie her sandals. The charge against her made the threat more real. Because followers of Christ refused to accept the emperor as a god, Christians were executed for being traitors of the Empire.

"One of Adiona's trusted slaves is waiting in the corridor to lead you through a secret passage to the street. He'll accompany you to the gladiatorial school. Antonius and I aren't pleased with the situation but we agree the *lanista* can protect you better in his own domain."

"What about Caros? I can't endanger him. If the authorities find he's hidden me, he'll be imprisoned."

"He's willing to take the risk."

"I'm not," she said stubbornly. "He's sworn never to be enslaved again. If he's imprisoned his old master will buy him and send him back to the arena for certain."

"If you don't leave he's bound to kill someone defending you and end up with the same fate." Tiberia pushed her toward the door. "Don't be an *idiota*. I want you safe. *Caros* wants you safe. Escape to the school and give us a chance to work out a plan to protect you."

Pelonia felt like a coward, but she couldn't find a hole in Tiberia's reason. At the door, she stopped just long enough to hug her cousin. "I love you, dearest. I want your every happiness. Tell Caros I love him, too. In case the worst happens—"

"Say no more." Tiberia's throat worked to swallow back tears. "I refuse to listen. All will be well. Just go before they find you!"

A tall, dark-skinned slave by the name of Aram led Pelonia through the dimly lit bowels of the palace. "Look there," he said in his thick Syrian accent, once they emerged outside.

She glanced over her shoulder to find the sun-washed steps leading to Adiona's palace a short distance away. A handful of soldiers, their red capes flapping in the breeze, waited on the top landing, near the front door. Others were already fanning out to surround the property just as Tiberia predicted.

"Come," the slave said, "we must walk. A cart or litter may draw added attention and we want to remain in the shadows."

After what felt like hours at a punishing pace along Rome's littered streets, Pelonia and Aram came to the school's massive front gates. The place seemed quieter than usual, but she'd been away for almost six weeks. Perhaps the throbbing pain in her head made her remember things differently than they actually were.

A guard opened the iron gate, his face solemn. The yard was a mess, not the neat, efficient space she recalled. Crates and barrels were stacked at odd angles. Shards of broken ceramic were strewn across the gravel.

An air of foreboding seized her. "I think we should leave, Aram. This doesn't feel safe."

It was too late. Soldiers converged from behind the stacked crates and surrounded the two of them. Fear exploded within her. One of the uniformed men knocked Aram to the dirt. Propping his sandaled foot on the back of the Syrian's neck, he pinned him to the ground.

Encircled by soldiers, she had nowhere to run.

A sinewy arm clamped around her waist from behind. "You're a slippery little thing, aren't you?" His harsh laughter rang in her ear.

"How did you find me?"

"We were warned you'd be at one of three places. The widow's palace, the senator's home or—"

"Here," she finished for him. Panic rising ever higher, she worked to remain above the abyss of terror that promised to drag her deeper into its depths.

As the soldiers bound her wrists behind her, she gave herself over to prayer. *Dear Heavenly Father, if it's Your will I die for Your name's sake, please let me do so with honor.*

Her ankles shackled with a short chain, one of the men lifted her off her feet and tossed her face-first into a wagon. Her head, already sore from the previous night, bounced against the rough wooden floorboards. Lewd comments and rough caresses on her bare calves prickled her skin with revulsion.

"Enough of that, men," said a voice of authority. "She was supposed to be delivered by the noon hour. Unless you want to face his ire yourself, we'd best take her to the magistrate as ordered."

* * *

The wagon rolled to a halt. Orders were barked and two of Pelonia's captors were assigned to guard her. Calloused hands hefted her from the wagon and stood her on the ground. Hot, queasy and faint from the long, bumpy ride in the sun, she trembled uncontrollably. She'd had too long to think about the horrors of her possible fate. Like the wolves snapping at the Christians in the amphitheatre, images of torture and untold agony plagued her.

The taller of her guards bounded up the steps leading to a public building in front of her. A chiseled stone sign above the entrance read, Magistrate.

Perspiration broke out on her brow.

"Get moving." The second guard shoved her and she proceeded him at a hobbled pace up the steps. The taller man returned from indoors, his red cape flowing out behind him. "Hurry it up, woman," he bellowed from the landing. "The magistrate's in a foul mood. He's been waiting all afternoon to hear your case."

Why? Why was the magistrate waiting for her? What was so unique about her situation?

The rope chafing her wrists, she entered the office. Her shackle rattled against the concrete floor and echoed off the barren gray walls.

Where is everyone?

Except for a few dour-faced clerks behind tables to her left, there were few witnesses. She'd never been to a magistrate's building and had no firsthand knowledge of how legal proceedings were carried out. Perhaps all suspected criminals were tried in relative private? No. Something was wrong.

A clerk stood and read her name and supposed crimes from a small scroll. A guard pushed her forward. The shackle caused her to stumble. With her hands cinched behind her back, she almost fell. Biting her lip, she prayed for courage and crossed the austere room to stand before the magistrate.

A rotund man with deep lines in his forehead, he smacked his lips and scrutinized her from behind laced, sausagelike fingers. Nerves stretched to the breaking point, Pelonia began to fidget under the weight of his glare.

"I think I've been lied to," he finally said with disgust. "I was told you were dangerous, a deviant intent on influencing a senator to commit treason against the emperor."

The seriousness of the charges made her tremble. No wonder she'd received a rapid trial. It was bad enough to be tried as a Christian, but inciting others to rebel meant instant death.

Suddenly the lack of observers gained new meaning. She suspected the office had been cleared to protect Antonius's honor, not her privacy. With so few witnesses, there was less chance of gossip to sully the powerful senator's name.

"You look more like a harmless butterfly to me." The judge licked his thick lips and allowed his eyes to roam up and down her person.

Repulsed, she lifted her chin and met his gaze with a cold stare. His suggestive smile faded. His expression hardened. He picked up a stylus and scribbled notes on a piece of parchment. The chair he sat on creaked as he leaned back to sneer at her. "So tell me, is your accuser a suitor who wants revenge because you've shunned him? Or are you truly a follower of that crucified agitator, Jesus of Nazareth?"

The temptation to lie called to her. Her own sense of self-preservation betrayed her. The fear of torture and death played havoc with her reason. An insidious voice whispered inside her head, *Won't God forgive you if you deny Him just this once?*

The magistrate's brow pleated with impatience. "Come on, tell the truth, girl. You've nothing to fear if you're a faithful subject of the emperor."

She tugged at the ropes binding her wrist. "I…"

"On the other hand, if you're a follower of Jesus, you'll follow Him straight to the arena."

Her head began to throb. Judging from his blunt tone, she didn't doubt he'd sent many Christians to their deaths. She struggled not to show her terror. A simple denial and her life would be hers again. As would the chance to be with the man she loved. Every facet of her being demanded she set aside her faith and follow her heart.

"Well, spit it out. I have other cases to try today."

Her resolve hardened to flint, she released a pent up breath. "I… I'm a loyal subject of the emperor."

"Silly wench. Why didn't you just say—"

"But Jesus is my God."

The guard shuffled his feet behind her. His shadow overtook hers on the floor as he moved closer.

"Are you certain you don't want to reconsider?" The magistrate smirked. "I'd hate to send such a beautiful woman to die."

She shook her head. "I won't change my mind."

He shrugged, then snapped his fingers. "Guard, take her to a holding cell in the arena. Tomorrow we'll see if she feels the same when she faces the lions."

Chapter Twenty-Four

Pelonia's guard led her down a dark corridor beneath the amphitheater. Bound and chained like the worst sort of criminal, she was trembling so hard she felt bruised from head to toe. The afternoon's games had yet to finish and the mob's roar dripped down to the holding pens like acid. Memories of the wolves ran rampant in her mind. She clung to her faith, praying incessantly to keep from going mad with fear.

The stench of urine and death gagged her. Weeping, angry tirades and insane ramblings escaped the condemned held in cells on each side of the narrow corridor.

The guard stopped abruptly and opened a cell to her right. Rodents shrieked and scurried to the shadows as torchlight invaded their subterranean nest.

"Welcome home, wench." The guard untied her hands and shoved her inside. Her ankles still shackled, she stumbled and slammed into the wall at the back of the tiny stall. "Don't worry," he said with a laugh, "you won't be here long. The mob will get their chance at you tomorrow. I hope your God appreciates you dying for Him."

"He did the same for me and you."

The guard grunted in reply. The door slammed behind him as he left, taking the light with him. Surrounded by darkness, she rubbed her arms to start the flow of blood after being bound and numb for hours. The chill of the place invaded her bones until her teeth began to chatter.

From across the hall, a tortured moan carried through the small, bar-covered opening in her door. Chains rattled and the cries for help from her fellow prisoners fell on deaf ears.

"Dear God, please help me," she whispered. "I need You like I've never needed You before. Please help me accept Your will. I offer You a sacrifice of praise, knowing that You alone are my Rock and my Salvation."

A sense of sweet peace settled over her and she recognized the influence of the Holy Spirit, her Comforter. In the months since her father's death, she'd known the Spirit was with her, but she hadn't *felt* His presence as she did now. A song of praise bubbled to her lips. Words of thanksgiving flowed from her mouth. The longer she focused on the Lord, the less she focused on her troubles or herself.

Caros left his horse with his Greek champion, Alexius, and pushed through the crowd leaving the amphitheatre. Charging down the steps that led to the behemoth's underbelly, he passed the waiting line and entered the editor's office.

"Get out," he ordered the client already in discussions with Spurius. Without hesitation, the man jumped to his feet, gathering an armful of half-rolled scrolls before he scuttled out the door.

Spurius leaned back in his chair, lacing his hands over

the mountain of his belly. "Caros, you're here. I didn't expect you this quickly."

"I came as soon as I heard from you. Where is she?"

"She's in a holding cell like the magistrate ordered."

His gut clenched at the thought of Pelonia in one of the pits. "How much for her freedom?"

"What's she worth to you?"

Everything. Caros shrugged. "Fifteen hundred denarii is the usual price for a female slave."

Spurius chuckled and shuffled a few parchments on his desktop. "But this female is most *un*usual, is she not?

He studied his crafty former master with growing impatience. "Spurius, I have no time for games. Tell me her price so I can take her and leave."

"Her price is...*your* freedom."

Staggered by the unexpected blow, Caros willed himself to stay in control. "Explain."

"It's simple. You declare your loyalty to me—"

"You mean enslave myself again." The very thing he'd sworn never to do.

"Whatever you want to call it is up to you."

"I call it extortion."

"Perhaps." Spurius picked up a piece of parchment from his desk and began to roll it into a tube. "But if you want to see your woman returned to you unharmed, you'll meet my terms."

"Then she *is* unharmed?"

"For the time being, but that can change with the wind."

"You black-hearted worm! She's an innocent—"

"She's a commodity." Spurius stood up to put some distance between them. "While you and I are men of business. If you wish to buy my goods, let's strike a bargain. If not, I need to get back to those waiting in line outside my door."

Seething, Caros surged to his feet, his chair falling backward to crash against the concrete floor. "Then name your terms, old man, *all* of them and be warned, I know what a backstabbing cheat you are, so I'll have a few of my own."

"Your woman must have gold between her legs. What else could inspire such ardor in the iron heart of Caros Viriathos?" The editor chuckled. "You haven't turned Christian, have you? Is that why you're concerned for her plight?"

"No," he answered, his voice cast in stone.

"Then you must be in love with the wench." Spurius's eyes took on a greedy light. "My terms are simple. Declare loyalty to me. Fight in the arena tomorrow for the amusement of the mob and your payment will be the girl. I'll take care of all legal ramifications if there are any, though I can't think there will be once I've paid off the magistrate."

On the surface, Spurius's terms were basic enough, but Caros saw through the loopholes immediately. "I'll agree to your terms—with some clarifications. First, I'll fight for you tomorrow afternoon for one contest and one contest only. Then I'll be a free man again. Second, I'll entertain the mob and make your riches for you. As my reward, Pelonia, my former slave—not just any girl—will be released and waiting for me alive, unharmed and well when I leave the arena. If I die, she'll be granted her freedom and returned unharmed to Senator Antonius Tacitus under the same terms she would have been given to me. Third, Pelonia will accompany me home tonight and return with me to the arena tomorrow. Fourth, this agreement will be put in writing and a copy delivered to my steward within the hour. Fifth, you will never darken my door or approach me to enter the arena again. If you do, you'll understand it's at your peril. And if you *ever* make another lewd suggestion concerning my woman, I'll make you wish you were dead. Am I clear?"

The editor swallowed hard and nodded. "Done, except for taking the girl home tonight. The magistrate's a stickler for body counts."

"Then release her to stay with her cousin at the senator's palace tonight and I'll take her place in the pit."

"Done!" The editor slapped his desk and did a little jig of glee. "Was that so difficult? Shall we have a drink to celebrate?"

Caros ignored the man and made for the door. He found Alexius waiting outside the editor's office. The corridor was less hectic, but a line remained to wait for Spurius.

"Who's he?" Alexius tipped his head toward a young man following them.

"Spurius's lackey. We're going to the holding cells. He's to speak with the jailer."

"Judging from your expression, the situation can't get worse."

"No," Caros admitted. "I've agreed to reenter the ring."

Alexius halted. "Impossible!"

"No. Spurius promised Pelonia's freedom if I fight one last time."

Alexius swore in Greek and hurried to catch up with Caros's quick steps. "So the dog's finally found your Achilles' heel. He's been after you for years to return to the games."

They both knew it was true. Only for Pelonia would he set aside his vow and become a slave again. Their rapid steps clipped along the concrete floor.

"I'm granting you your freedom," Caros said.

"I don't want it."

"As your master, I'm ordering you to take it."

Alexius frowned, but gave an ill-tempered nod of acceptance.

"While I'm in the arena, you'll be the *lanista* of the Ludus Maximus."

"You're mad!" Alexius's frown deepened.

"So everyone says. Now listen to me. We haven't much time. If I lose, Gaius will help you take control of the school. I've spoken with my steward in times past concerning this matter. He knows I intend for you to be my successor. I want you to train the men well. Pay special attention to the new man, Quintus. He has much to offer. Can I count on you?"

"How can I say no?" The Greek tried to smile. "You better *not* die...or I'll hunt you down in the afterlife and kill you myself."

"Ha! Even in death I'd best you." Grateful to have Alexius by his side, Caros thumped him on the back. "Don't worry, my friend, you won't have to be a free man for long. I expect to live and when the contest is over, I *will* want my school returned."

They stopped at the stairs leading down to the holding cells. Caros clapped his champion on the shoulder. "I'd like a few moments alone with Pelonia, but afterward you're to escort her to the senator's palace."

"This is madness. Why are you staying here when you have to fight tomorrow? You should be eating well and sleeping better in preparation. Just bring her home with us."

"No, it's part of the agreement."

"She's not going to let you take her place in the ring without a fight."

"She has no choice." Caros whipped the tail of his cloak over his forearm and started down the steep steps, the other two men following close on his heels.

At the holding level, the situation was explained and the jailer led him and Alexius through the complex maze of corridors to Pelonia's cell. Spurius's man returned to his master.

"Is that…singing I hear?" Alexius asked.

Caros listened to the faint song. "I believe so," he said with equal bewilderment.

"Obviously things have changed," the Greek said dryly. "There was nothing to sing about the last time I was here."

"Things haven't changed enough. It still smells like a sewer."

The melody grew louder. There was more than one voice and though the atmosphere was dank and cold, the usual moans and cries of the condemned were minimal.

"This way," the jailer said, leading them down a narrow hallway alive with singing voices. "You want to see the wench who started this racket. Before she got here, these Christians were resigned to their fate. Now they're praising their God like they've all lost their minds."

The key grated in the lock. Caros took the torch and sent the jailer on his way. To Alexius, he ordered, "Keep watch. I'll be a few moments, no more."

Caros pushed open the door and ducked to enter the cell without bumping his head. He placed the torch in the holder on the wall. His heart stopped when he saw Pelonia. Bathed in the fire's glow, she stood in the tiny cell, hands raised shoulder high, her eyes closed. Deep in meditation, she had yet to realize she wasn't alone.

She'd never looked more beautiful to him than she did in that moment. Surrounded by the moldy walls of her prison, he saw her for the indomitable spirit she was. He prided himself on strength, but next to her, he was a sapling compared to an oak.

Her sweet voice caressed his ears, stirring him to marvel at the greatness of her God, a God awesome enough to inspire worship even in the depths of a gaol.

Her song ended, though others down the corridor continued with their praise. Lowering her arms, Pelonia opened her eyes. A smile of such pure joy touched her face he was struck dumb by the splendor of it.

"Caros? What are you doing here?" She came to him, wrapping her arms around his waist to nestle close.

He closed his eyes and hugged her tight, dying a little inside when he realized that if the match didn't go his way tomorrow he'd never hold her again. He kissed the top of her head. "I came to rescue you. I thought you'd be terrified, but I see you've made yourself at home."

She laughed, but he felt the dampness of her tears through the linen of his tunic. "It's home now that you're here."

Startled by the admission, he lifted her chin and kissed her softly, his heart swelling with love until he thought his chest might burst with emotion. "Why didn't you lie this once and tell them—"

"Shhh..." She placed her fingertips over his lips. "You know why. I'd never deny my Lord."

He nodded, accepting her loyalty and belief in Jesus were part of what made her unique. "I know."

"But I *was* tempted."

"Of course you were," he said, doing his best to relieve the guilt in her eyes. "Who wouldn't want to cling to life when death is breathing down your neck?"

"No, I'm not afraid to die." She tried to smile. "I'm afraid of the pain beforehand, certainly, but not death itself. That's not why I was tempted."

"What other reason is there?"

Her eyes softened. "Until now I... I've had few regrets in life, Caros. I regret that my mother passed away at my birth and I never knew her. I regret not being able to tell my father how much I loved him one last time before he died. But in death tomorrow, I'll be reunited with them because they're waiting for me with the Lord."

"Then why—"

"Because my deepest regret," she continued, her bottom lip trembling, "is...is never having the chance to spend a lifetime with you."

His heart wrenched at her words. "I feel the same, love. Which is why I'm taking your place in the arena tomorrow."

The blood leeched from her face. "No! I won't allow it!"

He silenced her with a soft kiss. "You will, *mea carissima.* You have no choice in this. Alexius?"

Pelonia watched in horror as his champion entered the cell. "Caros? No!"

He nodded toward the Greek and Pelonia was swept from the cell. Her protests echoed through the pit's dark corridors. Her desperate sobs broke his heart, but for once in his life he was certain he'd done the right thing.

* * *

Caros couldn't sleep. Thoughts of tomorrow's contest crowded in on him like the cell's damp walls. Though not locked in, he'd promised to stay in the prison as part of the bargain. If he broke any part of the pact, experience had taught Spurius would use it against him. His cell door closed to keep the vermin at bay, he'd settled in for a miserable night of stones poking his back.

"*Lanista?* Where are you?"

"Quintus?" He rose to his feet, almost hitting his head on the ceiling. He pushed open the cell door. "I'm in here."

"Thank God." Quintus lifted the sack he held in each hand. "Pelonia sent bedding and food. I would have been here sooner, but I had to bribe the jailer."

Struck by her thoughtfulness, Caros nodded in understanding. "How is Pelonia?"

"She's worried, of course, but clinging to her faith. She's peeved for having to leave you down here. She told me to tell you she and Annia will be in prayer all night, and to assure you she'll return tomorrow."

"I never doubted her. Pelonia's the most honorable woman I know."

"Then you two are a good match. You're an honorable man."

Taken aback by the Christian's unexpected praise, he muttered his thanks, then asked, "Have you heard anything about the contest tomorrow? Spurius always promotes his fights well, but this one is short notice."

"I think everyone in the city has heard. Criers have been all over town announcing your glorious return from retirement." Quintus handed him a sack. "There were placards posted near the amphitheater. Seems you're to fight a handful of men at once and a slew of wild beasts."

"Is that all?"

"From what I can tell." Quintus tilted his head in the direction of the other cells. "Have they been singing long?"

"Off and on."

"Are the Psalms bothersome to you?"

"No, I find them peaceful."

Quintus opened the second sack. "This is the food. There's meat, bread, fruit and skins filled with fresh water. Enough for tonight and tomorrow."

Seeing the bounty, Caros joked, "Enough for me *and* the rats."

"Your lady doesn't want you to starve."

"Apparently."

"She's concerned about you."

"She needn't be. I cut my teeth in the games."

"She's more concerned about your soul than your hide."

Caros dug into the food and pulled out a loaf of dark bread. He ripped off a piece and chewed it while he eyed his slave. He swallowed. "I'm convinced there's no hope for me."

Quintus stilled. "You think you'll lose tomorrow?"

He leaned against the doorframe, careful not to bump his head. "No, my body will be fine. It's my soul that's lost."

"Why are you so convinced you're irredeemable?"

He shook his head. "I've killed many Christians. How could your God forgive me when I've killed so many of His own?"

"Is *that* why you've had difficulty accepting the Way?"

His chest unbearably tight from guilt, Caros nodded.

"Whatever you've done makes no difference. Paul also murdered many believers before he came to the Lord. And yet the Lord used him mightily."

Stunned by the knowledge Pelonia's great teacher had committed the same sins as he, Caros was afraid to believe his ears.

Quintus grinned. "You've no reason to doubt Jesus loves you. He has His hand on your life. If you believe in Him, He'll be faithful to forgive you no matter what you've done."

Caros felt buoyed by the hope of forgiveness for the first time. "Thank you, Quintus."

Quintus clasped him on the shoulder as he turned to go. "Open your heart and accept the love of Jesus. Forgiveness is yours if you'll only believe."

Later, alone, warm and fed, Caros leaned against a stack of pillows contemplating his numerous talks with Pelonia and his latest discussion with Quintus. Except for the occasional rattle of chains and the constant drip of water somewhere beyond his cell, the pit was quiet.

Open your heart and accept the love of Jesus. Forgiveness is yours if you'll only believe.

Quintus's words went round and round in Caros's head. Since the first time Pelonia had told him about Christ's love, he'd wanted to believe in the possibility of forgiveness. But, having killed so many Christians, he'd been convinced there was no help to be found in their God.

After thinking for so long he was beyond salvation,

the concept terrified him. What if he accepted, truly accepted Jesus as his God, only to find it was no more than a hoax?

He shook his head to ward off his doubts. Pelonia believed. Quintus believed. So had the many Christians he'd seen die in the ring.

Teetering on the edge between denial and what his heart told him was truth, he took a deep breath and prayed, "Jesus, if You'll have me, *I* believe in You."

Chapter Twenty-Five

Caros awoke the next morning, his mind and spirit at peace for the first time—like the shackles had been freed from his soul. Focusing on the contest before him, he accepted the years he'd spent as a gladiator were all part of God's plan for his life—all preparation for today's final battle.

To keep from being distracted, he allowed himself no more than a few moments to think of Pelonia. He looked forward to telling her about his newfound faith. He realized he'd told her everything about himself except how much he loved her. As soon as he saw her again he vowed to correct the matter and tell her every day for the rest of his life.

Hating the slave's garb Spurius sent, he dressed with grim resolve, unrepentant in the decision to break his vow if it meant rescuing Pelonia. Eager to see his mission accomplished, he stoked himself for victory until there was no room in his mind for failure.

Spurius collected him from the pit a short time later. Noticing the stack of pillows and discarded food cloths, the old man quirked an eyebrow. "I see if you lose today it can't be blamed on an uncomfortable night."

"I won't lose. I have unfinished business to attend to."

"Concerning your woman, no doubt. She arrived hours ago, in case you were wondering."

"I knew she'd come."

"Why? Because she'd be hunted down otherwise?"

"Because she's a woman like no other, Spurius. A woman of honor who lives by her word." The two men left the row of empty cells and ascended a flight of steps. "Where is she in the stands?" Caros asked.

"How should I know the exact spot?"

"Why do you sound suspicious, old man? Where is she?"

"The last I saw her, she was with her cousin," the editor grumbled.

"As long as she's safe."

"She is."

Unconvinced, Caros warned, "Don't forget our bargain. She's to be waiting for me alive and unharmed when I leave the arena."

"I've forgotten nothing. I'm hurt you don't trust me."

He motioned toward a bank of cages. "I trust you like I'd trust one of these predators at my back." Hearing the first muted cries of the mob, he grew impatient. "How many men do you intend for me to fight?"

"It wouldn't be a surprise if I told you." Spurius gave a crafty grin. "But I do have a finale to please every Roman's love of drama. You'll go back into retirement a god in their eyes."

"Don't do me any favors."

Spurius chuckled. "I'm not. I'm going to use your misery to lure the mob back into their seats tomorrow."

"You're a contemptible bit of slime, do you know that?"

"I've been called worse…just this morning, in fact."

Occasional snatches of sunlight began to cut through the gloom. Slaves tended the cages filled with bears, panthers, tigers and other wildlife from all over the Empire.

He could feel the crowd's excitement pulse through his nerves. The roar of agitated lions mingled with the spectators' cry a level above them. The smell turned from one of moldy decay to the mixed stench of dung, overripe bodies and blood.

"The mob is frenzied today. All fifty thousand seats are filled and the balconies are overflowing." Pleased with himself, Spurius grinned. "It's all because of you. I told you there was a fortune to be made if you'd come back and fight."

"I don't expect you to understand, you filthy cur, but I wanted a peaceful life."

"And you chose to train gladiators?"

"What else was I fit for after you kept me enslaved all those years?"

Spurius shrugged. "Your livelihood wasn't my problem. I had my own mouth to feed."

They came to one of the platforms used to lift combatants directly into the arena. Sand sifted through the cracks in the floorboards. The impatient chant of the crowd shook the foundation.

Slaves waited nearby with the armor and sword of a Samnite. Caros strapped a leather greave to his left leg before lifting his large visored helmet over his head.

Accepting his shield with his left hand, he gripped a *gladius* in his right. His fingers caressed the leather hilt like the hand of a contentious, but oft relied upon friend.

"No wonder the crowds always loved you, you look like Mars himself." Spurius motioned for the slaves to lift Caros into the arena. The ropes creaked as one set of pulleys raised the platform, while another set parted the floorboards above his head. "Your woman is truly blessed by Fortuna," Spurius shouted up to him. "Who else but you could have saved her from death in the ring?"

Our God, Caros thought as he rode toward the cloudless blue sky. Tense with the anticipation of battle, he acknowledged Christ could have chosen to use a miracle to save her, but He'd chosen to honor him with the privilege instead.

As the top of his head crested with the floor, the announcer introduced him along with his long list of titles: *Lanista* of the Ludus Maximus, The Bone Grinder, The Undefeated Champion of Rome. The mob's fanatical cheer swept across the expanse like a whirlwind. The platform locked into place. He raised the *gladius* in a salute, drawing even more applause and stamping of feet.

Marveling at the sea of people, he left the platform and anchored his feet in the sand. Eyes focused on the main gate, he watched slaves wrestle it open.

An iron chariot thundered toward him, spewing a cloud of dust in its wake. Behind the driver, two archers flanked his first opponent. Flaming arrows streaked toward him. He blocked them with his shield, extinguishing them in the sand.

The chariot raced past him, so close he jumped back to avoid being hit. Dressed as a beast from the underworld in a horned helmet with snarling teeth, his opponent leaped from the back of the chariot. He swung his long blade with no mercy. Caros met the attack. Blood pumping, he gave himself over to the thrill of the sport.

Blade met blade over and over. Caros swiped the other man in the arm, drawing first blood. The crowd went wild. An arrow pierced the sand near his feet. Blocking his opponent's weapon with his own, he turned just in time to deflect a second arrow with his shield.

The chariot returned, dropping off another set of fighters. Aware he'd promised Spurius to entertain the crowd, Caros fought all three men at once until a lioness was lifted into the arena.

Released from its binding, the cat launched herself into the fight. Grasping the wounded man from behind, she sank her teeth into his neck. The mob cheered for death and the man cried out in agony, but not for long.

Disgusted, but focused on his other two adversaries, Caros ignored the crack of bone as the lion tore into the dead man's flesh, and launched an offensive attack. Dividing the other two men, he wounded the first, weaker foe with a slice across the thigh and a blow to the chin. The gladiator staggered backward, falling to the sand.

The mob cried for murder. The sound of blood rushing in his ears, Caros ignored them. The sun beat down on him. His sweat flowed in rivulets. Raising the point of his sword, he went after the last man.

A giant from the untamed lands of Germania, Caros recognized the titan from previous contests. An expert with a trident and net, his opponent had only been defeated once, and that was by Alexius.

Eyes intent, he waited for the German to make the first move. The titan lifted the net. Swinging it in a circle above his head, he cast it toward Caros. Caros raised his shield and moved to avoid it, but the knotted rope ensnared him in its web.

Behind him, he heard the floor shift, another platform lift into place. Unable to turn in the jumble of cords and find his newest adversary, Caros expected the worst when the crowd stood and roared.

Slicing through the ropes that bound him, he threw off his helmet and worked free of the net just in time to avoid the trident piercing his chest. With a tactical swing of his *gladius,* he glanced over his shoulder. A rhino, its sharp horn glistening in the sun, barreled toward him. Reacting by instinct, he dropped his shield.

The mob gasped.

His free hand latched on to the post of the trident just below the prongs. He yanked with all his might and swung his massive foe toward the beast. The rhino's horn caught the German in the ribs. The momentum of the animal's pounding feet dragged the screaming man into the sand where he was trampled.

The mob chanted Caros's name with insane abandon. As he drank in air, he watched the rhino race toward the main gate where slaves angled it into a stall. He cast an eye toward the lioness. Lying in a circle of bloodstained sand, the cat continued to ravage its meal.

Trumpets blared, announcing a shift to the day's final entertainments. The lioness was caught and taken back to her cage. His interest keen, Caros watched a handful of slaves pull a covered wagon across the blood-spattered sands. At the same time, across the arena another hole opened in the floor.

The announcer began to weave a tale of a mighty gladiator whose prowess caught the eye of Venus. A hush fell over the crowd when they learned the warrior rejected the enamored goddess in favor of a human girl.

The crowd shrieked and clapped as the platform slowly lifted Pelonia into the arena. Dressed in a gossamer tunic, her black hair unbound and flowing in the breeze, she was tied to a stake, her hands trussed behind her back.

With dawning horror, Caros realized Spurius had cast him and Pelonia as actual leads in the drama. His feet heavy with fear, he ran toward her, listening keenly to what might unfold next.

The announcer's voice boomed across the theatre. "Furious, the goddess disguised herself as a predator and vowed to kill her rival."

All at once, the slaves tugged on the sheets covering the wagon. The billowing cloths fell away to reveal a large caged tiger. The cage door opened. The beast roared. Unlike the mob that was too far away, Caros saw the animal had been abused and frothed at the mouth.

The predator hissed and smacked at the slaves poking him with sharpened sticks. He leaped from his prison, landing between Caros and Pelonia. Straining every one of his sore and tired muscles, Caros picked up speed. The beast's golden eyes latched on Pelonia and bounded toward her. Terror kicked through Caros. He'd never get to her in time.

Terrified, Pelonia closed her eyes and gave herself up to prayer. At any moment, she expected the tiger's attack. Frozen, unable even to scream, she asked the Lord to protect Caros and see him safely from the arena. Animal footsteps galloped closer. She braced herself for pain.

Anger shot through her. How could she accept death like a coward? She forced her eyes open and… *"Cat?"*

The tiger leaped through the air, his roar sounding to her like a plaintive wail. He careened into her, driving the breath from her body in a groan of agony.

The spectators jumped to their feet, delighted by what at a distance must look like a fatal attack. As he usually did, Cat wallowed against her, rubbing his head and face across her chest.

Weak with relief, she tugged at her bonds, wanting to hug the dear animal. Seeing someone had abused him, her anger burned against the foul soul. *God help him if I ever find out who hurt my pet!*

Within the same heartbeat, Caros's shadow fell over her. He raised his *gladius,* intent on a deadly strike. The rage of battle still clouding his intense blue eyes, she could see he'd had no time to realize the animal was his own tiger.

"Caros, stop!" she cried. "It's Cat."

His facial muscles contorted with confusion, he managed to digest her warning and stop his weapon's mortal blow just before it sank between Cat's shoulders.

Seeing her love as a gladiator for the first time, she watched him grapple for control of the violence raging through him. Smeared with blood, his tunic torn, his fingers white from the tight grip on his weapon, he heaved in great breaths of air.

"Caros," she said for his ears only, casting away her fear. "Caros, we're all right."

Seemingly unaware of how close he came to death at the hand of his master, Cat bumped him with his nose.

Caros buried his fingers in the ruff of fur around Cat's neck. He opened his eyes and stared at her as though she'd just been raised from the grave. "You live?" he said in wonder. "I saw the tiger leap at you. I thought for certain you were dead."

The wild crowd forgotten, she gave him a gentle smile. "I'm well. We all owe thanks to you."

With tender care he cut her bonds and swept her into his arms. His quick steps took them to the sidelines, Cat trotting close behind them.

They crossed the threshold into the staging area. Caros buried his face in the curve of her neck. "Thank God you're safe."

Uncertain if she'd heard him correctly, she tipped her head to look intently into his eyes. "Which God do you thank?"

"Your God," he said, his low voice thick with conviction. "The true and living God whom I accepted last night as my own."

Overjoyed by the unexpected news, she squealed with delight. "How? Why? What happened to convince you?"

He carried her into a private alcove she guessed at one time served as an office. He set her on her feet and grabbed a towel from a peg on the wall. "Quintus visited me last night."

"I know," she said, stroking the top of Cat's head. "The Lord told me to send him."

He laughed, amazed by the God whose ways he had yet to fully comprehend. "Quintus explained that your teacher, Paul, was a killer the same as I before he came to believe."

"Well, yes," she said, her forehead puckered in her confusion. "Everyone knows… No, of course, you didn't know. How could you?"

He shrugged and used the cloth to wipe the sweat from his face, neck and chest. "I wish I had known. My guilt over killing so many in the past convinced me God would never want me."

"Oh, Caros! I'm sorry I didn't think to tell you." She wrapped her arms around his neck and buried her fingers in the damp curls at his nape. "Of course He wants you. He wants *everyone*."

"I believe it now." He held her tight, breathing in the joy radiating from the depths of her soul. "The question is, do *you* want me?"

She reared back, her smile soft and filled with love. "I—"

"Caros? Master, where are you?"

Caros groaned at the sound of Alexius's voice beyond the wall. He lifted his head. "Go on. Just ignore him."

"I—"

"There you are, Caros, Pelonia. By the gods, I've been looking for you everywhere."

"Go away, Alexius," Caros ordered.

"Is that all the thanks I get for switching out Cat?"

"Cat!" Pelonia shrieked. "My poor baby, I forgot all about him." She dropped to her knees in the hay beside the tiger and began to examine the cuts on his face. The tiger recoiled and growled low from the pain, but he allowed her to fuss over his wounds. "Someone abused him. I'd like to know who did this. I'd make them sorry for certain."

"I believe it," Alexius said. "After last night I'll never doubt you're a firebrand."

Caros raised an eyebrow.

"What?" Alexius frowned. "She seems like such a mild little bird, but you should have seen her giving orders. If I weren't four times her size, I think she might have scared me witless. I'm warning you, my friend, she should have been a centurion."

"Who should have been a centurion?" Spurius asked, pushing his way around Alexius.

"Pelonia," the Greek answered. "She's got quite a temper."

"After today, she has quite a reputation. Do you hear the mob? They love her. They believe she really tamed the beast."

Alexius sent Caros a meaningful grin. "She has. Can't you tell?"

Caros wasn't amused. "Spurius, what was she doing out in the arena or *anywhere* near a tiger."

The editor paled. He hemmed and hawed, all the while backing away from Caros's angry glare.

"We had a bargain, you worm."

"Yes, we did. And here she is, safe and well just as we agreed. Now, if you'll excuse me I believe I'm needed elsewhere."

Alexius chuckled. "That's one way to get rid of fleas."

"What happened today?" Caros asked his champion, a tinge of the blinding fear he'd felt still with him.

The Greek leaned against the stone wall. "I arrived early this morning to see how you'd fared in the night. On my way to your cell, I overheard Spurius telling the day's plans to his slaves. I reckoned the situation wouldn't end if I escaped with the girl, so I simply changed out the tiger."

"You're a genius," Pelonia said. She stroked Cat's ear. "But do you know who cut him?"

"No, but if I find out you'll be the first to hear." Alexius tapped his thigh. "Let's go, boy. It's time to go home."

Cat lumbered past, giving Pelonia a gentle bump that sent her toppling into the hay. Caros lifted her to her feet.

"One last thing," Alexius said. "Gaius had a chariot delivered to convey you home."

As soon as they were alone, Caros pulled her back into his arms. "Before they interrupted, you were saying?"

"Hmm… Yes, what *was* I saying?"

He squeezed her, making her giggle. "I was saying, you dear, wonderful man, that I want you, too. I want you today and every day from here on out."

"That's good." His chest ached with tenderness. "Because I love you, Pelonia. I love you more than my own life."

"I love you, too," she said, her eyes soft with emotion. "I've known since the night we stargazed together. It's been torture thinking I could never have you."

"I want you to be my wife, *mea carissima*, to share the rest of my days."

Happiness brimmed and spilled over into every part of her being. She wrapped her arms around his lean waist and burrowed against him, offering her Heavenly Father a prayer of eternal gratitude. "I'll marry you, my love. I'd already decided I'd never wed anyone if I couldn't have you."

"I'll always be yours. I swore you'd admit I owned you, but from the first moment I saw you, you've owned my heart."

He dipped his head to savor her sweet lips with a kiss.

Joy overflowed from the depths of her soul and she gave herself over to the happiness of being held by the one man she loved above anyone else.

"In case you ever doubt it, you *are* my life, Pelonia. Without you, I'd still be wandering in darkness, ignorant of the Lord's saving grace, lonely and hungry for peace.

Why He chose to shower me with His favor is beyond my ken, but I vow to spend the rest of my days thanking Him for the gift of you."

She tried to hide her tears behind a smile. "I wasn't much of a gift. You did pay three thousand denarii for me."

"Money well spent for a woman beyond price. Knowing what I do now, I'd pay a thousand times that amount and consider myself blessed."

As Caros swept her into his arms and carried her into the warm afternoon, she glanced toward the sky, certain both her fathers smiled down on her from heaven. The sting of her slavery was gone, replaced by the freedom to love a man worthy of her trust and respect. She sighed with contentment.

He brushed her temple with his lips. "What are you thinking, *mea carissima?*"

Loving his deep blue eyes, she brushed a thick lock of hair behind his ear. "Only that I'm blessed and happy."

"Good." He set her on her feet in the chariot and kissed her softly. "That's exactly how I want you to be."

* * * * *

SPECIAL EXCERPT FROM

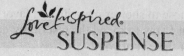

Love Inspired
SUSPENSE

*An Amish widow and a lawman in disguise
team up to take down a crime ring.*

Read on for a sneak preview of
Amish Covert Operation *by Meghan Carver,
available July 2019 from Love Inspired Suspense.*

The steady rhythm of the bicycle did little to calm her nerves. Ominous dark blue clouds propelled Katie Schwartz forward.

A slight breeze ruffled the leaves, sending a few skittering across the road. But then it died, leaving an unnatural stillness in the hush of the oncoming storm. Beads of perspiration dotted her forehead.

Should she call out? Announce herself?

Gingerly, she got off her bicycle and stepped up to a window, clutching her skirt in one hand and the window trim in the other. Through her shoes, her toes gripped the edge of the rickety crate. Desperation to stay upright and not teeter off sent a surge of adrenaline coursing through her as she swiped a hand across the grimy window of the hunter's shack. The crate dipped, and Katie grasped the frame of the window again.

"Timothy?" she whispered to herself. "Where are you?"

With the crate stabilized, she swiped over the glass again and squinted inside. But all that stared back at her was more grime. The crate tipped again, and she grabbed at the window trim before she could tumble off.

Movement inside snagged her attention, although she couldn't make out figures. Voices filtered through the window, one louder than the other. What was going on in there? And was Timothy involved?

Her nose touched the glass in her effort to see inside. A face suddenly appeared in the window. It was distorted by the cracks in the glass, but it appeared to be her *bruder*. A moment later, the face disappeared.

She jumped from the crate and headed toward the corner of the cabin. Now that he had seen her, he had to come out and explain himself and return with her, stopping whatever this clandestine meeting was all about.

A man dressed in plain clothing stepped out through the door.

"Timothy!" But the wild look in his eyes stopped her from speaking further.

And then she saw it. A gun was pressed into his back.

"Katie! Run! Go!"

Don't miss
Amish Covert Operation *by Meghan Carver,*
available July 2019 wherever
Love Inspired® Suspense books and ebooks are sold.

www.LoveInspired.com

Inspirational Romance to Warm Your Heart and Soul

Join our social communities to connect with other readers who share your love!

Sign up for the Love Inspired newsletter at **www.LoveInspired.com** to be the first to find out about upcoming titles, special promotions and exclusive content.

CONNECT WITH US AT:

Facebook.com/groups/HarlequinConnection

 Facebook.com/LoveInspiredBooks

 Twitter.com/LoveInspiredBks

LISOCIAL2018